DEC   2000

Muskrat
Courage

Also by Philip Lawson

Would It Kill You to Smile? (1998)

Muskrat Courage

Philip Lawson

St. Martin's Minotaur ✖ New York

www.stmartins.com

Library of Congress Cataloging-in-Publication Data

Lawson, Philip.
    Muskrat courage / Philip Lawson.—1st ed.
      p. cm.
    ISBN 0-312-26207-8
    1. Missing children—Fiction. 2. New Hampshire—Fiction. 3. Kidnapping—Fiction. 4. Georgia—Fiction. I. Title.

PS3562.A945 M87 2000
813'.54—dc21   00-024756

First Edition: June 2000

10 9 8 7 6 5 4 3 2 1

To Maxine Willis and Lou Haas
of Cherokee Village, Arkansas,
and to John and Mae Whitaker of Columbus, Georgia

And to Frank and Claire Phillips of Providence,
Rhode Island

Acknowledgments

Philip Lawson gratefully acknowledges the help of Colonel Joey Branch of the Troup County, Georgia, Sheriff's Department; Chief David White of the Pine Mountain, Georgia, Police Department; and an anonymous agent of the FBI in providing information about kidnap-investigation procedures. Misconstruals or misapplications of this information are solely the author's fault.

One

E arly in the day of the storm that stole Olivia, I watched in
horror as she barely avoided being trampled by the pony I
had given her as an indulgent consolation gift. At the moment
of her rescue, with her small body shaking in my arms, I realized
that this new task of fathering would demand all my wisdom, heart,
and courage.

But only her abduction later that day drove home the knowledge
that parenting—more exactly, my failure at it—could make me feel
like dying myself.

Or like killing the man who, using the storm as cover, had kidnapped her.

That October morning dawned too much like an idyllic autumn
Sunday: butterscotch light, a few stray vanilla ice-cream clouds, and
sparrows singing in the sycamores. It wasn't a Sunday, though, a
circumstance that left life's cheap irony incomplete. Instead, I faced
another prosaic Wednesday, which people with jobs call Hump Day,
the Heartbreak Hill in the Peachtree Road Race of their workweek.

But Wednesday held no such terrors for me, William Keats, Esq.,
man of leisure. My school-counseling career involuntarily on hold
but my bank balance buoyed by my recent modest inheritance, I
contemplated another day of reading and futzing about at household
chores and home improvements, of listening to music and preparing
a couple of unhurried meals. If only Adrienne could have enjoyed
a similar schedule. But although my contributions ensured the day-
to-day upkeep of the recently purchased old house we shared, as well

as a few renovations, Adrienne handled all the mortgage payments. The local First Peoples Bank would have frowned on two ne'er-do-wells in the same household.

Busy in our mint green kitchen at seven A.M., I looked up to see Adrienne pad sleepily through the door. Immediately I quit my breakfast assembly line for a hug. Adrienne, returning my embrace, raised wicked, nonculinary thoughts with a long kiss.

"Do we have time?" I said.

She smiled. "Not really, Will. You and Olivia may have nothing pressing to do, but I've got another long in-service day ahead, remember? That was just a foretaste of the time we'll have when I get home. If I can still keep my eyes open, of course. Besides, I've already heard Olivia puttering about."

"Damn! Well, anticipation will make the hours fly like, um, chickens hungry for their mash."

"Now there's an image worthy of your literary namesake. Coffee ready yet?"

"Any second now." Gliding back and forth between the Formica-topped center island and the stove, gracefully juggling coffeemaker, toaster, and two skillets, I whipped up a breakfast of raisin bagels, cheese-flecked scrambled eggs, and onion-laced homefries. So proficient at cooking had I grown over the past year that I could simultaneously prepare our meal and watch Adrienne sip her coffee as she scanned the *Atlanta Constitution*. With one smooth leg crossed over the other beneath her checkered flannel robe and her slipper bobbing to the St. Saëns symphony in our countertop CD player, she stirred emotions ranging from admiration to idolatry—a narrow bandwidth, maybe, but one that I enjoyed inhabiting.

Just as I slid three full plates onto the table, Olivia, clad in a fuzzy pink sleeping gown, skipped into the kitchen.

"Morning, Mom. Hey, Will. Smells good. Boy, did I have a funny dream last night!" She took her accustomed seat. "Roogy Batoon could fly!"

Olivia, Adrienne's daughter, had turned eight in mid-June. Because summer had unshackled us all from school, we had made an eight-hour trip by car to Disney World to celebrate. Watching her among the smaller kids cavorting there, I realized that the child with whom I lived had truly begun to mature. She no longer resembled the runty if precocious preschooler I had met when Adrienne and I started dating. In fact, she now manifested not only an emotional stability rare in one her age but also the first faint physical signs of young womanhood. These hints of an early adolescence scared me a little, but also more deeply endeared her to me, for in Olivia's fair hair and open smile I saw her mother's luminous girlhood photographs come alive.

Only in the squint about her eyes and her deft but outsized hands did Olivia favor her biological father, Byron Owsley. I hardly regretted in her appearance the absence of any other paternal signatures.

I sat down with my family. Olivia placed her hands palm to palm, then made a *gassho* over her food. Adrienne and I did likewise, then fell to eating.

"So Roogy Batoon could fly," I said. "Did she have wings?"

"Nope. I just climbed on her and she took right off into the sky."

"Where did she take you?" Adrienne asked with unfeigned interest.

Olivia's face clouded. "I can't exactly remember. Some new country." She brightened. "Maybe it was Oz!"

Adrienne lifted an eyebrow. "Oz again? That's all we ever hear about these days. Exactly what's so captivating about those silly books?"

Olivia frowned and hunched forward. "If you haven't read them, you can't know. They're just really cool." She pronounced *cool* in the late-nineties way, two syllables with the *l* at the end as a kind of half-swallowed afterthought.

"And that movie. I'm a little surprised your tape hasn't worn out by now. And that we haven't all turned as green as the Emerald City itself."

As the culprit who had introduced Olivia to Baum's *Oz* books in response to her fascination with the MGM film, I had to speak up. "I would have thought almost any sort of reading good for Olivia."

"Not to the point of obsessively rereading. It could make her neglect her other assignments."

Olivia straightened. "I'm five chapters ahead of the rest of the class in my geography book. And I just finished writing a report on *Harriet the Spy*! It's gonna get an A! Ask Will—he read it."

Lately I had helped Olivia with her homework while Adrienne either graded papers from her own sixth graders or prepared for her next day's lessons. "A-plus," I said.

Olivia crossed her arms in a gestural *So there.* Adrienne started to speak, but suppressed the urge, as if unwilling to further disturb the peace. I bit my own tongue. Exchanging neutral comments about the day ahead, we finished eating.

Adrienne went upstairs to shower and dress. Olivia joined me at the sink to help with dishes. We hurriedly finished that task, and I plonked Olivia in front of the television to watch a new incarnation of a childhood favorite of my own, *Captain Kangaroo.* Then I hastened up the back stairs to catch Adrienne alone in our bedroom before she descended again. Unfortunately, sex was almost the last thing on my mind.

Adrienne faced the dresser mirror opposite the door, showing me a sleek fall of wheat-colored hair and the trim lines of her backside. In the mirror, her fingers fumbled at the buttons of her jonquil-colored blouse. She had seen me enter but had not turned. I approached her from behind and put my hands on her waist. She essayed an unconvincing smile and continued struggling with her buttons.

"What's the matter, kid?" I asked in my calmest voice. "Did I step out of line?"

Finally buttoned, Adrienne turned. "No, Will. It's just . . ."

"Just what?"

"We can't have two contradictory lines of discipline when it comes to raising Olivia."

"Discipline? Where did discipline enter this morning's tussle? Olivia has more self-control and initiative than most kids twice her age. She finishes her chores and homework almost before they're assigned. She simply got excited about her dream and how it might relate to something that turns her on. The *Oz* books don't constitute great literature, but I sure loved them at her age, and only rarely does a scene from one of them induce me to rob a bank or commit an ax murder."

Adrienne looked at the waxed hardwood beneath our feet. "Maybe that's the rub. I never read the *Oz* books. And the *Oz* books may not represent the only thing I miss out on. You greet Olivia when the bus drops her off every afternoon. You see her for many more hours a week than I do. You two groom her pony together, you go for walks, you color pictures, you build Lego castles, you—"

"Do you mean to say I'm getting *too* close to her? Wasn't that the idea when we decided to move in together, part of the reason for combining households?"

"Yes. But sometimes I feel . . ."

I waited for her to finish.

Adrienne turned away and picked up her shoes. Stork-standing on one foot and then the other, she slipped them on. "Forget it. It's probably just a selfish maternal thing."

"Now that you've raised the issue, how can I forget it?"

Looking at me almost defiantly, Adrienne said, "All right, Will. Here's my fear, in all its ugly irrationality: I sometimes feel as if Olivia is being stolen right out of my arms."

An electric ripple traversed my spine. "By me?"

Adrienne leaned toward me. Tears glimmered in her eyes. "No. I mean, I don't know. Oh, Will, it's all such a damned complicated mess!"

I caught her and hugged her. "I think I understand. We haven't adjusted to this whole new arrangement. We still—"

"You mean *I* haven't adjusted."

"No, listen. The *three* of us haven't settled fully in. So the arrangement naturally admits of glitches. On top of that, you can sense Olivia stretching her wings, establishing different kinds of independence. Of course it troubles you. Only parents who build walls around their feelings can pretend it doesn't. But there's nothing unnatural about Olivia's blossoming and wing-stretching."

Adrienne pulled back and studied me. She had heard me shift into sagacious-counselor mode dozens of times, and more than once she had reined me in with just such a look.

"Unless it's me," I said shakily. "Unless I'm the unnatural element."

"Hardly. Half the kids in my school today live with step-parents or unrelated adult live-ins," Adrienne said. "It may be unnatural—whatever that word means—but it's not uncommon. And you're a prince compared to some of the guardians I've had the misfortune to lock horns with."

Prince implied chivalry, and I tried to rise to the call. "What if we got married and I adopted Olivia? If both of you could regard me as her legal father, not just the de facto man of the house?"

Adrienne laughed self-consciously. "I already regard you as her legal father, Will. But I don't want to make another mistake as humongous as the one I made with Byron. I fear—"

"Thanks. Thanks a lot."

"Please don't take it like that." She kissed my forehead. "I'm not saying never. I'm just saying not yet."

"Whenever you're ready, then. I just want you to know that."

"I know it. I've long known it. And I treasure the generosity of the offer, especially after I've behaved like such a bitch. Believe me, it would make my life easier among my sterner Protestant colleagues."

"So accept the offer."

She pushed me away with one finger. "Not yet." For now, at least, she had clotured debate. "Damn. I've got to reapply my lipstick. If I arrive late, Goldborough will lash my tail."

I decided not to press the issue. I could not singlehandedly resolve Adrienne's upsetting sense of estrangement from her daughter. I had a part to play, but not that of initiator.

"Principals live to lash tails. But if anyone's going to lay a corrective hand on your pretty tush, they'll have to see me first."

Adrienne grinned. "And you'd do what?"

"Set up a ticket booth and charge admission."

The sharp kick to my shin really didn't hurt that much.

Downstairs, Olivia's absorption in the antics of Bunny Rabbit and Mr. Moose reassured me that she had caught none of our adult wrangle. I dropped onto a hassock next to where she lay on the carpet. For five or six minutes, we silently watched television together.

Adrienne breezed in, clutching her book-satchel and purse, smiling as if nothing had ever troubled her. "Gotta run, guys."

Olivia hurled herself at her mother. The intensity with which they hugged startled me.

"Don't give Will any lip today, sweetheart."

The long-scheduled in-service day for teachers exempted every kid in Speece County from classes.

"I sure won't! Unless he starts something first."

I put up my dukes. "You and what army?"

Olivia returned pensively to her TV program. I walked Adrienne to the entryway where our coats hung, a place she insisted on calling the "mudroom." As she donned her jacket, I said, "Lasagna and a bottle of Chianti sound good for tonight?"

"Only if you're dessert."

I walked her outside and watched her drive away to the east on her twenty-minute excursion to Tocqueville Middle School. Dawn's clouds had since piled higher, thicker, and darker.

Back inside, I faced a freshly expectant Olivia. "When do I get to ride Roogy Batoon?"

"After lunch. I've got some chores to take care of first. Think you can keep busy till then?"

"Can I watch *The Wizard of Oz*?"

I hesitated a moment, then said, "Why not?"

"You won't hear a peep out of me for three hours!"

"Hey, I didn't say you could watch it twice."

Olivia's face crumpled.

"Okay. But *only* two times."

I left Olivia slotting the tape into the VCR. As I gathered up my tool chest, shrugged into a coat, and went outside, I wondered for the first time if Adrienne had a point about Olivia's fixation on Baum's fantasy world.

One of the gutters on the south side of the house had come loose from the eaves. Firmly planting my old wooden ladder, I eyed the sagging aluminum trough and wished for some of my good friend J. W. Young's mechanical expertise. I climbed the ladder to the eave.

An hour and a half later, after once banging my thumb hard enough to crack a pecan, I had almost completed the job. Scooping clotted leaves from the whole length of the catchment had added extra time to the task. This failed to surprise me. Back in my old place in Mountboro, I had quickly learned that a home constituted an altogether ravenous time-sink.

Atop my repositioned ladder, I paused. Above me, the whipped-cream clouds of the morning had curdled into a sullen mass of gray cottage cheese. The breeze had sharpened into an unignorable wind. I could not recall hearing the forecast during breakfast cleanup, when I had switched the radio on, but the portents suggested slop and slosh.

A hundred yards away, beyond a picket of bare white sycamores, the country road leading to our place showed an approaching blue pickup. Almost no one traveled our road at this hour, and I watched with interest—in fact, with muted suspicion—as the battered and paint-shedding GM truck drew up to the mailbox at the end of our driveway. For approximately fifteen seconds, the truck and its hard-to-see driver idled there.

Our mailman drove a white car with a steering wheel on the right side, and I had never seen a delivery person of any reputable express company in such a conspicuous wreck. Maybe, on a dare, a teenager with a Louisville Slugger at hand sat there nerving himself up to launch our mailbox into the trees. This possibility made me drop one foot to a lower rung.

The pickup, however, shuddered to life again and leapt away in a haze of red dust and webby exhaust. A misguided soul looking for someone else's place, I told myself, and promptly forgot the incident.

I returned to the job and, to escape the worsening weather, hurriedly finished. After stowing my ladder and tools, I went inside. Onscreen, Dorothy, back in Kansas, had just awakened from her gaudy Technicolor dream.

"Okay, Sprout, change in plans. You get your ride early, before the rain hits."

Olivia jumped up. "Rain? That's great! We can camp out in the treehouse then!"

"I don't think so. Your mom wouldn't appreciate either of us sporting a permanent lightning bolt through our middles. Not only does it hurt like a dozen vaccinations, but it makes it impossible to get through most doorways."

"You're crazy!"

"Think so?"

"Yeah. If you had a lightning bolt stuck in you, you could just turn sidewise to go through a door."

"Good point. Now, get dressed and meet me at the barn."

The hinges on the peeling barn door needed a shot of WD-40. I made another note on a long mental list. Inside the raftered enclosure, myriad scents assailed me: hay, dung, tar, decaying wood, spilled motor oil, the drying grass caught in the mower's blades.

From her stall, Roogy Batoon whickered and stirred. I filled a feed-bag with oats and approached her.

Roogy Batoon, a small sorrel filly, had entered our lives through a caprice of mine. One Friday in April, Olivia, rushing for a bus, had missed a concrete step outside her school. She broke her wrist trying to cushion her fall. The injury could not have occurred at a worse moment for her. As the emergency room doctors tended to her wrist, the other members of her choral group rode that same bus to the big city to attend a joint performance of the Atlanta Symphony Orchestra and the Men's Glee Club of Morehouse College.

The inconsolable Olivia broke my heart. Her physical and emotional pain, which she bore with better grace than I would have expected, prompted me to buy her an outrageously expensive gift. When the trailer from Big Bear Farms pulled up the following weekend, Adrienne had instantly fathomed the depths of my insanity.

"Well," I had said, "we've got that big empty barn out back and . . ."

To her credit, Adrienne had allowed me my grand gesture. "So you decided to fill it with a couple hundred pounds of love in the guise of horseflesh."

"Pretty much."

Olivia ran in from outside screaming deliriously: "Those guys are unloading a pony! Is it for me?"

"No. Our electric bill's too high. The pony's going to work a generator treadmill in the basement. Haven't you seen that setup yet?"

Olivia calmed herself and regarded me dubiously. "If I work the treadmill, can we set the pony free?"

"Absolutely, kiddo. Just stop leaving the bathroom light on when you go to bed."

Roogy Batoon took her unlikely name from a famous comic strip of my youth. On a recent trip to the bookstore, I had discovered that an enterprising small-press publisher had plans to reissue Walt Kelly's *Pogo* in sequence, and I had snapped up the initial volumes. As we read the strips together, an avian character from Baton Rouge named Roogy Batoon caught Olivia's fancy, and she had adopted the name for her pony.

Now Roogy nuzzled my hand and accepted her feedbag. I shoveled manure as Roogy Batoon chomped. Matching input and disposal of output, we finished at the same time. Olivia still had not joined me, so I opened the outer door in the pony's stall and shooed Roogy out to run in her enclosure. She took off like a goosed squirrel.

Some vague impulse made me look out into the corral.

Olivia tottered atop the fence, walking the narrow rail as if it were a balance beam.

I flipped. "Olivia, get down from there right now!"

Startled, she turned, toppled, and whomped at full length into the mire of the run. From the opposite side of the corral, Roogy Batoon cantered at alarming speed toward her.

Before I knew I had moved, I burst into the corral with the shovel in my hands. Maybe yelling like a novice bungee jumper and brandishing the shovel did not constitute the most efficient method of diverting Roogy from Olivia's path, but the tactics worked. My frantic behavior so disconcerted the pony that she drew up sharply, reared back, and retreated to the farthest recess of the paddock.

Instantly, I had Olivia in my arms. The fall had knocked the wind out of her, and only just now had she managed to draw a new breath. Her first halting words lifted something raggedly solid into my throat.

"Sorry, Dad."

"Not your fault, kid. All mine."

Needless to say, Olivia never rode that day. After getting her inside and into a bubble-filled tub, I stabled Roogy Batoon again. By the time Olivia emerged from her bath, to announce that she had no bruises and felt fine, the storm had arrived. Starting stealthily, it soon escalated into one of those El Niño–magnified downpours typical of the year, replete with throaty thunder, keening winds, and brilliant jags of lightning. At high noon, the day's light level suggested early twilight. I took solace from the fact that Adrienne's Camry had recently passed a full safety check.

Over a lunch of tomato soup and grilled cheese sandwiches, Olivia said, "We don't have to tell Mom about me falling, do we?"

"I guess not. No harm, no foul."

Olivia looked relieved. "Good. She worries too much." After several spoonfuls of soup and a bite of sandwich, she added, "Things don't always work out like they do in the movies, do they, Will?"

"Not too often, no."

A cutthroat Sorry tournament and a session reading from *The Wind in the Willows,* our book in progress, brought us up to mid-afternoon. The lights had flickered once or twice as we rolled dice and read, and I thanked the presiding deities of country living that our propane-fueled stove allowed us to cook even when the power went out. I eventually left Olivia to her own devices and ambled into the kitchen to start supper.

Time passed in a fugue of dicing and chopping, boiling and layering pasta strips. As the time approached when I could expect Adrienne, I repeatedly glanced outside. The gloomy, puddled lawn, its azalea and hydrangea shrubs long since stripped of blossoms, suggested the inevitability of winter.

Around four o'clock, two things happened.

The power went off, plunging the house into blackness, and I saw Roogy Batoon running loose in the backyard. Earlier, had I neglected to latch her stall securely?

"Olivia," I called, "get the big flashlight and stay put. I'm going outside for a minute." I did not tell her why, knowing that Olivia would insist on "helping" me recapture Roogy.

From the parlor, she said, "Okay."

Undoubtedly remembering my shouting and my shovel brandishing, Roogy Batoon skittishly eluded me for a good five minutes. At last I managed to herd her back through the wind-buffeted barn door.

Returning to the house I heard a slapping noise, like a flagpole lanyard in the wind. A portion of severed electrical cable hanging from our house whipped the clapboards repeatedly. Its other end lay on the lawn and arced lazily upward to the nearest pole.

I ran inside through the back kitchen entrance, and did not stop until I stood in the empty living room. Raindrops swarmed like hornets through the open front door. Muddy adult footprints tracked the rug. Olivia had vanished. Fleeting as a rare perfume, she had subliminated into thin air.

As I stood on the front steps with the rain pelting my face, Adrienne's car pulled into the drive.

Two

N early a year and a half ago, I passed through one of the most challenging periods of my life.

In the spring of 1997, my father, the publicly acclaimed but secretly deceitful Skipper Keats, had bowed off our mortal stage during one of his stale routines with his favorite ventriloquist's dummy, Dapper O'Dell. When Skipper's cerebral aneurysm burst, he and Dapper toppled to the boards before the crowd at the Gag Reflex, the second-story comedy club that my father and his partner Satish Gupta had turned into one of the most successful show-business bistros in Columbus, Georgia. Briefly, at least, the whole city had mourned, and when the irreplaceable Dapper went missing from Skipper's coffin on the day of their planned internment, I resolved to trace to their source all the tangled threads meta-phorically trailing from Dad's shabby tux.

Not one but two mistresses, I learned, had come between Skipper and fidelity to his marriage vows, the first during my boyhood and the second during a recent five-year period. My mother, LaRue, had tolerated the second affair because she loved both Skipper and his paramour, Sherri Gupta, the wife of Skipper's long-term business partner.

As I searched for Dapper, these revelations had staggered me. When she eventually learned of them, they also staggered my little sister, Kelli, a high school junior who had idolized Skipper as a performer, a philanthropist, and a doting dad.

LaRue, meanwhile, had retreated for the ensuing summer into

the recesses of Skipper's Keep, the decaying family mansion, where she played melancholy nocturnes on her baby grand, countless distracted hands of solitaire, and reluctant hostess to the well-meaning old friends who infrequently dropped by to cheer her up. Then, as if she had deliberately resolved to discard her widow's weeds, she started shopping again, visiting friends, and giving one day a week to the ministries of the Valley Rescue Mission. Credit belonged primarily to her own spiritual resources, a robust jumble of New Age credos that had once seriously annoyed me.

In January of this year, nearly nine months to the day after Skipper's fatal collapse, LaRue summoned me to the Keep for a talk. Eula, her cook, served us coffee and banana cream pie, and tactfully made herself scarce.

"Will, I believe I'm going away."

I took a sip of the expensive imported coffee that Eula had brewed. "Really?"

"When have I ever been less than an utter realist?" She gave me a self-mocking smile, primarily because an honest reply would have taken half the afternoon.

"Well—," I began.

"Bite your tongue. Now that neither finances nor domestic obligations make it impractical, I'm planning a long, relaxing, and, I hope, educational ocean cruise."

Aboard a floating elderhostel, I thought . . . but did not say aloud. In fact, the notion struck me as an eminently sane one for a woman in her position. Moreover, it would get her out of my hair and relieve me of the guilt I felt when I failed to visit her regularly. When next she smiled, I had the uneasy suspicion that she had just read my mind.

"Exactly how long a cruise?" I said.

From the drawer of a nearby secretary, LaRue hauled out a cascade of glossy brochures and psuhed them across the table to me.

"A flight from Atlanta to Miami in September," she said, "then a voyage aboard the *King Ruggedo* of the Royal Swedish Lines. We'll trace the coasts of Central and South America all the way around and finish six months later in San Diego."

"Six months!"

"You don't think that's too long, do you?"

"No," I said hastily. "No, of course not. Did you really plan this whole trip yourself?"

LaRue pointed her chin at me. "Actually, I had some help. Burling arranged many of the details. In fact, he's going to come along."

Burling Whickerbill, a bear of a man about my own age, had served the Keats family as general legal factotum for the past five years. In the wake of Skipper's death, he had unknotted many of Dad's tangled business affairs and now continued as our primary adviser and attorney.

"My God, Mother, as what? Your boyfriend?"

"You wanted to say gigolo, didn't you?" LaRue smiled. "Of course not. As escort and protector. I asked Cleveland Voss to lend Burling out for the duration of the cruise, and he, as a personal favor, agreed. I imagine that Burling will bring a computer along and get a lot of his legal work done right there aboard ship."

"Wait a minute," I said abruptly. "Who'll watch Kelli while you're gone?"

"Kelli's coming too. She finishes high school in June, and this fall she'll begin her freshman year as an unmatriculating student without portfolio."

"What?"

LaRue laughed at me. "Travel will function as her university, Will. What better time for it? And what better education can one get than the education of cosmopolitan firsthand experience?"

My initial resistance to this idea crumbled. In fact, the idea made perfect sense. If anything, I felt a mild resentment that neither Skipper nor LaRue had thought to take *me* on a cruise after *my* graduation from high school. But my parents had obviously learned from their mistakes with me, and Kelli had repeatedly profited from their gradual enlightenment. How, then, could I begrudge her the spoils of this process?

So, on the twenty-third of September, the first official day of autumn (and precisely twenty-three days before Olivia's kidnapping), I stood with Adrienne and Olivia in a waiting area on Concourse A in Hartsfield International and waved goodbye to the Delta jetliner lumbering down the runway with LaRue, Kelli, and Burling aboard. Their leavetaking exhilarated and saddened me, as if I understood that my freedom from my obligations to the Keats family would portend greater dedication and vigilance in the case of the Owsleys.

Three

P atches of amber and white light crawled our parlor walls. Emanating from the spinning dome atop the Georgia Power truck outside, these radiant surges provided the only illumination in the house. My Indiglo watch read five-thirty P.M., but my inner time sense told me that years had passed since Olivia's disappearance. Meanwhile, the roving lights from the truck steadily ratcheted up the intensity of my headache.

I held Adrienne to me on our couch as three bulky human shadows stood just inside the open door, occasionally shuffling their feet and conferring in husky whispers. Random gusts of wind swept past these men as if in search of additional household treasure. Neither Adrienne nor I cared. The storm had already taken our most precious possession.

From the yard, we could hear the crackling chatter of the radios in three patrol cars, the rattle of rain on their body metal, and the badinage between two Georgia Power linemen, one on a ladder and the other above him in a cherry-picker. Then, suddenly, the darkness ended: the house lights flared on, and the motor in the refrigerator clunked again into its senseless baritone drone. When the lineman outside collapsed his aluminum ladder, it sounded like the cranking of a torturer's rack.

With the return of our power, the three sheriff's department investigators—two in creased brown uniforms, one in a gray London Fog–style coat and a matching fabric cap—moved into action. The two in uniform took their directions from the tall, stern-faced man in mufti.

"Now that we can see what we're doing, I want you fellas to photograph those footprints on the carpet and to pick up soil samples. Keep your eyes peeled for fibers, butts, anything that looks like it doesn't belong. You know the drill. When you're finished inside, start on the yard and the outbuildings."

The chief sheriff's investigator turned away from his subordinates and advanced toward us. I took some hope from his self-assurance and looked sidelong at Adrienne to gauge her reaction.

Her bloodless face and taut dry skin made her frighteningly unfamiliar to me. Her lips repeatedly shaped the silent mantra "Olivia." She sat hunched forward, as if she had taken a solid blow to the gut. I tried to pull her to me again, but she stubbornly maintained her rigid, forward-leaning posture.

Nothing would purge the events of the past half hour from my mind. Seeing Adrienne's Camry, I had rushed bareheaded into the storm and down the long driveway toward her. Alarmed, she had instinctively braked her car and thrown it into park.

"Someone's stolen Olivia!" I shouted.

My self-evident panic convinced her instantly. Adrienne jumped from the car, hurried to me in the rain, and fiercely clutched my hands, meanwhile craning her head to survey every inch of the property within her view.

"Who?" she cried. "When?"

"Just now!" I said, shaking my head contradictorily, as if to negate what had happened. "Not five minutes ago."

Adrienne shoved me away and faced into the rain like the figurehead on a clipper ship. "Olivia! *Olivia!*" She swiveled toward another compass point. "Olivia, don't do this! Come back!"

Together, though not touching, we bellowed Olivia's name. Then, leaving Adrienne's car running, with its headlights glowing and its wiper blades tick-tocking, we raced into the house. Adrienne repeated my fruitless search of the interior, and I dialed 911.

The sheriff's department patrol cars and the chief investigator's unmarked companion arrived in fifteen minutes, the Georgia Power truck shortly thereafter. The two sheriff's deputies shone their flashlights all about the foundations of the house, just to make sure Olivia did not lie unconscious behind a hydrangea shrub. Rain ricocheted off their slickers and poured in veils from their hat brims. The stern-faced man in civvies directed us to the couch and told us to sit tight until the linemen had restored our power.

"We can't risk disturbing or obliterating evidence," he said. "If you have any patience at all, exercise it now."

Now, with light restored, the two deputy investigators began to sift and winnow our house for any signs of the person or persons who had stolen Olivia. I scarcely paid them any heed. My hands kept going to Adrienne's hunched shoulders, and because we could no longer huddle motionlessly in the gloom, I half wished that the darkness had continued. Now we had to confront our pain and act to remedy it.

The chief investigator knelt before us. Until that moment, in his gray raincoat and motoring cap, he had struck me as an automaton, a bloodless agent of the law, and my first clear sight of his angular jaw and the oddly dented tip of his nose had reinforced this impression. Only when he knelt, with an audible creaking of his joints, did his humanity assert itself.

"Captain Nicholas Cooper," he said, "chief investigator for this quadrant of the Speece County Sheriff's Department." He showed us a wallet-cased badge. "Sorry to invade your home like this, but given that someone has apparently kidnapped your daughter, you'd rather have us tromping around here than trying to collect information over the phone."

Without even thinking, I said, "Yes sir."

"Within the next twenty to thirty minutes, four or five more officers will arrive. They'd've come already, but this crazy storm has us stretched to the max. Rest assured, though, that we treat every child's disappearance with the utmost seriousness. Until the facts tell us otherwise, we regard all such reports as forcible abductions. To start, we'll turn your home and the entire surrounding neighborhood inside-out. More than likely, we'll call in the GBI to assist, and the search will spiral out from there."

This prospect did not so much hearten as appall me—Captain Cooper's words clearly spelled the end of our settled life—but Adrienne compelled herself to sit upright and spoke with only the faintest hint of a quaver:

"What can Will and I do?"

"Quite a damn bit." He rose with another stridulous creak and pulled a ladderback chair over. When he sat, his knees nearly touched Adrienne's and mine. "The three of us can take a powerful first whack at setting this calamity right." He produced a pen and notepad, then flexed the fingers of his right hand as if stiff wires articulated them. When he noticed me noticing, he said, "Early-onset arthritis. Runs in the family. This weather doesn't help any."

"I'm sorry," Adrienne said.

"The least of our worries," Cooper said. "For the record, tell me your names, ages, occupations, and exact relationship."

Adrienne recited her first three answers in a tone of rote obedience. She added, as if Cooper had failed to discern this fact, "I'm Olivia's mother. She's eight. She's only eight."

I took my turn, and even to my own ears I sounded like the robot voice heard in cybernetic elevators. Cooper jotted down my answers, though, and, because I had made the 911 call, urged me to detail my account first. I did so as succinctly as I could, in the same remote and mechanical accents, realizing as I spoke that my narrative represented Adrienne's first full acquaintance with the events preceding Olivia's disappearance.

Cooper said to Adrienne, "And you arrived home, Ms. Owsley, shortly after the purported abduction?"

The word *purported* slapped me hard, but Cooper was exercising an intelligent, self-protective discretion, and I resisted the impulse to contradict him, to defend myself, to protest too much.

"Yes," Adrienne said. "Just minutes too late to save her."

As if she might have succeeded where I had failed.

Cooper looked up from his notepad. "Please don't adopt that attitude, ma'am. Beating yourself up emotionally won't help pull you through this trouble."

"What will?" Adrienne said tightly.

"If a third party has indeed kidnapped your daughter, you need to embrace the fact that you bear no responsibility for the crime. None. You can't even lash yourself for the venial sin of temporary inattention."

"She wasn't here," I said. "What about me?"

Cooper gave me a thin but earnest smile. "So far as I can tell at this stage, same goes for you, Mr. Keats. Olivia had a competent and caring guardian watching over her, and she stayed sensibly inside during the beginnings of the storm. If under those conditions an outside party made off with her, *that* person—*that* sleazoid—has to answer for the deed, not either one of you."

Peripherally, I saw Cooper's deputies troop back outdoors after finishing their work inside. The crackle of police radios commingled again with the retreating static of the storm. When the door slammed, Cooper eyed me somewhat less benignly.

"You've told me that you and Ms. Owsley aren't married," he said.

"I've asked her. More than once. A dozen times at least."

"Easy. I'm not recruiting for the Moral Majority, Mr. Keats. I simply need to know if you're Olivia's biological dad."

The question made me flush, in part because I believed that nearly three years as Adrienne's lover and Olivia's stand-in father ought to increase my credibility as a parent, and in part because the question raised the sinister tabloid specter of the abusive step-father or male live-in.

"No, I'm not," I said as evenly as I could. "That honor belongs to Byron Owsley, who lives in Tocqueville on Jarboe Street." I happily gave Cooper the exact address. Byron's image had floated ghostily through my mind several times since the abduction; no more obvious suspect existed.

Cooper asked me if Byron and I maintained strained or cordial relations. He asked Adrienne if her ex had ever made any threats against either her or her daughter.

"I see as little of Byron as I can," I said. "When we do meet, he treats me with a certain formal curtness."

"No hostility?"

"More like mild resentment," I said, trying to be fair. "Generally, Adrienne passes Olivia over to him in some neutral spot for his alternate-weekend visitation."

Adrienne said, "I can't recall his ever making . . . a threat. I'd remember that, don't you think?"

One of the uniformed deputies reentered the house, edging awkwardly through the door with a familiar tool in his gloved hands: a pruning device with a fourteen-foot-long fiberglass pole and a cord-activated cutting beak at its business end. I had used it a month ago to thin the high foliage in the magnolia beside the house, then conscientiously racked it in the barn next to our weed-eater.

"Someone shoved this thing under the side porch, Captain Cooper," the deputy said, extending it toward us.

Cooper stood and examined the muddy instrument. "Take it along when we leave, Sergeant Pollit. Despite the dirt, we might lift some prints from it." Cooper turned back to me. "I assume you don't usually store that cutter where Pollit found it."

"No."

Pollit moved to exit, and Cooper, smiling faintly, crossed the room to hold the door open for him. Then he shut Pollit out and said, "I envision this sequence of events. The kidnapper determines that Mr. Keats and Olivia are inside, then enters the barn, looking to create a diversion. Except for the rain, he may have considered lighting a fire. Instead, he spots your pony and sets it free. Then the pruning hook catches his eye, and he figures he'll cut your power line. While Mr. Keats struggles to recapture the pony, he enters the unlocked front door and seizes Olivia. Out he goes, more than likely to a hidden vehicle."

I remembered an event from earlier in the day. "Working on the gutters, I saw a blue truck pause on the road by our mailbox!" At Cooper's urging, I recounted everything I could about the incident.

"Good." Cooper bit his bottom lip, then opened the front door again and summoned Pollit back inside. "Radio in this description of the girl and the clothes she had on. Also these specs on a truck that Mr. Keats saw earlier today." He handed a sheet from his pad to Pollit, who nodded his consent and exited much more smartly than he had with the pruning hook.

"What happens now?" I said.

Cooper spoke to Adrienne, as if her status as Olivia's mom called for him to reassure her. "Within the hour, roadblocks will snap into place on every highway and wheelbarrow track in the vicinity. We'll interview travelers. We'll question your neighbors. We'll notify the Georgia Crime Information Center folks and their national counterpart, the NCIC. Both maintain databases of missing children that law officers all around the country can easily access."

"All around the country?" Adrienne said. "Do you think this man intends to drag Olivia to some other state?"

"At present, I have no idea. But if we don't find your daughter within the next twenty-four hours, and if we have reason to suspect that the kidnapper has transported her across state lines, we'll call in the FBI out of Atlanta."

Those initials chilled me; they exponentially raised stakes that already loomed as high as the moon. Before I could speak a word of my dismay, though, at least three more sheriff's department patrol cars came whickering and strobing into the yard.

"Reinforcements," Cooper said. "If you'll excuse me, I'll go out and bring them up to speed." He studied Adrienne. "You all right with that?"

She nodded. "Go ahead."

Alone for a moment, she and I clutched each other. "God," I murmured into her throat, "I'm sorry. I'm so sorry."

Adrienne stroked my hair. "Shh."

We touched foreheads, not speaking, for three or four long minutes. Then came an inquiring rap at the door—a knocking more like that of a timid bellhop than a detective on the clock—and Cooper stuck his unreadable face inside. We separated, and he strode resolutely into the room.

Adrienne surprised me by standing to greet him. "Do you think we should expect a ransom demand?"

"I don't believe so, Ms. Owsley. Forget the movies. Most child abductions involve people known to the parents."

"Byron," I said, likewise getting to my feet.

Cooper flicked a glance at me. "Often an estranged parent *is* the perpetrator. For that very reason, we'll visit your ex this evening, Ms. Owsley, and grill him to a toasty brown."

"If he hasn't skipped the country entirely."

This time Cooper simply ignored me. "Your former husband *could* have Olivia innocently—if wrongly—with him. If so, we might have her safely back to you tonight."

Adrienne prayerfully gripped her own hands before her, and I put my arm around her shoulder.

Without bothering to knock, a burly, dark-haired man in his mid- to late fifties walked into the house, instinctively side-stepping the clayey footprints still visible on our carpet. Cooper introduced him as Colonel Lyman Stratford, chief deputy of the Speece County

Sheriff's Department, an investigator of almost legendary renown throughout the state. Stratford shook hands with Adrienne and me. A spectacular chaw of smokeless tobacco bulked out his cheek below his left ear.

Stratford addressed Cooper first. "*Almost* legendary, Nick?"

Cooper smiled. "Trying not to trowel it on *too* thick, sir."

Stratford grunted. "Facts are facts, though, and only a mule'd be stubborn enough to dispute 'em. I *am* a living legend."

Cooper saluted. "As you say, sir." On his way out, he gave us an ambiguous, deniable wink.

Alone with us, Stratford said, "From this point on, I run the operation, and I have questions for you that Nick couldn't dream of even after eating a handful of jimsonweed."

Indeed Stratford did. For virtually two uninterrupted hours, using a pocket recorder and a ready supply of tapes, he pumped Adrienne and me about our personal histories, our friends, relatives, and business associates, every single place that we had visited in the last eight years, and Olivia's teachers, pals, grades in school, sleeping and eating habits, enthusiasms, and dislikes. He also asked Adrienne for a selection of current photographs of Olivia, to supply not only his investigators but also the state and local media. We spent at least twenty bittersweet minutes picking through a shoebox of color snapshots and turning the felty pages of a big leather album.

During our lone break, Adrienne and I prepared and nibbled half-heartedly at a couple of green-banana and mayonnaise sandwiches. Midway through a bite, tears began to stream from Adrienne's eyes. But no other change in her face or manner occurred, and she matter-of-factly wiped away the tears with her napkin.

Stratford, who refused all offers of food and drink, recommenced his interrogation about thirty minutes later, focusing on addresses and telephone numbers of any of our relatives whom the abductor might approach for money or shelter. The revelation that my mother and kid sister had embarked on a six-month circumnavigation of Latin America prompted Stratford to shift his bolus of tobacco to the other jaw. Did he suspect their complicity, or automatically dismiss them as likely culprits? His stony expression defied interpretation.

Around midnight, the questioning—blessedly—ceased. Most of

the investigators had left, but seeing Stratford out and numbly receiving from him news that two deputies would remain overnight in case Olivia returned or the kidnapper attempted contact, I spotted Cooper in the yard.

Jacketless, I went down the steps with Stratford, then parted from him and trotted lightly over to Cooper, who had nonchalantly tacked toward his unmarked cruiser. Rain continued to fall, in Methodist sprinkles rather than torrents, and, hiking my flannel overshirt above my head, I noticed that one of the departing deputies had long since shut off the wipers and headlights on Adrienne's car. Inevitably, the patrol cars' Firestones had left ugly herringbone wallows in our flower beds.

At the door to his own vehicle, Cooper turned to face me. "How's Ms. Owlsey holding up?"

"Not too bad. By morning, she'll be running this case."

Cooper smiled his blade-thin smile. "We'll take good help from any quarter." We listened to the raindrops ploshing into the puddles around us. "By the way, was your father Skipper Keats?"

I recoiled, without quite knowing why. "Guilty as charged."

"Then you and I attended high school together in Columbus, Will. I'm Stan Cooper's son. Remember Cooper's Lumberyard, out on Victory Drive? My dad's still in business in the same location."

Inanely, we shook hands again, as if our previous introductions had failed to take. I mentally superimposed an old yearbook mug shot of the young Nicholas Cooper on the mature face before me, and the precision with which those features aligned startled me.

"You got your diploma a year ahead of me," I said. "Then you went out west somewhere. Right?"

"You could join our department on the basis of your memory alone, Will. California. Hollywood. I wound up on the police force there."

"What brought you back?"

"I never quite jibed with the weirdness in La-la land. A nasty divorce had something to do with it too. My repatriation, I mean."

"How long have you served with the Speece County boys?"

"A little over a year." His lips clicked together as if welded, and I realized that his native amiability aside, he disliked the reversal of roles that made me his interrogator.

"And here we stand tonight," I said mollifyingly, "reunited after a dozen years by a little girl's abduction. Life is strange."

Cooper massaged one lightly arthritic hand with the other, forbearing to comment on my platitude. "Good night, Will." He smiled that smile, then climbed into his car and rolled the window down. "We'll talk again soon."

He and two other deputies departed for their headquarters complex south of Tocqueville. I watched the parade of nimbused taillights recede into the drizzle, then walked back to the house to seek again—as I could envision myself doing repeatedly over the coming days—Adrienne's forgiveness.

Four

I once dreamt that I attended a party where a male corpse lay smack-dab in the center of an enormous Persian rug. None of my fellow partygoers paid the least heed to this pajama-clad body, but laughed and drank and bantered around it, as if it constituted a two-dimensional pattern in the carpet's weave. My efforts to alert everyone to the body's presence and to bring about its decorous removal all aborted. Finally, I too began to ignore the corpse. Now the same burdensome mix of dread and propriety in that dream had encumbered my waking life.

Sergeant Pollit and a deferential young cop whose name-tag identified him as Mazar had proceeded me into the house. I showed them where to find the coffeemaker, the drip filters, and the Folgers and advised them to help themselves to any snacks they fancied. Then I slowly climbed the carpeted stairs to the master bedroom.

Halfway up, I heard the telephones both upstairs and down ring in different but equally startling registers. I heard Adrienne scramble for the bedroom extension, but Pollit immediately snatched up the handset in the parlor.

A moment later he appeared at the foot of the stairs. "Mr. Keats, if you'd like to unplug the phones upstairs, we'll man the one down here so that the two of you can get some sleep." He had pale green eyes and a blond smear of a mustache that I had not noticed before.

"All right." As if we would easily sleep. "Who just called?"

Pollitt squinted up at me. "Captain Cooper. The DMV has provided us with a list of all the blue trucks in Georgia." Cooper may have said more, but Pollit did not choose to impart it to me.

Like a marble statue of herself on a medieval tomb, Adrienne lay in only bra and panties on our four-poster. She stared sightlessly at the ceiling as her right hand worked the wooden prayer beads of her wristlet *mala* and her lips silently recited a mantra. I shed my damp clothes and sat down on the edge of the bed in my ghostly white boxers.

Adrienne looked toward me. "I listened in on Cooper's phone call. They seem to be pursuing every lead they can."

"They should drive over to Byron's place. If it's empty, he took Olivia. If he's there alone, he knows where she is."

"You can't know that."

"I feel its truth."

Adrienne's next statement—half question, half assertion—threw me. "Because you found Skipper's missing dummy, you now seem to think you can play Sam Spade with Olivia's disappearance. Don't forget that she's flesh and blood, not teak and molded plastic."

I returned Adrienne's admonitory gaze.

She relented and reached for my hand. "I'm sorry."

I readily took hers. "You can't tell me you've cleared Byron of any culpability in this. Privately, I mean."

"Of course not. In fact—"

"What?" I prompted her.

"I neglected to tell Captain Cooper something about Byron." She took a breath and continued: "Byron disapproves of our living arrangements. He's told me more than once that you have no right to participate in Olivia's upbringing. As if he ever contributed more than an amorous spasm to her life or well-being!"

I could not keep myself from saying, "That's motive right there, Adrienne. Why didn't you mention it?"

"I don't know. I just couldn't accuse him outright."

"A statement of fact doesn't qualify as an accusation. Let Cooper and his associates decide what Byron's mean-spiritedness means."

An ambiguous silence grew between us. Then Adrienne said, "Byron thinks you're spoiled, and he's envious of our life together."

I scorned Byron's reported opinion as the result of spleen and jealousy, but it still rankled. "Do I care what Byron thinks? When Cooper and Stratford interview him, he'll reveal his true colors. Assuming he hasn't long since skipped."

Another silence. Then, plaintively, "God, I miss her. I miss her as much as if I hadn't seen her in a year. As if she were—"

"Don't say it."

Adrienne rolled off the mattress, seized a pale yellow sleep shirt from one of the bedposts, and shrugged into it. She padded over to the dresser and picked up a small, gilt-framed photograph of Olivia, which she scrutinized hungrily in the grainy half-light.

"Forgive me, Will, but I need to do this." She proceeded down the hall to a sewing room that we had converted into a *zendo* for Adrienne and Olivia, a space devoted to Zen meditation. There she would sit on a teal-green cushion and a mat of the same color before a simple altar: a low table bearing a Buddha, an incense pot, a vase of cut flowers, and several tokens of appreciation for the gift of the material world. These last included a seashell, a beetle's weightless exoskeleton, a vial of sand, and a comical windup dinosaur.

Although Adrienne wanted solitude, I knew that once settled in, she would find my half-apprehended presence unobtrusive. I gave her a few moments, and then followed her down the hall to the *zendo*. Standing in the gloom of the corridor, I watched her bow before the carven soapstone Buddha and place Olivia's photo on the table beside it. The she lowered herself gracefully to her cushion, arranged her legs into the Burmese lotus position (which she had often recommended to me as a less taxing variant of the familiar full-lotus), and cradled her hands in her lap, thumbtip to thumbtip.

I admired Adrienne's stillness, I envied her the serenity that her practice seemed to impart to her, and I felt an eddy of the concealed resentment—jealousy, even—that it often stirred in me because I could never effectively drift into the same unfathomable waters that she did. On the wall above her altar hung a peculiar hand-lettered poster: a family tree of practitioners whose root was Buddha and whose sinuous trunk grew upward through the millennial masters to Adrienne's own teacher, Jim Rakestraw, a Massachusetts man whom I had never met.

As Adrienne's *samadhi* almost perceptibly deepened, I felt my own heart jump behind its bars of cartilage and bone. The very soles of my feet burned.

Skipper and LaRue Keats had raised me, albeit without enthusiasm or conviction, in the basic protocols of Southern Protestantism.

Not the tub-thumping or shouting sort, but the tip-your-hat-to-the-preacher and don't-cuss-on-the-sidewalk variety. Somewhere in my youth, however, the idea of a pain-racked, human God had crucified itself in my heart, and my skeptical intellect had never really overthrown it. Not even my parents' conversion to the self-help mysticism of New Age spirituality during my high school years had dislodged this embarrassing figure from my imagination. I rarely attended church, or prayed, or read the received texts anymore, but the idea of God as a personality—a loopy, idiosyncratic, *loving* person—still mysteriously moved me.

Adrienne—in her adolescence a level-headed convert to Buddhism—accepted this fact about me. Her practice encouraged such acceptance. She liked that even as a hard-nosed modern Southerner, I respected her own spiritual path. She even found subtly flattering the fact that her practice inarguably attracted me—if only because I admired how sitting seemed to augment her galloping appetite for life. And so she frequently urged me to undertake within the framework of my unorthodox Christianity a Buddhist practice of my own. Since my father's death, these polite but persistent entreaties had only increased.

Standing outside Adrienne's *zendo,* a room where Olivia also regularly sat, I mulled these issues as I worked to quell both my sense of guilt and my embarrassing resentment. If Adrienne could center herself in this venerable way, why should I begrudge her the accomplishment? My own spiritual immaturity held no relevance. She looked simply lovely sitting there. She looked serene. She also looked remote, but that perception stemmed more from my egotistical bias than from the essential orientation of Adrienne's heart. Maybe she still refused my marriage proposals because of my lack of insight into such matters, large and small. This thought stung.

I turned on my heel, my nostrils full of incense and shame, and retreated to our bedroom. The house made intermittent wooden settling noises, as if to mock my own unsettled state, and sleep did not come.

Five

O ccasionally I heard Sergeant Pollit and Deputy Mazar moving about downstairs. I began to torture myself with speculations. What if the kidnapper did call, either to taunt us or to demand a ransom? If someone other than Adrienne or I answered, wouldn't he perhaps know and hang up? I pulled on a pair of flannel pajama trousers and left the bedroom.

The two deputies sat almost complacently over coffee cups and Keebler Pecan Sandies at the dinette in the kitchen. The young Mazar, sandy-haired and freckled, jumped to his feet, sloshing coffee in the process, while Pollit twisted around to face me with a competent smile and no signs of guilt whatsoever. I stated my concern.

"Any kidnapper who's not a total space cadet will automatically assume you've contacted law enforcement agencies by now," Pollit said.

"Meaning?"

"It won't surprise him to hear an unfamiliar voice on the phone. He may even relish talking to cops, especially if he likes to play mind games with authority."

"Or if *she* does," Mazar said.

Pollit grimaced tolerantly at the younger deputy. Mazar lowered himself back into his chair and concealed his sheepishness by helping himself to another cookie. His front teeth snapped off the first bite with a startlingly loud report.

When I made no move to leave, Pollit said, "Almost every call coming in here will concern routine procedural matters. But if you really want to answer the phone every time it rings, Mr. Keats, then just plug it back in. One stipulation, though. Don't answer until the third ring. That gives us time to pick up and monitor the call."

"Okay."

"In my opinion, though, the abductor wants you all to sweat some and won't even bother to call tonight, if he ever does."

"You don't think he wants money?"

"Everyone wants money. He may want you all's daughter even more."

"Or she," Mazar said. "It really could be a she. Some crazed, lonely woman who can't have children or who just miscarried or something."

"Jerry," Pollit said, "have another cookie."

I returned to the bedroom and plugged our telephone back in. Adrienne continued her focused, solitary sitting in the *zendo*.

Everyone wants money, I thought, once more lying alone on our king-size mattress in my boxers. That indisputable assertion included Byron Owlsey. My gut still persisted in assigning him a role in all this. Even if he had snatched Olivia for emotional reasons, I could not rule out monetary demands from him, now or later. Skipper's final bequeathment to me, along with my share of the settlement from Satish Gupta dissolving their thirty-year partnership, continued to cushion me against the financial hardships that otherwise would have attended the loss of my job. Byron knew of these windfalls; he may have both frowned upon and coveted them.

I let my mind glide back to the September evening over a year ago when I had revealed to Adrienne the details of my new financial condition. We sat at an isolated table in the dining pit of T. J. Crowley's in the Peachtree Mall in Columbus and nursed a couple of glasses of California Cabernet Sauvignon. Generous shrimp cocktail appetizers sat before us on glossy indigo china platters.

"Wow," Adrienne said.

"What's wow-able?"

"How often does this sort of thing"—she lifted her wine glass, nodded at her shrimp and the surroundings—"happen to a simple, apple-cheeked Massachusetts gal?"

"A gal of your caliber? Not as often as it should."

"How will I ever force myself back into a classroom on Monday?"

"Trust me, teaching's in your blood."

"Which, right now, consists of equal parts plasma and alcohol."

"Good. To quote the immortal Ogden Nash, 'Candy is dandy, but liquor is quicker.' "

"Unfortunately, T. J. Crowley's doesn't lend itself to instant gratification of that sort. Fortunately, my place does. Olivia's overnighting with her bosom pal of the month, Felicity Garner. *Mi casa es su casa.*"

"Nice. And nicer for being unexpected and convenient. But you know what I'd really prefer?"

"Complete hedonistic abandon, right? To quote the immortal Paul McCartney, 'Why don't we do it in the road.' "

"No, what I'd actually prefer is a place of our own. Emphasis on the 'our.' "

Adrienne took a long, deliberate sip of her wine. Just as deliberately, she ate a shrimp. "You want us to move in together?"

"More than that. I want us to buy a *house* together."

"Together? On my salary? Just because you're one of the nouveau riche—"

I clasped her hand across the tabletop. "The money means nothing to me if I can't do something decent for us. No, scratch 'decent.' Revolutionarily good."

"What about a job? You still don't have one. Don't you want to coast on your money until you decide what you really want to do?"

"I already know that. Eventually, I want to get back into counseling kids. But right now, I want to buy us a house."

"Gee, I think the banks are closed at this hour."

I plunged ahead. "I provide only the downpayment, see, a few measley thousand dollars. That leaves me plenty in the bank. You pick up the monthly mortgage payments, which won't amount to much more than you're already paying to rent your current place."

"Suddenly I feel like I'm dating Alan Greenspan."

I ignored her. "And if I move out of the old Keats squirrel barn in Mountboro, LaRue can rent it out to somebody else to supplement her savings. Everybody benefits."

"It all sounds fiscally irresistible, Mr. Chairman."

"Tease me all you like, but I want this, Adrienne. I want this the way—well, the way a coho salmon blazes red to spawn and die."

She laughed at my melodramatic analogy. "I'll go along with the spawning, but please don't up and die just yet."

I had won her over. Within a month we found the very house in which I lay on the interminable night of Olivia's abduction. From nearly the beginning until the abduction, our delectable new living arrangments had felt as settled as Greek history. . . .

At some point I dozed off. When I awoke, lifted from sleep by a shapeless apprehension rather than by any vivid nightmare, the bed-side clock radio read 4:17. Adrienne had either never rejoined me in our bed or else abandoned it again during my restless slumber. Still muzzy, I put my feet on the cold floor and shuffled down the hall to the *zendo*. Only the soapstone Buddha greeted me.

I walked back down the hall and peered into Olivia's room. Adrienne lay fetally curled in our daughter's bed, clutching Olivia's photo just under her chin. The sight made me briefly fancy that Olivia had returned to us as a young woman exactly resembling her bereaved mother. I went to the narrow bed and gently touched the woman's shoulder.

"Adrienne."

She closed her eyes tighter, drew her shoulders in, and mumbled unintelligibly. Olivia's name formed on her lips, though, as did the heartbreaking word "lost." I crawled into the bed beside her, to embrace and gently rock her. Amazingly, in this way I fell asleep beside the woman who steadfastly declined to become my wife.

Sunlight stabbing into the room—upon whose blue walls we had painted puffy clouds and Technicolor hot-air ballons—revealed that yesterday's storm had moved on. I could hear the shower running, and my watch told me it was 6:23. I pulled myself up like an am-bitious puppet, returned gracelessly to the master bedroom, and dressed in yesterday's clothes. Despite the sun, the day looked cold. Blessedly, my flannel overshirt had nearly dried, and my woolen socks still felt soft and natural.

Sergeant Pollit and Deputy Mazar had left the kitchen. I poured myself a tarry cup of leftover coffee, sipped it, and spit it into the sink. As I contemplated the orange-juice carton in the refrigerator, Mazar reentered, looking as sunken-eyed and fatigued as a sandbag-ger on all-night levee duty. Clearly he had not even dozed.

"Thanks," I said, sticking out my hand. "Thanks a lot."

Somewhat bemusedly, he shook with me. "Captain Cooper's going to find your little girl," he said. "You should hear about some of the cases he cracked in California."

"Don't you and Pollit get a break?"

"Our relief will arrive within the hour, sir, and the roadblocks we set up last night will stay in operation with rotating personnel all day."

I stated the obvious. "Nobody called."

"No sir. Could happen, though. Could happen this morning."

"I appreciate the watchful waiting you and Pollit did. I mean that." Like a politician on automatic, I reshook his hand. Mazar politely indulged me.

"Good luck, sir. I wish you all the best of luck." He exited without my ever learning what had brought him to the kitchen, if not simply to check on whoever had descended.

Adrienne still had not come down, and I had no appetite at all. I suddenly recollected, though, that one other member of our afflicted household might want breakfast: Roogy Batoon.

I squelched across the lawn to the barn. Inside, Roogy Batoon greeted me heartily, alternately tossing her head and bumping her muzzle into my chest. I gave her a feedbag and tried to picture Olivia running to embrace the pony after her ecstatic reunion with Adrienne and me. Like one of Olivia's Nerf toys, however, this vision had no heft, primarily because I could construct no plausible scenario for Olivia's return.

Outside again, I ambled to the base of a tall but spreadeagle oak beyond Roogy Batoon's paddock. Ten feet off the ground perched Olivia's treehouse, its scratchy rope ladder dangling to my waist. On moving to this country place outside Tocqueville, I had wanted to transport my own childhood treehouse from behind Skipper's Keep to the property I now owned with Adrienne. In one of his few displays of selfless paternal love, Skipper had initiated the building of that treehouse, and I still had fond memories of it. Unhappily, it had deteriorated too badly to survive such a move. For which reason my ever-amenable pal J. W. Young had helped Olivia and me construct a new and improved version in this ancient, labyrinthine oak. Afterward, J. W. had bestowed an unexpected compliment: "Son, if

I hold you under my wing for eight hours a day for a decade or so, you might could grow into a halfway decent country carpenter."

I grabbed the ladder and sent it swinging. The little house above me looked as desolate as the farmhouse at my back. Who knew when Olivia would inhabit either of them again?

Back in the kitchen, I dropped two Pop Tarts into the toaster and started a fresh pot of coffee. Watching the coffee drip, I realized that after showering and dressing, Adrienne would have returned to the *zendo* for another stint of sitting. I could have prayed, I suppose, but I manifested as little skill at that as I did at disciplined meditation. I lacked commitment, conviction, and patience.

Adrienne exhibited all these qualities. Zen did not, as some people believed, blunt or vitiate her emotions. In fact, she probably felt things more keenly than did nonpractitioners. However, ordinarily she held the reins on her feelings, rather than their exercising a tyrannical control over her. Additionally, Zen allowed her to focus on matters immediately at hand, to the exclusion of past or future distractions, and guided her to a self-submerging compassion for all of the material world, animate and inanimate. Living day to day with Adrienne, I had seen her distill these theoretical benefits of the Zen way into the real-world practicality that some proponents had termed "grandmother wisdom." How could I fail to envy her?

Pouring a cup of coffee, I recalled a parable that Adrienne had told me on the day of my father's burial in Mountboro, for it had an almost prescient application to the kidnapping of our daughter.

"Very long ago," Adrienne began, "a Zen master with a devoted wife and several rambunctious children experienced the untimely death of his youngest son. This event devastated him. He mourned with conspicuous fervor for an unseemly length of time. In fact, his students could not square his extravagant display with his low-key teachings."

"Students never change," I said.

"Listen, don't talk. So the disciples gossiped. They consulted skeptically among themselves. Then, summoning their joint nerve, they approached the heartbroken master. 'Master,' they said, 'have you not told us that life is an illusion?' He raised his tear-stained face and replied, 'Yes, of course, for life is indeed an illusion.' The students exchanged perplexed looks, and the bravest of them said, 'If all is illusion, sir, why do you weep so unrestrainedly over the death of your son?' " Adrienne fell silent.

"What did he say?" I asked her.

"He said, 'This is the most painful illusion I have ever encountered!' "

As if this memory had summoned her to join me in our own present painful illusion, Adrienne came up behind me and put her hands on my shoulders.

"Good morning, Will."

"That's debatable, but thank you for saying so." I drew her around and kissed her. She broke away, pale but dry-eyed, wanly smiling.

"There are good days and better days. I have to keep believing that."

Her words put me in mind of the credo of the Native American warrior: *Today is a good day to die.* I kept the association to myself. Aloud, I said, "Yeah, me too."

I poured Adrienne a small cup of coffee, which she doctored with skim milk and a spoonful of tupelo honey, and the toaster launched its hot prefabricated missiles. The contrast to yesterday's breakfast, neither of us mentioned: it surrounded us like a poison fog. We ate in silence.

Eventually I said, "Adrienne, why did you keep Byron's last name?"

She looked up as if I had clapped a pair of cymbals together. "You just can't get past Byron, can you?" The irritation in her voice almost gratified me; not flawless, she still had idiosyncratic sore spots of her own.

"I've never understood why after your divorce you didn't revert to your maiden name. Was it for Olivia? After all, Adrienne Thompson has a pleasant enough ring."

"It was partly for Olivia," she admitted. "Half at least."

"And the other half?"

"Adrienne Thompson, Will, was a gullible twenty-one-year-old who fell for the sweet-talking, handsome exterior of an egotistical scoundrel. That Adrienne Thompson lacked the brains to leave this guy until she had endured three years of verbal abuse and deception." She set her cup down with a heavy clink. "But that Adrienne

Thompson no longer exists. Along about that third unbearable year, she died, while the semi-enlightened Adrienne Owsley lived on."

"Adrienne," I said apologetically, regretting my question.

She ignored my attempt to halt or divert her. "You fell in love with a woman named Adrienne Owsley, Will, and that same woman intends to retrieve her missing daughter from whoever took her."

This statement put an emphatic period to our talk. It also led me to believe that in her heart of hearts she too suspected Byron of this new betrayal.

Six

Sergeant Pollit stuck his stolid head into the kitchen. "Our replacements just got here, folks, and Jerry and I wanted to tell you all goodbye. Hang in there." Jerry Mazar, peering over Pollit's shoulder, gave us a cheerful two-fingered salute. Then both departing men edged aside, allowing the newcomers to enter.

"Morning," a uniformed woman said in a file-on-burred-metal contralto. "Sergeant Lisa Sleator at your service." She circled the dinette and knelt beside Adrienne as a male deputy moved to fill the empty doorway. "How you making it today, honey?"

Sleator's frosted brunette hair—cut short and recently blown dry—glinted in the sunlight; a hint of eyeshadow purpled her thin lids and brought out the lavender in her irises. Tucked under her right arm, her Smokey the Bear hat resembled a big Daliesque soup tureen.

"Moment by moment." Adrienne spontaneously embraced Sleator. Hearing herself addressed as "honey" had not put her off—maybe just the opposite.

Sleator nodded at her partner. "That's Deputy Kinney."

Kinney nodded curtly, his thick arms folded across his even thicker chest. He wore the raw face of an Australian lifeguard and the empty disinterest of a well-fed hammerhead.

"A shy GBI agent named Trent Badcock is in your front room handling call-tracing," said Sleator. "I think he's taken your most comfortable chair."

"He's more than welcome to it," said Adrienne.

"More forensic people will arrive shortly," Sergeant Sleator announced, "to take care of some investigative procedures we couldn't accomplish last night. Don't let the kidnapper's silence get you all down. Good things are happening even as we speak."

"Like what?" I said.

"Haven't you all seen the news?" Kinney said, almost accusingly.

"No," Adrienne said. "Should we have?"

Kinney took a step aside, granting us passage to our own parlor. "Why not take a gander for yourselves?"

The four of us filed into the living room where the big, gray-black Phillips Magnavox already cast its cathode glow and its antic buzz into the otherwise gloomy room. A bespectacled, curly-haired man in a brown suit and an unfortunate maroon-and-yellow tie had comandeered the remote. Upon our entrance, he scrambled to his feet like a babysitter's trespassing boyfriend. A strip of antisnoring tape crossed the bridge of his nose.

"Oh," he said. "I—this must be yours." He extended the remote.

"Relax, Trent," Sleator said. "Turn it up so they can hear it."

Badcock increased the volume. The female anchor on the Atlanta NBC affiliate's lead-in to the *Today* show distinctly said, "—Olivia Owsley," thereby cuing a fresh placarding of our daughter's smiling face for the viewing public. Adrienne blanched. The anchor, in voiceover, summarized the facts of the abduction and recited a pair of telephone numbers that any witnesses or tipsters could call.

"By now," Sleator said, her arm comfortingly around Adrienne's waist, "hundreds of thousands of people across the state have seen Olivia's picture. A tremendous plus for our side."

The enlarged photo, grainy and washed out, faded, and the co-anchors of the *Today* show replaced Olivia's image almost as if it had never occupied the screen at all. They promised an interview with a best-selling author, cooking tips, and an analysis of the latest crisis in the Middle East.

"Turn that off," Adrienne said.

"Yes'm." Trent Badcock pointed the remote and annihilated the picture. A gauzy false twilight filled the curtained room, and for one long moment we stood together like strangers in an elevator. Badcock placed the remote atop the set, mumbled an apology, and wandered over to the phone to fuss with his aluminum-cased tracing unit.

Sergeant Sleator spoke to Adrienne and me. "Don't take this wrong, folks, but we'd like the two of you to come to our headquarters this morning for polygraph testing."

"A lie detector," I said. "You suspect us of lying?"

"Just you," Kinney said, then guffawed.

My hands involuntarily fisted. Sergeant Sleator's intercession stopped me from doing anything foolish. "Please excuse Mouth Almighty," she immediately said.

Kinney guffawed again, but nervously.

Adrienne further defused the situation by asking, "Do you plan to subject my ex-husband to a polygraph test too?"

"Yes indeed."

"He's still around, then?" I said.

"You bet. The Tocqueville police found him at home yesterday evening. He's already undergone an opening round of questioning."

Adrienne and I exchanged a glance. If Byron had not taken Olivia—and his presence at home seemed to absolve him of the actual kidnapping—then recovering Olivia would undoubtedly demand more effort, more resources, more time.

"Do Will and I have to report for the test the same time Byron does?" Adrienne asked Sleator. "I don't want to have to deal with his accusations."

"His grandstanding," I said.

"Not a problem. We'll conduct these tests over the next several days. Besides, I overheard Captain Cooper expressing his intention to allow Mr. Owsley to stew a little first."

I said, "Why not examine Byron early and push this investigation to a swift conclusion?"

"The boss wants to uncover a fact or two to sharpen our approach," Sleator said. "Ms. Owsley's ex may cut himself on an unexpected question. Good polygraph strategy sometimes requires a little patience."

"Should you be telling us these things?" Adrienne said. "Potential suspects."

Sleator grinned. "Honey, you got book rules and real-life rules. I trust my instincts, which give you two a gigantic edge over old Byron."

I stood with my hands in my pockets. Adrienne nodded thoughtfully, then went upstairs to change clothes for a trip to the new sheriff's department complex. Sleator stepped outside for a smoke. As Kinney vanished into the kitchen and Badcock continued trifling with his equipment, I stared at the Magnavox. Something about its bulging, lidless eye teased my memory.

The VCR. Olivia, before going outside and falling in the mire of Roogy Batoon's corral, had watched a portion of her tape of *The Wizard of Oz*. Reluctant to break away from her favorite scene, she had taken longer to join me than I had expected. I knew with absolute certainty which scene had so enthralled her, but to test my intuition I turned on the set, partially rewound the video in the built-in VCR, and hit the *play* button.

Over an hour into the film, Dorothy and her three self-consciously refurbished comrades stand outside the Wizard's Emerald City palace, obeying a doorman's command to await the Great Oz's pleasure. The Cowardly Lion sings "If I Were King of the Forest" and then elaborates feistily on courage, his definitive theme. Watching this familiar piece of business, I froze. Olivia loved what came next, and when Bert Lahr in his prosthetic jowls pronounced the riddle that we gleefully cried in unison nearly every time we watched together, I literally had to bite my lower lip:

"What makes the muskrat guard his musk? Courage!"

I abruptly killed the picture, the sound, and, very nearly, the painful memories. Deputy Kinney had reentered the room; he and Trent Badcock both had their eyes on me. What juvenile whim or character flaw, they no doubt wondered, had induced me to watch a snippet of this particular film in the wake of Olivia's premeditated theft? I looked hard at each man in turn, and they averted their eyes.

Muskrat courage. A paradox, a seeming oxymoron. Lions have courage. Or, like Baum's confidence-crippled king of the beasts, obsessively seek it. Elephants, tigers, rhinoceroses, fighting bulls, wolverines—frightening animals from the mongoose to the Minotaur—enjoy legendary reputations for courage.

But the muskrat? Lowly water-dwelling rodent, secretive vegetarian, harmless furry swimmer amid the reeds? Was it not more preyed upon than preying? If so, why would the Cowardly Lion cite it as an example of stealthy, aggressive, and notably abundant courage?

Olivia, no pushover for either the hard sell of Madison Avenue or the rhyming pop of Hollywood songwriters, had initially balked at this whimsical assertion.

"No lion would look up to a muskrat," she had protested.

"What about a Cowardly Lion?"

"Nu-huh! He only *thinks* he's a coward."

"What if I said the muskrat has the admirable existential courage to be itself and nothing more than itself?"

Olivia thought a moment, then said, "*Every* animal has that kind of courage, Will. Only people try to be something they're not."

"Very astute."

"I know. Like at school, Stanley Roberts, he pretends he's dumb, not smart, so the other boys won't call him Teacher's Pet."

"Well, that kind of pretending *is* dumb, which suggests that Stanley's *not* really smart, which further suggests that he isn't pretending."

Olivia squinted skeptically, then returned to task. "The Cowardly Lion thinks the muskrat has a *special* courage. Can't you explain it to me? I thought you understood this stuff."

I struggled to redeem myself. "The muskrat has muskrat courage, Olivia. He's small and relatively helpless, but when somebody unfairly shoves him around, he stands fast. He never spoils for a fight, but he doesn't run from one either."

"He guards his musk!"

"Abso-dang-lutely. He doesn't have claws like a mole, or fangs like a wolf, or armor like a tortoise, but when he believes in something, by golly the little guy stands up for it. And that applies even when his own pelt isn't at risk. If he sees a gator menacing his wife or kids, what do you suppose he does? Cuts and runs?"

"No sir! He guards *their* musk too!"

"You bet. Keep your paws off my family's musk, you big creep!"

"Right!" Olivia stopped bouncing and studied me with an almost poignant bemusement. "What *is* musk, Will?"

At this point in my reverie, Adrienne came back down, wearing her blue denim jumper and a long-sleeved ribbed white jersey. Her prayer beads peeked from beneath the end of one sleeve. Her gaze drifted indifferently past Kinney and Badcock as she plainly looked for Sergeant Sleator, who just then providentially made her return.

"Hook us up to your infernal machines," Adrienne said. "No one at work expects me in today. Imagine that."

"Muskrat courage," I said aloud. Everyone looked at me as if I had spoken Martian, for not even Adrienne recognized this peculiar expression as a heartening private catchphrase between Olivia and me.

"I just mean that we could all use a little muskrat courage about now," I said by way of unhelpful explanation.

"Any brand of courage will serve," Adrienne said, "if you believe in it."

Seven

When Adrienne and I moved in together, I traded in my '94 Saturn for a used Toyota Tacoma truck in good condition. A pickup better suited my new lifestyle as a househusband and country steward. With it, I could haul lumber, grain, hay bales, pine straw, guttering, PVC fittings and pipes, burlap-wrapped shrubs, and tag-sale furniture. I could drive out into our fields to set salt licks, replace termite-riddled fence posts, unclog foliage-littered drainage ditches, or stand silent before a pale blue wall of sky.

Visibly anxious about leaving our house in the care of three law-enforcement officers, Adrienne preceded me down the broad steps to the Tacoma. In the set of her shoulders and in her stride, I detected resentment—an emotion I knew she despised in herself—at the very presence of these watchful cops in our home.

"We'll survive this," I said, leading her to the truck.

"I don't doubt it." She halted and looked me full in the face. "But at this moment, Will, *our* survival doesn't concern me much." As she gripped the handle of the passenger door, I remembered that one of Olivia's favorite toys, a stuffed Cat in the Hat figure, lay on the cramped rear seat of my Tacoma.

"Wait." I tried to reach in and nudge the Cat in the Hat to the floorboards.

"I've already seen it, Will. Please don't treat me like an emotional invalid." She climbed into the forward cab and secured the Cat in the Hat in her lap. I slid in next to her and turned the key in the ignition. "Unless you want to move into a hotel, we'll continually bump into Olivia's stuff, until she comes home to us."

I put my hand on her knee. "Sorry. No hotel. No more clumsy evasions."

We drove east on West Point Lake Road toward Tocqueville. Adrienne clutched the Cat in the Hat the way my father had sometimes clutched Dapper O'Dell, his signature ventriloquist's figure, and the way many of the distressed children in my office had clutched the felt or artificial-fur puppets I had given them to calm them.

In 1995, Speece County dedicated a new Sheriff's Office and Jail Facility directly behind the site of the old County Stockade. The complex consisted of several vaguely art deco buildings with enamel panel facings of cobalt blue and charcoal gray—suggesting an ironic architectural reprise of the Civil War—and high slit windows. Because it sat off Highway 27, we had to take a looping perimeter road past a number of factories and industrial headquarters to reach the access drive to the new facility. Approaching it, I felt like an interloper, without passport or visa, in a foreign military state. Adrienne's hunched shoulders and locked knees hinted at her own distress.

"It looks like a camp for Chinese dissidents."

I could hardly dispute her assessment. Hurricane fence surrounded the contoured cell blocks and the parking lot behind the Legolike fortress of the Sheriff's Office. Coils of razor ribbon garnished the top two feet of the fence.

" 'If you build it,' " I said, pulling into an asphalt lot the size of a soccer field, " 'we'll fill it.' The nation's latest get-tough-on-crime motto: 'Please fence me in.' "

Adrienne said, "Still, I can think of at least one sleazeball I'd gladly fence in forever."

"No argument there." I waved at the expanse of shimmering asphalt. "We can thank God for one small favor."

"What's that?"

"Not a single camera crew or satellite truck in sight. I feared this place might be swarming with them."

"Maybe their *absence* should worry us."

"Like the Japanese alarm cricket whose silence spelled trouble? I hope not."

We walked across the asphalt lot and then along a pebbly sidewalk to the binocular case–shaped lobby. To enter either the sheriff's hermetic office to the left or the immaculate tiled jail to the right, you had to state your business to a uniformed woman in a control booth. If she approved, she would spring one of the reinforced glass doors on the far side of the anteroom. Beside her booth hung a poster warning deadbeat dads to make their child-support payments or forfeit their drivers' licenses. An image of a guilty John Doe's license bore a "Suspended" stamp, and beneath it ran the admonitory legend "Pay Up or Walk!"

For all his shortcomings, Byron Owsley had never failed to make his child-support payments. He generally handed over a check, or a money order, or even a fat wad of cash when Adrienne transfered guardianship of Olivia on alternate weekends. No nailing him on this charge, unfortunately.

"We've come to see Captain Nicholas Cooper," I told the matron in the booth. "He expects us."

After securing permission via her mike and headset, she pressed a button to open the left door. We stepped through into an echoey, air-conditioned space. Before we could sit down in the connected, tweed-upholstered chairs here, Cooper emerged from a door deeper within the complex. He could not have slept much last night, but he still managed to look rested. He wore a strained but amiable smile and a white knit shirt with "Captain Cooper" above its pocket in blue.

"Ms. Owsley, Mr. Keats, thanks for coming."

"Have you learned anything new?" Adrienne asked him.

"Let me answer that question after we've administered your polygraph tests." Cooper smiled to soften any inadvertant rebuke. "Please follow me."

He led us into a windowless maze: overhead fluorescents, featureless walls, and blank industrial doors. A sense of plunging into a machine-augured rabbit hole overcame me. I took Adrienne's hand as a way to bolster my nerve and orient myself. As we walked, Cooper explained that, although only three years old, the facility already held its maximum population of prisoners.

"If you build it, we will fill it," I said lightly.

"Amen," Cooper said. "We have beds for three-hundred, thirty-two of them in a cell-block for women. Right now, though, we're holding three-hundred and twelve prisoners, forty-one of them female."

"We've come a long way from Mayberry."

Adrienne yanked my hand. "Please excuse him, Captain Cooper. Some of your Deputy Kinney's wit may have rubbed off on Will."

"Ah, Mouth Almighty." Cooper shook his head. "Rest assured I'll speak to the boy." He returned to his spiel. "Of course, we get city cases from Tocqueville, DUIs and drug runners caught by the highway patrol. Robbery suspects, wife-beaters, prosties, and even an alleged murderer or two from places as cozy as our county subdivisions."

We stopped in the entrance to a carpeted bay divided into working cubicles for the senior investigators. Each cubicle had a desk, a computer, and pegboard walls festooned with idiosyncratic items: birthday cards, calendars, theater tickets, family portraits, photocopied poems, children's artwork, and an assortment of bumper stickers:

START IN ON CRACK, YOU MAY NEVER GET BACK
MAKE MY DAY—HUG A COP
DRUG INVESTIGATORS DO IT UNDERCOVER

Chief Deputy Stratford spotted us and emerged from a full-sized glass-walled office just off the bay. He shook my hand as if intent on crushing it to grape-pulp, then lifted Adrienne's as if to kiss it.

"Ms. Owsley. Sure hope you got some sleep." He waltzed the chaw on the left side of his mouth over to the right.

"Some. Do we really have to do this? Take lie-detector tests?"

"Actually, no. In fact, we usually wait two or three days before even suggesting such a step."

"What makes Olivia's case different?" I asked.

Stratford looked at me ruminatively. "Not a great deal. My 'legendary' instincts give me good feelings about you all. So your own innocence constitutes only half the issue. I figured if you all willingly submitted to testing early on, that would give us some leverage with Ms. Owsley's ex and other potential suspects."

"Like who?"

"I don't care to divulge that yet," Stratford told me brusquely.

Adrienne said, "I hate to feel compelled. But if it gives you leverage over Byron—"

"Some," Stratford said. "A little."

"—then we'll take your tests. At least I will."

"I will too," I said, feeling like the Boy Wonder to Adrienne's Caped Crusader.

Captain Cooper said, "We have an experienced polygraph examiner down from the GBI office in Atlanta. He'll conduct your tests—separately. We'd like you to go first, Mr. Keats. You okay with that?"

Despite my innocence, my guts churned like potatoes in a metal hopper. "Sure. Will Adrienne have some company, or will she have to sit alone?"

"I'll chat with her," Cooper said. "The time'll fly by."

Stratford grunted. "Looks like you all've got no need of me." He retreated to his office, a spacious room so well-stocked with stuffed spoils of the hunt—the head of an eight-point buck, a crow on a varnished dowel, a squirrel clinging to a tree-trunk segment—that it could have passed for a taxidermist's shop.

Cooper escorted Adrienne to an untenanted cubicle with two chairs and me to a powder-blue sweatbox with a mirrored observation window concealing anyone behind it. The GBI examiner— a tall, fine-featured baby-faced man wearing pleated khaki trousers, a short-sleeve shirt, and a Day-Glo orange tie—tinkered with his machine. Cooper nodded me to a chair beside the machine and ducked out, closing the door.

Without introducing himself, the GBI agent attached his machine's various leads to my body and sat down in a chair in front of mine. I stared at the razor rash on his pink nape and wondered if his bad manners stemmed from thoughtlessness or a deliberate attempt to unnerve me.

"Please note, Mr. Keats, that you can monitor the machine's responses to your answers as they emerge." The examiner's voice reminded me of the full-bodied tones of the narrator of a PBS nature program.

"Why would I want to monitor them?"

"To see how you're doing. When they can view the results, most examinees relax a little and respond to our questions with greater openness."

"I planned on telling the whole truth whether I could watch your Tinkertoy in action or not."

Testily, the examiner said, "I'll begin with a few baseline questions, and you'll see pretty quickly how to interpret the graphs." He took an audible breath. "Are you William Jennings Keats?"

"Yes."

"Do you live in Moscow, Idaho?"

"No."

Six or seven similar easy-to-answer questions followed, and the examiner pronounced himself satisfied with the polygraph's adjustment to my specific physiological responses. He then asked another five or six simple but pertinent questions—at which point he framed one that blindsided and baffled me.

"Isn't it true that you were recently in communication with a man named Polk James?"

I said nothing. The examiner started to repeat the question, but I interrupted him: "I don't know *anyone* named Polk James."

"We need a yes or no answer, Mr. Keats." He asked me his disturbing question again.

"No," I said emphatically. The polygraph needle reacted with an alarming jag before falling back into an even chitter testifying to my truthfulness. The examiner asked me three more unremarkable questions and signaled an end to our session.

Once free of the lie detector's grasp, I stood gratefully. Captain Cooper appeared at the door and led me through the windowless labyrinth back to his own office, a space smaller than Stratford's but more attractively decorated. Handsome prints of different species of trees ran along three walls at eye-level: oaks, sycamores, elms, and others. Cooper gave me a cold canned citrus drink and told me that another officer had deliberately conducted Adrienne to the polygraph room by a different route. Sipping my drink, I realized that I had unwittingly sweated both my tee and my short-sleeved oxford shirt straight through.

"Excuse me a minute." Cooper left me sitting alone at his desk. On it rested file folders in neat stacks, a Swingline stapler, a box of

3-½" computer disks, and a framed photo of a much younger Cooper standing next to an instantly recognizable Buddy Ebsen on a busy television-studio lot. Ebsen had inscribed the photograph: "All thanks to Officer Cooper. Barnaby Jones couldn't have solved the case any quicker." Quite a testimony; quite a trophy. On the other hand, the Hollywood souvenir mattered far less to me than the mindset of Adrienne and the whereabouts of Olivia. I held the cold soft-drink can to my forehead and closed my eyes.

A rap on the frame of Cooper's door—who knew how much later?—startled me into looking up. There stood Adrienne, flanked by Stratford and Cooper, frighteningly like guards returning a prisoner to her cell.

"Passed with flying colors," Adrienne blew on the nails of one hand and buffed them on a jumper strap—although a sudden flash of her eyes betrayed her underlying anxiety.

"Now if you'll come with us," Stratford said, "we have a significant piece of evidence we'd like you to identify."

I got up, went to Adrienne, slipped my arm around her waist, and fell into step with her behind the loose-jawed, big-hipped colonel and the trim, efficient captain.

Eight

We exited from the ground floor into a fenced parking lot around the corner from the visitors' lot where we had left the Tacoma. October sunlight glinted from the razorwire interthreading the chainlink. The dazzle made us all shield our eyes.

"There," said Stratford, pointing, "you see that one?"

I squinted and peered. So did Adrienne and Cooper. At that moment, clouds drifted between us and the sun. Among a fleet of departmental cruisers and a motley asortment of impounded vehicles, I caught sight of an isolated blue pickup. The truck simmered lopsidedly on the asphalt, one rear tire gone flat. I recognized it as a ten- or twelve-year-old GM model, and further recognized it as the pickup that had idled briefly beside our mailbox yesterday morning. I told Stratford and Cooper so.

"You sure?" Cooper said.

"Either the very same one or its identical twin."

"Excellent," Stratford said. "Let's go back inside."

Adrienne said, "But who does it belong to?"

"Polk James," I said simply, somehow certain no one would have reason to contradict me.

Back in Cooper's office, Stratford pled other responsibilities, assured us that Cooper would answer all our questions, and swaggered off. Cooper propped his bottom on the edge of a printer table while Adrienne took his desk chair and I pulled up a battered folding chair.

"One of our deputies found the truck shortly after six this morning in a brush thicket on Rutherford Henry's farm five miles down Antioch Church Road from your own place. Henry uses a walker to get around and watches TV with the sound at top volume. As you correctly surmised, Mr. Keats, the truck has its registration in the name of Polk James, but Mr. Henry neither saw nor heard it trespassing on his property during the early stages of last night's storm. He had no idea that James had abandoned the truck only sixty or seventy feet from his little house."

Adrienne said, "How do you know that Polk James was actually driving it?"

"We got good prints from the steering wheel, the door handles, and the tailgate. His and no one else's."

"Then Polk James kidnapped Olivia," I said.

"We can say so with near certainty." Cooper paused. "Especially since we found prints that match the ones Olivia gave us during last year's drive to fingerprint every school-age child in the county. We lifted them from the truck's dashboard and inner passenger door."

Soundlessly, Adrienne began to cry.

"As a clincher," Cooper continued, "we have two sets of footprints, one of them identical to the ones on your carpet, and the other a child's. They lead across a swatch of Mr. Henry's muddy pasturage to another family's house. The Cotlands', to be specific. Do you know them?"

"We know almost no one out that way," I said. "We don't really have neighbors, we have road shoulders and fences."

"Modern life," Cooper said matter-of-factly. "Anyway at five-thirty this morning, David Cotland telephoned us to report that someone had stolen his wife's silver Chrysler LeBaron. She'd left it in an unlocked garage about fifty feet from the house. Apparently, as with Mr. Henry, the noise of the storm effectively covered the theft of the car."

"Did Polk James *plan* these shifts and dodges?"

Cooper looked at me. "Highly unlikely. It strikes me as strictly a matter of necessity proving the mother of grand larceny. When James's rotten rear tire blew, well, he dumped the truck and dragged Olivia through the rain to victimize the Cotlands."

"*Damn!*" Adrienne cried. She brought her fist down on the hard desk blotter, and the framed photo depicting Cooper and Buddy Ebsen jumped and fell over. "Sorry." She righted the picture and shuffled it around absentmindedly. "Sorry," she repeated.

"Perfectly okay," Cooper said. "Please don't sweat it."

Adrienne resolutely straightened her back. "Who *is* this Polk James person, anyway? What does he want with Olivia? How did he even know she existed?"

"Let me show you what we have on him." Cooper approached his desk and punched up a color mugshot of the suspect on his computer monitor. He swiveled the screen to face us more directly. I drew my chair up closer, but Adrienne recoiled. A demon had materialized on the screen. "Not exactly a Pierce Brosnan look-alike, is he?"

The face on the screen, ostensibly human, resembled that of an elderly chimp, a specimen low on the simian pecking order, a creature that had endured a lifetime of humiliation and abuse from its age-mates and juniors alike. Sparse black hair overlay James's sweaty scalp; his pendulous ears sprouted coarse tufts as if in mockery of the loss on top. In any other circumstances, a face to pity. This morning, though, knowing what I had just learned, I hated the ugly little man. Had he occupied the chair next to mine, I would have tried my damnedest to strangle him.

Beneath the mugshot glowed vital statistics and an exhaustive record of James's priors. Cooper summarized for us: "Forty-eight years old. Five feet six. One hundred and seventy pounds. Brown eyes, black hair, a light scar on his jaw."

"He looks sixty!" Adrienne said.

"James lives on the eastern outskirts of Tocqueville with his mother, Alice-Darlene. They rent a shotgun house with asbestos-shingle siding and a rusted tin roof. James has seldom held a job for more than six months, mostly menial positions like fruit picking, janitoring, dish washing, and sewer-line laying. For the past two or three years, he's made a skimpy living doing freelance hauling with his truck."

I said, "And, obviously, he has a criminal record."

" 'Fraid so. It's as thick as the Greater Atlanta phonebook and extends all the way back to his teens. Until now, most of his crimes have fallen on the petty side. Shoplifting, public drunkenness, writing bad checks. Trespassing. Disturbing the peace. All offenses of that magnitude."

"The NBA should recruit him," I said.

Cooper ignored me. "Once he tried a bit of breaking and entering. A routine city-police patrol nabbed him on the porch of a middle-class home with his pockets full of cheap flatware and his arms around an expensive microwave oven. He was duck-walking with it, trying to get it down the steps without it going smash on him. For that brilliant heist, he did a year-and-a-half up in Jackson. Apparently that jail stint five years ago put some of the fear of the Lord into him. He served his parole and hasn't tangled with us since."

"You mean you haven't *caught* him at anything."

Adrienne said, "What could have motivated him to take Olivia?"

"A year ago, Lamar James, Polk's father, died of liver failure from chronic alcoholism. With his death, the family finances went into a tailspin. Government checks stopped coming, and their landlord recently threatened to evict them."

"Could you evict James's face from this screen, please?" Adrienne said. "I don't imagine we'll soon forget it."

"Sure thing." Cooper toggled up a screensaver: blue sky and clouds that served only to remind me of the painted walls in Olivia's bedroom.

"But what made Polk James think stealing Olivia could possibly rescue his mother and him from their troubles?" Adrienne asked.

"Simple," said Cooper. "The distinct likelihood of winning a large ransom for her safe return."

"From us?"

"From the son of the renowned Skipper Keats. Your daddy entertained people in this part of the country for years. Most west Georgians—seeing him on television, reading about him—considered him a wealthy man. When he died, they naturally assumed his surviving family—including his only son—would inherit his wealth. Polk James's daddy died penniless. His son's twisted sense of justice probably demands a redistribution of the wealth. Or so I currently theorize."

"Almighty Jesus."

Adrienne extended both hands to me. The tear streaks on her face made it resemble a pale and melancholy mask. I took her hands, pulled her to me in the castored chair, and lightly kissed her forehead.

Cooper politely ignored this exchange. "In my opinion, Ms. Owsley, Mr. Keats, Polk James stole Olivia intending to confine her in some out-of-the-way safehouse and then to present you with a ransom demand. Until that happens, though, we can't do much more than put out an APB for the Cotlands' stolen car—which we've already done—and work our way through James's network of acquaintances. I say acquaintances because he doesn't appear to have any close friends at all."

After a beat or two, Adrienne said, "Tell me something, Captain Cooper."

"Certainly. Whatever I can."

"Has Polk James ever molested a child?"

"No, ma'am. At least, we have no knowledge of such behavior. And if he'd ever molested a child here in Tocqueville—even if the parents hadn't pressed charges—you can bet that word would still've circulated and ended up in our files. Nobody loves a pedophile, except maybe another."

"What if he'd killed his victims?" I said reluctantly.

"He didn't. We have no outstanding unsolved child murders in this county. Keep in mind too that James has never—as far as we know—committed a violent crime against a person. That bodes well for recovering Olivia unhurt."

Adrienne nodded, but fidgeted with her prayer beads.

"Did the roadblocks you set up produce any results?"

"Some nebulous ones. But remember: last night we'd primed our deputies to look for a dented blue pickup, not the Cotlands' stolen LeBaron. Of course, they also had orders to stop and closely question any driver transporting an elementary-school-age girl."

"A Chrysler with Polk James and Olivia in it didn't prompt a challenge?"

"Actually, a Chrysler did pass through our checkpoint on Lower Antioch Church Road around seven last night, heading west. We've already suspended the young deputy who waved it through without a registration check."

"What had Polk James done with Olivia?" Adrienne asked.

"Probably gagged her, tied her up, and put her in the trunk," Cooper said, averting his eyes.

Nine

Back at our house, we found in our yard not only the expected law-enforcement vehicles but also a squat green rustbucket—in its former life one of the earliest Honda Civics—which I knew on sight as my friend Hutchinson Payne's little car. Hutch himself sat on the upper step of the porch, his hairy ankles visible above his mismatched socks and his lank torso cocked to one side like that of a well-used cloth doll. His silver-shot amber beard, bib overalls, and blue-and-green-checked flannel shirt made him resemble some archaic wainwright or farmer.

"Look," Adrienne said, "he's heard about Olivia and driven all the way out from Mountboro." I could not say whether I entirely welcomed Hutch's presence. Olivia's kidnapping had scrambled my social instincts.

As Adrienne and I neared the steps, Hutch rose and slid his hands into his overall pockets. In his creaky, split-seamed boots, he rocked on the highest step. Meanwhile, his shy smile repeatedly formed, faded, and reappeared.

"You could have gone in, you know," Adrienne said. "We've already got well-meaning strangers in the house. An honest-to-God friend would've warmed the whole place."

"Kind of you to say so," Hutch replied. "I had such a hard time simply deciding to come that inviting myself in didn't seem an option. If you want me to go, just say the word."

"No, please stay," Adrienne said.

I climbed the steps and impetuously hugged my friend. We must have made a disconcerting picture, the back-to-the-land yuppie and the double-jointed hillbilly philosopher, but I didn't give a damn what Sergeant Lisa Sleator, Deputy Kinney, or GBI man Trent Badcock thought, even as I paranoiacally supposed them peering out at us between the curtains.

Hutchinson Payne had driven twenty-five miles to see us, from his parsonage to our farmhouse. Widowed pastor of the First Baptist Church in Mountboro, he hardly qualified as my daily spiritual adviser—technically, the Methodists still claimed me—but he and I had nevertheless developed a strange fishing-and-debating society that seldom met more than every third or fourth month. In times of crises, though, Hutch ministered unobtrusively to me. I would never forget that he had quietly attended my father's funeral in Columbus.

Adrienne took Hutch's hand and led him to the row of cane-bottomed rockers weathering to a fine dish-water grayness on our wraparound porch. In three of these chairs we sat and rocked like Confederate veterans on a Georgia town square.

"If you all don't regard it as prying," Hutch said, "just how do things stand?"

Sometimes finishing each other's sentences, Adrienne and I recounted the story of the kidnapping and the investigation to date. As he listened and rocked, Hutch gently chewed his bottom lip. The sun climbed, dragging shadows across the porch floor.

"Sounds fairly promising," Hutch eventually said. "A known suspect with a simple motive and no apparent violent or predatory tendencies. Plus the police have a pretty good lead on the direction he's fled."

"Grabbing a little girl out of her house strikes me as violent," Adrienne said tensely. "So does pulling her across a field in a storm and locking her in a trunk."

"Of course," Hutch said. "Of course." Adrienne relaxed, accepting Hutch's implicit apology. "I just trust that your little girl will return to you. Out of the storm a survivor. I don't offer this as mealy-mouthed comfort either. I sincerely believe, as you must too."

"Thanks, Hutch," I said.

Adrienne looked out across our property, humming something

unintelligible. A hawk, fluffed in its plumage like a vagrant in a hand-me-down coat, sat on a power line surveying the marshy countryside.

Hutch got up and stood in front of us. "Perhaps we could pray together. If it soothes no one else, it would soothe me."

Gratefully, it seemed to me, Adrienne took his extended hand. I dropped my chin to my chest and felt his other hand firmly grip mine. At least a minute passed before Hutch spoke again: "Holy God, we don't pretend to understand evil. We don't pretend to understand even our own confusion and terror in evil's presence. We can't know Olivia's pain and dismay in the grip of this evil. But you know, Lord. You alone know. We petition you for two things: strength and endurance, and Olivia's safe return. Lord, put remorse in her kidnapper's heart and have him send her home soon. Amen." Hutch released us and stepped back.

"Thank you," Adrienne said.

"I'll take my leave now. Call me if you feel the need."

He climbed into his squat green car and bumped out of our yard in a spreading plume of white exhaust. In the wake of yesterday's storm, he undoubtedly had repair work to do on the homes of a half-dozen parishoners with tempest-battered roofs and shutters.

Adrienne fixed Sleator, Kinney, and Badcock open-faced tuna sandwiches, despite their various protests that they could feed themselves or had packaged snacks in their cars. A tray of carrot sticks, olives, and pickles accompanied the sandwiches, as well as a pitcher of pink lemonade from frozen concentrate. Because Polk James still had not called with a ransom demand, the investigators' presence had begun to feel oppressive, as if we were barracking Hessian troops. By the end of their lunch, which we did not share, even the boorish Kinney had picked up on this vibe of irritation. Seeking to counter it, he volunteered to wash dishes. Sergeant Sleator endorsed his offer.

"Let the men clean up for a change, right, honey? And why don't you two try to bag a nap? We've got all the bases covered."

We went upstairs, past Olivia's empty room, with its painted armadas of clouds and hot-air balloons, and lay down side-by-side on the four-poster, with the telephone unplugged. I set the clock radio's alarm for 1:00 P.M., and for a little over an hour we actually slept—a ragged rather than a blissful slumber, but sleep nonetheless. At the shrill cheeping of the alarm, I sat up and put on my shoes. Adrienne opened her eyes and gave me a sweet but abstracted smile.

"Maybe we should eat," I told her.

"Okay. Something cold, though. I'd like to sit for a while."

In the kitchen, I prepared a Waldorf salad, found two small containers of blueberry yogurt, and spooned canned peaches and mandarin orange slices into a pair of metal sundae cups. I set these items on a wooden tray in the now desolate-looking refrigerator, until Adrienne finished her half-hour stint "eyebrow to eyebrow with the sages." Then I wandered into the living room.

Badcock sat on the sofa jockeying a Game Boy. Sleator and Kinney slashed playing cards at each other across our coffee table. All three looked abashed to see me, but Sleator quickly recovered her poise and threw down a face card that made Kinney groan.

"Our replacements come on at three," Kinney told me, less to impart the information than to avoid having to deal with Sleator's cunning play.

The parlor looked a mess. None of our barrackers had seen fit to tidy up. An arrangement of dried flowers had toppled from a lamp table. Various sections of yesterday's *Atlanta Constitution* draped the furniture. Polk James's clay-encrusted footprints, as offensive as semen stains on a rape victim's dress, especially galled me.

"May I vacuum?"

Sergeant Sleator looked up bemusedly. "Of course, honey. Forensic and the photographers have done everything they possibly can."

I ran the roaring vacuum all around the room, coming as close to the deputies as I could without sucking their uniforms into its bag. It felt good to restore a semblance of order to this corner of the world; it gave me some hope that our fractured emotional universe might eventually recohere.

When I had finished, I picked up the newspaper pages, righted the upended flower vase, and straightened cushions on the disheveled chairs and sofa. Badcock looked up from his game with a smile, but would not shift his butt an inch for me—until the telephone rang. Then he jumped as if pitchforked.

Sleator somehow beat him to it. "Uh-huh," she said. "Uh-huh.

Yes sir. No sir. Uh-huh. Uh-huh. Uh-huh." Extending the phone to me, she announced, "It's Detective Cooper. He wants to talk to you or Ms. Owsley."

I took the phone. "Will Keats here."

"Thought you might like to know that we've found Mrs. Cotland's stolen LeBaron," said Cooper in a strained and weary voice.

My heart somersaulted. "And what else?"

"Nothing else. We don't have your daughter, but there's no sign she's been harmed."

"Great. Excellent, in fact."

"But James has bumped up the pot, Mr. Keats."

"How do you mean?"

"He abandoned the Chrysler in Alabama. Crossing state lines automatically brings in the FBI. The case no longer belongs exclusively to Georgia law-enforcement agencies."

"Will the feds take you off it?"

"Hard to say."

I considered this answer, then said, "I hope not."

Cooper chortled self-consciously. "Well, I hope the same, Mr. Keats."

"Anything else? Anything at all?"

"The Chrysler wound up on the edge of a fish-hatchery pond outside Rainbow City, Alabama. Their police department has already started conducting interviews, setting up roadblocks, consulting with other agencies and on-line information sites. And—" Cooper hushed.

"And what?"

"Kidnappings always bring out the kooks. A self-annointed psychic supersleuth by the name of Oscar Greenaway called us about ten minutes ago."

"Who?"

"Greenaway, Oscar. He lives in Atlanta and specializes in finding missing persons. Claims to pick them up on his clairvoyant sonar. A kook. He's had one or two debatable successes, though, and if we get desperate enough you might want to let him do his thing."

"Have we reached that point so soon?"

"Not by miles. You all hang in there." He rang off without bringing Sleator back on the line.

I returned to the kitchen. Adrienne came down as I set out our cold lunch. She heard with thoughtful equanimity Cooper's new information.

"What about us? What do *we* do?"

"Keep on keeping on, I guess. And following Hutch's example, it wouldn't hurt to pray."

Adrienne finished eating. "That's pretty much the game plan I had in mind, Will. Would it upset you if I went back to the *zendo* for a while?"

"Go ahead. Sit for us all." If not for work and family obligations, Adrienne could meditate for several consecutive hours. Three or four times a year, she undertook a day-long retreat in Atlanta with experienced fellow practitioners. At home, though, she confined her sitting to a half hour each morning and night, frequently with Olivia on her own mat beside her. I might mildly envy or resent these sessions, but I also understood that during them Adrienne grappled meaningfully with issues vital to all of us.

"What about you?" she asked me.

"Well, for starters, we need groceries—for hungry deputies as well as ourselves. And pony chow. And maybe some sort of tasty alcoholic painkiller. I thought I'd drive back into Tocqueville."

"Okay," Adrienne said. "You've always meditated better with your hands on a steering wheel than your fanny on a *zafu*. Just be careful." She kissed me and let me go.

In town, I made the rounds of several stores, from Farmers Supply to Crazy Carl's Party Shop to Kroger's. In every one of these establishments I had the irrational feeling that other customers had mysteriously winkled out my identity and gathered in small clumps to gossip about the kidnapping. If I whirled to catch them out, though, they instantly dispersed. Paranoia, your name is Will Keats.

The parking lot at Kroger's teemed with vehicles of every make, model, and year. I parked in the only vacant spot I could find, hard by a malodorous Dumpster, and left Olivia's Cat in the Hat on the front seat as sentinel. About an hour later, I trundled out of the store with a laden cart and secured my purchases in the truck bed with an arrangement of plastic crates and colorful bungee cords of my own invention. I then took out my keys and opened the driver's door.

Cat in the Hat had vanished.

Before I could frame another thought, Byron Owsley stepped from behind the Dumpster, clutching the stuffed toy by its neck. He gave me a thin, malevolent smirk.

"Lose something, Keats?"

Ten

I flinched. And flinched again when Byron hurled the Cat in the Hat at me over the hood of my truck. If I had not reached up and caught it, the doll would have struck me in the chest. At once repulsed and infuriated, I tossed the toy through my truck's open door onto the passenger seat and clambered in behind the steering wheel. I yanked the door closed and jabbed my key at the ignition switch.

Byron swept around the Toyota's grille and seized the strut of my sideview mirror. A mask of phony contrition had slid down over his earlier look of contempt.

"I hope you won't lodge theft charges against me, Keats."

"Move your hand and step back."

"I know that taking Olivia's stuffed toy was technically theft, but I really don't have many mementos to—"

"Can it, Byron."

"Why so huffy? No friendly twinge for her honest-to-God daddy?"

"Listen, you pick up Olivia a couple of times a month for one reason only—to get Adrienne's goat. And maybe even to poison Olivia against her mother and me. You don't know what you've got in that girl, Byron."

Without releasing the mirror, Byron took an exaggerated step back. "Maybe you don't either. Why else would you have let some scuzzball into your fancy house to steal what's not even yours?"

That sucker punch stole my breath. I used the moment to study Byron. He had four or five inches in height on me and forty more pounds of well-distributed muscle. He had banded his coarse black hair, with reddish highlights like those in a Kodiak's pelt, into an eighteen-inch ponytail; his sideburns, meanwhile, had the length and thickness of Velcro sneaker tabs. On the forearm closest to me, a red-and-blue tattoo of a stallion gleamed amid sun-bleached hairs.

"Nothing to say to that, Keats?"

I shook my head disgustedly.

"Why do you think I despise you all or that Olivia despises me? That whatever the crime, I stand guilty as charged? That no simple human connection links me to my daughter or to Adrienne? Or even to you, Mr. High-and-mighty, Will-*yum* Keats?" Something suspiciously like hurt altered Byron's angular face, and for reasons beyond fathoming I chose to treat this mask as genuine.

"What do you want, Byron?"

"I've wanted to talk to you ever since all this went down. My truck's in surgery at the garage over there"—he nodded at the Dodge dealership across Paris Avenue—"and when I saw you pull into the Kroger lot, I said, here's my chance."

"What could we possibly say that would do either of us any good? If you know anything about the kidnapping, go straight to the sheriff's office and spill it to Captain Nicholas Cooper."

"Fuck Cooper. I need to talk to cops like you need another trust-fund check."

We had reached an impasse. Byron possessed—although I had never known this before—an ill-disguised antipathy to the law verging on paranoia. He also exhibited another attitude—one I had long suspected—of abiding resentment toward me as both a privileged rich kid and the undeserving usurper of his place as Adrienne's lover and Olivia's dad. He claimed to want to talk, but his barbed-wire eyes said he would rather inflict pain.

"Where can we go?" I said.

"Carry me back to my place on Jarboe Street. The mechanics won't get a new fuel pump into my heap for a couple of hours, and the cheap bastards won't give me a loaner."

"All right," I said grudgingly. "Get in. Just remember that anything you say bearing on Olivia's kidnapping I'll automatically pass along to Cooper."

"Fair enough. I've got nothing to hide." Byron finally released my mirror and, rubbing his naked forearms, trudged back around the hood of the truck to the passenger door. He swung his Levi-clad legs in and squeezed his broad-shouldered torso in after. A surprising eddy of late-autumn air swirled in with him: November crouched just a few days over the horizon. Tenderly, Byron moved the Cat in the Hat figure to avoid crushing it and balanced it on his knees, much as Adrienne had done earlier. He modeled a leather vest over his sleeveless, pearl-buttoned denim shirt, but neither garment had kept gooseflesh from stippling his biceps. That gooseflesh and the toy in his lap made me suddenly aware of him as a vulnerable human being.

"Let's get rolling, Keats," he said.

After glancing away from Byron and engaging the clutch, I recalled from a host of pieced-together conversations with Adrienne much of her ex's history. Some of it edged into my consciousness from Byron's proximity to me, almost as if his body heat and his ill-suppressed spite also projected his biography.

Twenty-two years old in 1985, Byron glanced around his Alabama town—a trackside hamlet only an hour from Tocqueville—and found it wanting in local color, opportunity, and romance. Gorbachev had just come to power in the Soviet Union, the man who eventually presided over the dissolution of the Red superpower. The American president, the retrospectively ailing Ronald Reagan, continued to shake his fist at the "evil empire" while lauding the Nicaraguan contras as "the moral equals of our Founding Fathers." The economy had stagnated, the federal deficit had soared to an all-time high, and the country had become a debtor nation for the first time since World War I. The stylish cynicism of *Miami Vice* typified network television, a hole had just opened in the ozone layer over Antarctica, and the feel-good humanitarianism of "We Are the World" reigned as the global anthem.

Landlocked Rainbow City, Alabama, noted these blips on the cultural radar, but only just. Byron and his provincial fellow citizens got more worked up—as he later recounted to Adrienne—over a beloved soft drink. To Byron and his cohorts, Coca-Cola's replacement of its ninety-nine-year-old formula represented a high-handed desecration. Outraged, Byron toppled New Coke displays in local grocery stores, and on one drunken occasion climbed to the roof of the dilapidated Magnolia Hotel and shot out the tires of a New Coke delivery truck with his father's 30.06. He escaped fines or jail time for the first escapade by painting the shutters on the local police chief's private residence. The more serious offense went unsolved and unlinked to him. Only months later, as a young man making a meager living planting pine seedlings for a timber enterprise, did he understand that he had comported himself like a loser and a fool, passionately upset over a can of caffeine and colored corn syrup.

This modest epiphany moved Byron to change his life. He told his parents, Millie and Goodloe, goodbye and left home to enlist in the navy, which to an ignorant landlubberly kid from the pine scrubs seemed an exotic alternative to civilian life, maybe even the only one. He swept almost effortlessly through basic training, and earned a much-coveted berth on the cruiser *USS Wichita*, then anchored at Norfolk, Virginia. The ship and its southern port represented the height of tolerable cosmopolitanism to Byron, who had never before ventured any farther over the Alabama state line than Panama City, Florida, to the south and Atlanta, Georgia, to the east. When, under new orders, the *Wichita* dieseled away to Yankee waters off Newport, Rhode Island, he briefly regretted his enlistment and suffered four hours of intense homesickness.

Whatever the initial shock, the northern clime and New England society did nothing to moderate Byron's rambunctious personality. (Only basic training had accomplished that feat, and only for its swift duration.) Several postings to the brig for infractions ranging from obscenely heckling some visiting schoolchildren to shoving a lieutenant j.g. on a gangway convinced him that he could not make a career in the navy's tightly structured hierarchy. He declined to re-up when his two-year hitch ended. Honorably discharged— barely—and footloose in New England, he rejected a plea from his diabetic mother to come back to Rainbow City. Millie pled with him, he rationalized, only to secure his help caring for Goodloe, now a febrile and embittered victim of colon cancer. For six months after his mustering out, Byron wandered incommunicado and virtually guiltless. He wound up in Lowell, Massachusetts.

This down-at-the-heels ex-milltown, famous primarily as the birthplace of Beat writer Jack Kerouac, offered measurably more opportunities than a commercial heat-sink like Rainbow City—even during an economic downturn. Thanks to his military training as an assistant machinist and shipboard plumber, Byron had picked up a number of rudimentary metal-working skills; he exhibited an almost inborn flair for bending to his will iron and steel, copper and brass, tin and aluminum. Deliberately, he stopped one day at a blacksmith shop called—humorously, although Byron did not at first get the joke—the Oil Can Foundry, whose proprietor and master smith, Guy Huberdeau, watched Byron perform a few simple operations at the forge and hired him as helper-apprentice.

Six months under Huberdeau's tutelage—six months working contentedly at a job he liked—beveled away many of Byron Owsley's rough edges. When he met Lowell native Adrienne Thompson, then twenty-one, at an art gallery whose decorative garden gates he was helping to install, he unaccountably behaved himself and charmed her. He kept charming her until, in 1988, she married him. He did not entirely descend back into macho surliness and impatience until after Olivia's birth in February 1990. Not long after that—under a mysterious pall that Byron still had not fully explained to Adrienne—the three Owsleys fled both Lowell and New England.

Byron took his family south, as if the need for adult refuge had pushed him willy-nilly back to his roots. He settled wife and child not in Rainbow City, however, where his father had died and his mother endured in failing health, but in Tocqueville, Georgia, a town of twenty thousand with several small new factories along its semirural industrial boulevard and a revived textile mill on its western perimeter. Adrienne, taking over Byron's old role as outsider, watched as he used the last reserves of their capital to establish his own penny-whistle blacksmith shop, an enterprise that his lack of acumen and his ever-increasing prickliness almost sabotaged at the outset. Relations between Byron and Adrienne soured along with the business, although not solely for financial reasons, and one year after the Owsleys' move to Tocqueville, the couple separated. The divorce came soon after, and one-year-old Olivia took nothing from the trainwreck of this marriage but a hopper car of dubious genes.

Despite the divorce, Adrienne stayed in Georgia. She owned a small automobile, a graduation gift from her parents that she had scrupulously maintained even during difficult times. Building on two years of community college in Lowell, while scrabbling by on money from her folks, AFDC, and Byron's child support, she attended Troy State College in Phenix City, Alabama, and quickly earned a teaching certificate. With a position in the Speece County School System teaching middle-school children, she worked her way out of near-poverty, shedding along the way most of her self-recrimination and self-doubt. In fact, she did better than Byron, whose business turned only enough profit to buy him groceries and the occasional off-brand six-pack. Had he not purchased outright his tumbledown home-cum-smithy on Jarboe Street, no sane landlord would have agreed to rent it to him.

Byron's hard-luck tale, as I had assembled it over time from Adrienne's reluctant hints, reminded me of a smart-alecky saying of Dapper O'Dell, my father's favorite ventriloquist's dummy: "There's no situation, however bad, that with a little dedicated effort you can't make worse." The few times Byron and I had actually met, my discomfort had expanded so conspicuously that it must have cramped his own sense of self. As we drove toward his shop, he seemed to detect my current uneasiness and repugnance.

Looking at me speculatively, Byron said, "Relax, Keats. I don't bite."

A line from a Disney tune, one I had often sung to Olivia, popped into my head. "Never smile at a crocodile," I said aloud.

Byron glared, then laughed once from his belly. "If you'd ever faced a gator for real, Keats, you'd know that sometimes you smile at them just to keep from peeing your pants."

Surprising myself, I laughed once too. "I'll remember that." A little of my resentment dissipated, but I still wondered if Byron had really encountered me accidentally. Were his metaphorical fingerprints totally absent from Olivia's abduction? And what besides blame-laying, self-justification, and aspersions on my upbringing and character did he have to say to me? I turned off Paris Avenue onto Pulaski Street and angled south through traffic.

Byron seemed to regard my laugh as something of a compliment. Leaning back and studying me, he said, "I hear your hotshot Captain Cooper plans to drag me in for a lie-detector test."

"Why not? Adrienne and I went in for ours this morning."

"Actually, I knew that."

This assertion, whether boast or lie, startled me. "How?"

"I'm wired, Keats. Not much in this town escapes me." We rode in silence for a long city block. Then he asked, "So how'd you and Ade fare on the liar's quiz?"

"If it's any of your business, we both passed." My voice had suddenly thickened. Byron's use of an unfamiliar nickname for Adrienne had sent queer pricklings through me. It implied between them a level of bygone intimacy that I had accepted intellectually but had never viscerally felt, a past that excluded me.

"Congratulations. All that clean living pays off, I guess."

"I turned in my Boy Scout badges years ago, Byron. But"—I raised two fingers to my brow in a self-mocking salute—"I just might occasionally recognize the difference between truth and a lie."

"Lucky you." Heedlessly, Byron shifted Olivia's Cat in the Hat to his left knee and began bouncing it, as he might have once bounced Olivia. Neither of us speaking, the Tacoma cruised nearer and nearer Jarboe Street and the Byron Owsley smithy. Once again, my uneasiness began to build. Byron continued bouncing the stuffed cat, harder and harder, as if the truck's floorboard fed his leg a galvanic charge.

With no apparent goad or trigger, I remembered the groceries in my loadbed. "Ice cream," I announced.

"What?" Byron looked at me as if I had spoken Tagalog.

"I bought ice cream at Kroger's. I left it in a sack in back. It'll melt before I can get it back to Adrienne."

"Stop," Byron said. "Hang a right into that vacant lot."

Mindlessly, I obeyed, and my Tacoma jounced to a standstill in the middle of a weedy corner lot where joe-pye grew and maverick jobbers occasionally sold cheap work clothes off the backs of trucks. Byron set Olivia's toy on the dash and got out. In the rearview I saw him rummaging through my boxes until he found the ornate pint of Cherry Garcia ice cream. He yanked it from its sack and brought it back with him into the cab.

"Let's eat it, so it won't go to waste." From his jeans pocket Byron extracted a Swiss Army knife, from which he pulled down a short-handled spoon. Then he peeled off the lid of the pint and dug out a heaping spoonful, which he immediately shoveled into his mouth.

"We'll take turns," he said, offering me the spoon.

"You go ahead. Eat all you want."

He did, taking his time. The flesh on his arms grew as thick as a gator's hide.

Eleven

With one hand on the steering wheel, I waited. Byron ate the entire pint of Cherry Garcia, licked the spoon with an exaggerated show of tongue, then crumpled the carton and tossed it out the window. I grimaced.

"Relax, Keats. I'll pay your littering ticket." Grinning, he folded the spoon back into the knife case and repocketed it.

"Forget it. Just buy Olivia an extra cone the next time you have her over."

Byron swallowed his grin. "Why are we still sitting here? Let's get a move on."

As we left the lot, Byron's goosebumps took on Himalayan proportions. I kicked the truck's heater up, noting peripherally his strong and well-tanned arms. The energy radiating from him had sufficent force, I briefly imagined, to shatter the windshield into powdered sugar.

"I saw a six-pack of Heinies in your truck bed among all those lousy hothouse vegetables you're toting."

"So?"

"I sure could use a beer to cut all that sweetness."

"Do I look like your bartender?"

Byron snorted. "You wish. Even Michelle down at the Black Bear Tap looks tougher than you do."

"No argument there," I said. "I've *seen* Michelle."

The sign for Jarboe Street popped up suddenly ahead of us, to our left. Byron ceased begging for beer and jabbed a finger to make me heel the truck over into the side street.

The reputable citizens of Tocqueville called Byron's neighborhood Dogtown. Adrienne had once described it to me as "potentially improvable." I agreed, and then proposed that by the same standards the Love Canal could be called a "convalescing waterway." In Dogtown, unpaved alleys intersected stingy streets with more than their share of potholes. A few shabby businesses—a shoe-repair shop, a tailor's cramped closet, a convenience store dispensing malt liquor and lottery tickets—alternated with shotgun hovels, deteriorating clapboard duplexes, and the rare shingle-sided bungalow with a well-broomed dirt yard. A poster on a telephone pole advertised a rhythm-and-blues concert to benefit a shelter for battered women.

Byron watched me study his neighborhood, monitoring my swings between fascination and revulsion. He asked me belligerently, "You think maybe Hanoi Jane Fonda got it right?" he asked.

"When?"

"When she claimed parts of Georgia looked like the Third World."

"Poverty doesn't have a nationality. Believe me, Byron, as a counselor, I've paid home visits to places straight out of a Bosnian war zone, houses that make these shanties look like the Biltmore."

"I wouldn't know, Keats. I'm Dogtown through and through."

Byron's testiness overlay bruised pride. Where, he must wonder, would I rank his place, the house-cum-workshop where Olivia stayed on her weekend visits, on my own professional scale of livability.

And then we came upon it. A century or so ago, the building had started life as a horse barn or a carriage house, maybe even a fire station. Over the years, amateur carpentry and slipshod masonry work had altered it, and not for the better. Weathered plank siding, the same antique silver as the rockers on my porch, cloaked the lower story, boxing in Byron's workplace, "Owsley's Anvil & Bellows." That legend flaked away from a metal sign dangling from a single metal chain above the smithy's wide double doors. An immense padlock secured the doors, and soot-stained windowpanes shivered in the autumn wind. Beyond the windows lurked the silhouettes of a forge, several suspended tongs, and a hive-shaped brick kiln.

The second floor—Byron's living quarters—insulated its inhabitants from the elements with scavenged vinyl siding in three ill-assorted colors: teal, orange, and rose. The dunce-capped exhaust of a woodstove poked out of the southern wall, releasing twists of pecan or hickory smoke into an even grayer sky. An exterior staircase, crudely scabbed on, led to a porch with no more square footage than a stovetop. A ripped screen door fronted a slick brown hollow-core door whose veneer curled upward from the bottom.

I pulled up in front of the rough double doors. "Okay if I park here? Customers don't seem to be scrambling over each other to get in."

"Business sucks this time of year. Besides, anybody with any swank in this town already owns an Owsley original."

"Really? Like what?"

"An ornamental gate. A fireplace facing. Or maybe a lampstand from my Blue Period. The real trouble is, folks'd rather throw stuff away than fix it. Or they buy cheap plastic shit to begin with."

We got out of the truck. Byron stalked off toward the stairs. Three or four steps up, he looked back. "Come on, Keats. And haul those beers up with you." When I clicked my heels and saluted, he said, "Listen, good guests take a gift along when they go visiting. Ade always made sure we did."

Although Byron's second use of his private nickname for Adrienne seemed calculated to irk me, I laughed and said, "I think you ate yours in the truck." Then I snagged the six-pack from the truck bed and followed him.

The staircase's ominously mushy steps took me to the landing, where Byron and I jostled as he opened the screen door. How easily, I realized, he could have pitched me over the flimsy rails into the red-clay yard. *No idea what happened, Officer. Beside me one minute, broken-skulled and bleeding down on the ground the next. Must've got dizzy and tripped.* I shuddered and tightened my grip on the rail.

Byron pushed the inner door open and pulled me into the main living area of the old carriage-house loft. "DeLynda!" he shouted. "DeLynda, we got a guest! A geek bearing gifts!" We stood waiting on the edge of a large beige-and-blue circular braided rug coming unstitched at its seams. Byron held me lightly in place by my shoulders, as if he feared I and the coveted six-pack might suddenly vanish. "*DeLynda!*" he shouted again.

"You didn't say anything about fetching company home," a female voice called from deeper within the apartment. "Give me a sec, okay?"

Byron shrugged and gestured me toward a sofa resembling a hirsute, deboned hippo. When I dropped down onto this piece, my knees rose as high as my chest. Byron removed a beer from the sixpack in my lap, twisted off its cap, and brandished it at the room and its furnishings.

"My castle."

A scarred oaken table occupied the center of the rug. Atop the table sat a box of Cheerios and two yellow plastic bowls, abutted by a breadboard bearing half a loaf of marble rye and a stick of air-chapped cheese. A handsome stained-glass lamp—probably of Byron's own manufacture—hung over these items. The chairs, a pair of yard-sale ladderbacks, stood away from the table at estranged-looking angles. Beyond them on a dais of purple-red bricks squatted the laboring woodstove, a scuttle of short pecan logs beside it. The whole room smelled, not unpleasantly, of smoke, cheese, and scorched metal. This last smell coiled off the stove, but also seeped up from the foundry below.

As he gulped from his bottle, Byron lifted his eyebrows in a maddeningly superior you-know-how-women-are expression that almost prompted me to rebuke him. Instead, I said, "Byron, what do you want from me besides beer and ice cream?"

"You know, Will-*yum*, you're carrying around a heap of bad karma. Maybe I can help you deal with it."

"Look, if you want to strangle me for letting someone steal Olivia out from under my nose, get in line. You might have to elbow *me* aside. I couldn't feel worse if—"

Byron's live-in emerged from the depths of the loft. Striding in stylishly chunky high-heels, she stretched taut the high-sheen black fabric of her pants, which flared above their cuffs into bellbottoms. I tried to stand, but the sofa would not let me. The bottles in my lap rattled like untuned chimes. "Don't get up," the woman said, as if I could. She and the shelf of her breasts cast me in shadow. Her translucent white blouse and the lacy ivory bra beneath it invited my gaze, but I tried to focus on the raccoon mask of her blue eyeshadow and the down-tumbling mass of her strawberry-blond curls.

"DeLynda Gaye," she said, unabashedly sticking out her hand. I tried to take it, but the embrace of the sofa allowed me only to brush her burgundy-painted fingernails. "And who're you, fella?"

"Will Keats," I said, still trying to get up.

DeLynda looked down at me in complete puzzlement. Then she turned to Byron. "The guy who lives with your ex? The one who let some jerk kidnap Olivia?"

"I invited him," Byron said. "For his beer. Have one."

DeLynda contemplated the carton in my lap. "Well, sure. Don't mind if I do." She reached down, her hand lingering a second longer than necessary, selected a bottle, uncapped it, and brought it to her lips. She sipped, just barely tilting the bottle. "You sure let one darling little girl get away from you yesterday, Mr. Keats." De-Lynda's presence in this room confounded me as much as mine did her. Her familiarity with Byron and her evident ease in the apartment bespoke a relationship of some duration and depth, and yet Adrienne had never mentioned DeLynda Gaye to me. Perhaps she knew nothing of the arrangement, even though Olivia told her mother almost everything . . . or so we had assumed.

With some difficulty, I set the carton of Heineken aside and struggled to my feet. "I don't appreciate the tag-team abuse. Maybe I should just leave."

Byron used his free hand to push me in the chest. When I surprised him by staying upright, he put his face to mine and said, "You screwed up, Keats! That's not abuse, just the truth!"

As calmly as I could, I said, "Don't make the mistake of thinking you could have prevented the kidnapping."

"It didn't happen on my watch, did it?" He walked several steps away and chugalugged the remainder of his beer. DeLynda removed another bottle from the carton and carried it to him. He took a greedy swig, rocking a little on his heels. A distraction of some ambiguous kind seemed to roil in him, and he again intercepted my gaze and held it.

"Do you have something specific you want to say to me?" I asked him.

"The sheriff's department thinks Polk James took Olivia, don't they?"

"Polk?" DeLynda said incredulously. "Poor bow-legged little Polk?"

I approached Byron. "How the hell do you know about Polk?"

Byron half-turned his shoulder. "Nothing much that goes on out at the cop coop escapes me. I've got my contacts, and I've got—" He broke off teasingly. "Anyway, there's something about Polk's involvement that likely'll come out sooner or later, and I figured you should hear it from me first."

Coldly, I said, "Okay. Tell me."

"I know Polk a little. He lives on the outer edge of Dogtown. Sometimes we'll run into each other at the Club Elite or the Fire Tower Lounge." He drank a mouthful and set his bottle down next to the breadboard. "A few weeks ago I got polluted and ranted on to Polk about rich sons of bitches and their unearned inheritances." He paced back to DeLynda Gaye and twisted his index finger in a ruddy spiral of her hair.

"You're saying you mentioned me to Polk James?"

"Yeah. I may even have led Polk to suppose he could shake you down for some of your daddy's swag. Not that I encouraged him to try it, you understand."

Byron's confession enraged me. I picked up a bottle from the couch and squeezed it by the neck as if it were the throttle of a runaway train. I envisioned crashing it against the table and screwing its jagged end into Byron's stomach. Words emerged from my throat like bees from a tumbled hive.

"You muscle-bound oaf! Everything that happened yesterday was your fault!"

Byron closed with me so quickly and with such force that I dropped the bottle and fell back onto the couch with almost his full weight pinning me.

"Listen to this sorry loser, DeLynda. Thinks he can unload his blame on me, cover *me* with abuse." He pressed his broad forearm across my throat, his eyes as flat and lusterless as dirty stone buttons. "Take it back, Keats, before I crush your sorry windpipe!"

My hands came up to clutch Byron's arm. Like an iron bar, it resisted my efforts to dislodge it, as if the blacksmith's rigid materials had infused his arm. For the second time within minutes, his face hovered only an inch or two from mine, wolfishly contorted.

"I won't," I managed to choke out. Then I threw Byron's own taunt back at him. "That's not abuse, just the truth."

The pressure increased on my windpipe as Byron gripped the wrist of his levering arm and bore down even more savagely. "Admit you screwed up, Keats! You and you alone."

DeLynda floated into my strangely checkerboarded vision. "Stop that! Byron, let him up! *Let him up!*"

Byron paused without releasing me. "Dee, butt out! Go rinse out your pantyhose or something."

"He called you on something stupid you admitted yourself," DeLynda persisted. "You got drunk and put a really terrible notion in poor little Polk's silly noggin. So stop that macho shit and get over it."

"Listen, woman—"

"For once, use your brain, not your biceps. You think I want to see you in jail for assault or murder? My stake in this thing is just as big as yours, you dumb hammerhead."

For whatever reasons, DeLynda's appeal worked. Byron stopped strangling me. He pushed my face to one side, scraping it on the sofa's rough upholstery, then reared back and regarded me with chagrined disgust. I massaged my throat, conscious that a livid bruise would soon discolor it. Byron pushed himself up and backed away to the join between one wall and the canted ceiling.

"Okay, okay, *I* screwed up royally *too*. But when I get Polk James in my hands, DeLynda, I won't stop short like I've done with this smug pissant."

I levered myself off the ensnaring sofa. "Byron, if you feel any regret for mouthing off to Polk James, tell the authorities—*before* Captain Cooper asks you in for your lie-detector test. You might actually help Olivia that way."

DeLynda looked between Byron and me, radiating a mysterious aplomb, as if she had intervened in—or even precipitated—similar disputes a hundred times in the past and walked away from them all without so much as a lipstick smear. Her bearing suggested a woman of at least thirty, but on another level of appraisal I suspected she had barely attained her majority. As I studied her, she grabbed a long rust-colored cabled sweater off a shabby wicker trunk and gracefully slipped into it.

"I'm walking out to Tilden's for some sandwich meat," she told Byron. "You fancy deviled ham?"

Her matter-of-factness seemed to cow Byron. "Sure. Whatever."

DeLynda grabbed her purse and walked fluidly toward the door. There she paused and looked back at us. Even through her lavish makeup, her eyes sparkled and her small nose and mouth hinted at a curious girl-next-door sauciness. "You all play nice while I'm gone." Neither Byron nor I said anything. "You hear me, Byron?"

"Sure," he said. "Go for your walk."

DeLynda blew him a debonair kiss and went out. Her high heels clattered down the steps with the staccato rhythms of a Rockette's. When we could no longer hear them, I gestured to the toppled bottles on the couch. "Drink them all, Byron. I've got to hit the road." I couldn't resist adding, "Adrienne's waiting for me."

Byron declined to parry this jab. He may not even have recognized it as one. Instead, when I moved to follow DeLynda down to Jarboe Street, he looked me full in the face and said, "Don't you want to see Olivia's room?"

The question stunned me. On the ride over, I had imagined checking out the conditions Olivia endured while overnighting with her father, and then discussing them clinically with Adrienne. Byron's assault had seemed to negate that possibility. However, he had just offered me a chance to do what I had hungered to do from the beginning.

"All right," I said. "Show me."

Byron swept aside a beaded curtain, through which DeLynda had earlier passed, and nodded me inward. A short windowless corridor ran straight back to a bathroom, whose toilet sat exposed in that doorway. Immediately on my left, a cluttered and disheveled room revealed itself as Byron and DeLynda's. A queen-sized mattress with neither frame nor box spring dominated the floor, a black slip garnishing one corner like the petals of a dahlia.

A disconcerting thought struck me. This loft had been Adrienne's first home in Georgia. In this very room, she and Byron, man and wife, had slept, quarreled, laughed, fought, and made love. Feverishly irresolute, I came to a dead stop.

Byron brushed past me to a second door. He grabbed the knob, lowered his chin, and appeared to compose a short speech in his head: "Keats, we've done the best we could by Olivia with what we've got. I mean the absolute best. I never wanted Olivia to cringe at the idea of living with her daddy."

Byron opened the door, and I moved past him into an immaculate, highly polished box fifteen feet on a side. Heart-pine floorboards gleamed a beautiful amber-gold, gauzy yellow curtains framed a single window, a Little Mermaid bedspread stretched across a pallet in a homemade frame with the tautness of a drill sergeant's model. An array of stuffed animals perched on a bookshelf containing a library of battered Golden Books alarmingly below Olivia's current reading level. A small table featured a tiny bona fide china tea-set meticulously placed and aligned. I had no idea how to react. Although the attention to detail exhibited Byron's high regard for his daughter, the overdetermined hothouse aspect of the room suggested a smothering possessiveness—not only affection, but ripe emotional greed.

"Pretty, Byron. You love her a lot or you'd never have put this much time and energy into making her room so handsome."

"Thanks." The word conveyed resentment, humility, and embarrassment all at once.

"But Olivia doesn't belong to you anymore, if she ever did."

Byron flicked me a hostile look. "I know. I know that. And that of course is the fucking problem, isn't it?" We stared at each other. "So please just get the hell out of here, all right?"

I happily obeyed him, leaving Olivia's room, parading without a backward glance through the parlor, and slipping out onto the chilly landing. The air bludgeoned me, and I briefly stood there, seeing Byron in the middle of that spooky dollhouse chamber, his mind imagining it as an otherwise perfect golden ring missing its one multicarat diamond.

Twelve

I n my truck again, I made a U-turn and headed back up Jarboe
Street toward Pulaski. Virtually naked oaks and sycamores
formed a stark trellis over the street, and five or six black men
in watchcaps or ear-flapped hunter's hats huddled around a fire in
a rusted oil drum. A full block ahead of me strode a confident female
figure in black bellbottoms and a bulky sweater the color of oxidized
iron. Once or twice she looked back over her shoulder toward the
foundry. A curious tilt to her head implied not fear of the derelicts,
but expectancy: DeLynda Gaye was watching for me. When she
finally spotted my truck, she stepped off the ill-repaired sidewalk
into the street and thrust out her thumb. I cruised up to her and
stopped with my passenger window lowered.

"Hey, sailor, going my way?" Shivering, DeLynda pulled her
sweater more tightly around herself.

"Women who use that pick-up line *open* their sweaters, DeLynda.
They don't draw them closed."

"Maybe I'm conflicted."

I laughed. "Get in." I pushed the passenger door open.

DeLynda climbed in next to me and automatically scooped the
increasingly bedraggled Cat in the Hat into her lap. It had received
more attention in the past twenty-four hours than Olivia had given
it in the past month. "Cain't hardly call it a convenience store when
you have to hoof it six blocks for a stick of gum."

"It amazes me you're willing to hoof it at all. Most folks your age
hate to walk anywhere. And through this neighborhood too—"

DeLynda's blithely tossed her head. "It's more dirty and rundown than dangerous. And those fellas back there—everybody around here, in fact—treats me better than decent."

"Scared of Byron's fists?"

"Not at all. They just appreciate a lady."

I made no reply to that, but drove toward Tilden's.

DeLynda's long nails raked the plush on the back of the Cat's head. "If you got no wheels, you walk. Hell, I'm used to it. Even when Byron's bucket of bolts isn't sitting on some grease monkey's lift, like as not it's sporting a flat or an empty gas tank." Her cheap perfume went up my nostrils like ginger straws. "Just how old do you think I am, anyway?"

"Twenty-one," I said instantly. Women younger than twenty-one take that assessment as a compliment. Happily, so do older women.

Raucous laughter spilled from DeLynda. "Thank you! Thank you, you sweet-tongued rascal."

"Did I miss by a mile?"

"Mile and a half. I'm twenty-six."

"Twenty-six. You're still a baby."

DeLynda snorted. "Baby gator, maybe, horny hide and all. I've seen more than my share of the hard and hairy times, Mr. Keats—as the Gold Rush whore once said. So watch out for cute little animals hiding big teeth. They might snap off something you'd rather not part with."

"Amen," I said. A quarter mile on, I pulled into Tilden's parking lot. The store's managers often attempted to discourage after-dark robberies by positioning clothed mannikins at various spots beyond its plate-glass windows, but only a thief with severe myopia would ever fall for this ruse, and even I, a rank outlander, had heard of the practice. DeLynda made no move to open her door, as if expecting me to comment further on her veiled confession of a dubious past.

"The experience hasn't really told on you," I finally said. "Not physically, anyhow."

She laughed again. "Wow. My charms have won me another admirer. Any chance a gallant Good Ol' Boy such as yourself might offer to wait here while I shop and then give me a ride home?" My expression must have betrayed my reluctance. DeLynda grabbed my arm. "How bad do you want to get Olivia back, Mr. Keats?"

"I'd drive you to the North Pole and back."

"Why, Santa, I didn't recognize you." DeLynda released my arm and opened her door. "Wait on me. I need to tell you some stuff."

I considered following her inside, both to make sure she didn't skip on me and to replace the ice cream and beer Byron had consumed. But Tilden's stocked Colt 45 in lieu of Heineken and Popsicles rather than Ben and Jerry's, so I cooled my posterior in the rapidly chilling Tacoma.

DeLynda practically skipped back to the truck when she saw that I had stayed. She hopped in with her plastic bag of purchases and said, "Drive us around, okay? I don't want any of Byron's buddies to see us sitting here together."

"You've got it." I pulled onto Jarboe, then swung a right onto Pulaski and cruised with her acrid perfume in my nostrils again, along with more subtle pheromones that faded to inconsequence when she began to talk.

"We've lived together, Byron and me, over his blacksmith's business about six or seven months now. So I know Olivia. On her weekends with us, I fixed her breakfast—eggs and toast, mind you, not just cold cereal. I took her to the park a lot. We liked to shop together. Once Byron drove us to the Hollywood Connection down in Columbus. Oh, yeah, we also liked to go to the skating rink here in Tocqueville."

"Forgive me, DeLynda, but she never mentioned you or any of these special trips."

"Well, I asked her not to."

The fact that Olivia had obeyed DeLynda flabbergasted me; most eight-year-olds kept secrets no better than a colander holds water. "That's amazing," I said. "What kept her from squealing on you? She usually tells Adrienne everything."

"The truth, probably." DeLynda leaned her head against the passenger window.

"The truth?"

"One day Olivia asked me if I'd ever had a real job like her mama's or like yours before the school board canned you. So I told her. Told her how I got my start in a club called Tuxedo Junction, in Birmingham, where the girls waiting tables wore nothing but shirtfronts and bowties. I learned my moves in that place. Then my daddy found out the real lowdown on my 'waitressing'—who knows how?—and drove all the way from Wedowee to coldcock a bouncer and drag me out of there wrapped in a coat. Before he could stuff me in the car, two other employees flattened Daddy and hustled me back into the Junction, where Mr. DeGrazia blamed me for the ruckus and gave my pretty butt the ax. Which upset me no end, and a passel of customers to boot."

"I can only imagine."

"I took my severance pay and caught a bus to Denver." DeLynda rubbed her palms on the shiny black material sheathing her thighs. "A girl at the Junction had told me about all the money in town and all the good-looking skiers who went clubbing there. I didn't meet any—greenbacks or hunks, either one—and ended up turning tricks on Colfax Avenue. At least I ordered every manjack I serviced to put on a jimmy cap. My last blood test showed me clean, thank God. Anyway, I got fed up, caught another bus, and came back south."

"To Tocqueville?"

"Hot-lanta first. Then a girlfriend asked me to go to Columbus with her. Said she had a surefire exotic-dancer gig for us down there. Wouldn't you know, the boss of that soldier-trap hired me and not her. I haven't laid eyes on her since. I worked at that club a year or so, took a travel break, and then went back to the same grind. But a new club on Victory Drive started scouting local talent and after a month or two hired me away from the old place."

"Fascinating stuff, DeLynda. But what does any of this have to do with getting Olivia back?" By chance, we swept past the headquarters of the Tocqueville police at the foot of Prendergast Street. The dour gray facade of that building seemed to curdle something within DeLynda, who sat mute for an entire block. Then she picked up the Cat in the Hat again and cuddled it to her throat and upper chest.

"A lot, I think. I don't know, though. I could be wasting your time, Mr. Keats. Maybe you should take me back to Byron's now."

I turned into a filling station, crept like a miser past the pumps, and regained Pulaski, to retrace our path. Suddenly DeLynda started talking again.

"Better pay and my name in the poster cases outside the new club convinced me to switch. Not my real name, of course. I stripped as Ruby Slippers. 'Ruby' for my hair, tinted a little darker than you see it now, and 'slippers' for a pair of sequined ballet shoes that I never took off, whatever else in the way of clothes I lost during a performance. Those shoes symbolized something to me. Dignity, probably. Guys offered me as much as a C-note to come out of those slippers, Mr. Keats, but I never did."

"Good for you."

DeLynda flicked me a look to determine if my comment contained any ridicule or censure. Satisified that it did not, she said, "Mr. Saudek—he ran the Glass Cat—agreed that keeping the slippers on added to my mystique. It drew a dozen or more GIs, salesmen, and truckers every night. In fact, Mr. Saudek paid me weekly bonuses that made it easy for me to ignore the foot freaks."

To keep speed demons from running up the Tacoma's tailpipe, I moved into the right lane before the railway overpass and slowed to twenty-five.

"You've probably already guessed this part," DeLynda continued. "One night a little over a year ago, Byron walked into the Glass Cat. He sat right at the runway between two dweebs in JC Penney suits, like a stallion between two ponies. He didn't drool, he didn't hoot, his eyes didn't bug out. He didn't even pull that I'm-a-sophisticated-stud shit, either. He just—well, he just *appreciated* me. Back in the dressing room, one of the busboys brought me a silver box with black and silver ribbons around it. Know what I found inside?"

"I have no idea."

"Byron had run to a nearby drugstore, the only place open at that hour, and bought me some apple-scented foot lotion, a Snickers bar, and a Hallmark card with a ballerina on it. His note inside the card said, 'Any gal all night on her feet / At the end of her shift deserves a treat.' He wrote that poem himself, it wasn't already there from the card company." DeLynda exhaled deeply and touched the stuffed toy's soft hat to one corner of her eye. "Now I ask you, did that show class or what?"

"It's unquestionably pure Byron," I said.

"Amen. Muscles *and* charm in the same package. The very next weekend he attended another show, his last, and we started dating. After we became an item, he wouldn't come to the Glass Cat anymore. 'I want the reality of DeLynda Gaye, not the fantasy of Ruby Slippers.' He didn't even mind all those other guys goggling at me. He knew I loved *him*. He just hated the way the dancing wore me out. He said if I quit he'd support me. Claimed his blacksmithing money would let me live like a Dixie princess, especially if I moved in with him. A few months of dating and whatnot convinced me to accept his offer."

"How could you possibly go wrong?" I said.

DeLynda shuddered and bounced the Cat in the Hat on her knees. "Have I made Byron sound perfect? He's not. He has a nasty streak, all right. It mostly showed itself after I moved in with him, sometimes expressway-wide. After he drinks a little, even just one beer, he tends to explode. Usually just ugly talk and shoving. But what I really don't like—something he kept hidden early on—is that he don't make all his money blacksmithing."

"No?"

"Sometimes he disappears three or four days running and comes home with major folding money that he carries me out to dinner on. Real nice dinners, but the conversation always lacks a little something. 'Where'd you get the cash, honey?' I ask nicely. 'Running guns to Cuban exiles,' he says, and laughs. Usually I laugh too, but it scares the pee out of me. He might really be doing something mighty like his silly brag, maybe even something that could get him killed. And, Jesus, the nightmares—"

"Yours or his?"

"His, Mr. Keats. I don't have any such weight on *my* conscience. But Byron tosses and pitches. Sometimes he even hollers in his sleep. 'Mr. Kingston,' he calls out, 'let me be!' Or, 'Erroll, you son of a bitch, go to hell!'"

"Do those names belong together?"

"They go together all right, and they mean something to me. Erroll Kingston lives and works in Atlanta. A bigshot, at least to the upright types who can't see into the cracks where he *really* operates. Out of sight, Kingston has his crooked feelers in a lot of pies. I've heard rumors—" DeLynda stuck, then completely changed tacks. "One Saturday night at the Glass Cat, a buzz about the owner coming to watch us started up. None of us girls had ever seen the guy before, since Mr. Saudek managed the club night to night. Anyway, as soon as this fifty-year-old character wearing his black winter coat like a cape and this fly five-hundred dollar hat walked in, well, we knew. We'd've known even if he hadn't had a bunch of shade-wearing bodyguards and ass-kissers all around him. Under his hat brim, he had Jack the Ripper eyes and a mouth like a big pale suckerfish."

"Mr. Congeniality," I said.

"Listen, that joker sent shivers from my scalp to my toes. He could've nodded his head and one of his stooges would've gutted me or Tiff or any of us gawking dancers just to satisfy Mr. Boss Man's whim. That scary guy's name was Erroll Kingston."

I clutched the steering wheel harder. "And you think Kingston has something to do with Olivia's disappearance?"

"I don't know. I just have this really bad feeling."

"What about Polk James? The sheriff's department has his truck, his fingerprints."

"Polk James couldn't mastermind a kidnapping any more than you could run Byron's forge."

"Thanks."

"No offense, Mr. Keats. Just remember the name Erroll Kingston. Byron hates him, or resents him, or something, and that scares me as much as Byron's mysterious money-making trips."

A block or two back, we had entered Dogtown. I drove as slowly as I could without provoking a cacophony of horns.

"Let me out here," DeLynda suddenly said. "I don't want Byron to catch us."

I did as she said. Clutching her grocery sack, she strode away without a single backward glance. Her determined swiftness afoot left me no time to ask, *Catch us at what?*

When I drove back out to the house, the dropped flag on our mailbox signaled that Bob French had made his delivery. By long-standing agreement, I collected the mail, even when Adrienne was home. I couldn't reach into the box from the elevation of the truck, so I parked it at the top of the drive with its motor running.

The box held a small pile of letters, solicitations, bills, and advertising circulars. One item popped willy-nilly into view as I dropped the sheaf onto the seat of the Tacoma. A picture postcard of a docked cruise ship with palm trees and blistering-white tropical buildings in the background. I flipped it over and read its message:

> Having a wonderful time. Quite content, by the way, that you all remain in Georgia while we three navigate the sea lanes. On Bonaire in the Netherland Antilles, a Bahá'i "pioneer" received me into her home. Such an interesting, *interesting* faith, Bahá'i!
>
> Hello to you all. Give Olivia a big hug for me. Do I have a conch for her! And T-shirts galore! You wouldn't believe!
>
> Lovingly, LaRue

I immediately shoved the postcard into the Tacoma's glove compartment.

Thirteen

At nine o'clock the next morning, a Friday, Captain Nick Cooper showed up on our porch with a formidable African-American man of forty or forty-five. In our front room, the sheer mass of this broad-shouldered newcomer instantly shrank our furniture and the parlor itself to a stage set for puppets. If someone had inflated a Macy's Thanksgiving Day Parade balloon in our faces, the effect could not have been more dramatic.

"I'd like you all to meet Asa Fearing," Cooper said.

"Asa *D.* Fearing," Fearing said. "The 'D' stands for Daniel, my daddy's name. I'd dishonor both him and the Bible he always carried if I introduced myself without it."

Cooper smiled. "Sorry, Asa. I won't forget again."

"Not a problem. We only just met. Besides, if you do forget my daddy'll speak through me again and set you straight right quick."

"Agent Fearing comes to us from the Atlanta headquarters of the FBI. They've assigned him to investigate Olivia's abduction, now that we know our prime suspect carried her into Alabama."

When Adrienne stepped forward to greet Fearing, he engulfed her pale hand in his brown one and then decorously released it. "My condolences on your trial, ma'am. I've come to help you pass through it, much as an unexpected figure in the fiery furnace helped Shadrach, Meshach, and Abednego. Not, of course, that I claim a special invulnerability."

Adrienne's face brightened. "Would you like to sit down, Agent Fearing?"

"Not just yet." He looked at me. "Mr. Keats, you too have my sympathies, as well as my personal assurance that this case will occupy all my waking moments—maybe a few of my sleeping ones—until we bring your daughter home."

"*Safely* home," I said.

"Yes sir, safely home."

Fearing did not look to me like an FBI agent. He did not wear the stereotypical black, gray, or blue suit that television has conditioned us to expect. Instead, he sported a bright rust-and-orange jacket, a cinnamon crew-neck sweater, pleated khaki slacks, and mahogony loafers with bright new pennies slotted into the insteps. His neatly trimmed hair had a faint henna cast that the color scheme of his clothes heightened.

"I thought FBI agents worked in pairs," I said.

"Some of us do. I have a partner myself. Currently, he's recuperating from a minor gunshot wound."

Adrienne said, "How soon do you think you can track down this Polk James person?"

Fearing swung his big head back and forth like a buffalo testing the wind. "Excuse me, ma'am, but projections and speculations just put a straitjacket on everyone. Consider the Ramsey case. Who would've imagined that one could drag on so long?"

At this reference to the little girl infamously murdered in Colorado, the temperature in the room dropped five degrees. Maybe Fearing simply wished to induce some hard-nosed realism, but Adrienne blanched and I had a visceral urge to escort him from the house. Startlingly, though, Fearing clapped his hands together, producing a Concorde-magnitude sonic boom.

"But just because we can't name the precise moment when the Lord will favor us with victory, don't assume we can shilly-shally around or surrender to despair," Fearing said. "I intend to pursue Polk James like a hound of God. We'll start with a thorough reinvestigation of the premises."

Although he must have carefully studied the evidence already gathered, Fearing ambled purposefully through every room in our house. He examined every photograph of Olivia, counted and identified all her toys, books, and clothes. The attention he gave to seemingly minor details both alarmed and heartened me. Could the eye of an experienced federal agent cull from the trivia that the sheriff's department had already sifted a fresh and vital clue?

Nick Cooper left shortly after Fearing commenced his own intrusive scrutiny of our lives. Because I had wanted to talk to him about DeLynda Gaye's suspicions, I regretted his departure. Did Cooper know about Byron's live-in girlfriend? If Byron had not already hoodwinked or suborned Cooper's deputies, surely they would soon haul DeLynda in for a lie-detector test. Then the information about Byron's problematic second job and his mysterious links to a man named Erroll Kingston would emerge. Or would they? Maybe only my own intervention would force Byron and DeLynda to disclose what they knew. I would speak to Cooper later.

In the *zendo,* Fearing stood between Adrienne's mat and Olivia's smaller one, staring with half-bowed head at the Buddha on the table shrine. The back of his skull resembled a soft-sculpture bowling ball, his neck a mahogany plinth.

"Your daughter practices sitting meditation too?"

"Yes sir. As faithfully as her mother."

"But she also reads books, watches videos, writes stories, paints pictures, and plays the violin."

"A normal little girl," Adrienne said.

"*Extra*ordinary, I'd call her. Got herself a pony too, I hear."

"That's Will's doing."

Fearing looked at me with something like rebuke, as if my purchase of Olivia's pony had ineluctably set this whole affair in motion. I tugged at the turtleneck I had donned that morning to conceal the bruise Byron's fingers had left on my throat.

"This pony have a name, Mr. Keats?"

"Roogy Batoon," I said.

"Roogy Batoon." Fearing elaborately drew out the syllables of the silly name: "Rooo-gy Ba-*tooon.*" I began to perceive in him a buried vein of comic irony. "May I see this beast with the mythical name?"

"Of course."

Adrienne said, "You take him down, Will." Clearly, she intended to meditate before her altar as soon as we left. Not wishing to delay her, I escorted Fearing from the *zendo* and down the back stairs.

"Roogy Batoon figured in the abduction," I said in the narrow stairwell. "Polk James released her from the paddock to get me out of the house."

"James looks like a regular General Schwarzkopf. Turning the pony loose, snatching the pruning hook. Everything fell into place for him. Almost certainly he'd cased your homestead beforehand. Or he had an insider's knowledge of the place's layout."

I stepped out into the kitchen and turned to face Fearing, who still bulked large in the stairwell. "What do you mean by that, Agent Fearing?"

He held up a hand as imposing as a stop sign. "Not that either you or Miz Owsley had anything to do with the abduction, if that's what's ruffled your tailfeathers. But tell me, Mr. Keats. How many tradesmen, day laborers, or delivery boys have wandered onto your property over the past six months? Could Polk James have weaseled information from any of them? Could he have enlisted one as an accomplice? Humor me a little here."

Admirably time-conscious, Fearing pushed past me and out the back door. I trotted after him.

Already in the paddock, Roogy Batoon lifted her sorrel head, pricked up her ears, and cantered toward us at a playful angle, rhythmically flicking her tail. Fearing paused, roared a laugh that startled both Roogy and me, then strode to the fence so aggressively that the pony veered off. No matter. Fearing vaulted into the muddy paddock with the gravity-defying grace of a tank launching itself from a ski jump. Roogy spooked away on a diagonal canter.

"Come to Asa, darling," Fearing boomed. "I don't eat horsemeat unless it's barbecued."

Roogy circled the paddock twice, hugging the fence. Improbably, she drew near to Fearing, shaking her head in irritation or bemusement. Finally, against all my expectations, she stuck her muzzle under Fearing's uplifted right arm. He laughed in long baritone ripples and hugged the pony to him. "My beauty, my beauty," he crooned, stroking her jaw.

I leapt the fence too. Fearing and Roogy alike regarded me as if I had intruded on a lovers' tryst, Romeo and Juliet on the farm.

"Will this help us find Olivia?" I asked.

"Joy brings insight," Fearing said. "Who knows?"

"Insight can't drive a car and scour the back roads of Alabama."

"Mr. Keats, some people—maybe you?—expect FBI agents to act like robots. Well, I'm sorry, sir, but it just ain't in my nature." Fearing slid his hands to either side of Roogy's face, back toward her jaws, and lifted her head affectionately. "You tell him, sweetie."

I waited. What else could I do with an FBI agent who had turned our paddock into his private petting zoo? Then Fearing let go of the pony's head and ran one hand down her back in a caress that provoked voluptuous tremors throughout her pelt. For a moment, Fearing looked ready to leap on Roogy's back and gallop around the yard like a hired horsebreaker. Instead, he walked to the paddock gate and eased himself through it into the yard. I followed him out.

"Does Olivia ever ride the pony?" Fearing asked.

"Whenever I let her. She loves Roogy."

"Smart girl. Does she ride well?"

"Better than passably. Wednesday she missed her ride because of a tumble from the fence. She would have headed right back out if I hadn't insisted on washing the mud off her and making her rest." I struggled with the abrupt realization that Olivia might never ride Roogy again.

"Everything I learn about your daughter leads me to reckon she may prove as instrumental in her own rescue as anything you or I can do."

I stared at Fearing disbelievingly. "You expect an eight-year-old to counter her own kidnapping?"

Fearing laughed. "Not to counter it, no sir. To use her native gumption to survive. To jam a monkey wrench sidewise into Polk James's plans."

"What if she doesn't? What if she can't?"

"I'll bet on Olivia. Do you want to bet against her?"

I shook my head and gazed between barn and house at the pine-furred land distantly bordering Alabama. Dead kudzu vines hung from the nearer trees like cut telephone cables. "I'd never bet against Olivia. I just don't like the odds."

Fearing laid his hand on my shoulder. "God's my bookie, Mr. Keats."

I surprised myself by laughing. "Let's go back to the house."

In our living room again, Fearing asked, "How'd your daughter spend those crucial final hours with you, Mr. Keats?"

"Not final, I hope. She passed some of the time watching *The Wizard of Oz*." I nodded at the television. "She only stopped when I called her outside."

"If you ask me, that nonsense obsessed her."

Fearing and I turned around. Adrienne sprawled deep in a well-upholstered easychair catty-corner to the set.

"Couldn't you sit?" I said.

"Too jittery. Believe me, I wish I could."

Fearing folded his hands before him and rocked back on his heels. "As my daddy always said, 'If you can't get *over* your blues, get *behind* them.' "

Adrienne gave him a wan smile. "Thanks for the advice."

"My daddy gave it to me free, ma'am, and I pass it on at the same price. No thanks necessary." Fearing turned again to me. "Did you pull the cassette, Mr. Keats?"

"No. I rewound it ten minutes' worth, then replayed it until the tape counter read zero again."

"Could you do that for me now?"

"Sure." I picked up the remote and repeated actions that had earlier baffled a sheriff's deputy and a GBI agent. Fearing watched Bert Lahr in his Cowardly Lion getup sing "If I Were King of the Forest," and then extol the glories of muskrat courage. Muskrat courage. A day ago, that phrase and its associations had buoyed my spirits. Not now, however. This morning it simultaneously mocked me and incited my guilt.

During the replay, Adrienne averted her head and covered her ears. Fearing nodded sagaciously, as if the *Oz* clip encoded an arcane map to Polk James's current whereabouts. When, at the end of Lahr's scene, I cut the power to the VCR, Adrienne dropped her hands into her lap and Fearing rubbed his palms together like an enthusiastic tax collector.

"Olivia's movie reminds me of a joke I heard recently," he said. "Would you all like to hear it?"

Adrienne looked up at him with wary amazement. "Sure. What mother of a kidnapped child wouldn't?"

I said, "Right. Maybe you know a good one about the Lindbergh baby."

Our sarcasm did not deter Fearing, who actually crossed the room to stand before Adrienne. "This enormous mother of a tornado, see, swoops down and catches up former President Reagan, Speaker of the House Gingrich, and ol' Bill Clinton. It whirls the three bigshots all the way to Oz and drops them plumb in the wizard's lap. The all-seeing Oz ain't fazed, of course, and he booms, 'What can I do for y'all? Speak up now!'

"Reagan takes a step forward, a sort of tottery one, and asks the wizard if he can give him a brain. Wiz says, 'No problem.' Then Newt pushes up front and asks for a heart. Mr. Wizard says, 'Sure!' "

Fearing swiveled his gaze from Adrienne to me, gauging our reactions. "Now Billy C., he don't move. He just sort of cranes his head around like he's missing something. Finally the wizard loses patience and yells, 'And what exactly do *you* want?' Ol' Bill, still gawping about in puzzlement, says, 'Where's Dorothy?' "

Silence. Fearing did not move. Even as the silence lengthened, he stood poker-faced, neither crowing nor contrite. Then Adrienne began to laugh. She covered her mouth, but her guffaws burst out anyway. Within seconds she had slid out of the chair to the floor, where she rolled about mirthfully. I began to laugh too. Adrienne had given me permission. Fearing still did not move. His expression neither condemned nor sanctioned our laughter.

Eventually, Adrienne regained control of herself and sat up with her arms around her knees and her eyes coruscating. "Thanks," she told Fearing.

"Okay," Fearing said. "*That* you can thank me for."

Fourteen

Standing alone on the porch, I watched Fearing drive away in a white Ford LTD bearing government plates. His departure left me shaky and irresolute, and I suddenly knew why.

For the first time since Olivia's kidnapping, Adrienne and I faced the prospect of a substantial block of time alone together. All the deputies and investigators had taken their leave, all our friends had already visited or called. Police technicians had established their beachhead—a tap on our line, that ominous recorder next to the telephone—and left their robots both to guard and to monitor us. Now, Adrienne and I had no one to distract us from our loss or from our raw emotional interdependency. The weekend stretched before us as cheerlessly as a desert. We each saw Olivia's recovery as an indistinct mirage above this wasteland, a cruelly shimmering illusion, and we loathed each other for our lack of faith.

Neither of us reacted well to the torment of the abduction. Adrienne seemed ready to crumple into Zen-drugged lassitude; her habitual serenity, however, had eroded into little-girl fidgetiness or long-enduring pessimistic funks. I moved the other way, plunging into frenetic activity, darting off helter-skelter like quail at the sound of a shotgun blast. My separate interviews with Byron and DeLynda had occurred as a result of my unexamined longing to act rather than to think, and my current fretfulness a mere seventy-two hours after the kidnapping stood in marked contrast to Adrienne's uncharacteristic passivity. How would we relate to each other later today? Tomorrow? The day after? Would our moods and outlooks eventually dovetail, or would the fracture between us widen and swallow us?

Further, issues that we had once tacitly cloaked to maintain family harmony had begun to squirm for release. What positive feelings, if any, did Adrienne continue to nurture for her manic ex-husband? Did she know of Byron's new lover? If so, why had she never mentioned DeLynda's existence to me? Did she mistrust me in my role as Olivia's surrogate father? Did she hope by her silence to spare my feelings or to mask her own? What of my own recent secrecy? Try as I might, I could find no rational explanation for concealing from Adrienne my whereabouts or my doings.

Home yesterday afternoon from Kroger's and Owsley's Anvil and Bellows, I had said nothing of my run-ins with Byron and DeLynda. (Also, I had hidden in the Tacoma's glovebox LaRue's postcard, yet another concealment.) True, Adrienne had not asked me to explain my tardiness—whether because she trusted me or because she could not abandon the TV set and the slim possibility of an illuminating bulletin, I still didn't know—but I had hardly given her a chance, hurrying upstairs to put on the black turtleneck jersey, then returning to the kitchen to put away the groceries.

Out of guilty solicitude and habit, I prepared a small supper from canned beans, canned Mexicorn, and frozen franks, and then washed dishes. Later, separate again, Adrienne vegetated in the *zendo*, while in the dark parlor I nursed a scotch and listened to melancholy jazz: Miles's *Kind of Blue*, Coltrane's *A Love Supreme*. Only after turning off the CD player and climbing the stairs did I discover that Adrienne had fallen asleep on our bed. I undressed and joined her, but set my internal alarm so that I could arise before her and put on my bruise-obscuring turtleneck. Pulling it over my head, I wondered how many times Byron's violence had prompted *Adrienne* to dress for concealment.

The various evidences of our recent estrangement unnerved me. As I looked upon Adrienne, I resolved to bridge the chasm widening between us. When I sat down on the mattress beside her, her coiled body and tear-streaked face shredded my resolve. What could I possibly do or say to console or hearten her? She had drawn her shoulders up to her ears, and her forearms wrapped her belly as if holding in an abdominal rupture.

Frightened, I touched her shoulder. It relaxed a little. Her wet eyes opened. Then she let go of herself and grabbed for me as a shipwreck victim might clutch a floating spar. We embraced awkwardly, Adrienne pushing up from the bed to place her wet cheek next to mine and her lips to my ear. In fact, she nibbled at my ear, tickling me so that I hunched my shoulder in self-defense.

"Don't pull away, Will."

I nuzzled her hair and stroked the back of her head. "I've missed you," I whispered. "Really missed you."

She whispered back. "How much togetherness can you stand?"

"What?"

"If we stay busy together, we can survive this nightmare. Eventually, Cooper or Fearing or one of those guys will bring her home to us. Meanwhile, let's work together sprucing up this place, till we're too tired to think. Sweet old Mr. Goldborough has told me not to come in for the next several days."

I tried to look her squarely in the eyes. "You ready for me if I shift into commander-of-the-fort mode?"

"Sure." She smiled. "Right now, I *need* someone to tell me what to do."

"You got it. But only when it comes to fixing up Cold Comfort Farm here. For everything else, I'll need *your* guidance."

We kissed. Then, still fragilely smiling, Adrienne pushed me away and dressed in threadbare jeans and a denim shirt. Downstairs after breakfast she added a windbreaker and mud-encrusted boots.

That difficult first weekend we killed with hammer and saw, rake and shovel, pitchfork and pruning hook. We buried it under compost, mulch, and pony manure. On Sunday evening, after two days of nearly uninterrupted work, we stood exhausted in our accomplishment. Neither of us mentioned that over the span of our labors not one fresh word from the sheriff's department or the FBI had reached us. Fear, meanwhile, had prevented us from simply calling and asking for news.

On Monday morning, I took an early shower and stepped naked from the stall to find Adrienne at the medicine-cabinet mirror with her toothbrush. She blinked at me as if I had materialized from another dimension, then gestured at my throat with the toothbrush. I lifted my hand to the bruise: a perfect opportunity for truth-telling.

"I slipped and whacked myself with the pitchfork handle, forking hay for Roogy," I lied. "No idea until now that it'd caused a bruise."

"That jersey you wore hid it." Nothing in Adrienne's expression or tone conveyed accusation. "Here, let me smooth some ointment on it." She found a tube of Neosporin and applied some cream to my throat with a feathery gentleness that aroused me. Adrienne responded to my obvious excitement by embracing me; the tube of antibiotic fell to the tiles. We waltzed clumsily back into our bedroom. On our bed we continued to move more like waltzers than starved dogs, and the curious graciousness of the sex—which, ironically, I had initiated with a lie—reopened old channels of sympathy. We finished almost together, and held each other for an hour.

This intimacy set the mood for the next several days. We talked more, often about Olivia. Whereas I deliberately called up and dwelt on past happy moments, Adrienne insistently, even defiantly, projected Olivia's life into the future, as if visualizing her future would actually bring it about. We never argued, though, and our mealtimes reacquired their importance as periods of laughter and information-sharing. Indoor and outdoor work, along with visits from friends like the Youngs and the Lapierres, helped pass the time, even if the hours still limped by.

At least once a day, Adrienne's parents, Neil and Ruth Thompson, telephoned from their New Hampshire farm just north of Lowell, Massachusetts. Inevitably during each call, just as they had during the call Adrienne placed to them the day after Olivia's abduction, they volunteered to leave their apple orchard in the care of Adrienne's brother, Aaron, an untested twenty-year-old, and fly down to Georgia. Olivia had visited with them at least once a year since the Owsleys' departure from Lowell, and the Thompsons would do anything for their grandchild, including offering themselves to Polk James as stand-ins. Given the couple's age and her father's questionable health, Adrienne always demurred. Besides, they had disapproved from the start of her relationship with Byron—wisely, Adrienne had long since conceded—and of her decision to remain in Georgia when she might have returned north. The strain of these old disagreements still lent an uncomfortable torque to all her familial interactions: not estrangement, but an edgy politesse. In fact, I got along with my mother better than Adrienne did with either of her parents, even though a gummy web of affection obviously bound them all.

On Thursday evening when the telephone predictably rang, Adrienne shot me a quasi-annoyed look, then answered it. Dropping down onto a nearby chair, she said, "Hello, Mother," her face evincing resignation. I climbed the stairs and picked up the bedroom extension.

"—*some small advance by now,*" Ruth Thompson said. "*If the Boston police had this case, they'd've already solved it.*"

Adrienne said, "The Georgia police are working as diligently and intelligently and creatively as any northern ones."

"*Doing what? Adding another inch to their bellies sitting around the hogpen swilling moonshine.*"

"No stereotypes, please, Mother. Captain Cooper and his crew don't resemble your prejudices in the least. And neither does Agent Fearing."

"*I had some hopes for him. At least he doesn't hail from Dogpatch. What has he told you lately?*"

"Very little. Yesterday he said that to all intents and purposes Polk James and Olivia have vanished from the planet."

"*How comforting.*"

"Comfort comes cheap. We insist on his telling us the unvarnished truth."

"*Well, what does that ex-Hollywood deputy with arthritis say?*"

"Not much more than Fearing. He admits he can't imagine what sort of extortion scheme James has in mind."

"*They're feeding you pap to cover up their own ineptitude! Let us come down.*"

"To lend your investigative expertise? Please, Mother, try to let go of that idea. The police need only a small break to get the case moving again."

"*I suppose . . .*"

When Adrienne came upstairs after this call, she sat down beside me on the bed, her brow as furrowed as corduroy. I put my hand on her knee and said, "Parents know just how to soothe their adult kids, don't they?"

After squinting at me in ritual annoyance, Adrienne guffawed. Laughing, we rocked in each other's arms.

Halloween fell on that coming Saturday. I bought a pumpkin the size of a medicine ball at a convenience store and carried it home in my truck. Adrienne, out on an errand of her own, did not see me wrestle it inside and into the middle of our kitchen table. During her absence, I carved into the pumpkin diamond-shaped eyes, bovine nostrils, and a vast snaggle-toothed grin. I dripped candle wax into its cavity, seated the candle there, and carried the jack-o'-lantern out to the front porch in the descending twilight. When I lit the candle and set the cap in place, the pumpkin emitted a pleasant yammy smell and countless jitterbugging flashes.

We lived too far out to attract many trick-or-treaters, but I hoped that at least a few would come by to see my handiwork. A car pulled into the drive. Sitting on the top step, I recognized it as Adrienne's Camry and watched as she parked it in its customary place. She emerged, retrieved a grocery bag from the backseat, and took two or three strides toward the front porch.

"Trick or treat," I said.

Adrienne spotted the lantern and stiffened as if a high-amp current had gone through her. She proceeded jerkily up the walk, climbed the porch steps, and dropped the bag of groceries in my lap. Before I could stop her, she squatted and shoved the pumpkin off the porch. It hit an ornamental stone that Olivia and I had painted to resemble a comical frog and cracked open with a loud hollow snap, sending the cap rolling across the lawn and extinguishing the candle. Adrienne's hands hung limply over her knees. She stared out into the dark, her breath faintly luminous.

"You had no right to do that, kid."

She gestured at the smashed goblin head. "You had no right to do *that*." To celebrate a children's holiday, she meant, when our own child no longer had the capacity to join in.

"I think I did. Would Olivia want us to turn a holiday she loved into a wake?"

"Don't patronize me, Will."

"If we have to cover ourselves in ashes every holiday, we may as well buy a whole shitload tomorrow. Veteran's Day, Thanksgiving, Hannukah, Christmas—shall I go on?"

"I won't listen to this." She rose and strode past me.

I set the grocery bag aside, looked over my shoulder, and shouted, "*Stop right there, Ade!*"

She swiveled on me. "Don't ever call me that. You might as well call me idiot or bitch."

A knot as heavy as a ripe pumpkin formed in my gut. I had trespassed against her own self-concept. "Adrienne, I'm sorry."

She looked at me without expression, then stepped into the house and slammed the door. I let her go. For the next half hour I remained on the porch staring down on the shattered jack-o'-lantern.

That night, in bed, Adrienne reared over me naked and cupped my face in her hands. "Forgive me, Will. Please forgive me." With her silent tears flowing, we made love for the second time since Olivia's abduction.

On Monday, Adrienne returned to teaching. At first, she told me that evening, dealing again with lesson plans, fifty-minute class periods, and all the accumulated paperwork of her absence had struck her as labors tantamount to pushing a battleship up Stone Mountain. As the day wore on, however, fellow teachers had appeared to offer condolences and encouragement, and even her students—the naturally fractious as well as the predictably respectable—had displayed an attentiveness and sensitivity that heartened her, even if an earlier group counseling session rather than individual compassion had prompted this sympathetic attitude.

"We cried again," Adrienne said. "Even some of the tough ones I never could reach before. It helped."

"Don't worry," I said. "They'll turn on you soon enough." That line prompted us to laugh together, which also helped.

For me, though, Monday had crawled. Desperate for relief, at one point I actually considered calling the Thompsons. Another day of such deadly inertia would undercut my sanity.

By Tuesday morning, I had made up my mind to *do* something to get Olivia back.

Fifteen

After Adrienne left for work, I set off for the Speece County Sheriff's Office and Jail Facility. Like an analogue of Poe's telltale heart, the postcard in the glovebox repeatedly drew my attention from the road. Finally, I could no longer stand its accusatory call. I pulled to the side of the road, removed the card, tore it into pieces, and scattered them to the November winds. LaRue would have to consult her own scrapbook for memories of her trip.

The woman in the control booth in the foyer passed me through as soon as she saw me, and Cooper, dressed in his signature gray slacks and white knit shirt, came out to escort me into his office. Once seated, he flexed the fingers of his right hand as if they pained him. "Wish I had some news, Will. About the only development concerns Byron Owsley. He came in for his polygraph test yesterday."

"Did he pass?"

Cooper narrowed his eyes and frowned. "Technically, yes. But—"

"But what? It's either yes or no, isn't it?"

"Not really. We know of cases where experienced people have beaten the machine. For instance, certain drugs alter the physiological responses the machine relies on. Some folks don't even need chemical help, though. Cool-headed larceny and a certain amount of self-delusion let them hoax the machine. Byron's testimony never wandered into falsehoods—according to the polygraph and its technician. But I watched the whole performance, and my gut tells me he served us a tossed salad of fictions."

"Doesn't that allow you to arrest him and subject him to more intensive interrogation?"

"On what grounds? His lies probably didn't even involve Olivia. Guilt about felonious business may have nagged at him. So, for the moment at least, Byron remains a free man."

"And what about his girlfriend?"

"DeLynda Gaye?"

Cooper's knowledge of DeLynda's existence reassured me of his competence, just as it relieved me of the necessity of informing him of her. How I could have reasonably explained any close acquaintance with Byron's live-in eluded me. "That's her name—unless Byron's got more than one woman on his hook."

Cooper smiled. "I don't think Ms. Gaye would stand for that. She strikes me as a woman quite capable of extracting a certain, ah, fidelity from her man. We've already taken a preliminary statement from her, one that confirms Byron's alibi for the night of the kidnapping. We'll definitely haul her in for her own polygraph test eventually. But in my estimation—and Chief Deputy Stratford agrees with me—she's a peripheral figure."

"I don't think she had a hand in Olivia's kidnapping either. But as Byron's lover, she probably knows all his dirty secrets."

Cooper massaged his knuckles harder, as if my persistence aggravated his pain. "Damn, I wish somebody made WD-40 for joints! Again, Will, what relevance does DeLynda's knowledge of Byron's questionable activities have in Olivia's case? Granted, Byron's probably running a dozen different scams to stay afloat. That forge of his doesn't mint pocket change these days. But right now taking him down for even a dozen larcenous offenses doesn't concern me. I want Polk James."

I leaned forward. "So do I. Which is why I came to ask your permission to interview a couple of people about Olivia's disappearance."

"I don't advise it. Your good intentions aside, you could inadvertently compromise the case. You could even blow any hope of a successful prosecution."

"If you had anyone in custody to prosecute."

"True enough. But my lack of news doesn't mean the GIBs and FIBs haven't made some deliberate, low-key progress you could still somehow botch. No, Will, go home and put up storm windows or paint your fences. Don't try playing detective."

I declined to move.

Cooper crunched his knuckles and swiveled away. "Stubborn as a certain kid at Columbus High who kept flinging himself at the crossbar until he'd knocked it off the uprights a dozen times. Remember that, Will?" Cooper shook his head with grudging respect. "Who exactly did you want to talk to?"

"Polk James's mother."

"Ah, the eccentric Alice-Darlene. We've talked to her. Three or four times. Once under the polygraph."

"With what results?"

"Oh, she probably lied a time or two. But not about Polk's whereabouts. She honestly doesn't think her son did it. Just as honestly, she doesn't know where he's gone. In fact, she wanted us to list him as a missing person and start looking for her poor boy in local quarries and pine stands."

"I'd still like to talk to her. And to that freelance psychic you mentioned."

"Oscar Greenaway."

"Right. Folks looking for a cancer cure go to Mexico. Desperate parents consult anyone they think might help."

Cooper, still facing away from me, wrapped his stiff fingers with a thick rubber band. "An American citizen with no intention to harass can talk to almost anyone he wants."

"So you've given me permission?"

"I've made a simple statement of fact about Constitutional rights."

When Cooper refused either to speak again or to face me, I got up and walked toward the door. Suddenly, Cooper swiveled about and said, "Will."

"Yes?"

"You never did make it as a high jumper. But everyone on the whole damned track team admired your tenacity."

Knowing the address, I could have gone directly to the James shack on the eastern flank of Dogtown. But my own innate thoughtfulness and a prudent concern for my own hide led me to drive first to

Tocqueville Middle School. I parked on an access road near the running track and jogged across the browning autumn grass to the windows of Adrienne's classroom—as I had often done to avoid checking in at the office.

This time, however, a rail-thin fiftyish rent-a-cop with a pistol on his hip intercepted me, calling out in a high-pitched voice for me to halt. I obeyed without hesitation.

"You a reporter, mister?"

"No. Trying my best to avoid them. I just wanted a quick word with Adrienne Owsley."

The security guard looked me over skeptically. Then recognition dawned on his face, and he smiled. "Sure. Go ahead. Just be quick, okay? Goldborough will can me if anyone except Miz Owsley and her kids sees you out here without authorization."

"Thanks. I'll try not get you in any trouble."

As we approached the building, someone in Adrienne's room levered a window out, for her students had already witnessed my unexpected powwow with the guard, and Adrienne herself knelt in front of this opening to talk with me.

"What's going on? Have you heard something?"

My unexpected appearance had falsely raised her hopes. "No. But I have a new idea or two." I recounted my interview with Cooper.

"Don't act alone," Adrienne said through the window gap. "If you'll wait until after school, I'll go with you."

A little girl with beaded dreadlocks came up behind Adrienne and placed a hand on her elbow. "Did that man kidnap your daughter, Miz Owsley?"

"No, Lakeisha. He's working to get her back." To me, Adrienne said, "Alone, you could intimidate Mrs. James. She won't relate to you. But she and I are both mothers with missing children."

"Polk James as a child," I said. "There's an angle I'd've probably never seen. Okay, I'll wait."

Adrienne smiled, blew me a kiss, and closed the window. Lakeisha, meanwhile frowned through the glass at me, still dubious of both my innocence and my utility.

At 4:30 P.M., Adrienne and I crossed the line into Dogtown. The neighborhood encompassing the James house proved even more dispiriting than the streets leading to Byron's home: stunted trees, broken or rusty fences and gates, overturned trash barrels, unraked dirt yards, starved-looking pets or strays, abandoned trucks and cars moldering under dead kudzu.

"Charming," Adrienne said ruefully.

"No slums in Lowell?"

"Oh, sure. Byron and I just escaped living in one, thanks to an affordable last-minute rental coming available in a better place. But it was a close thing, and I feel for these people."

I found the James shack by its smudged stenciled number on the curb. It reproduced the style of its neighbors, but on a scraped hill thirty or forty feet farther back from the street. On a narrow slat porch wider than the house itself dozed a ribby mongrel dog, part greyhound or whippet. Yard debris included a bashed-in cardboard box overflowing with aerosol cans and a lawn chair minus its webbing. As we left my truck, the dog crept off the porch and slipped beneath it without even barking at us.

The woman who answered my knock resembled a senile gnome. Her vertically striped red and white pedal pushers and her black T-shirt did nothing to flatter the upright tube of her figure. Nor did her frowsty red wig sufficently soften her features to prevent us from seeing in them the simian lineaments of her son, Polk James.

"What do you want?" The way Alice-Darlene James took in our faces—first Adrienne's and then mine—betrayed that she recognized us as Olivia's parents.

"Could we come in a few minutes?" Adrienne said.

"If I wanted you all to. Not sure I do, though."

"This whole business must pain you as much as it does Will and me."

"It'd pain me a lot less if people like you all'd quit reminding me of it."

A burst of thin rude noise erupted from within, powerfully drawing Alice-Darlene's attention. "You all're making me miss my show just when the shouting and shoving's getting good. Come on in if you want." She barged back inside, letting the screen door slam in our faces, and we followed.

Yellowed roller shades excluded all sunlight so that only the oval picture tube's undersea glare lit the room. Tattered magazine illustrations of Hollywood celebrities decorated the inexpertly finished gypsum-board walls, which showed hundred of nail holes and every tape ridge. Dozens of photographs in filigreed five-and-dimestore frames cluttered the top of an antique sideboard missing one leg and resting at that corner on a stack of mail-order catalogs. Mrs. James flounced down on a horsehair loveseat opposite the TV, which sat on a coffee table with absurd ball-and-claw feet. Adrienne and I lowered ourselves onto a kitchen chair and a ripped blue-plaid hassock flanking the loveseat.

"*I sold him to you, Mama,*" a young woman on the screen said. "*But that never meant you could keep him after he gave little Amy herpes.*"

Mrs. James leaned forward as a middle-aged woman on the show seized the teenage speaker by the hair and the two chunky figures grappled back and forth across the studio stage like posturing professional wrestlers. Adrienne and I exchanged a look behind Mrs. James's back, but held our tongues. When the on-screen fight gave way to a commercial, Mrs. James used a remote to mute the sound, but did not turn away from the set or ask us a single question. I boiled to speak, but Adrienne shook her head. After the commercials, Mrs. James boosted the sound, and we watched the show all the way through to its operatic conclusion, whereupon she blanked the screen with an equally operatic flourish of the remote.

"Watching that mess helps me forget my own," she said.

Adrienne turned to her gently. "Do you have any idea where your son may have taken Olivia?"

Alice-Darlene hit the arm of the loveseat, raising a plume of dust. "Nowhere! He didn't take her nowhere!" She shuffled her pudgy feet, clad in transparent jelly shoes just like those that Olivia often wore. "Cain't you all get that through your heads? Polk's got nothing to do with your troubles!"

I said, "Ma'am, a sheriff's deputy found your son's truck five miles from our place the morning after someone stole our daughter."

"They stole your girl, they could steal a truck too!"

"The only adult fingerprints in the truck belonged to your son, Mrs. James."

She shrugged. "Maybe the thief wore gloves. They's plenty of folks smart enough to outfox the police."

I paused. What Mrs. James theorized may have merited a moment's consideration. But Occam's Razor—and common sense—dissuaded me from multiplying potential culprits.

Alice-Darlene pushed herself to her feet and paced away from us. "Polk's had his troubles, sure. We all have. But the police keep picking at him. A bad thing happens anywhere in Tocqueville, they show up on our doorstep. Now a bad thing's happened to Polk—I just know it!—and they've turned everything against him."

Adrienne intervened before I could again speak bluntly. "Mrs. James, forgive me for asking this, but have you ever known your son to hurt a child?"

"Not a babe, not a child, not even a grown-up man his own size. He once kicked a dog somebody sicced on him. 'Side from that, no ma'am. He might've shoplifted something Lamar or me needed a time or two, but he don't do violence. You can put that in the bank and pull a draft on it." Mrs. James ran a thumbnail between her two front teeth and pointed her chin at the photographs atop the sideboard. "You think me and Lamar raised trash? We brung up a good boy and did it on next to nothing. Look for yourself. Go on. Look!"

Adrienne and I both went to the display, where we surveyed the Polk James Gallery. A remarkably apish little boy tumbled in the grass, climbed on monkey bars, hoisted a bamboo pole on the edge of a pond, stood barefoot in patched overalls with his spindly chest showing between the straps. Older, Polk uneasily consorted with more attractive and healthier-looking classmates. In none of these dingy prints did he show his teeth in a smile, but in several an ambiguous grin flickered about his lips, a wan spark of vitality flared in his eyes. The mugshot on Cooper's monitor had made Polk James appear dead-in-life, whereas Alice-Darlene's collection of candids hinted at a real if battered intelligence.

"What happened to the boy we can see in these shots?" I turned back to Mrs. James.

She sighed, and her shoulders slumped. "Acne blistered his face and neck, even his back. He lost most of his hair before he was nineteen. Girls didn't like him. His daddy drank too much. What *didn't* happen to him?"

"You didn't desert him," Adrienne said. "You stood by him."

Mrs. James lifted her head again. "I'm his mama. Standing by their children is what mamas do."

"And I'm Olivia's mother, Mrs. James."

The comparison registered. "I hope you find her. I don't know where to tell you to look, though. If somebody snatched her and Polk together, Polk'll try to help her get away. You can count on that." She picked the remote off the horsehair loveseat and dully mashed button after button, as if hitting them in some cryptic sequence would restore her son to her.

I blurted, "Why would Polk carry Olivia to Alabama?"

Mrs. James looked at me glassily, her mouth fell open, a bubble of saliva glinted in the cavity.

"Thank you for your time," Adrienne said. "We'll let ourselves out."

In the truck again, motoring away from Dogtown, Adrienne said, "Since you lost your job, you seem to have forgotten everything you ever knew about empathizing with people and gaining their trust."

"I always do better with kids. And I didn't have my soft puppets with me today. Besides, I really hate wasting time when I know somebody's lying."

"She's not lying, Will. She truly believes that somewhere inside Polk James—the sullen, main-chance-seeking adult—lurks a little boy with a fishing pole."

"Cripes," I said.

Adrienne forcibly wobbled my knee, as if manipulating a joystick that might alter my emotions. "Cripes yourself, William Keats. I'm trying hard to believe the same thing."

Sixteen

When we got home, I prepared a honeymoon salad (lettuce alone) and zapped a pair of Swanson dinners (the same bland Salisbury steak and mashed potatoes that my otherwise overparticular father had unaccountably enjoyed, and which LaRue and I had often perforce shared). To offset this unexceptional food, I opened a good but inexpensive bottle of Merlot and, glass in hand, offered an impromptu blessing:

"Lord, watch over us despite our flaws, bad taste in vittles not the least among them. Amen."

Adrienne echoed my amen, then said, "Thinking of Skipper?"

"How'd you guess?"

She forked up a piece of steak dripping with cornstarch-rich gravy. "He comes up with this meal as reliably as the meal itself."

I washed down my own forkful with a hefty slug of wine. "I can't stop evaluating and criticizing my father, but after visiting the James household, I'm inclined to cut Skipper a little more slack. Plenty of worse dads out there—Lamar James for a prime example."

"So many ways for a parent to screw up. So few ways to get it right."

Several minutes passed before I said, "I need to hear what Oscar Greenaway has to say about Olivia's whereabouts. Do you want to go along on another wild-kook chase with me?"

"The psychic? You've got to be kidding. At least twice since the kidnapping he's called, and as politely as possible I've told him to bug off. I can smell a money-grubbing charlatan without standing in the same room as one, Will."

"He's gotten results before."

"Ten years ago. And even then, according to Stratford, he did better pinpointing the location of bones than of living people."

"Even that—"

"What? Has its benefits? Maybe so. Believe me, I'd rather know the harsh truth than stumble along year after year in the grip of some pathetic hope. But I don't think Oscar Greenaway has it in him to help us."

"Would you object if I went to see him?" Adrienne looked up at me over a forkful of mushy bright-orange carrots. "Just to cover all the bases?" I added.

"I'd actually appreciate your doing that," Adrienne said. "So long as you *didn't* insist on my going along."

I relaxed, satisfied that I had secured Adrienne's permission to mount a solo assault on Greenaway's mythic sanctum, a place that had garnered some bemused press as far away as New York, Miami, and Los Angeles.

The next day, with Adrienne in school, I found Oscar Greenaway's unlisted telephone number on a single sheet of letterhead from the sheriff's office; Cooper had halfheartedly given it to us shortly after Greenaway contacted him. He hated to abet in any way the notoriously publicity-hungry psychic, who habitually pressed his business card upon any stranger who looked the least interested in his services.

I counted six rings before Greenaway picked up and said, "Oscar knows who's calling and why, but please confirm. The manner in which you deliver your message contains important clues about your mentational turmoil. Please be brief, however, for time never relents."

"Will Keats," I said. "I wanted—"

"To consult Oscar about your missing daughter. Naturally, naturally. What took you so long?"

I decided not to tell Greenaway that he represented a desperate last resort. "I had to convince Olivia's mother."

"Miz Owsley. A sharp tongue, there. No slur intended, Mr. Keats, for Oscar comprehends her distress, but she treated Oscar most ungraciously."

Greenaway's insistence on referring to himself in the third person stalled me for a moment. "Then please forgive her, Mr. Greenaway.

I have her convinced of your talents now. I simply referred her to the Helandra Bullington case—"

"Oscar's greatest triumph! No one else knew the heiress lay buried in the woods with a breathing tube down to her coffin. Only Oscar could direct her rescuers to the site!"

"Exactly. For that very reason, Mr. Greenaway, I hope you can lead us to Olivia."

"An exceptional little girl! Oscar feels he already knows her. Even broadcast pictures fail to diminish her aura. Ever since the news broke, Oscar has been concentrating almost continually on her image. But the visuals provide insufficient threads to connect his spirit to hers. What of her toys?"

For a moment, I was thrown. "What about them?"

"Did she have a favorite, preferably one that mimicked a living thing? Not a truck or such, you see, but the representation of an animate creature."

Immediately, I proposed the Cat in the Hat.

Just as quickly, Greenaway said, "Has anyone handled this toy lately?"

I pictured the popular cat bouncing on the knees of Adrienne, Byron, and DeLynda. "Yes, several people."

"No good, no good. Think again!"

It hit me forcefully: Olivia now owned the only one of my father's ventriloquial figures that had ever truly engaged her interest.

"Well?" Greenaway said.

"Nobody's touched her good pal Davy Quackett since she went missing."

"Excellent, excellent! Oscar recalls Davy with considerable fondness. Your father animated him most endearingly. Bring Mr. Quackett with you. Hear Oscar though: handle him sparingly yourself!"

"When?"

"Why, now, of course! Did you not hear Oscar tell you that time never relents?"

Most of the homes in the Druid Hills neighborhood of Atlanta, near Emory University, featured Tudor-style architecture. Driving past the big brick homes with diamond-shaped windowpanes, slate roofs, and crisscrossing timbers, I felt like Twain's displaced Connecticut

Yankee. Although I knew that lawyers, doctors, and university profs lived in this neighborhood, I half expected to see Henry the Eighth enthusiastically directing a beheading on one of its immaculate lawns.

Oscar Greenaway's property stood out in this simulated patch of Merry Olde England like a cracker box on a shelf of blown-glass vases. A tall granite wall surrounded his domain, and a host of stamped-iron weathervanes—crows, whales, horses, even a lobster—surmounted its parapet at irregular intervals. The wall itself wore animal-shaped placards bearing slogans in red or yellow enamel paint as bright as lollipops. I parked at the opposite curb and stepped out carrying Davy Quackett in his full frontier regalia. Only then did I pause to read some of the mottos:

Alcoholism & Altruism Alike Delude.

A Stitch in Time Could Close My Bolthole.

To Pee or Not to Pee—That's No Question.

Could God Create a Stone So Heavy That
Mere Mortals Would Mistake It for His Brother?

Above this wall rose a flagpole displaying a bright green pennant with a large white gothic G inside a solid white O. From my current vantage I could see neither the house nor its grounds, so I crossed the street to an unlatched built-in gate that admitted me to the courtyard.

A flagstone path led me through a copse of rhododendrons to a broad patio. Around this terrace stood numerous poles supporting gourd birdhouses, Native American spirit catchers, or Tibetan prayer flags. Beyond the patio, Greenaway's one-story house, a mix of Spanish Colonial and Romanesque architecture, sprawled against a backdrop of ginkgo trees; the terra-cotta half-barrel tiles of its roof peeked through this leafage, while from a back corner rose a clock tower, whose clock face, I noticed with amusement, had been divided into thirteen hours.

I crossed the patio to the front door. Here hung an archaic bell-pull, which I dutifully yanked.

"*Enter!*" a concealed speaker commanded me. I went in.

Greenaway greeted me not in the cool foyer with its Maxfield Parrish–esque murals of arcadian dreamscapes, but from the arch of the room beyond it. Although five-seven or -eight, he stooped like a gnome, pear-shaped in pleated gray-and-white-checked trousers and a piratical purple shirt. His wan but stubbled face floated like a moon above the shirt's high collar, while atop his head perched a Mongolian cap adorned with old campaign buttons, including *I Like Ike, All the Way with LBJ,* and *AuH2O.*

Greenaway blinked, jigging his rank white eyebrows up and down. "Oscar bids both of you welcome."

I almost looked behind me. Then I registered Davy Quackett's fifteen-pound weight anew. "Thank you." Impulsively, I fumbled for Davy's headstick and threw my voice, causing the duck to utter his own lisping "Thankth."

"Very nice lip control," said Greenaway, as if he and I were fellow illusionists. For now, though, I chose to believe that beneath his professional duplicity there still glimmered a spark of real clairvoyance.

The parlor surpassed even the exterior of Greenaway's place in outlandishness. Sunlight poured in from tinted skylights of leaded glass. Carved chairs and settees reproducing furniture from the nineteenth-century China trade labored under cushions featuring incongruous Navajo designs. Ferns and tropical flowers grew from huge brass planters incised with a bewildering pantheon of Hindu deities; the planters themselves hunkered around the mosaic floor like pieces in a bizarre chess match. Finally, five or six glass cases containing memorabilia from Greenaway's career—clippings, testimonial letters, photographs—stood in off-center alignment against three of the four walls.

In fact, though, the most outrageous items in the parlor were not the furniture but an assortment of lime-green and banana-yellow budgerigars—budgies—that swung on or strutted along an equal number of hetereogenous open perches. These birds, like parakeets on steroids, squawked or slyly chattered, eyeing us with affection or malice.

Greenaway led me to a divan and said, "Rest your corporal self, sir." After I had obeyed, he sat down in uncomfortable proximity. "Now, disburden your soul to Oscar."

"You already know why I've come," I said impatiently. "I want you to help us find Olivia."

"In due time. First, Oscar must acquaint himself with her wooden friend." Greenaway took Davy Quackett. Cradling the dummy, he moved its limbs through a full range of motions, then placed his lips to the rim of Davy's coonskin cap and whispered, then lowered his own ear to Davy's beak.

"Mr. Greenaway—!" I began.

"Shhhh. Davy Quackett has told Oscar all that Oscar needs to know. Now comes the scrying." Greenaway placed Davy on the divan, rose painfully, ambled into a farther room, and returned carrying a lawn ornament.

Once, many respectable households had boasted gazing balls in their front yards, but I had not seen one since childhood. These emerald-green spheres generally perched atop a column and mirrored their surroundings. The one in Greenaway's hands reflected my own fish-eye portrait, Greenaway himself, and distorted recesses of the parlor.

Greenaway sat between Davy and me, the gazing ball in his lap. He took my left hand and Davy's right, peered slump-shouldered into the ball, and spoke in a ghostly tremolo:

"Olivia loves and misses her Cat in the Hat. Likewise, she loves and misses her Davy Quackett. She loves her mama, her dada, and her silly Willy-yum too. She misses them as well."

"Mr. Greenaway, it hardly takes a psychic to—"

"Shhh," said Greenaway before adding, "And of course she loves and misses her Roogy Batoon."

Neither Adrienne nor I had ever mentioned the pony's name to Greenaway. Certainly, he could have chanced upon it in a newspaper story or through contacts with the police, but his saying Roogy's unusual name aloud still gave me pause. I listened closely as he continued his "scrying":

"Olivia fears that you will forget to curry or feed her pony. She fears that Roogy Batoon will pine away to pelt and bones from missing her so much. She worries less about her own health than she does poor Roogy's. What comfort may Oscar pass along from you to Olivia about this beloved animal, sir?"

Every last budgie in the parlor had fallen silent. Despite all my earlier skepticism, I leaned over the ball and said, "Do you see her? Can you tell if she's all right?"

"Clouds drift between Oscar and Olivia, Oscar fears. He sees a small room—dilapidated, dirty, dark."

"Where, for God's sake?"

Greenaway held up a flaccid white hand. "What else does Oscar see? Water? Yes, water—but not now, in the future. And along with the water, sir, fire."

My bout of credulity suddenly lost its hold. Water and fire, the two oldest symbols in any charlatan's repertoire. I released Greenaway's hand and digustedly got to my feet.

Greenaway jerked as if he had received a blow to the head. He almost dropped the gazing ball. Instinctively, I caught it before it could hit the floor and shatter. It burned an icy coldness into my palms, and I hastily placed it on the cushion next to Davy. The budgies began to twitter and grate again.

Greenaway peered up out of his ambiguous fatigue. "Oscar hopes his scrying has satisfied you, Mr. Keats."

"I found about as much as I expected to."

"Then Oscar requests that you remit his standard fee."

"Which is?"

Greenaway scratched his jaw. "A round hundred, sir. Oscar's birdies require a prodigious quantity of seed."

I extracted five twenties from my wallet. "Not bad for five minutes of shameless quackery." I retrieved Davy from the divan and shifted him possessively to my hip.

"Call it what you will, Mr. Keats. But Oscar still enjoys a visit from Helandra Bullington every week without fail."

Seventeen

Olivia leaps into our four-poster and puts her forepaws on my naked arm. When I roll over to determine the identity of my harasser, she dances on my chest and stomach, often nearly slipping off but regaining purchase and excitedly licking my face. She has come in the form of a small stiff-haired dog with pointed ears, brushlike whiskers, and breath smelling faintly of peppermint and stale lunchmeat. A terrier, maybe. I grab her forelegs to keep her from leaving claw marks on my unprotected torso.

Don't wake Mama, says Olivia the dog.

She'll want to see you, I protest. *She'll want to know you're safe.*

Let go of me, Will. You're pinching me.

When I release her, Olivia whirls around, bounds from the mattress, trots exploratorily about the room, and pauses before a mahogany chifforobe that I do not recognize as ours. Before I can stop her, Olivia paws the righthand door open and squeezes inside the chifforobe, vanishing into dustbunny limbo as the door swings shut again. I roll off the bed, cross the room, and yank open both of the heavy doors.

Asa D. Fearing sits in a lawn chair just inside the piece. *She went that way, Will.* He nods over one shoulder at the bleak hinterland deeper in. When I duck my head and enter the chifforobe too, he fades from sight like an unsmiling Cheshire cat. Cautiously, I proceed into the storm-riven interior, which now opens out as limitlessly as a winter ocean. Despite my mounting reluctance and fear, I continue to pursue the runaway terrier that spoke to me with Olivia's voice. A brutal wind keens in my ears.

Fifty or sixty feet in front of me, DeLynda Gaye appears, as brilliant as a Vegas angel cast in neon. *Keep going,* she advises me. *You'll find her.* But as I approach, she fades just as Fearing did, and the storm at the far back of the chifforobe builds in strength and intensity, spreading and rising. Its magnificent ragged thunderhead boasts lightning-red eyes and a snaggle-toothed grin identical to my carved jack-o'-lantern, a face that bridges the entire sky.

My bones rattle inside this buffeting amassing darkness, and suddenly, at some unreachable immeasureable distance, a small dog barks. . . .

Olivia the lost dog. I sat up, wiping my hands down my chest and arms like someone frantic to dislodge a spiderweb. Adrienne lay beside me, her eyes wide open.

"Will, what's wrong?"

"Nothing. A bad dream."

She snuggled closer. "Then tell me about it."

How could I confess that I had seen Olivia as a disobedient little dog in a frightening welter of wind and rain? "You know, kid, I'd really rather not."

She propped herself on her elbows. "Sometimes a bad dream can offer startling insights."

"Criminy, don't pull that sensitive-shrink crap on me again."

Adrienne lowered herself back down and scrunched away. "Forget it. Stew in your own sour nightsweat."

"Please," I said, suddenly remorseful. "I just don't know what good it'll do me talking about my nightmare."

"Maybe it would do *me* some good."

I took her chin between thumb and forefinger. "Okay, but let's go downstairs. I could use a cup of high-test."

Thirty minutes later, we powwowed on the living-room floor, Adrienne's back against a padded easychair and mine against our low-riding sofa. November sunlight varnished a pottery lamp and her sallow face. Tom Petty and the Heartbreakers crooned on low volume in the background. I cradled a cup of hot coffee, Adrienne a mug of green tea. (She avoided coffee because caffeine produced nonmalignant fibroid masses in her breasts, even though she still occasionally put away half a pound of M&Ms at a sitting.) From the kitchen wafted the smell of ready-made cinnamon rolls baking. Anyone viewing this scene minus the audio would have supposed us as blissful as transfigured saints.

"Okay," I said after several slow sips of coffee. "Serve me a topic and I'll volley."

Adrienne set her tea down. "I never realized there was a net between us." Quietly—unobtrusively—she began to cry.

"Sorry, kid. Bad choice of metaphor."

Still crying, she stared sidelong out our picture window. "It was witty enough. Semiwitty," she amended. "Today, though, I just can't appreciate it. Probably not tomorrow either."

"Okay, *I'll* start the conversation." I told her of yesterday's visit to Oscar Greenaway's place, omitting nothing.

She returned her gaze to me. "Maybe you should've questioned him more closely. That stuff about fire and water . . . I don't know, maybe it does mean something, Will."

Was Adrienne having me on? I couldn't quite parse her voice or her body language. "The hokiness of 'fire and water' in particular put me off. You don't imagine the fool actually foresaw something, do you?"

"There are more things in heaven and earth, Horatio."

"Than there are in a Mountboro delicatessen? Didn't the Buddha say that?"

She laughed and picked up her tea again. "Will, I'd like us to spend Thanksgiving with my folks and my brother, Aaron."

"Sure. Invite them down."

"No. I mean in New Hampshire, Will. At Singing Trees Orchards outside Lowell."

Pow! A wind-expelling punch to the gut. I formulated a dozen reasons why this idea could never fly. What if Polk James chose the Thanksgiving break to sound his ransom demand? What if Olivia escaped and made her way home to an empty house? What if Captain Cooper or Agent Fearing needed us for additional information or an important brainstorming session? Who would feed Roogy? Additional objections occurred to me as Adrienne coolly studied my face.

"I could go alone, Will, but I'd like to have you with me."

My coffee tasted more bitter than alum. All my stubbornness and caution had bought me to date was the needless disappointment of the woman I loved. "Thanksgiving in Lowell. *Mmmmmmm.* Should we squeeze in a side trip to Plymouth?"

Adrienne smiled, genuinely. "Only if you consent to play the tourist."

"Tourist? Hey, I plan to make an impassioned speech on Native American rights, then blow up Plymouth Rock."

"Terrorists from Dixie don't get the kid-glove treatment in New England, Will. Horrible tortures await you in our clammy unheated gaols." (I could almost hear the archaic spelling.)

"Worse than sharing a house with your mother?"

The cushion from the easychair sailed harmlessly over my head. "You troglodyte. Going home for the holidays makes perfect sense. Even dogs go home to lick their wounds. Why can't I?"

"No reason at all. As soon as we've eaten a couple of cinnamon rolls, I'll call the travel agency."

That close to the holidays, booking seats proved costly, but I understood from a counselor's perspective that Adrienne needed this short-term regrafting to her roots. She needed mother-love, father-love, even kid-brother-love; a respite from the unilluminating tedium of the kidnap investigation; a holiday from her anxiety-inducing exposure to our house and everything in it redolent of Olivia. I foresaw similar, if less intense, benefits for myself. A change would do both of us good.

Although Adrienne's school did not start its Thanksgiving break until Wednesday afternoon, Mr. Goldborough granted her—illegally but decently—an extra three days before the holiday. We left Atlanta Hartsfield International on a Delta flight to Boston, then, on the evening of Friday the twentieth. Our vacation would last nine full days. Although the Thompsons had wanted to send Aaron to pick us up, I insisted on renting a car, knowing that we would need a vehicle of our own.

As for our roles in the investigation—roles increasingly more passive than we liked to admit—no one in a position of authority objected to our departure. After all, we supplied them the relevant phone numbers and addresses, and everyone from Lyman Stratford to Nicholas Cooper to Asa D. Fearing to anonymous GBI grunts probably breathed a collective sigh of relief to have us out of their hair.

Aloft on the crowded airliner, I said to Adrienne, "Now that we've left, they can all relax."

"Who?"

"The cops."

"Don't defame them, Will. They want to collar Polk James as much as we do."

"Yes. But do they want Olivia as badly?"

Adrienne placed a hand on my knee. "How could they?"

I peered out the cold square of window. As our jet banked and climbed, the urban sprawl beneath us twinkled like radiant circuit diagrams. Could I see all the way to Tocqueville? I doubted it. But I could imagine both our empty house and Roogy Batoon shivering under her blanket in her mouse-haunted stall. A few hours from now, roundly cursing my name, J. W. Young would arrive in pre-dawn darkness, prior to whatever handyman's jobs he had lined up for the day, to care for Olivia's beloved pony.

My worries turned elsewhere. I had never traveled any farther north than New York City, and that visit had occurred almost twenty years ago, when Skipper dragged me along on his last all-out effort to persuade a hotshot booking agent to land him either a prime-time TV appearance or a noteworthy movie role. (That trip had ended in disaster, souring us both on the Big Apple.) Further, I had never met the Thompsons or Adrienne's brother, and I worried that they might view me as the ne'er-do-well son of a semi-celebrity or as the prime villain in Adrienne's decision to stay in Georgia. Over and over, I rubbed my palms down my slacks.

Adrienne grabbed my wrist. "Settle down. After Byron, you'll look like Leonardo DiCaprio to them."

I thought about that. "Name someone older."

"Harrison Ford?"

"Not quite that old."

"George Clooney?"

"Perfect. Hand me my stethoscope."

A stewardess wheeled her cart nearer and began popping the ring tops on miniature beverage cans.

"How about a drink instead?" Adrienne asked.

"Sold. Then I'll really begin to operate."

. . .

The clamorous Boston airport brought my anxiety back full strength. Adrienne secured the keys to our rental car, a Dodge Neon, while I shivered each time the nearby door slid open to admit another blast of piercingly Arctic air.

Once in the cramped Neon, Adrienne at the wheel, I notched the heater up to high. "Do folks up here bother to sell refrigerators, or do they just leave their perishables on the windowsill?"

"Don't be a baby. This is a mild autumn night."

We picked up Route 93 north, and I tried to settle in for the ride. Shortly, we turned onto Route 128 west and then onto Route 3 north. Strange towns with odd names sped by in the dark: Woburn, Billerica, Chelmsford. Even at ten-thirty at night, the freeways rocketed with traffic, and I could sense an ambient alienness that made my nape hairs prickle.

"Relax. You're still in the same country."

"Only if you think the treaty at Appomattox Court House really ended the War Between the States."

"You mean the Civil War."

"Georgians regard that term as a self-deluding oxymoron, lady."

"Come on, Will. Look out there and tell me what you see."

I obeyed her. "Headlights. Taillights. Running lights."

"There you go—that's America to a T." Adrienne laughed and said, "A Model-T, I guess. Anyway, we'll soon enter the wilds of New Hampshire."

"Lions and tigers and bears, oh my."

We shot through Lowell itself, the town where Adrienne had grown up, married Byron, and given birth to Olivia. Eventually, we crossed into New Hampshire, exiting the interstate for the darkness of a two-lane with so little traffic that we might have invaded the Twilight Zone. I fell asleep.

A tapping on the glass awakened me. The Neon had come to a full stop, the rataplan of its engine eerily muted. A tall pale man in his seventies peered in at me while tugging fruitlessly at the door's outer handle. Adrienne flicked a switch next to her, and my door opened, flooding the car with Arctic air.

"Welcome," said the coatless man. "You look like you could use a nice warm bed."

Eighteen

I awoke in a strange room with salmon-colored poppies on its wallpaper. Travel-fatigued under the unaccustomed weight of two or three quilts, I retained a vague memory of Adrienne's earlier departure from our nest. Her familiar scent still clung to her pillow, but the smell of baking apples—with a cinnamon grace note—nearly overwhelmed it. Sunlight streaming through the tall second-story dormers prompted me to get up. I peeled away the quilts, swung my feet to the floor, and padded over to a window in my T-shirt and boxers.

A swatch of brown lawn rolled away from the house. On the grass, a crude pumphouse, or toolshed, and a phalanx of bare trees. Here and there on their stripped branches a few forlorn apples clung, leftovers from the season's main harvests; they still resembled sand-yellow, olive-green, or brick-red ornaments, though. I imagined picking one or two for Roogy Batoon, extending the fruit on my palm and hearing the explosive crunch as she halved it with one bite. Light ricocheted among these trees like glints on a vast web-work of spider silk.

Thoughts of Roogy reminded me again of Olivia's kidnapping—an inescapable heartbreak no matter how far we traveled. Would her grandparents, whom I had yet to face, hold me chiefly responsible, as the Protector Who Failed? I dressed, slowly, in a long-sleeve flannel shirt, a pair of jeans, wool socks, and creased moccasins, all from my carry-on bag.

In the upstairs corridor I felt comfortably at home. Despite superficial differences, this house shared with my grandparents' old house in Mountboro and our current farmhouse near Tocqueville a patina of loving human use. Creaking floorboards and overpainted moldings intensified this impression. Although Adrienne had never lived in this particular house, it symbolized for me, and possibly for her, the tradition- and memory-filled home where she had in fact grown up in Lowell.

"Hey, Mr. Houseguest-guy, need directions?"

I turned around. A tall young man with a riot of pale blond hair shaved close and high around his ears and neck slouched in profile against the frame of an open door. Despite the chill, he inhabited only a pair of paint-splattered khaki trousers and an armless undershirt emblazoned with the image of videogame vixen Lara Croft. His almost prehensile toes clenched the floorboards, and his wheat-stubbled lantern jaw gleamed in the sunlight cascading through his room.

"I beg your pardon." The formality of my phrasing made even me wince.

"Don't do that," the young man said. "I'd have to grant it, host to guest, and you may not deserve it." He lifted an eyebrow.

"You must be Aaron." I reached to shake his hand.

He folded his arms across his chest. "That's what everyone insists, especially my folks. But I always get the feeling they're talking about an Aaron I don't know."

"At your age, I felt the same way."

Aaron barked a quasi-contemptuous laugh. "But you've got all the answers now, right?"

"Hardly." I refused to lower my gaze from his. "I've just learned to live with the unease."

This response seemed to resonate with him. He pushed away from the door and levered himself toward me. Blotches of red, yellow, blue, green, and orange flashed on his khakis and sleeveless tee, and when he stuck out his hand, his arm had the slinky strength of a new garden hose. We shook, and he loomed over me like a Swede in a boxcar.

"Want to see my studio?"

"Absolutely. But will they miss me at breakfast?"

"Breakfast's history, houseguest-guy. My folks've written you out of it faster than Stalin erased his worst enemy. Come on."

My first glimpse of the south-facing room that Aaron called his studio wowed me. Nonfigurative canvases as bright and variegated as cockatoos under klieg lights leaned against the walls. Abstract mobiles of copper, glass, and clear plastic hung from the ceiling. Grotesque but affecting sculptures in concrete and modeling clay, a few studded with found objects ranging from safety pins to Popsicle sticks to old circuit boards, skulked on tabletops and shelves like a secret convocation of aliens. A relatively uncluttered area in front of three curtainless dormers functioned as a workspace.

Aaron hitched his thumbs in the straps of his shirt. "Waal, pardner, how do you like my little spread? Raising up quite a crop of art, ain't I?"

"I can only compare it to one thing."

He squinted at me suspiciously. "What's that?"

"An explosion at a Froot Loops factory."

Fortunately, Aaron laughed—with real pleasure rather than self-protective contempt. "I'll quote you in the publicity for my first show."

"Ah. And when will that occur?"

"Whenever some local gallery owner proves he's got something other than baby shit for brains."

I moved near an acrylic-and-paper figure, something resembling a Technicolor fish crossed with a Stealth bomber. "Do the locals really react so negatively to your work?"

"Unlike most of my peers, I deal in joyful illumination. Right now, though, the market appears to favor self-pitying darkness. I guess them's the breaks. No one will truly appreciate my stuff—let alone buy it—until I relocate."

"New York?"

"San Francisco has the niftier allure. Hey, I could get off on hanging with the Juxtapoz crowd."

I had no idea who or what constituted the Juxtapoz crowd, but refrained from revealing my ignorance. "If you didn't expect a king's ransom for them, Aaron, I see several pieces"—waving my hand—"that I wouldn't mind buying. Maybe that would give you a stake for your move."

"Gee, Mr. Rockefeller, how can I ever thank you?"

I chalked the sarcasm up to Aaron's youth and self-consciously artistic temperament. "I'm serious."

"Groovy. But the only ransom you should be thinking about is the ransom that brings Olivia home."

I stared at Aaron as coldly as a hired killer. Although he tried to hang in there, my intensity—my honest-to-God anger and outrage—rattled him. Eventually, red-faced and trembling, he looked away.

"If the money I inherited—money I never went looking for or coveted—could bring Olivia back, I'd stand at the crossroads in the pouring rain with a suitcase full of unmarked bills. But so far, Aaron, nobody's said a fucking thing about wanting my daddy's money for Olivia's return. Nobody."

Aaron continued to study his bare feet. "Sorry. Just mouthing off. Next time tell me to shove it."

"I think I just did." Luckily, my stomach chose that moment to snarl loudly. "I'm going down for breakfast. Want seconds?"

"No thanks. If I have to eat another bite of Mama Ruth's apple strudel, I'll puke."

"You make it sound so appetizing."

Aaron hastened to reassure me. "Oh, no, it's great. But the seven-hundred-and-forty-ninth piece tends to stick going down."

Adrienne, Ruth, and Neil huddled around the solarium table over late coffee and the remnants of the famous house strudel. "Hello, sleepyhead." "Welcome, William." "Good afternoon, young man." None of them got up, of course, but Neil pulled out the chair next to him and nodded me into it. The solarium abutted the kitchen, which featured a butcher's block with tiled sides; painted apples decorated every other tile. The towels hanging near the sink had an apple motif, as the did the coffee mugs and placemats before me.

"I'd've made it sooner but I ran into Aaron," I said.

As he poured my coffee, Neil's callused hand hid the carafe's plastic grip. "Right. Aaron can certainly talk your ear off."

Ruth said, "Getting Aaron to talk is like pulling hen's teeth." Then she looked at Neil and said, "Oh." Adrienne laughed, and Ruth said "Oh" again, this time with an involuntary rouging of her papery cheeks.

"To my untutored eye," I said, "you have something of a genius upstairs." (I had struggled not to say "you all" even though the context demanded it. Adrienne's folks probably already thought me a sodbusting redneck or a julep-sipping bigot.)

Neil grimaced. "They say genius involves pain, but ours is a pain in the sacroiliac."

"Neil," said Ruth, pushing a huge slice of strudel toward me on a plate with a border of painted apples. Above pouches of loose flesh, her brown eyes implored me to partake. "Eat, William. I'll fix you an egg and sausage too."

"The cake's plenty, ma'am. We usually just eat cereal."

"Unless Will cooks," Adrienne said. "Get him out of bed and he can whip up an omelette to shame Julia Child."

Small talk. Pleasantries. All to avoid thinking about the oppressiveness of our current situation. I gratefully took part in the ritual, listening intently as well as sometimes piping up with what I hoped were defensible opinions of my own. At length, the Thompsons began to speak of the conflicting circumstances that had led them, over a decade ago, to abandon their hardware business in Lowell for this agrarian enterprise in New Hampshire.

"We wanted to get Adrienne away from that loutish brute Byron," Ruth said.

"We didn't relish going bankrupt in downtown Lowell, you mean," Neil said. "We didn't want to die of gunshot wounds or emphysema or stress-induced strokes."

"As if running an apple orchard at our ages with very little know-how didn't subject us to *worse* stress!"

"Know-how? The trees have the real know-how, Ruth. The few minor practicalities we needed to learn, I picked up in two weeks, just from reading and talking with other growers. No, I don't regret anything about our move. If we'd done it sooner, we might have kept Adrienne from going south." He shot me an appraising look. "As for Picasso up there, moving sooner would've made no difference. I figure he was doomed from about age three."

Ruth blurted, "If we'd moved sooner, this horrible thing would never have happened to Olivia."

Neil, Adrienne, and I all looked at Ruth as if she had just unapologetically broken wind. She looked back with a self-effacing smile that I saw as the template for Adrienne's most characteristic smile.

"Mother," Adrienne said, "what happened to Olivia stemmed from the cruelty and irrationality of one disturbed person. Something similar, or worse, could just as easily have happened in Lowell."

"I think not," Ruth said primly.

"Explain to me how you can say that, Mother."

Ruth's self-effacing smile tightened. "Bad as it is, Lowell is still part of New England."

"And no one like Polk James lives in New England?" Neil said.

"Maybe in the city," Ruth conceded. "But most likely not in New Hampshire, and certainly nowhere near Singing Trees Orchards. We have a safe home here."

Neil patted his lips with a green napkin printed with clusters of apples. "Sometimes the worst things happen at home: accidents, betrayals, hurtful words—even murder, Ruth."

She shuddered. "Not if good people live together honorably."

"Will, Olivia, and I tried to do that in Tocqueville, Mother, but evil still found a way through our defenses."

Ruth Thompson began to cry. She picked up an apple-printed napkin and daubed at her eyes. "I hate that monster, Polk James! And I won't feel any different toward him even if God tells me to practice forgiveness!"

"Please, Mother, let's leave God out of this."

"I agree with Adrienne," Neil said. "We never get anywhere when we drag the so-called Almighty into our talks. Never." He folded his napkin beside his crumb-freckled plate.

This contretemps gave me a chilly insight into some of the factors—other than an innate spiritual bent in a non-Western direction—that had pointed Adrienne down the path of Buddhism. The contrast between her father's hard-nosed agnosticism and her mother's pietistic Lutheranism had clearly torn at her throughout her girlhood, leaving her as cold toward Western churches as an empty tin offering-plate. I identified with her dilemma, for my own parents had adopted a synthetic New Age creed, all glitz, gunpowder, and feel-goodism, that brooked no impertinence or even questioning. As at my house, religious discussions among the Thompsons must have devolved into fiery debates or dinner-table wrangles. The difference between Adrienne and me was that she had encountered or built up through her Zen practice a workable faith that still eluded me: I envied her that faith even as I sought my own.

With difficulty, Ruth controlled herself. "All right," she said coldly, "what do you kids plan to do today?"

Adrienne pinched a piece of burnt cinnamon off the cake and put it on the tip of her tongue. Then she ate it and said, "If you all don't mind, I'd like to take Will into Lowell and show him where I grew up."

I could have kissed her for that "you all."

"Go ahead," Ruth said.

"I thought maybe your boyfriend might like to help with the cider pressing at some point," Neil said. "We'll make the usual party out of it, invite some interesting folks."

"Sounds like fun," I said.

Neil stood up. "If you'll excuse me, I need to go listen to my trees." He smiled cryptically.

When Ruth began to gather up the dirty dishes, Adrienne moved unobtrusively to help her. "Go into Lowell and enjoy yourselves. We'll see you later today."

"Can we pick up anything in town for you, Mother?"

On her way to the sink, Ruth paused. "Believe it or not, we don't have a holiday turkey yet. If you select a nice frozen Butterball—oh, about eighteen pounds—Neil will reimburse you."

"No way," I said. "My treat. And that won't begin to repay you all for your hospitality, Mrs. Thompson."

Ruth smiled at me self-effacingly, but made no reply. We continued carrying dishes to the sink. I washed, Adrienne dried, and Ruth placed everything in the cabinets or drawers where they belonged.

"You do have gracious Southern manners," Ruth finally said when we had finished.

"Thank you, ma'am."

Later in the driveway, wearing a coat of Neil's because the one I had packed was too flimsy for the weather, I turned to Adrienne and said, "I didn't think your mother would really serve turkey for Thanksgiving."

"What did you expect?"

"I figured she'd whip up the whole meal out of apples. Apple fritters, applesauce, apple jelly, apple omelettes, apple frappé, apple pandowdy, apples Benedict, applejack, app—"

Adrienne stuffed the sleeve of her coat in my mouth and dragged me sputtering to the little Dodge Neon.

Nineteen

T raveling on the twisting pine-galleried Nashua Road, I said, "Your folks seem to've survived this year's harvest—no canes, crutches, or body casts."

Adrienne, concentrating, turned onto Route 38. The closer we got to the small city of Lowell the more crazed and ill-mannered other drivers became. Did Yankees have to qualify officially for their licenses? If so, then a certificate of insanity or surliness had to represent the one obligatory document.

"Dad looks fragile," Adrienne finally said, "but he can work with the best of them. Aaron helps incredibly. He *likes* to pick. It gives him a good excuse to leave off making art for a time. Neighbors come in to help, knowing that Dad will do the same for them. And in the grand commercial scheme of things, Singing Trees Orchards don't cover that many acres."

"Despite the plural?"

"Alyson's Apple Orchard up in Walpole sprawls over five hundred acres, compared to my parents' fifty. Oh, the liniment bottle and heating pads undoubtedly saw some heavy use a month ago, but life has eased off on my folks since then. Don't forget: Thanksgiving originally honored the finish of the harvest."

"Do the Thompsons have a lot to be thankful for this year? Moneywise, I mean."

"They did okay, I guess. Dad never discloses exact figures to anyone but Mother. I know they have fallback reserves. When he worked in the hardware store, Dad socked away a little every month, and Mother earned decent money as an administrative bookkeeper at the Technological Institute. Besides, they cling to every penny like barnacles to a boat hull."

I laughed, sunlight flashing through the windshield on my hands. "Must be generational. Skipper played the barnacle too, but, unlike your folks, he also mimicked that unlovely critter's ability to scrape your hide right off."

The scattered commercial buildings flanking Route 38 south of the New Hampshire line—the road had somehow turned into Lakeview Avenue—multiplied, and the open spaces separating them dwindled until, scarcely noticing the transition, we cruised into an urban landscape. A "Lowell City Limits" sign hove into view to formalize the change.

Here on the northern periphery of the onetime mill village, no structure stood very tall; and although this neighborhood in no way reproduced the squalor of Dogtown, neither did it suggest Rodeo Drive. The businesses—dry-cleaners, cafés, auto-repair shops—maintained a tenuous grip on profitability. The houses among them—mostly multifamily rentals, judging from the multiple mailboxes and power meters—showed the dilapidation that only absentee landlords and hardscrabble tenants can together engineer.

"So far I'm impressed."

"Sorry. I should have asked the Chamber of Commerce to force the magnolias into a second bloom for you."

"Did you *like* this place?"

"Loved it. Grew up here. Made friends here."

"Met Byron here. Had Olivia here."

Adrienne cast me an annoyed glance. "Can't deny it."

"Well, Shangri-la it's not."

"I always assumed Columbus, Gee-Ay, held that title."

I worked an invisible dummy in my lap, making it say with no accompanying lip movement: *She disrespected my old homeplace so I knocked her flat.*

"Ha ha. C'mon, give grimy old Lowell a chance. You haven't seen the charming parts yet."

"Like the Byron Owsley Memorial Drunktank?"

Adrienne blistered me with a hide-scraping scowl. "That's the final incredibly stupid jealous comment I intend to stomach on this trip, mister. Let's slay this whole Adrienne-loved-Byron dragon once and for all."

"Fine." I couldn't quite bring myself to regret my quip at Byron's expense, but my gut clenched and my fingertips whitened, for who knew what revelations lay ahead?

Adrienne said, "Hang on," and took a sudden left off Lakeview: once, I knew, the address of her father's hardware store. Neither of us spoke. We prowled through a warren of residential streets, seeing children at play and a few strolling adults, among them two or three anomalous-seeming Asians.

Adrienne read my mind. "In the eighties, a lot of Cambodian immigrants arrived. The candy store where I used to buy my daily Butterfinger now rents some really wild chopsocky videos."

One final turn brought us onto Lupine Street. Adrienne parked in front of a three-story duplex bearing the numbers 7 and 9. A dizzying unease—like the one I'd told Aaron I'd learned to live with?—settled upon me.

"People call this district Centralville, and directly around the corner is Christian Hill. After we married, Bryon and I lived right here at Nine Lupine. The second floor. I still remember how grateful we felt to find a decent place."

"Can we get out and look?"

"Sure."

We exited the Neon, and I studied the big house set amid its tidy but unremarkable neighbors. In the midday sun, its shingled facade gleamed a flat brown; its trim, shutters, and porch railings a nearly phosphorescent white. Unpainted latticework partially hid the foundation supporting the lower porch. Because Adrienne had once lived here, for me the house had an eerie hyperreality totally at odds with its nondescript architecture. As I gaped like a rube, a middle-aged woman in a second-story window stared down on us with a thin-lipped expression right out of a Depression-era Walker Evans photograph. I ignored her stare to note the toys in the yard and the family washes hanging in plain view.

"Not exactly Monticello, but the roof looks in decent repair."

Adrienne smirked. "Listen, this place draws almost as many visitors as Monticello."

"You're kidding. Why?"

"Its historic associations."

"Let me guess: Amy Lowell once smoked a cigar here."

"Amy lived in Brookline, you Philistine."

"The Kennedys held invitation-only orgies on all three floors?"

"Can that. You'll wind up in one of our canals in a concrete overcoat."

"Horrors. Okay, dispel my ignorance."

"You're gawping at the birthplace of Jack Kerouac. His mama delivered him in the same room where Byron and I conceived Olivia."

"Maybe I didn't need to know *quite* that much about the place, Adrienne."

Give her credit: she recognized that, whether with Freudian ulteriority or real inadvertence, she had wounded me, and she took my arm in hers and said, "Will, I'm sorry. That was . . . boorish, insensitive."

"Try 'heartless.' Try 'unconscionable.' " But I brushed my lips against her temple, and the woman in the second-story window ducked out of our sight.

" 'Cruel,' " she said. " 'Cold-blooded.' 'Pitiless.' "

"Knock it off. I can't believe Jack Kerouac lived here. In college, I read and reread *On the Road* and *The Dharma Bums* like quasi-sacred texts." I gawked a moment longer at Saint Ti-Jean's shrine. "Why hasn't Lowell bought this place and turned it into a museum?"

Adrienne folded her arms across her chest. "Maybe because Olivia hasn't lived long enough to write the Great American Novel and stake her own claim to the place."

A silence fell. At last I said, "Thanks for showing it to me," rocking desolately on my heels. "Maybe we should go."

"Yes," Adrienne said. "We should."

We climbed into the little car again and drove wordlessly back to Lakeview from Lupine Street. Kerouac had lived only forty-seven years. So far, though, he was thirty-nine up on Olivia.

We visited Adrienne's schools: Lowell High, that long stretch of dull yellow brick where Kerouac too had daydreamed of escape and transfiguration; also, the plain Jane campus of Lowell University, where Adrienne had completed two years of higher education before conceiving her daughter and dropping out. Later, in the Tyler Park district, we sat in our car outside the handsome bay-windowed home where the Thompsons had confronted life during Adrienne's girlhood and adolescence.

"Fifteen Georgia Avenue!" I said. "Good Lord, our meeting was predestined."

"Romantic malarkey." But she smiled as she said it.

We drove next to the art gallery where Adrienne had met Byron Owsley: Bridgeport's Exhibitions. The gallery's window—true to Aaron's assessment of the local aesthetic climate—showcased one depressing canvas, a rectangle of black with feverish slashes of ochre and sulfur. Adrienne and I studied this masterpiece, looked at each other, shrugged.

For last, she saved the queer establishment on Beaver Street called the Oil Can Foundry, which its owner, Guy Huberdeau, had wedged into the husk of a defunct filling station: a tiny office and commodious twin bays. On the corner of the lot still stood the tall ancient sign, "Haffner's Gasoline," with a mule of extinct neon tubing over the legend, *"It Kicks."* Around the lot or next to the building squatted or leaned or reared hefty examples of Huberdeau's handiwork: decorative iron wheels, scroll-laden gates, a birdbath fit for a roc. We parked near the birdbath.

At this foundry, Byron had apprenticed as a blacksmith, earning enough to support his new family and hewing briefly to respectable middle-class protocols. Adrienne made no move to leave the car, staring at the picture window filling the place where the lefthand garage door had hung. Apparently, Huberdeau had installed this window to give visitors a view of his forge. But, from the car, we could not see anyone through the smudges and sundogs on the glass; a sudden eruption of sparks, however, told us that Huberdeau or an assistant had come to work today.

"Aren't we going in, kid? I'd like to meet the legendary Guy Huberdeau."

Adrienne gripped the steering wheel more tightly.

"I mean, anyone altruistic enough to serve as Bryon's mentor deserves a firsthand look, right?"

"When we lived here," Adrienne said after a beat or two, "I held Guy dear to my heart." She pronounced his name like Asian butter, *ghee*. "But I can't help worrying that he might think my sudden reappearance pretty brazen."

"Why? I don't get it."

"Byron and I skipped town. I never even told him goodbye."

"Ouch. Had things reached such a pass?" She nodded. "And in all the time you've lived in Georgia?"

"Eight years without contact. Not even a holiday card."

"Then what makes you think he's still alive?"

Adrienne indicated the welding sparks. "Someone's in there. And when you've seen a man bend a poker with his bare hands, you tend to suppose him indestructible."

"You've got nothing to worry about. Huberdeau sounds like an altogether decent fella."

"The decentest. But—"

"Turn on the old Adrienne Owsley charm. He'll forgive you in a heartbeat."

"Let's hope so." She got out, set her shoulders, and strode toward the foundry's picture window. I followed. At the greasy wall, we shielded our eyes, peering in at a huge car-part sculpture of a mechanical horse, sparks spewing behind it like electrified sea spray. When they faded out, Adrienne rapped smartly on the glass, and a medium-sized figure in a battered welder's mask and a scorched leather apron emerged from behind the metal horse. The blue-white pinpoint of plasma at the tip of his torch burned into my retinas. I had to look away.

Adrienne rapped on the glass again, harder, as if fearful that Huberdeau might ignore her. Instead, he extinguished the torch, set it down, and walked over on formidable bowed legs, his hairy forearms glistening, his biceps stretching the fabric of his black polo shirt. When he lifted his helmet, he revealed the face of a weary old soldier, eyebrows like arcs of grizzled rabbit fur, and eyes as stingingly bright as his torchtip.

"Busy!" he yelled, squinting out into daylight. "Damn busy! Come back Monday!"

Adrienne shouted, "I owe you some money!"

Huberdeau's eyes narrowed. "For what? I don't recall doing no work for you."

"You loaned me fifteen dollars for groceries until my husband got paid!"

Huberdeau peered at Adrienne more intently, then raised both fists as if ready to shatter the glass wall between us. With his nose only a quarter of an inch away, he caught himself and yelled, "Come to the office, you!"

Adrienne and I complied. Huberdeau's office contained a spring-shot couch, a cheap wooden desk piled high with paperwork, a shaggy Norfolk pine in a vintage Coke cooler-cum-makeshift planter, and one dented folding chair. As we entered from the parking lot, Huberdeau barged in from the garage, tossing his mask aside and opening his arms like Zorba the Greek. He bear-hugged Adrienne, lifting her a foot into the air and turning her around as if she weighed no more than a scarecrow. Then he set her down, stepped back, and drank her in. Self-consciously, she smoothed her wool plaid skirt and clasped her elbows. At that moment, I had no more reality for either of them than an imaginary subatomic particle in an unreachable alternate universe.

"You scamp, you damn near broke my heart!"

"I hesitated even to come by. I—"

"You visit Lowell, you don't stop and see me, I'd sure as hell find out and chase you back to Cajun country."

Adrienne shook her head in amusement. "You must know I don't live in Louisiana, Guy."

Huberdeau waved off geography as inconsequential. "Now you're here, who cares about all my horrible sleepless nights? One whole decade of silence."

"It was only eight years. And I'm sorry, truly sorry."

"I know, I know. You think I don't figure Adrienne Owsley has plenty on her plate, too much to fuss with a old codger like me? Anyway, like ants to sugar, the young mens crawl to you, keep you damn busy." Huberdeau looked at me. Finally.

"Guy, this is William Keats—my fiancé."

Huberdeau engulfed both my hands with his, and we shook that way. "You treat this smart pretty girl much better than her first old man, you hear? Next time I learn she get hurt, I don't pull no punches, me."

Adrienne blushed, from pleasure as well as embarrassment. "No threats necessary, Guy. Will's okay."

"Strictly a peace-loving man," I said.

"That's good, that's mighty good." He beamed. "Now you two come look at my latest project. Hurry."

Huberdeau hustled us into the foundry, which featured both old-fashioned implements—anvils, post vises—and modern ones, including a computer-driven lathe. We admired the spirited horse sculpture that he had shaped out of pistons, chromed bumpers, and rusty leaf-springs. Huberdeau circled it, pointing out details and frequently reversing directions.

Adrienne said, "You used to shoe horses, now you build them."

Huberdeau ceased pacing and frowned. "I stopped shoeing horses years ago. Not for me no more, no."

I wanted to ask why, but sensed that neither he nor Adrienne would welcome the question.

One hand on the fake horse's neck, Huberdeau tried to restore the convivial mood of a moment past. "Where's your baby girl, eh? One sweet charmer she must be by now, I bet, just like her mama."

Adrienne started to speak, but could not. She looked to me, and, as tersely as I could, I explained about Olivia. Huberdeau's face grew redder and redder, his throat cords flexing, his cheeks alternately inflating and falling slack. At length, he raised his fists as he had done earlier at the window.

"Jesus Christ, I find that *cochon,* I cut his balls off!"

Adrienne put her hands to her face. "Where's your bathroom, Guy? I need a minute here. Maybe five."

"Of course, of course." He pointed her to the john, tucked away in a box-lined alcove near the office, and added, "Forgive me for mentioning anything that hurts, eh?"

Adrienne smiled at him wanly as she left us and crossed to the restroom. After the door closed behind her, Huberdeau grabbed me by the bicep; he thrust his big face into mine, meanwhile pulling me aside as if for even greater privacy.

"You there, Keats, you listen close to me. I got to give you some important facts, yeah. But not where *she* can hear, not here, not today."

I couldn't shake his grip. "Then where? And when?"

"You meet me tomorrow for lunch, right? The Club Diner, near City Hall. At noon."

"I don't know these places."

"You find out. Don't let me down, eh?" At last, he released me and stalked away, profoundly agitated.

We actually had time to talk at some length, but Huberdeau apparently thought speaking behind Adrienne's back—her literal back, anyway—an unmanly violation of her status as a friend of longstanding.

Adrienne came out of the john and rejoined us, squeezing a damp tissue in her hand. "Guy, we plan to stick around the whole week. We'll sit down to talk soon, but, right now, I've got to go. I've got to . . ." She stopped.

Huberdeau patted her back. "Don't try to explain, you. Both of you come back when you can. I got plenty to keep me hopping— but for you guys I'd drop anything, anytime."

He conducted us both out to the car and held the driver's door open for Adrienne. On the passenger's side, I remained standing until Huberdeau caught my eye over the cartop and mouthed the word "tomorrow." I nodded and slid into the Neon. Adrienne turned the key in its ignition, and we soon drove off.

"Do you think," I asked as we passed through downtown Lowell on the way home, "you could point out City Hall to me?"

Twenty

W e bought a frozen Butterball turkey at a Stop 'n' Shop, popped it into the trunk, and headed for the New Hampshire border and Singing Trees Orchards. A dozen questions fretted me. What ruse could I devise to reach Lowell alone? What did Guy Huberdeau want to talk to me about? How could I rendezvous with him without divulging my trip's purpose?

At the end of the private lane to the Thompson farmhouse, where it intersected the Nashua Road, we came upon a roadside stand unlike any other. It had the standard dropdown window, a rustic plank counter, and several inside shelves for the Thompsons' paper sacks, bushels of apples, and plastic jugs of cider, but its facade bore upon it primitive portraits in plywood, papier-mâché, and amber or green plastic from softdrink bottles, portraits of Neil, Ruth, and Aaron. On the roof, a rainbow-shaped sign in eccentric calligraphy proclaimed this stand "Official Outlet for Singing Trees Orchards Products." The whole mishmash reminded me of a weird Howard Finster opus. Last night in the dark and again this morning heading out, I had failed even to notice the stand.

Now I said, "Aaron's handiwork?"

"How'd you guess?" Adrienne pulled up alongside the stand, lowered her window, and said, "How're sales, Mom?"

Ruth sat on a stool inside, bundled like a Russian princess for a cross-country troika ride, mounds of apples not quite blocking her from view. She said, "Let's just say buyers haven't descended on us like they usually do for the wedding-dress sale at Filene's Basement."

"Why don't you go in?"

"Neil insists we keep going right up to Thanksgiving."

"We'll bring you a hot drink."

Ruth held up an insulated travel cup. "All set, dear. I'm an old hand at this." She blinked. "Did you get the turkey?"

"A beauty. We're going to slip it into the fridge."

"Don't forget to get your money from Neil."

"No need," I said across Adrienne. "My treat."

Adrienne said, "See you later," waved, rolled up the window, and accelerated carefully up the graveled lane. "Can you believe that?" she said. "A woman Mother's age sitting in the cold and damp. They should both be retired. Sometimes I wish they'd never bought this place."

"As the man said, 'Better to burn out than to rust.' "

"Spare me the literary allusions."

"I have. Neil Young said that. Or sang it."

"Wow. You and Aaron can spin some vinyl together."

"Don't date yourself."

"I'd rather date you." She winked at me. "Hey, I admit I'm a relic, and proud of it."

"But a spry relic, right?"

Adrienne laughed. "Wouldn't you like to find out!"

A few yards from the house, Neil Thompson greeted us wearing only a short blue Thinsulate vest over his flannel shirt, and no hat at all. The pinkness of his scalp through his thinning hair gave him a tender Kewpie-doll look.

"Care to join me in gathering a few final windfalls?"

"Sure, Dad. Just give us a minute or two."

Inside, we stowed the turkey in the refrigerator, among Tupperware tubs of applesauce, to let it begin its leisurely thaw toward Thursday morning.

Then we caught up with Adrienne's dad, now trundling some empty bushel baskets in a wheelbarrow. I kicked along behind the two of them, basking in a wan November sunlight strangely different from that I knew in Georgia. At this latitude, in fact, it felt like something altogether else, the medium into which one slips at the instant of death or the tenuous blaze behind one's eyes at sexual climax in the dark. Falling through the bare branches of the apple trees, this light seemed grainy and dust-freighted, and I wondered how Aaron Thompson could conjure from it his almost tropical visions of slapstick joy.

Neil halted and said, "Take a basket and start filling it, kids. Don't reject an apple unless it's wormy or the deer have mumbled it up. The public won't see these, Will, they'll go into our cider press."

"Right."

Adrienne and I began foraging for fallen fruit. Because I had never thought much beyond Macs and Granny Smiths, the variety of apples that the Thompsons grew surprised me. The varietal names that Adrienne called out rang almost bardically, like kcnnnings: Black Gilliflower and Northern Spy, Zabergau Reinette and Ginger Gold, Liberty and Maiden's Blush, Karajin de Somerville and Esopus Spitzenberg.

The vinegary-sweet scent of decaying fruit and the earthy aroma of leaf mulch, along with the smell of my sweat and Adrienne's too, sharpened my other senses. I envisioned a life harvesting apples, taking solace from honest work among the tree trunks holding up the cold New England sky. "Stem end and blossom end, / And every fleck of russet showing clear." I could almost hear the trees singing in the late autumn breezes, not as soloists but as constituent strings in a vast harplike choir. I felt a long way from Tocqueville and the frustration of my protracted job search. A long way from the guilt and turmoil of Olivia's kidnapping. For this rare boon, I owed the Thompsons' singing trees, which crooned a cradle song promising me one night of unbroken sleep, a sleep free of dreams of a dog-child lost in a world-engulfing storm.

Sunday passed for the Thompsons as just another day. We ate again the familiar breakfast of applesauce and strudel cake, but this time with scrambled eggs, bacon, and yogurt cups. Aaron had only black coffee and a bowl of Grape Nuts, cracking wise about the "pomi-vores" around him and "Daddy Appleseed."

"Know why Dad never wears a hat?" Aaron asked me.

"No, why?"

"He still hasn't found a cooking pot that fits him."

Amused, I extended the joke: "Would he wear it with the handle to the front or the back?"

"Oh, Dad's no slacker. Front, definitely the front."

Neil harrumphed good-naturedly, but Ruth—for appearance's sake, I thought—said, "That's quite enough disrespect toward your father, young man."

Aaron ignored her. "If God had put *me* in the Garden of Eden, we'd still be there. I'd've thrown Eve's lousy apple right back into the underbrush."

"Let's leave God out of this," Adrienne said slyly, and, to my amazement, every Thompson at the table laughed.

After breakfast, Adrienne and I handled cleanup while Neil and Ruth read the *Lowell Sun* or the *Boston Globe* and did the crossword puzzles. Putting dishes away, I decided that I would offer as my excuse to drive into Lowell the need to buy a pack of condoms. A bad, awkward, embarrassing excuse, and a lie—because I had, in fact, brought condoms with me. Thankfully, after I'd slid the last plate onto its stack, Adrienne turned to me and said: "How would you feel if I went up to our room and sat for a couple of hours? It would settle my mind, in addition to making me *much* better company later."

"Sure," I said. "What if I took the car and went exploring?"

She kissed me on the forehead. "Have at it. If you want a destination, try driving north to Benson's Zoo."

Around eleven, Adrienne went upstairs to sit, and I climbed into the car to retrace yesterday's route to Lowell. On the way back from the Oil Can Foundry, Adrienne had showed me City Hall, and today, with the city center nearly deserted, I easily found a parking place in front of the castlelike building with its nubby roseate walls and prominent clock tower.

The Club Diner occupied a corner on the knot of roads crossing in front of City Hall. A white shoebox of a building on a brick foundation, with planters full of dead flowers under its windows and maroon panels running about its roofline, the Club Diner had a prominent sign inviting patrons to "Try Our Sirloin Tips—$6.25" and boasting of its fifty-fifth year of operation. I climbed two steps to its front door and entered.

A steamy blast of food-fragrant air greeted me. I scanned the interior. Huberdeau sat in a booth upholstered in brown vinyl, a cup of coffee occupying his full attention. I took off my borrowed gloves and strode toward him. At his booth, I extended my hand and said, "Mr. Hu—"

Huberdeau grabbed my wrist and pulled me down to the same split cushion on which he sat. The fragrance of sintered metals pervaded his clothing, reminding me of the not-unpleasant smells I'd noticed in Byron's loft apartment.

"Right on time," he said quietly. "You're a good boy, you."

"That's me in a nutshell: Mr. Reliable." He let me remove his hand from my wrist. "Mr. Huberdeau, do we have to share the same bench?"

He lowered his voice further. "You bet we do. This story I want to tell, no one but you should hear it."

The waitress arrived, gave us a bemused look, and nodded when Huberdeau suggested that I order either the chili or the vegetable soup. I opted for soup, Huberdeau for chili, and the waitress lay silverware down along with a basket of homemade cornbread squares, left us briefly, and returned with my drink, a tall milk. When we had our privacy again, Huberdeau admitted that our visit yesterday had thrown him for a loop.

"Your girl, Adrienne, she was one bright spark in my life. But that rat-bastard husband of hers—"

"Ex-husband, thank God."

"Sure, sure. But the memories I keep of him and the trouble he brought—very painful. Nowadays, what's he doing?"

"Hanging around the edges of our lives, brightening the corners where he lurks."

Huberdeau snorted a laugh. "He brightened some goddamn corners for me, all right. You heard me say I don't shoe horses no more? Well, blame it on that goddamn Byron Owsley."

The waitress returned, smiling as if our companionability must represent a late father-and-son reconciliation. My soup's smell enticed me. Despite the big breakfast I had eaten, hunger seized me again. "Enjoy." The waitress left. I buttered some cornbread, reached for my spoon. Luckily, Huberdeau ate lefthanded so that we didn't jab elbows into each other's ribs as we dug in.

"Byron was a good apprentice, he was," Huberdeau said. "Quick to pick things up—worked hard too—but that was all a big act, which fooled me good. I started to give him customers all his own, like this Cambodian guy name of Charlie Bun who had his own stable of racehorses. Bun came to this country rich already, not like so many of his countrymen. That I didn't like. How's a man get rich in a pisshole like Cambodia? Only by ripping off his brothers, his sisters, his country really big-time, eh? But Bun's horses needed shoes so I took him for a customer. Anyhow, too late I found out something bad. Bun pays Byron a coupla grand to mis-shoe somebody else's pony."

I stuck my spoon in my peppery soup. "Why would he do that?"

"This pony belongs to another customer of mine, Charlie Bun's top rival in the racing biz. His horse—"

"What sweethearts, Charlie Bun and Byron Owsley both."

"*Shhhhh!* Listen! This horse, she's the favorite in a race at Suffolk Downs, our local track north of Boston, eh? She looks fine in preliminaries, she gallops out the gate okay, but after this job Byron done on her shoes, she goes really wobbly in the homestretch, crumples down, pitches her jockey. Charlie Bun's rival has to have her shot right there at the track, a million dollars of horseflesh lost to pain and suffering; to deception, you know. Ol' Bun cleans up on bets—fucks his rival really good too—and Guy Huberdeau comes out of this cesspool with like shit all over him, yeah. The police start poking around but can't find no real evidence that me or Byron done anything wrong on purpose. Okay? Not okay. If we wasn't total bastards and crooks, we must be just a coupla goddamn screwups. For next year or two, people look at me funny. I know what everybody's thinking too: How much did Charlie Bun pay for my soul? I lost plenty of business, including my deal with the owner of the dead horse, and a few friends too."

"So you fired Byron?"

"I kick his ass out the door so hard his own shoes almost stay behind. I tell him to get his greedy butt out of Massachusetts and quick. He just nodded, not surprised, like maybe he was thinking already along those lines."

"A young man with a wife and a baby daughter?"

"Save this pity, Mr. Keats. Like I said, Byron was leaning south already. And I got heart, me. I gave that scumbag a grand to take care of his family. On top of what Charlie Bun paid, Byron had him a good stake, he did."

"How much of this does Adrienne know?"

"Me, I say not a lot. You think Byron confesses his nastiness like he won some award? No way. He made me the villain, probably, which is why your girl not writing or nothing for ten years never surprised me. I figure it's the price I pay for acting the good guy, me."

Huberdeau fell silent, and both of us ate, finishing our meals to the clinking of silverware and the white noise of the fan in the ventilator hood.

At last I said, "Why'd you tell me this story, Mr. Huberdeau?"

He put an arm around my shoulder and leaned close. "I want you to know what this bastard can do. Someone's kidnapped Olivia, eh? How much you bet old Byron's involved?"

"Hey, I've thought the same thing. But Byron's got what looks like an airtight alibi, and the police need evidence to—"

"Then you help them find it. Don't let Byron escape again from whatever shit he brings down on himself." Huberdeau pulled his arm away and nodded peremptorily. "Now let me up. This talk it brings back the pain. A lot. I got to go hammer something, me."

I slid out, as did Huberdeau, who dropped several bills on the table. After telling me to have a happy Thanksgiving and to take care of Adrienne, he brusquely exited the diner.

I sat down again, semistunned. The waitress sauntered over, plucked up the money on the table, and said, "Old Huberdeau's a good tipper. He even left enough to cover your dessert. Want some apple pie?"

Twenty-One

On Monday morning, Adrienne leaned over in our soft up-stairs guest bed and scratched the tip of my nose. "Will, I want to go see another old friend today."

"Male?"

"As a matter of fact, yes."

"Oh God," I groaned. "Didn't you hang out with any persons of the female persuasion when you lived here?"

"Unh-unh. They claimed I stole all their boyfriends or didn't know how to mix-n-match outfits, one or the other."

"The former, no doubt. Does this old flame have a name? And where do you have to go to see him?"

"Where do *we* have to go, you mean—I want you to come along. His name's Jim Rakestraw, my old Zen teacher. He lives with some students in the Lowell Zen Center on Gumpus Road."

"*Gumpus?* As in 'Lumpus'? As in 'Humpus'?"

Adrienne pinched my cheek, forcefully. "Behave! I've always wanted you to meet Roshi Rakestraw."

"But has old Humpus Gumpus Roshi Rakestraw always wanted to meet *me*? That's the question."

"Ask him yourself."

Gumpus Road wound through a residential section of Lowell that we had not yet visited. We parked in front of a wide winter lawn stretching like a heath to a rambling one-story house. Perfectly maintained, it featured a wraparound gallery, white clapboards, and an elegant hand-lettered placard next to the entrance: "Lowell Zen Center." Adrienne rang the bell, triggering a soft three-note chime from inside. I shifted from foot to foot, feeling like a Burmese peon seeking admittance to the Imperial Officer's Club of Rangoon; I also wondered what I really knew of the practices and teachings of those studying here. The Four Noble Truths, the Eightfold Path, the Three Jewels—I had gleaned these concepts from my talks with Adrienne as little more than phrases. Here on the thirty-third day after Olivia's abduction, they all felt as irrelevant to me as last summer's boxscores.

The door swung open, revealing a petite, red-haired woman in jeans and a short black robe. She smiled at us politely, formally, almost coldly. "Hello. I'm afraid you've come at an inconvenient time. You see—"

"The midmorning chant is about to begin," Adrienne said.

The woman looked at Adrienne more closely. "I've seen your picture. You used to sit here, didn't you?"

"Years ago. I'm Adrienne Owsley. This is Will Keats."

"Would you like to chant with us?"

"Absolutely. Will?"

"I'll take a rain check. Assuming there's a place where I can, uh, sit and wait."

"Of course! Come in. Please call me Suzy."

Inside the entrance stood a five-by-twelve dovecote for shoes. We removed ours and slid them into empty pigeonholes. I noted that the room off the front hall featured a burnished hardwood floor, a few Swedish-modern chairs, and one well-stocked bookcase beneath a large Japanese print: a fat grinning beggarman, striding into the marketplace with his stick-borne bindle. I recognized the print as the Tenth Oxherding Picture, a symbol of enlightenment.

From deeper within the house came the plangent call of a gong. Suzy and Adrienne harkened to it physically; their chins lifted and their faces lit up.

"It's time now," Suzy said. "Pick up a visitor's robe outside the *zendo*."

Adrienne pecked my cheek. "Forty-five minutes, Will? Think you can last that long?"

I pulled her to me and whispered, "When have I ever?"

She looked at me quizzically, then punched me lightly in the chest. "Just behave, okay?"

Alone, I walked over to the bookcase. Along with scores of Buddhist titles (some familiar to me from Adrienne's library), it held several photo albums with dates on their spines. I sat down with the 1988–92 album and began leafing through it.

Inevitably, I came across the first of many shots of Adrienne: thinner, more vulnerably girlish, she carried a bundle of shingles up a ladder to the center's roof. In other photos, she appeared at Zen Center cookouts; shoulder to shoulder with fellow students on the lawn; or, in a shot bearing the legend "Public Chanting Demo at Mechanic's Hall," smiling onstage with the entire student body. I also took from the album a good Identikit image of Roshi Rakestraw: a thin, rawshanked man with flyaway gray hair and a face alternately ecstatically goofy and dauntingly intense.

A muffled, many-voiced murmur—fading, swelling, cresting—accompanied my perusal of the album. A full forty-five minutes must have passed because, with an abrupt terminal exclamation, the chanting ceased. I stood. A number of chattering people trickled out of the *zendo*. Adrienne did not appear. I sat back down. I stood back up.

Twenty minutes went by, and I began to think that she had opted for the "sneak-out-the-back-Jack" method of leaving her lover. So, contemplating barging into the *zendo* for answers, I ambled down the hall and bumped into a slender, familiar-looking man.

Rakestraw wore a more elaborate version of the student robe, with a round ceremonial clasp on its breast. Burgundy windsuit pants peeked from beneath his robe. Gangly and loose-jointed, Rakestraw carried a shiny knobby stick of real heft. He smoothed his unruly hair, smiled, and said unhesitatingly, "William Keats, I presume."

Briefly, his certainty took me aback. I recovered, shook his hand, and said, "Roshi James Rakestraw."

"Call me Jim. Please don't worry about Adrienne. After we talked, she decided to remain in the *zendo* for a short period of meditation."

"Short? How short?"

Rakestraw laughed. "Under the aspect of eternity, a gnat's eyeblink."

"Did she tell you about Olivia's kidnapping?" The compassion in Rakestraw's eyes induced me to add, "Or the unending godawful *pain*?"

Gently, he took my arm and led me slowly back down the hall and over to the bookcase in the waiting room. Here he let go of my arm and plucked a volume from the shelf, as if he had chosen it at random. He leafed through it, tilting the book so that its back jacket disclosed to me a photo of the smiling Dalai Lama: a smile undeniably joyful.

At that moment, the anteroom underwent a small transfiguration, as if someone had lifted a corner of the room an inch. Rakestraw had *meant* for me to register the Dalai Lama's smile, to apprehend in it the immense love that he had mustered in the face of his own personal and national tragedy. Or maybe I had simply read into the moment a significance that it mimicked possessing rather than owning in truth. How would I know? Was life nothing but a complicated Steven Wright joke?

Rakestraw smiled, not unlike the Dalai Lama, and shelved the book. "Let me show you around, William."

In a minor daze, I dogged along beside him. Besides the *zendo,* which I never actually saw, the Lowell Zen Center consisted of an office, a recreation room (Ping-Pong table, TV and VCR, card table, couch), and a cooking/dining area. Fresh-cut flowers graced every room. We wound up in the kitchen watching members prepare food and inhaling piquant cooking smells.

"You and Adrienne must stay for lunch," Rakestraw said.

"We accept," Adrienne's voice called out cheerily. "Will never refuses a free meal, Roshi." Adrienne embraced me from behind, adding, "Man, do I feel better, almost like I'd spent a weekend at a spa. On a gift certificate."

She *looked* better, more relaxed. Her skin glowed. I tried to say something welcoming but managed only "Hi."

Rakestraw rapped my shoulder softly with his stick. "No work, no food. Come on."

We pitched in. I cut carrots to dip in hummus while Adrienne seasoned a big pot of miso soup. Rakestraw prepared loaf after loaf of garlic bread, obviously his speciality. Then the whole community gathered and, seated on the floor on cushions, offered a blessing and fell to. Later, we poured tea into our soup-slicked bowls, both to rinse the bowls and to savor the tea.

Sitting full-lotus, Rakestraw rapped his stick on the floor. "Recently I read a poem by a Chinese man named Han Yu, who lived nearly twelve hundred years ago. Although not a follower of the Buddha, Han Yu nonetheless speaks wisely to us today." Rakestraw smiled ambiguously in my direction.

"Recite the poem," Adrienne said.

"Believe me, I never intended not to." Everyone laughed, and the poem followed:

> "Don't shoo the morning flies away
> Nor swat the mosquitoes in the evening.
> Between the two, they fill the world.
> So many, should you fight them all?
> And yet, how short a time they live.
> While they last, give in and let them bite you.
> October, and a cold wind wipes them out.
> You don't remember, then, they ever were."

No one applauded. But everyone had heard, and everyone seemed to listen beyond the poem's final echo. Rakestraw rapped his stick on the floor again. "Time for cleanup. Let's get to it."

As before, Adrienne and I pitched in. Then, Rakestraw walked Adrienne and me out to the car. I breathed in the cold air, the smells of pine and river. The incense-laden air of the Zen Center had intoxicated me in more ways than one, but the natural smells of the outdoors restored my sobriety. I liked Rakestraw, but realized that the zone of altered thinking that his Zen Center embodied had not arrived with me at the Neon. How, then, did Rakestraw manage to transport that uncanny zone with him?

Beside the car, he hugged Adrienne, his hair ruffling in the wind. He turned to me and said, "You have scarecrows in your part of the country, don't you, William?"

"Thousands."

"They accomplish their jobs by pretending to be human, don't they?"

"I suppose you could phrase it that way."

"Well, William, so do we."

While I puzzled over that one, he turned back to Adrienne and said, "Seeing you again, I remember many beautiful days. I foresee many more to come. Practice hard, Adrienne."

Once in the car, Adrienne took a moment to get the key in the ignition. From the porch, Rakestraw waved to us, making great wallowing circles with his arms, as if imitating a helicopter or washing a picture window.

"Look at that clown," Adrienne said affectionately.

On the way back to Singing Trees Orchards, snow began to fall, first in huge lazy flakes, then in alarming flurries as thick as television interference.

Twenty-Two

Snow fell all that Monday afternoon, ceased in the evening, threatened on Tuesday without following through, and on Wednesday morning, as the Thompsons quibbled about how much onion to dice into Ruth's Thanksgiving dressing, whispered down on the farmhouse and apple trees like cottony confetti. We made no more trips into Lowell, and Aaron and I fell into a routine of playing dominoes or watching TV. Adrienne spoke on the phone to old friends, helped her mother, or practiced *zazen* like a marathoner.

Once, as if the idea had just seized him, Aaron looked up at me over an asymmetrical schema of dominoes and said, "I'm surprised her butt doesn't go numb."

"Adrienne transcends numbness through sheer will."

"Sheer stubbornness, maybe. Why don't *you* sit?"

I liked Aaron despite his youthful prickliness. He had started to like me. I said, "I do sit, just like now. I just have to keep busy while I'm doing it."

Aaron planked down a domino. "Thirty points. Too bad you can't keep busy with more skill. I'm gonna whup your Southern-fried butt so bad you'll *wish* it was numb."

In three more plays, he kept his promise.

When Thanksgiving day arrived, I felt that we had anticipated it for months. What a relief that the five of us would finally sit down to an obscenely rich dinner, ritually stuff ourselves, and so fulfill our obligation to celebrate. Good smells pervaded the house, from roasting turkey to faintly scorched pumpkin pie. TV commentators for the noon pro-football game nattered in the background, and Ruth bustled back and forth to the kitchen just as if she hadn't already placed one steaming bowl of every prepared item on the table. I could hardly wait—not so much for dinner as for Ruth to sit down and stay down. Finally, she obliged us.

"Well"—Ruth put her lacy napkin in her lap—"I suppose a meal like this deserves a proper sendoff."

Hard-eyed, Neil said, "Do you mean a proper *blessing*?"

"Well, yes, if someone would care to offer one."

Aaron, parodying a hillbilly at mealtime, picked up a knife in one hand, a fork in the other, and held them upright on either side of his plate. "How about, 'Good bread, good meat, good Gawd, let's eat!'?"

Neil snorted, more in appreciation than censure.

Ruth said, "Maybe Adrienne's current favorite would do us the honor of returning thanks."

"Wait a second," Adrienne said. "*Current* favorite? As if I pick up and discard boyfriends every other day?"

Neil, looking up, appealed to the chandelier. "Someone'd better manufacture a little goddamn piety soon or we'll have nothing to eat but congealed grease!"

"Please, Will," Ruth said. "As our guest."

Her request found me at a loss for words. However, I had come through as a eulogist at my father's funeral and, later, at the Gag Reflex substituting for an ailing comedian, so I bowed my head and trusted to providence:

"Dear God, bless this wonderful-smelling food and these caring people. Bring Olivia home to us unharmed. Bring her soon."

"Amen," said Ruth and Adrienne together.

I unbowed my head to find Aaron giving me a thumbs-up. "Good one, Will. Short but sweet."

Neil said, "Thanks, Will. Would someone pass the turkey before I faint from hunger?"

"I'll second that motion," Adrienne said, concentrating on her breathing.

Ruth lifted the massive platter and passed it to Aaron. "See what a good job Will did carving. Such *big* slices." This remark felt like a veiled criticism, but her smile offset it. "Has Neil reimbursed you for the turkey yet?"

"Mother, please."

"We'd prefer that he didn't," I said. "We'd like to—"

"Guests don't pay," Ruth said tightly.

"Ha!" said Aaron. "Only if you don't count their slave labor picking up windfalls."

"That's enough, young man."

After that, only the clatter of utensils on china and the faint football-stadium racket from the TV interrupted our silence. Until the telephone rang.

Ruth jumped up and reached the portable phone's handset before the third ring. "Thompsons'," she said, then listened for a moment before approaching the table and giving the handset to me.

Who would call me in New Hampshire? "Will Keats," I said.

"This is Asa D. Fearing, Will." The agent's voice cut through me with the precision of an electric carving knife. *"Can I get from Lowell to the Thompson place without a snowplow, or should I wait for spring?"*

I turned away from the table, conscious of everyone's eyes on me. "Fearing, what's happened? Do you have good news?"

Adrienne's shadow fell into my lap. Her hand touched my wrist as if subtly asking for the phone. I gave her a stupid smile, but kept my grip on the handset.

"No, not exactly," Fearing admitted. *"I need to talk to you all in person."*

"Ask him if Olivia's okay," Adrienne said. "Damn it, Will—ask him! He knows better than to scare us to death!"

Fearing said, *"We have no evidence of any harm to Olivia, Mr. Keats. But we've encountered—developments. I just can't say any more over the phone."*

"Olivia's okay," I said to Adrienne. "He wants to drive up."

"Who is it?" Ruth said. "Should I set another place?"

"Tell whoever's on the line to join us," Neil said. "The more the merrier. Aaron, drag in another chair."

"I think you can make it," I told Fearing. "Just a while ago, plows and sanding trucks growled past the house."

"All right," Fearing said. *"Save me a chunk of bird and a dab of*

jellied cranberry sauce because I am indeed a-coming. Just give me a half hour or so." He broke the connection.

I handed the phone back to Ruth, who cradled it in its base. "Who was it, Will? Can't you say?"

"The FBI man in charge of Olivia's case. Your home cooking drew him all the way from Georgia."

Ruth no more believed this than she believed that apples grew on streetlamps. Nevertheless, she went into the kitchen and came back with another place setting, which she squeezed between her own and Aaron's.

"Agent Fearing may need *two* plates," I said. "He can probably eat an entire wildebeest all by himself."

"Please don't try to joke, Will," Adrienne said.

Neil and Aaron resumed eating, but much more slowly than they had before.

In less than twenty-five minutes, Asa D. Fearing arrived in a gunmetal-blue late-model Oldsmobile. Adrienne and I, bundled against the cold, awaited him outside. The sky had spit snow all morning: erratic bursts that the wind keening through the orchards sent flying like tattered grave wrappings. Fearing climbed out wearing an XXL parka with a furry hood that surrounded his face like sunflower petals around their dark central button. Swinging his inflated-looking arms astronautishly, he trudged toward the house, said hello, and stamped inside ahead of us.

Before he could even remove his parka, Adrienne said, "What do you have to tell us? What made you leave Georgia?"

"Consequential matters, ma'am, but not mortal ones—at least not where your Olivia's concerned." He glanced about. "Could we maybe sit down in a place where I can tell my story to everyone at the same time."

"Of course," Adrienne said, helping him out of his coat. "My mother wants to feed you."

We led him into the dining room, where he shook hands with Neil and Aaron, then gingerly lowered himself into a chair at the place set for him. Ruth heaped his plate with turkey, dressing, mashed potatoes, green beans, and cranberry sauce; she poured him a glass of Westport Chablis and sat down next to him. We'll talk as

I eat, he told us gesturally, spreading a napkin in his lap and surveying his food with evident pleasure.

"All right," I said. "Where's Olivia?"

"We still have no idea." Fearing popped a black olive into his mouth as an appetizer. "But we know where she's *not.*"

"Meaning?" Adrienne said.

"Late yesterday afternoon, an Alabama deputy from Cherokee County found Polk James alone in a hunter's cabin up near Weiss Lake." Fearing grimaced. "Somebody'd shot him once at the base of the skull. The newspapers like to call it 'execution-style.' "

"Holy Jesus," I said, and Adrienne squeezed my hand hard. I pictured poor monkey-faced Polk James with a hole in his head, and shuddered. Not that long ago, I'd seen a Labrador retriever shot in the same fashion, and the thought of a human being meeting that kind of heartless end unnerved me.

"Whoever shot Polk James," Fearing continued, "apparently took Olivia with him. All the blood at the scene matches James's. The shanty was a godawful mess, but not just from the murder. Over the years, hunters have really abused the place. That Alabama deputy found ripped mattresses, a door full of dart holes, a tub of filthy dishes, some battered cookpans, piles of old clothes—a regular Judgment Day mess to sort through for clues." He sipped his wine and made a face, either because of its taste or his image of the squalid cabin. "I won't lie. Finding James qualifies as a break. Finding him dead—murdered—with Olivia toted off under the arm of some evil bastard whose badness we ain't even begun to measure, that's downright *lousy* news, and I hope you all'll forgive me for bringing it here today."

"Of course," Adrienne said. "You've shown real dedication."

For the Thompsons' sake, I said, "You didn't have to do this in person. No Bureau policy requires it of you, right?"

"Generally, I do what my gut tells me, Mr. Keats, and my gut insisted I need to see you all face to face."

I eased into my old spot across from Fearing. "You still don't think Olivia has it in her to foil such monstrous people, do you? An eight-year-old girl versus an assassin or two?"

"Sometimes even smart *adults* can't wriggle out of a kidnapping alive." Fearing took a bite of turkey and chewed it thoughtfully.

"Back home, I thought she could maybe help herself out of this predicament, but that assumed she faced only Polk James. Now, we don't know who holds her or what sort of scruples this person's got. Only a bigger fool than me would say Olivia has even a one-in-a-million shot at helping herself."

"So what should we do?" Adrienne said.

"Besides finishing Thanksgiving with your family? Nothing, darling. Just let us fellas who get paid for it stay after the bad actors who crashed James's party. You all can worry about it just as well up here as you can in Georgia."

"What if the new kidnappers make a ransom demand?" I said. "Shouldn't we get ready to receive it?"

"Very good point." Fearing tapped his fork on the edge of his plate. "Finally, though, it's you all's call."

Adrienne moved to Ruth and put her arm around her. "Mother, we have to go. Dad, do you understand?"

"I understand a lot more than some people give me credit for," Neil said.

"Ditto." Aaron clasped his hands in front of him and shook them as a way of signaling his support. "You guys gotta do what you gotta do."

Fearing said, "If you all pack and follow me to Logan, I can get you on a nonstop Delta flight to Atlanta early this evening."

"At least finish your meal and have some dessert," Ruth said. "Surely we all have time for that."

Fearing forked up three or four green beans. "Ma'am, I won't disappoint you on that score. I've spent my share of holidays on the road, and there's hardly no sadder feeling. So I never refuse a home-cooked meal."

Neither Adrienne nor I could take another bite now, but we sat with Fearing and Adrienne's family as they finished eating, then climbed the stairs to our room and packed. Out every window we passed coming down, long scarves of snow twisted dreamily among the otherwise naked trees.

Twenty-Three

Having survived both the New England cold and almost a week with the quasi-dysfunctional Thompsons, I basked in Georgia's fine weather and our recovered privacy. During our absence, a spell of Indian summer had come upon the lower Piedmont, and when I awoke beside Adrienne, a breeze through our partially open bedroom window brought with it an illusory sense of well-being. Then I remembered Polk James's murder, and Olivia's second kidnapping

I got out of bed without waking Adrienne, dressed, and made my way clumsily downstairs. After starting the coffeemaker, I went out back to the stable. Roogy Batoon heard me enter and cantered around her hay-crowded stall, head up, snapping her tail like a fly whisk.

"Come to Daddy, baby," I crooned. "Come to Daddy."

Roogy approached, jerking her neck back like a near-sighted person trying to obtain focus. She calmed as I stroked her. The silkiness of her mane told me that J. W. Young had kept her both well-fed and well-curried. She whickered once, shook her muzzle, banged her jaw softly against my shoulder.

"Did you miss us, baby?" I fed Roogy a molasses ball. "Not much, huh? J. W. kept you company, maybe even read you old Lewis Grizzard columns." (Excerpts, no doubt, from *Shoot Low, Boys, They're Riding Shetland Ponies*.) I opened the gate to her stall, and, with a spirited double kick, she broke from confinement into the spectacular sunshine.

.   .   .

At ten o'clock on that same Friday morning, Adrienne and I telephoned ahead and drove to the Speece Country Sheriff's Office and
Jail Facility to confer with Nicholas Cooper. On the flight home,
Fearing had told us that Alabama law-enforcement officials, at the
urging of Georgia's Attorney General, the GBI, and the FBI, had
transferred the main responsibility for solving James's murder, as
well as all pertinent evidence, to the agencies already handling Olivia's kidnapping. Because the criminal trail had originated in Speece
County, and any prosecution of the case would occur here, Alabama
surrendered jurisdiction, even as its police continued to assist.
Adrienne and I were grateful not to have to deal with a whole new
set of names and faces.

Cooper greeted us in the anteroom and took us to his office.
Today he wore a powder-blue oxford shirt with a red and blue silk
tie. He had left the top button of his shirt undone, though, and
yanked the tie's knot away from his Adam's apple. As soon as we
had sat down, I preempted any opening pleasantries:

"When was Polk James killed?"

Cooper furrowed his brow as if my question had given him a
headache. "We found him Tuesday. He may have been dead
longer."

"Any idea who did it?"

"Agent Fearing surely told you most of what we've learned. The
shooter used a thirty-eight-caliber weapon and forced James to kneel
to take the bullet. Right now, we have no prints, no motive, no clue
how the killer tracked James down, and no idea where he may have
taken Olivia."

Adrienne said, "Please, Captain Cooper, bring us up to speed on
all that's happened since Tuesday."

Cooper alternately twirled a rubber band around a forefinger and
wrapped his swollen knuckles. "Given the way you two plunge headlong into every aspect of our investigation, I'm not all that comfortable telling you those things."

"Look," I said, "you cleared our visit to Polk James's mother. You
don't think that our asking her for help led in some way to his
murder?"

"Who can possibly say? When someone outside the police factors odd figures into the equations we've carefully set up, it puts our computations out of whack."

"*Odd figures!*" Adrienne said. "Additional information is a handicap to you guys?"

Cooper wearily shook his head; then he inadvertently shot his rubber band off my left shoulder.

I stood up and banged my fist on his desk. "Who factors the oddest figures into your pretty equations, Nick? People trying to help you because they so badly need *your* help, or psychopaths who unpredictably kidnap, kill, and disappear?"

"Why not tell us everything you can and trust us?" Adrienne said.

Cooper said, "Will, I'm sorry. Please sit down." I obeyed. "I realize that neither of you thinks passive hand-wringing is an acceptable coping style, and we need your help as much as you need ours. But if I confide in you all, you've *got* to keep your mouths shut. No leaks to the news media, to friends, even to loved ones. Can you all abide by such a complete gag rule?"

Without even consulting, Adrienne and I agreed.

Cooper fidgeted with a replacement rubber band. "You'd have probably learned on your own that Byron's skipped town. An hour after news of James's murder reached us, we tried to collar him for additional questioning and came up empty-handed."

Adrienne gripped her own shoulders. "I can't imagine Byron killing James. I just can't."

"Frankly, we didn't think he had either," Cooper said, "but his flight put the idea in our minds—along with the tempting notion that Byron now has Olivia."

"Do you really think he does?" I asked.

"Parents take some extreme measures to regain control of their kids, but no, personally, I don't."

"Why not?"

Suddenly self-conscious, Cooper dropped his rubber band back into the drawer. "As with the first kidnapping, he has an airtight alibi. From all we can determine, he never left Tocqueville until *after* the murder. Even if he did slip over to Weiss Lake and kill James, why not bring Olivia home and turn himself in? He could've claimed self-defense or diminished capacity. No Speece County jury would've ever convicted him. Who wouldn't go berserk running up on the man who'd held his daughter captive for a month?"

I said, "Have you talked to DeLynda Gaye again?"

"Of course. She vouches that Byron was in town until Monday, and she doesn't believe he even owns a handgun."

"He had one in Lowell," Adrienne said.

Surprised, Cooper looked at her. "What kind?"

"I don't know. Firearms give me the shivers. I never recall seeing it here in Georgia, anyway."

These matter-of-fact nods to Adrienne's past affiliation with Byron might have put me in a funk, but I leaned forward and said, "Do you have any *proof* that Olivia ever occupied the cabin where James was shot?"

"Yes, we do," Cooper said.

"Would you mind telling us about it?" Adrienne said.

Cooper yanked open a drawer in his desk and removed an opaque evidence bag. We gaped at it, imagining a hank of Olivia's hair, a piece of her clothing, a severed ear. Then Cooper opened the bag and slid its contents onto the surface of his desk without touching them. Adrienne and I stood up to examine the contents and found ourselves peering down on a miniature notebook—a Marble Memo, with a black-and-white cover—and the nubs of two pencils, one with red lead, one with green.

"I sent Deputy Jay Covington to Alabama on Tuesday. He found these items tucked into a slit in a mattress Olivia must have slept on," Cooper said.

Adrienne extended her hand. "Let me see them."

"Ma'am, I can't," said Cooper, deflecting her. "I really have no authority to show you folks this stuff, much less let you handle it. I've only done what I've done to—"

"To prove Olivia was in the cabin," I said.

Cooper nodded us to our chairs, then foraged out some tweezers with which to return the evidence to its bag. "The handwriting in the Marble Memo—very neat for a kid in her straits—perfectly matches the samples you gave us. Each entry begins with a notation of the month and day, so far as she could keep track of them. The last one, dated the twenty-second, Sunday, seems to describe her surroundings at Weiss Lake."

"But what else does she say?" Adrienne's voice broke. "Can't you give us five minutes to read it?"

Cooper's lips quirked in chagrin. "Thanksgiving's thrown us off a day or two—not an excuse, just an explanation. The lab hasn't even seen that little book yet. Our forensics people would string me up by my toes if they knew I'd done this." He returned the evidence bag to his drawer. "Before anyone else examines the notebook, Fearing and his boys will have to sign off on their need to know."

Adrienne said, "Does *Fearing* even know about the notebook yet?"

Cooper flushed. "No, ma'am. Not yet."

Along with his virtual admission of foot-dragging on submitting the notebook for analysis, this news stunned me. "Jesus, Nick," I said, "did you hope to score points against the FBI by withholding Olivia's witness in the notebook?"

After rolling his chair away from us, Cooper stared at one of the elegant tree prints decorating his office. "No. The notebook goes to the lab as soon as you all leave. Fearing and company will have access to the results as soon as they become available. But Jay did exceptional work finding it, and I plan to see that he gets proper credit."

"Great," said Adrienne. "Even if it delays the investigation and puts Olivia's life at even greater risk?"

"It hasn't come to that. It *won't* come to that. On my word of honor as an agent of the law."

Adrienne and I traded a half-incredulous glance. After a beat or two, Adrienne tapped her fist on her chest above her heart. "God help you if you fail to keep that word, Captain Cooper, or if you overestimate your own abilities."

Cooper castored his chair back around to face us, but waited a moment before whispering, "Yes, God help me."

To play on the guilt he evidently felt, I asked if we couldn't have a photocopy of Olivia's notebook. "That would be like getting a letter from her. In a sense, Nick, it would bring her home to us before she returns in person."

"Although I don't think I could stand it," Adrienne said, "if she wrote of cruelty or suffering or fear."

"She writes with humbling courage," Cooper said.

"Well, then?" I prompted him.

"Let me consult with Agent Fearing. Meanwhile, for all our sakes, please tell no one about our discovery." Cooper stood, an obvious invitation for us to leave.

Adrienne and I walked back to the Tacoma under a high pale sky; the sun throbbed quietly, and clouds drifted in wan flotillas. Not until we pulled out of the parking lot did Adrienne speak.

"Who do we trust here, Will? The glory-hungry local deputy? Or the FBI agent who has no idea what the deputy's kept from him? Both? Neither?"

"Ourselves," I said. "And Olivia."

Adrienne snorted ironically, then put her foot to the Tacoma's gas pedal.

Twenty-Four

At 10:00 A.M. Saturday in the Ever-Rest Cemetery on the eastern edge of Dogtown, Alice-Darlene James buried her son. Wearing a navy-blue polyester pants suit, she gimped into view on the arm of a black-clad preacher whose worn trouser cuffs scarcely reached the knobs of his ankles. The only other attendees included two elderly black women, a young man in greasy coveralls, and three folks of an age to have gone to school with Polk James.

The grave cut deep into the red Georgia clay, but Alice-Darlene stared off through a broken hedge of chokeberries at the traffic on a bridge over a switching yard.

" 'You believe in God, believe also in me,' " read the chinless acne-scarred preacher. " 'My Father's house has many rooms . . .' "

A hydraulic machine lowered the unadorned gray casket into the ground. Alice-Darlene watched this process, then stepped forward and kicked a clod into the grave, where, in striking the casket, it broke into clayey shrapnel.

Someone at my shoulder whispered, "Surprised to see you here." Nicholas Cooper, in a dark suit and tie.

"I could say the same," I whispered back.

"Professional duty. Have to check out the mourners. You?"

"I didn't want Mrs. James to suppose her son meant absolutely nothing to anyone beyond herself."

Cooper interthreaded his fingers and flexed his hands palm to palm. "Good enough. I don't see Miz Owsley."

"She doesn't share my overactive sense of duty."

The preacher eyed Cooper and me rebukingly. "From dust we came, beloved, and to dust we go back. May the Lord see fit to refigure Polk James into a resurrection body on the glorious day of final triumph."

Later, Alice-Darlene recoiled when Cooper and I appeared before her to offer condolences. Then she poked Cooper in the chest with a stubby finger. "You all set this up to make my boy look like a good-for-nothing." To everyone else, she said, "Two of the cowards that killed my boy've come this morning to mock him. This's what I think of 'em." She spat on Cooper's shoe, hooked her arm through the young preacher's, and ambled with him to the ancient Oldsmobile Eighty-eight on the cemetery's border. Cooper pulled a threadbare handkerchief from his breast pocket and wiped his shoe. In the absence of other mourners, he dropped the used handkerchief into the grave. "Good thing I buy these by the dozen, eh, Will? Anyway, hope you have a better day than I'm likely to."

After Cooper sauntered off, I stood at Polk James's graveside for three or four minutes staring at the tumbled soil and the cheap bouquets. Looking up at last, I saw a young woman on the edge of the cemetery near the chokeberry hedge. She hurried off as if my gaze had spooked her. Trim figure. Flared pants. Skintight jersey top. Masses of bouncing coppery hair.

DeLynda Gaye, I thought. And none other.

Classes resumed the Monday after the Thanksgiving holiday, and Adrienne joined her fellow teachers at Tocqueville Middle School. I distracted myself by patching some holes in the earthern walls of the storm pit under the kitchen with fresh concrete. My enthusiasm for this project lasted until lunchtime. Then I climbed out of the muddy pit, raked spider silk from my hair, showered, ate, and drove into Tocqueville.

I gravitated irresistibly to Dogtown and Jarboe Street, where nothing had changed since my last visit. I parked in front of Byron's blacksmith shop, which seemed as ancient this morning as a Pompeian ruin, and climbed the outer staircase to the second-story landing. I rapped on the door like a claims server, not really expecting anyone to answer.

When the door opened, I stepped back, startled, and so did the woman on the other side, DeLynda Gaye.

"Oh, my God, it's you—Adrienne's boyfriend."

"William Keats."

"Of course. Sorry I forgot your name. It's just that—"

"No need to explain. May I come in?"

"Sure. When you started pounding like that, I thought maybe the police had come back." She opened the door wider, revealing herself dressed as casually as a vacationing high school girl in faded jeans and an untucked blue-and-green flannel shirt. Her hair hung naturally to her shoulders rather than curling onto them like a cider-scented wig of cedar shavings. "Come on in." Barefoot, DeLynda led me in, walking rather than strutting, plainly heading for the sofa on which Byron had nearly strangled me.

I stopped. "Couldn't we sit at the table?"

"Sure." She sniggered, but let me pull out a chair for her. We sat across from each other over a spill of newspaper sections. Its crossword puzzle showed some penciled entries. Noticing my gaze, she flinched. "It pays to increase your word power," she said. "Now, what can I do for you, Mr. Keats? That the vice boys wouldn't bust me for, I mean."

"Or that Adrienne wouldn't turn me into a eunuch for?"

"How would she even know? The babe's not clairvoyant, is she?"

"*Clairvoyant?* You must really dig crosswords. What's happened to you since the last time we talked, DeLynda?"

"Besides Byron's cutting out? Well, my anxiety level shoots up whenever he leaves. So does my IQ, but most guys really don't care to hear about that."

"I might. Right now, just tell me where Byron went."

"The cops asked me that a dozen times. I'll tell you what I told them: I have no idea. I don't think he murdered Polk James, though, and he hasn't contacted me once since skipping town—if he even has."

"What else could have happened?"

"Anything. The same slime who killed Polk James may've dropped Byron down a bottomless well. You or me or Adrienne could follow poor Polk down into it next."

"I doubt that."

"You probably doubted Mr. Bill would entertain a kneeling pic-colo player in the Oval Office." DeLynda folded her arms across her chest, as if to cloture debate.

"So much cynicism so young," I said. When DeLynda snorted in disgust, I changed tack: "Tell me something else. Tell me what you know about Erroll Kingston."

"What I know, I've told you."

"The last time we talked, you told me to remember his name."

"Maybe I did, but the less you know about that major sleaze the sweeter you'll sleep."

"You suggested that Kingston may have had something to do with Olivia's kidnapping."

"Did I? I don't remember. Why would a fatcat in a sharkskin suit kidnap a part-time underling's little girl? He sure as shit doesn't need the money or the aggravation."

"Maybe because the underling asked him to?"

DeLynda got up and walked over to the beaded curtain veiling the hallway. Then, with several strings of beads in her hand, she turned and looked back at me. "Wrong, Mr. Keats. Don't try to pin Olivia's kidnapping on Kingston. You'd do better to ask a gator to guard your ham sandwich. Besides, Byron loves Olivia, he'd never ask Kingston to take the kid anywhere."

"Less about Byron, more about Kingston."

DeLynda thought for a moment. "He grew up in a little town near the Okefenokee, Waycross or Fosterville. That's where I think Byron went whenever Kingston called him—to the swamp. He al-ways came home wearing camouflage and stinking of bug spray."

"The Okefenokee's a four-hour ride. Hunters wear camouflage and bug spray right here in Speece County."

"Maybe they do, but Byron went down to that swamp."

"How do you know?"

The beaded curtain rattled as DeLynda passed through it. She returned a moment later carrying a battered hiking boot, which she tossed onto the table. I picked it up. The steel in the boot's fortified toe showed through the stripped-away leather, and a large portion of its complex tread was missing. *You'd do better to ask a gator to guard your ham sandwich.* It looked as if whoever had worn this boot had stuck his foot under a lawnmower, but of course other possibilities existed.

"Alligator?" I asked.

DeLynda said, "Either a swamp lizard or—"

"Or what?"

"Or Ugly Erroll himself."

"Where did Erroll Kingston grow up?" I asked Nicholas Cooper about thirty minutes later.

"Why do you ask?"

I recounted my conversation with DeLynda Gaye. Cooper sighed exasperatedly. "I know you need a job, Will, but the department's not hiring amateur dicks. In fact, if you keep up this freelance snooping, you could wind up a guest of the county."

"If I've stepped on any of your leads or done anything illegal, arrest me," I said.

"For pity's sake, don't go histrionic on me."

"I mean it. If I've broken the law, arrest me. But I haven't, have I? I'm not asking for secret information. I could probably learn Kingston's entire life history in a few hours at the library, but I thought you could save me some time."

"I can," Cooper said. "The GBI has investigated Kingston on half a dozen counts—from growing cannabis to peddling flesh to money-laundering—without quite putting together a trial-worthy case against him. He's smart."

"But a country boy?"

"Yeah. DeLynda had the goods on his birthplace. Nowadays, Kingston would like most folks to suppose him a native Atlantan, but he was born in Fosterville in Chesser County. Grew up there, went to school there, eventually had a small legal practice there and another in Waycross. A town can't get any closer to the swamp than Fosterville without having tea-colored water trickling through its streets."

"DeLynda thinks Byron may have run back and forth to Chesser County for Kingston."

"She does, huh?"

"Insisted on it. Have you investigated the notion?"

"More than likely," Cooper said. "But I'll telephone Sheriff Donovan in Fosterville and ask him to check it out with an eye to confirming or discounting the possibility."

"Tell Agent Fearing too."

"Of course."

"What else have you got going, Nick?"

"Two dozen other other lines of inquiry. Byron's disappearance troubles us, sure, but he makes a practice of absenting himself and cropping back up a few days later. Try to trust us a little—me, this department, the GBI, the feds."

"Sometimes I wonder why I should."

Cooper slid open a drawer and lifted out a manila envelope. "Maybe this will help." He tossed the packet to me. "Go ahead. Take a look."

I undid the string clasp and withdrew a sheaf of photocopies. In spite of the lack of contrast between the ashen letters and the white paper, Olivia's handwriting jumped out at me, as inspiring as her personal good wishes on a Father's Day card.

Twenty-Five

I took the photocopied notebook back to our farmhouse. Maybe I should have waited for Adrienne to arrive home from work before reading it, but I sat cross-legged in the middle of our living room, held the faintly oily pages in my hands, and let Olivia speak to me:

Oct 26

I have been with Mr. Poke, he seys to call him that, 5 days I think. At first he scared me alot, he smells bad & looks like the gorillas in George of the Jungle. Now he doesn't scare me so much, he smiles & tells me jokes which mostly I don't laff at. I cry alot. I cry on bed, even eating, & before going to sleep. Mr. Poke doesn't like to see me crying at all. He seys it hurts him. He aks what he can do to make me stop it. I tell him to get me some pencels & paper witch he did, he got me this little notbook with pencels red & green.

Give me a kiss, he said then, just to show you don't hate me. I WOULDN'T. Giving somebody something doesn't mean they have to kiss you, especialy if you hurt them before you ask it. Maybe I DO hate him.

This entry occupied two facing pages in the Marble Memo, but Xeroxing the flattened diary had reproduced both on one 8½" × 11" page. The microscopic printing showed Olivia's best effort at compressing her usual sprawling cursive.

Had she known, even in that first week, that her ordeal might last longer than a month, two months, half a year? I hoped that in shooting for endurance Olivia did not let slip any serendipitous opportunity to escape. Terror, if she had ever felt it, had given way at the time of this entry to bewildered tolerance of a stranger who resembled and apparently smelled like an ape.

That Polk James had demanded a kiss from Olivia both outraged and frightened me. Did his request embody the pathetic desire for approval of his evil deeds, or the first sick overture of a child molester? Olivia had resisted it, whatever James meant by it, but did that bode well or ill for her? My hands now shook so hard that I kept reading only with difficulty.

Oct 27

Up til now I have 1. run through mud, 2. rode in a car trunk, 3. slept on hay like Roogy eats. I miss my Mama & also Mr. Will. I miss them alway. I want to ask Mama if she misses me too? Mr. Will, what about you? I bet they miss me the way I miss them. But I can't hear them anser, they're too far away even if they try to speke. The quiet here has insect sounds inside it, still its real real quite.

Often I think of Roogy my pony my friend. Just as often I dream. Roogy runs, she galapps, she stands by my bed & watchs over me like an angle with 4 legs. But I know she is NOT there, just in my dream. I say to her while she stands there—How much do you miss me Roogy Batoon? How much how much how much? She ansers, she winnies. Sometimes then I smile inside.

Oct 28

I feel like a year has crepp by. We move from our first place in Alabama to somewhere esle. Mr. Poke seys to keep the police off balance. This is smart he says. Over & over alot he seys it. He reads magzines or doses while I write in my notbook or try to sleep. We eat 1. crackers, 2. Froot Loops, & 3. other stuff from pakages or boxes.

At night the frogs sound just like they do at our house,

the frogs, the crikets, & all the other scrapey bugs. I hear
critters crash through the woods, even up on the porch.
Or maybe its people looking for me. So Mr. Poke whip-
sers Be quite. I ask him when could I go home & he seys
Maybe never, maybe youll get a new home soon. I don't
like his anser. At all.

Each page of Olivia's diary—the record of her captivity—had pas-
sages, even if only a line or a phrase, that wrenched me apart, snapping my brittle stoicism like a Thanksgiving turkey's pullybone. To
keep reading, I had to hold some pages flat to the floor with my
unsteady hands.

Nov 4
    Tonight the moon glows round through the window
of the litle room where I'm trap beside Mr Poke in the
big one. He snores like Roogy making snores. It makes
me scared. Deers and maybe hungry bears come walking
by. The moon has clouds go over it too. So for a while I
have no lite to write & I must stop.
    Mama I want you or Mr. Will or my Daddy. I want
Roogy to crash through the window & fly me home like
a pretty pony eagle. She is so strong & pretty.
    Mr Will seys the muskrat has courage. Not much mus-
cle or claws or wolf teeth and no turtle shell, just muskrat
courage. I shuld have it too. Why not. Mr. Will seys
anybody small should. What else could I have tonight? I
don't have it though, even if I sing about it real quiet so
Mr. Poke can't hear. The moon shines in like a high
streetlamp shining.

I kept reading, of course. I read about ants trailing through the room
in which Polk James nightly locked Olivia, about how she had to
pee at night through the shanty's gapped floorboards, about thirst
and cold and hunger, and about how Mr. Poke returned after a scary
absence to untie her and present her with a McDonald's Happy
Meal and a warm chocolate milkshake. I read about her growing
fear that she would die when November began to turn really cold

and Mr. Poke neglected to stoke the fire because he was reading his "cutie" magazines or drinking from whiskey bottles arrayed like soldiers on a kitchen shelf in the otherwise slovenly cabin.

Occasionally, according to Olivia, Mr. Poke brought her into the bigger of the two rooms, propped her on his knee, and told her lopsidedly bloodthirsty fairy tales: a version of Hansel and Gretel in which only Gretel survived; a tale of a crippled ugly duckling that grew up not into an elegant swan but an immense sword-beaked heron that slaughtered all those earlier guilty of ridiculing it. He told these stories, Olivia implied, very slowly, as if making them up as he went along—as if, I thought, struggling to shape the inchoate anger inside him. Finished, he kissed her abruptly on the forehead, returned her to her stinking cell, and rattled among his liquor bottles, eventually performing a bungling clog dance around his own prison chamber, where he functioned as both Olivia's warden and his own.

When Adrienne got home, she found me sitting before a stack of facedown pages. Without a word, she picked them up and read them through twice in twenty minutes. She finished this exercise in tears, wiping her face with the backs of her hands and holding her mouth open in an unconscious ploy to keep from choking on her own emotion. I had never seen her look so anguished, but she finally regained control, picked up the final page, and read the last entry aloud with such an aggrieved sense of purpose that, just to listen to her, I had to clutch my own elbows.

" 'Somebody has come. Somebody has found us, but not anybody I want to. He yells at Mr. Poke. He tells him what to do. When he's done yelling I know he'll come into my room and tell me what to do too. Oh muskrat courage, won't you take me home?' "

After writing these words, Olivia must have crouched down and stuffed her Marble Memo and her pencils red and green into her urine-stained mattress, pushing them as far back into the smelly cotton innards as she could reach.

"At least she doesn't mention the shot," Adrienne said. "I don't think I could stand that."

"If she'd waited that long, she'd've never had time to stash her notebook in the mattress."

"Do you think she knew what the killer intended for Polk?"

"How could she?" I said. "But she must have realized that the yelling in the other room meant something more serious than a mere argument between grownups."

"She stayed calmer than I could have."

"Actually, she emulated you," I said. "I'd say all those hours she spent sitting Zen paid off."

Adrienne placed the final sheet facedown on the others. "But you and the *Oz* books taught her—see the final entry?—muskrat courage?"

"Yeah, muskrat courage."

"So we both helped," Adrienne said. "Mom and Dad alike."

Yeah. Mom and Dad alike. How long could we hope to bear such titles? Even on sufferance, as I bore mine?

Twenty-Six

On Saturday, December 5, we left our farm soon after an early breakfast and drove down Corridor Z through Columbus, Albany, and Tifton to Pearson, where we followed U.S. 441 southeast through scrub land bristling with plucked-looking pines, stunted oaks, and, toward trip's end, a patchy groundcover of saw-palmettos. We nosed into Fosterville, the seat of Chesser County, around noon, not yet within sight of the western edge of the Okefenokee but near enough to smell tannic acid, cypress knees, and lizard flesh.

The town boasted two Baptist churches, a Church of Christ, a Methodist church, a trailer park squatting on a shield of dirty white sand, and a cinderblock skating rink where a tattered poster on a padlocked door advertised an event two years past. A new high school with a corrugated tin roof abutted a barbecue joint and a Dairy Queen. Offices for a chiropractor, a real estate agent, and a lawyer specializing in personal injury cases occupied the same frontage as a beauty parlor and tanning salon, a body shop, and a credit union. Strangely for these turpentine flats, the courthouse and jail manifested the redbrick style, with clocktower and fluted columns, more common in upland Georgia counties.

Riding shotgun in her Camry, Adrienne said, "This town feels like a far outpost in some foreign empire."

"Like stepping from your own backyard into a Paul Bowles novel: Bedouins beneath a sheltering sky."

"Yeah." Adrienne's stomach rumbled low. "That last stretch of sword plants got tedious fast."

"Okay," I said. "Let's find somewhere to eat before we drop in on Sheriff Donovan."

On the main drag, we selected a café called the Tupelo Gum. It had customers coming and going, the sort of crowd that has grown up on country-fried steak, mashed potatoes, and turnip greens. Liking such fare ourselves, we parked and entered.

The waitress who sidled up to our booth kept brushing strands of oily brown hair away from her forehead, tucking them behind her ears. No more than twenty-five, she wore a small silver stud in one nostril. Her eyes gazed as far beyond us as Fosterville lies from Atlanta. Maybe she expected some eelgrass Elvis to roar up on a Harley and spirit her off to Mobile for a weekend of gambling and oyster shucking.

Adrienne plucked an old snapshot of Byron from her purse and showed it to the waitress. The photo flattered Byron, who'd posed bare-chested next to an old car. Adrienne had kept it, she told me, because Olivia had once asked her not to destroy or dispose of it. "Have you ever seen this man?"

The waitress glanced indifferently, then reconsidered and took Adrienne's wrist to pull the snapshot nearer. "No, but maybe I'd like to."

"Believe me, you wouldn't." Adrienne gently pulled her wrist free.

"Then why're you all looking for him?"

"Suppose I told you he owes us money," I said.

"I'd ask if you're putting up a reward for our help."

I turned to Adrienne. "So much for civic virtue and simple hospitality to strangers here in Fosterville."

The waitress scratched her jaw with the eraser on her pencil. "Maybe you all'd better order. If there's no reward, I could at least use the tip money."

Adrienne and I exchanged another look. This fey young woman with misapplied eye shadow and the soft beginnings of another chin had just leapt to an unjustified conclusion. Certain now that she would give us no help, we placed our orders—country-fried steak for me, a chef's salad for Adrienne—and sat back to breathe in the low-country ambiance: the scald of Frialator oil, George Jones on the jukebox, and the crude jocularity of several fleshy sunburnt men in overalls, camouflage fatigues, or blue jeans and ill-fitting Sunday dress shirts. A few of the men periodically looked our way, more curious than disapproving, although one beardless Paul Bunyan with a blond buzzcut gave me definite pause.

"Let me see that picture," I said.

Quizzically, Adrienne handed it over. I slid out of our booth and held the photo up.

"Excuse me, folks!" Adrienne lowered her forehead into her hands. "Could I have your attention, please?"

The blond lumberjack at the counter pushed up from his stool and boomed at me over three booths, "If you mean to say grace, mister, you should know that it ain't necessary. Every item on the Tupelo Gum menu comes pre-blessed."

I tried to ignore him. "I wanted to ask you all if anyone in here has seen this man."

The giant at the counter took a wallet from his overall pocket and flipped out a veritable hinged card deck of photographs. "Have *you* seen these youngsters, mister? I've got four big-eyed kids at home and never miss a chance to show their faces to a fellow photo lover."

Many of the diners hooted gleefully. A few shot me at least quasi-sympathetic smirks. "Jimmy Wayne," one of the latter group said, "leave the poor fella be."

"Pardon me," I started again. "I just wanted to—"

"Please, Will," Adrienne whispered. "Sit down."

"Share some pictures around," Jimmy Wayne said. "A noble goal, mister, so long as the half-naked guy in your picture ain't wearing a *thong*. Or less."

"His name is Byron Owsley," I inanely tried to continue. "We need your help to—"

"Because we insist on decent photos around here, not outhouse pinups, female or otherwise."

Our waitress bore down on Jimmy Wayne from the kitchen. "Give the man a break. He showed his picture first, and everybody here's already seen your brood a zillion times."

Jimmy Wayne gave her a mock-chivalrous bow. "Yes'm." He applied a supple reverse flip to his photos, which accordioned into a compact square that he recaptured in his wallet. He grinned at me enormously, like a sack full of possum heads. "Didn't mean to send a hurricane into your hammock, mister, but in Chesser County every tub's got to learn to sit on its own bottom."

What the hell did *that* mean? Our waitress hurried past Jimmy Wayne and set our meals in front of us. Defeated, I slid back into our booth and returned the photo of Byron to Adrienne.

Jimmy Wayne had one last sally: "Sorry, captain. You must feel as left out as the third verse of a Cokesbury hymn. That food should revive you, though." He then sat back down, to resume what looked like a civil conversation with the man beside him.

"Way to go, Sherlock," Adrienne murmured.

We began eating dispiritedly, but the food did perk us back up, and I placed an extra two dollars atop our check. Filing out, we noted that Jimmy Wayne had also left, without trying to regale us again with his photos.

As we walked to our car, a thin young man with the face of a hairless well-groomed otter came down the alley from the rear of the café and snapped his suds-flecked apron to draw our attention. We halted, and the red-armed kid furtively approached.

"Fayelle says you all've got a photo of a guy you're looking for," he said.

Adrienne handed her snapshot of Byron to the dishwasher. He studied it intently, then said, "I seen this dude. Him, or his older brother."

"When?" Adrienne asked him.

"Last spring," the kid said nervously. "He ate right here in the Tupelo Gum. I bussed his table. I remember him because he had a belt buckle like a lizard eating its own tail. Said he forged it himself. I said I liked it. He said he'd make me one. 'Course I never saw him again."

"Where'd he go when he left here?" I asked.

"Into the swamp, I guess. Said he liked to pole himself deep in, to Josiah's Island or some other such place, and listen to the owls talk."

Adrienne pressed him: "Do you remember anything else at all about this man. Did he say if he knew anyone here? Did he talk to anyone else in the restaurant? Please think. A little girl's life may hang in the balance."

"A waitress had to've talked to him, but they get running and don't always pay close attention."

"What about you?" I said.

"Well, just before he left, he claimed he knew the swamp so good there warn't nobody could find him in it if he didn't fancy getting found. Not in a million years."

Sheriff Donovan failed to embody the Wyatt Earp persona that, perhaps, Fosterville could have used. He more closely resembled an effete stockbroker with a perpetual scowl on his catfish lips, the sort who both annoys and disappoints his investors. He stood only a little more than five-and-a-half-feet tall. His starched and creased uniform, everywhere black and tan, fit him as if he had had it tailored in Hong Kong. His office in the rear of the Chesser County Courthouse had the dimensions of an outsized dumbwaiter, but he swaggered around it with a hand on his gun butt and a peppermint candy clacking aginst his teeth.

"Sure, Cooper called me. Even faxed me a photograph of your ex, Ms. Owsley. I haven't had time to frame it yet, but I glance at it occasionally to keep me from obsessing on local cases with a *real* chance of being solved."

"Your attitude could use an adjustment," I said.

Donovan stopped pacing and faced me. "So could my salary. So could our departmental budget."

Adrienne said, "We don't want much, Sheriff Donovan—a little of your attention. A man at the Tupelo Gum told us he saw Byron here in town last spring."

"Eight or nine months ago. Tourists happen. Not many of them make a habit of revisiting Fosterville, though."

"Byron's no tourist," I said impatiently. "He told the man at the café that he could lose himself in the swamp if he wanted."

Donovan laughed. "Hell, no trick to that. The Oke'll help you every step of the way. You've heard the story of the drunk looking for his lost keys at night? He does it under a lamppost because he can see better there. So mount your manhunt for Byron in Alabama or Massachusetts. He's lived in those states too, and the light's probably better in both of them."

"Look—," I began.

"You look, Mr. Keats. The swamp comprises almost five hundred thousand acres. The National Wildlife Refuge the feds carved out of it hits almost four-fifths of that. Which thousand acres do you want to wade into first? Start today. I can give you the name of a woman over in Eppley who breeds bloodhounds."

Adrienne said, "A well-trained group of searchers—"

"Stop! We have no warrant for Byron Owsley. Nor does he rank officially among the missing. And you want to send in the National Guard and the Boy Scouts?"

"In lieu of your department?" Adrienne said. "Sure."

"Even professionals can bungle around for months," Donovan said angrily. "Take the FIBs looking for Eric Rudolph in the Nantahala, which is about the Okefenokee's size."

"If nothing else," I said, "couldn't you just examine the entry points nearest Fosterville?"

"There are dozens!" Donovan clacked his peppermint and wiped his bottom lip. "And you can count the same number around Folkston, Waycross, or Fargo—to no avail. Forget it."

A logging truck growled through town, its gears ratcheting shrilly. The smell of either a paper mill or rotting peat moss drifted into the airless room. Donovan waved one hand, as if to sweep the stench away.

"Go home, folks. Go back to Tocqueville and let Cooper, the GBI, and the feds continue doing their jobs. If you keep trying to steal their thunder, Mr. Keats, eventually you'll take a lightning bolt up the butt."

I ignored this crudity. "Do you know Erroll Kingston?"

"Why in God's name," said Donovan, staring at me hard, "have you asked me about Erroll Kingston?"

"He comes from here. Byron may have worked for him."

"And?" said Donovan haughtily.

Adrienne said, *"And* if Kingston ever comes back to Fosterville, Byron just might come with him."

Donovan stalked to his desk and fell into his chair, his pot belly—actually more a mixing bowl—bulging against his belt. From an ashtray bearing the legend "Panama City, World's Whitest Beaches," he fumbled a candy, then unwrapped it and popped it into his mouth.

"Kingston grew up poor in the shadow of timber company land. By twelve or thirteen, he hunted and fished weekly in the swamp, the story goes, and a timber company bigwig hired him as a guide for business visitors. Kingston took advantage of this break—worked hard, studied hard. His benefactor sent him to university, where he did well enough to get into law school. He came home, practiced here and up in Waycross, acquired shares in the timber company, scooped up some land in various fire sales, and made some powerful friends. But he never stopped hobnobbing with alligator wrestlers and rattlesnake handlers. He liked such folk as well as he did bank presidents and timber tycoons.

"Fifteen years ago," Donovan went on, "my predecessor, A. W. Boatwright, investigated Kingston for suspected marijuana growing and cocaine smuggling, as well as for poaching and white-slavery connections. Boatwright went after Kingston mostly on rumor and circumstantial evidence, though, and he could never prove a damned thing. A year or so later, Kingston left Chesser County to start some sort of multicorporation in Atlanta. He comes back a couple of times a year to lollygag in the Okefenokee, hunting and boozing and whatever. Rejuvenating himself, they say."

To the sheriff's quick history, I added DeLynda Gaye's account of Kingston's visit to the Glass Cat, assembling a portrait of an unpleasantly powerful but not necessarily evil human being. "It's a rags-to-riches story," I said. "The American dream. So why does the guy spook everybody so bad?"

"He never spooked Boatwright," Donovan said. "But Boatwright should've probably let Kingston spook him."

"Why? What happened to Boatwright?" Adrienne said.

"Six or so months after Kingston moved to Atlanta, Boatwright died in an auto accident. The brakes on his patrol car failed on a high-speed chase up Highway 441."

"And you suspected foul play?" I said.

"Damned straight. You see, Mr. Keats, those brakes went out on the evening after a full vehicle inspection."

Twenty-Seven

We drove ten miles up State Highway 177 to Stephen C. Foster State Park. After paying the two-buck parking fee, we walked around aimlessly near some primitive cabins and a sort of marina from which excursion boats and canoes launched expeditions into the swamp's cypress-edged, Darjeeling-hued reaches. But we had no time to go in very far before nightfall and, in any case, no one to help us navigate the watery prairies.

Forlornly eyeing the boats in the marina, I understood that we had planned no better than kindergarteners. The one positive point about our quixotic mission was that, in early December, we had few gnats or mosquitoes to chivvy us as we stood lamenting our lack of foresight.

Meanwhile, the park brooded about us like a kingdom under a spell, Spanish moss hanging like hoary beards and cloud reflections sculling through the water like empty dugouts.

With one bleary-eyed stop in Dawson for Subway sandwiches, we drove back to Tocqueville and arrived at twenty minutes to midnight at the farm on Antioch Church Road. I made a quick visit to Roogy Batoon, waking her when I flicked on the stable's lights. I stood beside her, murmuring endearments, then realized that she had gone back to sleep afoot and that I would join Roogy in vertical slumber if I did not join Adrienne in our own bed horizontally. As soon as I'd lain down beside her, in fact, a vast impenenetrable swamp opened out in my starless mind.

.   .   .

Nicholas Cooper telephoned us on Sunday afternoon. For the first time in months, I had gone that morning to the Baptist church in Mountboro to hear Hutchinson Payne deliver one of his laconic, judiciously reasoned sermons. Adrienne had remained on the farm, taking care of chores and then retiring to her *zendo*. Her zeal for sitting reminded me of the legend of Bodhidharma's nine years in a cave, after which superhuman stint his legs fell off. I hoped that Adrienne's legs, and I as their chief admirer, escaped this ignoble fate.

Even though Hutch had that very morning preached withholding judgment until one had all the facts, Cooper's cheery "hello," in combination with Adrienne's isolation upstairs, irked me, and I barked, "Damn it, Nick, this call'd better contain something uplifting!"

"I've asked both Stratford and Agent Fearing about giving Polk James's impounded truck back to his mother."

My silence lengthened.

"Will? You still there?"

"This news is supposed to put wind beneath my wings?"

"Think about it. Alice-Darlene will have something tangible of Polk's. She'll have transportation again."

"Do you really regard such charity as policework?"

Cooper waited a moment before replying. "I guess so. Doesn't it strike you as uplifting?"

How could I reply to that? I had wanted Cooper to tell me that someone had found Olivia alive and unharmed. Instead, he had told me of a favor that he wanted to do for the dead kidnapper's bitter and self-deluded mother.

"Earth to Will, Earth to Will—"

"What about the truck as evidence? What about the integrity of the whole damned investigation?"

"We've crawled that truck two dozen times, from grille to tailgate. We've dismantled and reassembled it. Now Polk James is dead, and the perpetrator of the relay kidnapping—Fearing calls it that—has almost certainly never put a foot in Polk's blue pickup. Why *not* give it to Alice-Darlene?"

I remained silent.

With audible heat, Cooper said, "Unless you think we should seize it for victim compensation?"

"No," I said, shamed. "Give it to her."

"I just didn't want you and Adrienne to think we'd cut you all out of the loop," Cooper said more gently.

"Thanks."

"Meanwhile, the case proceeds better than you might suppose."

"Sure," I said.

"Nothing else for now. Sorry for the intrusion." Cooper hung up, like a gentleman.

After a while, I did too.

On Monday, the fifty-seventh anniversary of the raid on Pearl Harbor, I awoke feeling similarly strafed and battered. Given the inescapable burden of Olivia's absence, Adrienne went off to school as cheerily as I could have hoped, kissing me full on the mouth and encouraging me to have a good day.

But my gut ached with an intermittent throbbing, and an old ligament tear in my knee registered sharp twinges at capricious intervals. I knew these pangs had a psychosomatic origin, but that knowledge failed to dispel them. Knowledge is power only if you know how to use it. An unarmed sailor on a U.S. carrier, dodging machine-gun fire from a Japanese Zero, faces a clearer course of action than I did. Despite the eminent peril to his life, I envied that phantom sailor. My joblessness felt as conspicuous as a dose of leprosy, and as shameful.

I did have one plan, but it scared me. It scared me so much that it kicked my physical symptoms up an order of magnitude. Even in the safety and solitude of my own house, I had begun to hobble around like a crippled basketball guard with shin splints and a bad case of food poisoning.

About 10:30 A.M., the telephone rang again. Moving from one chair back to another, I picked it up on the last ring before the answering machine would have taken over. Mrs. Lapierre, my boss at Oakwood Elementary before budget cuts eliminated my position, came on the line.

"William, good news." She told me that Community in Schools, a program funded by the state and various local enterprises, had just lost an employee in a counseling slot. "Do you have any interest in interviewing for the position?"

"Of course," I said. "When?"

"On Thursday morning, in the old administrative building on Cofield Bridge Road."

"Give me a few specifics about the job."

"Brace yourself. CIS has even fewer financial resources than Speece County. If Ocie Lee Degginger decides she likes you, you'll take a pay cut for performing services almost identical to your old duties. And you'll work summers in several community programs."

"I can handle that. How big a pay cut?"

"Eight thousand dollars."

I whistled. "Why not just make the job an unpaid volunteer position?"

"Does the money matter all that much to you now?"

I thought about that. "No, not really."

"Plan to interview with Ocie Lee on Thursday at ten. I'll set it up for you."

"Thanks. Would you call me Wednesday to remind me?"

"Absolutely. Ocie Lee despises tardiness." I heard a chair scrape. Then Mrs. Lapierre said, "Good luck. If you get the job, I'll do all I can to have you assigned to Oakwood. You'll have your old office back."

My windowless broom closet. Hallelujah. In the background noise on our line I heard a teacher page Mrs. Lapierre over the intercom. Quickly, I said, "Will taking the CIS job keep me from taking the next permanent school position?"

"Quite the contrary. Will, I've got to go. My blessings on you and Adrienne both."

This remark constituted Mrs. Lapierre's only acknowledgment, veiled or otherwise, of our plight. But I could hardly blame her. We had one child in jeopardy; she had scores.

When she got home, I told Adrienne about the possibility of recovering my career as an elementary school counselor. She may have deduced this news, however, from the fact that I had brought out from storage all of the hand puppets—Paloma the Penguin, Frederica the Ferret, Windy the Troll, etc.—which I used along with my ventriloquial skills to counsel children. In fact, I had arrayed them in a line to meet her as she entered the house. For my sake, the news delighted her. Even the huge salary drop struck her as of no real consequence. Besides, eight thousand less a year looked good next to an infertile goose egg.

"How will you like it," I said, "if I have to work this summer and you don't?"

"No problem. Olivia and I will travel. Disney World again, maybe a trip to the ancestral Thompson estate. How does a cycling tour of the English Lake District sound?"

"I hope you have an independently wealthy boyfriend."

"Oh, I do. Sort of. And soon enough he'll have a job of his own again."

"Lucky fella." I leaned forward and kissed her.

"Whoa. Won't dinner burn?"

"Not unless the pizza chef at Domino's falls asleep."

Later in the evening, I told Adrienne an egregious lie about having to drive to Atlanta tomorrow to take care of some banking business related to my sister's trust fund.

Adrienne told me to enjoy my trip, maybe the last I could make before my Community in Schools job made me a day laborer again. I said I would, mentioning side trips to a favorite bookstore and to a tavern near Emory for roast beef and ale.

Not once, however, did I mention Erroll Kingston.

Twenty-Eight

In our Greater Atlanta telephone directory, I had looked up Erroll Kingston. No private listing existed, but no one could fail to see the bold-faced entry for "Kingston Ventures," whose address in Marietta, north of the city, I wrote down on a business card and stuck in my wallet. I had also mentally mapped out a route from Antioch Church Road that would deliver me swiftly to the front door of Kingston's headquarters.

So far as I knew, no one in the FBI, the GBI, or the Speece County Sheriff's Department viewed Kingston as any sort of suspect in Olivia's disappearance. But DeLynda Gaye had tied Byron to him in some ambiguous context; a dishwasher in Fosterville swore that he'd seen Byron there in Kingston's hometown; and the sheriff of Chesser County had virtually indicted Kingston for drug trafficking and the assassination of the only law-enforcement officer who had dared go after him. Who knew what other scabby activities Kingston engaged in?

Because I couldn't rule out kidnapping, I had decided to go see him. I didn't expect him to answer a direct question truthfully, but merely hoped my presence would startle him into some gaffe or quasi-admission that might jar the investigation out of the numbing stasis into which, in my view, it had fallen. And I prayed that my well-intentioned meddling brought no harm to Olivia.

In the pickup, I rehearsed what I wanted to say to a man with more power than anyone I had ever met. My father had wielded both authority and influence, but not to the extent that Kingston could apparently swing his; and Skipper Keats, all his double-dealing and self-seeking aside, had regarded guns with the same distaste that I did. So I traveled scared.

Cruising on I-85, I passed Turner Field, shot through the tunnel below the capitol dome, and hurtled toward the dormitory ramparts of Georgia Tech, skyscrapers pirouetting in slow motion on every side, the vehicles around me sliding up or back as if on wires. Where I-85 and I-75 divided, I angled into a lane leading to the Northwest Expressway and gunned toward the silver- or ebony-skinned office buildings of Marietta.

Kingston did not hold court in a single office or suite of offices: he owned a formidable tower complex on several acres of Georgia soil reclaimed from the brick and concrete laid down by greedy developers before him. Set about with ginkgo, dogwood, peach, redbud, and crepe myrtle trees, Kingston's grounds also featured Japanese bridges, rock-backed waterfalls, and flower beds sporting both late blooms and hothouse inserts. A pyramidal structure out front— more sculpture than sign—proclaimed the complex "Kingston Ventures." Above this title, a stylized silhouette of a castle and the initials KV in ghostly-fine script reigned as the corporate logo.

Knowing that I often worked better improvising, and fearful that a call would strike Kingston as a warning shot across the bow, prompting him to take off for the Okefenokee, I had not telephoned ahead (as if even a call from the president or a Mafia don would have intimidated him). Maybe he had already coincidentally fled, in which case my trip would prove as fruitless and misdirected as our recent visit to Fosterville.

The visitors' parking area admitted me easily: no guards, no gate, no sullen ticket-taker in a high-tech concentration booth. The lot had so many spaces that every cultist genuflecting at the altar of KV's wealth could have parked there. I found a spot near the central tower, a glass ziggurat with alternating terraces of jade-green and mirrorshade-silver. These surfaces reflected the surrounding landscape, offering the illusion of a distorted world only a membrane away from our own.

In the tower's lobby, I encountered a security kiosk and a series of handsome metal detectors resembling Zen Buddhist torii. I got past the kiosk and the first faintly humming torii simply by smiling and emptying my pockets. Farther on, a young woman in a kelly green pantsuit tended an information counter disguised as a white-marble fortress. Potted ferns as large as beach umbrellas flanked the counter, beyond which gleamed a bank of golden-doored elevators.

"May I help you?" asked the brown-skinned woman at the counter.

"I'm here to see Erroll Kingston."

"Do you have an appointment?"

"Do investors require appointments?"

The comely woman narrowed her eyes. "Your name, please."

"Will Keats. I want to back a project important to Mr. Kingston. I believe he'll make time for me—if, of course, he learns of my arrival."

Speaking into a tiny lapel mike, the woman relayed my request to someone with more authority. She listened to this other party's reply through an earplug, meanwhile staring at me blankly.

Then she said, "Repeat your name, please."

"Will Keats. William Jennings Keats."

Dutifully, she relayed a second question: "Any relation to the late ventriloquist Skipper Keats from Columbus?"

"His son."

She passed this news along and finally said, "Take the central elevator to the twenty-seventh floor."

"Thank you." Rarely had claiming Skipper as my father afforded such relief from anxiety.

It was short-lived. The speed with which the spacious express elevator rose set my stomach rolling. Nor did the prints of jungly Henri Rousseau paintings on the walls, including one I knew as "The Sleeping Gypsy," do anything to calm me.

When the door opened at the top of this ride, I found myself facing an expanse of moss-hued carpet. Original paintings lined the walls, a grabbag show ranging from the representational to the abstract—an Andrew Wyeth farmhouse next to a Pollock-style drip painting, a Mark Rothko beside a Leroy Nieman, along with stuff I couldn't imagine anyone wanting to frame much less own—as if the collector had assembled this show at the urging of twelve different consultants, seven of them blind. Trying to picture how Adrienne's brother, Aaron, would react to such an exhibit, I saw him jabbing a finger down his throat.

"Mr. Keats, hello!"

I turned around.

From the reception area behind me strode a muscular young man in khaki pants and a lime green polo shirt with a castle emblem on its breast. He introduced himself as Troy Blevins.

"Mr. Kingston's got someone in conference." Blevins gestured back toward his desk, then led me toward it, adding, "Could I get you something to drink while you wait."

My dry mouth spoke for me: "How about some water?"

"Sure. Have a seat. I'll be right back."

In his absence, I studied both his palette-shaped desk and the paintings on the wall to its right. If they were meant to impress clients, they must have often done so negatively.

"Here we are," said Blevins, handing me a bottled water. The receptionist had returned with another man, shorter and stockier than he, wearing an expensive charcoal suit and a pewter gray tie, but breaking the crisp line of his clothes by carrying his hands deep in his trouser pockets.

"Mr. Keats, I'd like you to meet Marion Lewis."

"*Monk* Lewis." Lewis flourished a callused hand and shook with me. "The last person who called me Marion was my third-grade teacher. Even she stopped after December." His hunched shoulders and bullet head made him look more like a dandified orangutan than an investment counselor.

Lewis seemed unaware that his chosen name had also belonged to a nineteenth-century Gothic novelist. I declined to break the news to him. However, I noticed that despite his relative youth he had an uneven bald spot on his crown, a tonsure that probably accounted for the nickname. His bare scalp had a creased and leathery look.

"Mr. Lewis, my pleasure."

"Call me Monk. Everyone does—Mr. Kingston, my nephews, this nellyboy here." Troy Blevins smiled tightly. "You told Angela downstairs you wanted to invest some money with us. Exactly which of our ventures did you have in mind?"

"Forgive me for asking, but exactly what is your connection to Erroll Kingston?" I sipped from my water bottle.

Lewis smiled, showing stained horsy-looking teeth. "Ah, a man who likes to play things close to the vest. But you'll soon learn that Mr. Kingston and I keep no secrets from each other. Let's go talk to him."

Abruptly, Lewis seized my elbow in a firm but nonthreatening way and steered me through an arch beyond the receptionist's desk. Here he squired me about a smaller room with lighted antique china cabinets against every wall and a Persian carpet on the floor. The cabinets displayed many different kinds of porcelain ware: trays, plates, and saucers, all on hinged wooden stands; bisque figurines standing unaided; and assorted pilgrim bottles, teapots, bowls, and vases on velvet boxes. Maybe I'd stumbled into a department store bridal registry.

"Some people think of me as Kingston's cat's-paw, Mr. Keats— the second-rate lieutenant of a brilliant CEO."

What did Lewis want me to say? I stared at him neutrally.

"Maybe you think the same thing."

"Forgive me again, Monk, but I've only just met you."

"Look here." Lewis led me to a cabinet showcasing a piece of blue and white porcelain in the shape of a flat-topped globe. The globe rested on a stand whose base resembled an upturned bowl. "Do you know what this is, Mr. Keats?"

"I confess I don't. China isn't a passion of mine."

This sentiment struck a chord with Lewis. "It isn't one of Mr. Kingston's either. He likes paintings. But this shit"—waving at the globe, at the whole display—"turns me on. Funny how one guy can like one thing and another intelligent guy something completely different." He peered at me as if for confirmation.

The moment felt surreal. "I guess it is," I said.

"Mr. Kingston knows paintings, but I know porcelain. I can tell you where each of these beauties came from, how freaking old it is, even the name of the factory or artist who made it. And, believe me, some of those French, German, and Eye-talian fellas had real tongue-twisters for names."

"I'll bet," I said, praying for a savior. None appeared.

Lewis nodded at the globe stand again. "What do you *think* it is. I bet you have no idea."

"Actually, I don't." I took another sip of water.

"Guess," Monk Lewis insisted.

Bizarrely, an image of Oscar Greenaway arose in my mind. "Some sort of fortune-telling device?"

My guess delighted him. "Where in hell did *that* come from? No way!" He spieled as if quoting from a museum catalogue: "It's an eighteenth-century wigstand, made in China for the European trade, decorated in underglaze blue—Ch'ing dynasty, costly as sin." He strutted standing still. "Even Mr. Kingston couldn't tell you more about this shit than I just have."

"Congratulations," I said.

"Thanks. Now, take my advice. Don't talk paintings with the boss. You might embarrass yourself again."

Lewis led me from the china room to Kingston's ornate door, where he rapped out a catchy code. A solenoid clicked, the door swung open, and I quickly set my water bottle on the receptionist's desk and followed Lewis through it.

Kingston's sanctum had nearly the floor space of the china room and the art gallery together. Erroll Kingston sat at a high-end workstation supported by an acrylic pane that rested on two enormous cypress knees. Around the walls, right up to the picture window behind him, ran a series of dioramas displaying animals common to the Okefenokee, from rattlesnakes to whooping cranes to white-tailed deer. Even more unnerving, the articulated skeleton of a fifteen-foot alligator hung from the polarized skylight above Kingston, like a dragon descending on an emperor's throne; this beast clutched in its jaws the skeleton of a smaller animal, maybe a raccoon.

Without looking away from his monitor, Kingston said, "Thank you, Monk."

"I stay, right?"

"Absolutely. We might wish you to fetch us something to eat or drink." Kingston wore a mint green linen shirt with the sleeves rolled up to his forearms, gold lamé suspenders, and a silk tie swirled with grays, greens, and silvers. His swept-back platinum hair had the appearance of a soft gleaming helmet. He clicked the mouse in his hand to exit his software, and looked at me with eyes the color of swampwater. His eyes felt harder and less human than the glass ones peering at us from the dioramas. "Will Keats," he intoned, "son of Skipper."

"And of LaRue," I said. "If you don't mind, I'd prefer to talk to you in private."

"Of course you would. Half the businessmen in Georgia would like to get me alone—and not just to talk. But I think maybe your alleged interest in investing with us conceals an ulterior motive, Mr. Keats. So Monk stays. If you truly wish to put some of your money into one of our ventures, name it now."

The word *ventures* got a lot of play around here. Taking a deep breath, I pondered a reply.

"I'm waiting, Mr. Keats."

"The Glass Cat."

Kingston looked to Monk Lewis, who said, "Your strip club in Columbus."

"Ah." Kingston clucked his tongue. "You think small, William Keats. How would your mother—LaRue?—feel about family money flowing to such an establishment? In fact, I offer no investment opportunity that would repay you a tenth so well as putting it into the search for Olivia Owsley."

This statement stopped my breath. With some effort, I said, "You know about the kidnapping?"

Kingston shrugged. "I make it a point to know about all that happens in my domain, Mr. Keats. Knowledge is not only power, but—potentially at least—salvation. Your story interested me personally. I recall the late Skipper Keats and Dapper O'Dell with considerable warmth."

Warmth did not seem a salient Kingstonian attribute. "Thank you," I said. "Does talking to me mean you'll try to help us find Olivia?"

"However I can, of course. But beyond posting a reward—does fifty thousand strike you as adequate?—the extent to which I can offer you all any genuine help remains hazy. No one, you see, has ever mistaken me for the police."

Even realizing that Kingston's failure to seat me—or any visitor?—was meant to shorten my stay, I persisted: "May I ask you a couple of questions?"

He leaned back showily in his chair. "Ask away."

"Do you know Byron Owsley?"

"The kidnapped girl's real daddy? No, I don't. Why should I?"

"Byron's girlfriend says he worked for you."

"In what capacity, Mr. Keats? Cutting my lawn, polishing my Lexus? Forgive me, but my reputation as a master of details aside, I don't know everyone who works for me in *this* tower. Monk, have I ever mentioned Byron Owsley to you?"

"No sir."

Kingston made a so-there-you-have-it gesture, then pointedly glanced at his watch.

"Then do you know Byron's girlfriend, DeLynda Gaye? She worked at your club under the stage name Ruby Slippers."

"Her I *do* recall." A saurian glint lit Kingston's pupils. "For all the most obvious reasons."

"You always remember the girls," Monk said supportively.

"Oddly," Kingston went on, "she never chose to introduce me to her boyfriend. For reasons just as obvious, perhaps."

"Adrienne and I have heard—from DeLynda Gaye, among others—that Byron's made several trips to Fosterville, your hometown." I had no intention of telling him about our quickie trip there on Saturday.

Kingston looked up at the skeletal alligator, as if beseeching it to devour me. "That implies a link to me about as much as two vacations to Rome mean that one is on intimate terms with the Pope, Mr. Keats."

I said, "Now, there's a megalomaniacal comparison."

Kingston lurched forward in his immense chair. "Don't try to psychoanalyze me, you ignorant asshole!"

This outburst rocked me, but I worked not to show it. Off to my left, Lewis took two steps nearer.

Then Kingston willfully reined in his anger. "Simply because you've read newspaper articles about me, don't assume you know me. *Nobody* knows me, not even Marion here, who seldom ventures far from my side unless I command it or grant him permission."

"I apologize," I said.

"Unless you want me to reconsider offering that reward, maybe we should cut short this interview."

Quickly, I said, "Skipper also hated clients who wasted his time.

I came for Olivia's sake, but Skipper would have encouraged me to invest some of my inheritance in enterprises as aggressive as yours. I wasn't lying about my interest in Kingston Ventures."

Kingston leaned back again, as if the mention of Skipper had appeased him. "But you didn't want to invest in the Glass Cat, did you? So what about Shalimar Oil? Or Alberta Kelleher's Patchwork Creations? Or—" He stopped himself. "Monk, get Mr. Keats a brochure detailing our investment opportunities. I don't have time to *recite* them."

"Yes sir." Lewis found such a brochure in a display rack on a nearby diorama and brought it to me.

To me, Kingston said, "Read about our holdings, pick something you like, and telephone the investment number in the brochure." He smiled, if only with his mouth. "Now, if you can find your own way out, I need to confer privately with Monk."

"Yes sir." With no other option, I retreated.

"Oh, Mr. Keats." I looked back. "I may have forgotten Byron Owsley, if I ever knew him. You, however, I won't forget."

As soon as I neared his desk, Troy Blevins looked up, smiled, and handed me my water bottle. "A lot of folks coming out of there need to replenish their vital fluids."

"Thanks."

"I guess Monk gave you the grand Fiesta ware tour?"

"You bet. He must not dust his collection often himself or few pieces would remain intact."

Blevins laughed. "No argument there."

I finished my lukewarm water and set the bottle down. I waved my brochure. "Give me a tip. Which *venture* has made Mr. Kingston the happiest lately?"

Blevins crossed his well-buffed arms. "Mr. Keats, I'm not an investment counselor. I—"

"Please, one no-fault tip, a clue for the clueless."

"Strictly confidentially," Blevins said, "I'd suggest Patchwork Creations."

"Mr. Kingston likes that one?"

"Big-time. It's a fashion firm over in Little Five Points. He thinks

Alberta Kelleher, the woman who runs it, an absolute genius at couture. Her new line this fall blitzed everyone."

"No kidding? How so?"

"Miles and miles of genuine lizardskin."

Twenty-Nine

W alking across the parking lot of Kingston Ventures, I tried to convince myself that the links I had mentally forged among Byron, Kingston, and Alberta Kelleher—with Troy Blevins's final remark as my anvil—really existed.

My best arrangement of the links: Byron ventured into the Okefenokee at Erroll Kingston's behest to obtain skins, hides, and plumage from protected species, products Kingston then funneled through underlings to the KV subsidiary, Patchwork Creations, and its head, Alberta Kelleher. Crazy? My paranoia run amok?

I didn't think so, and because I still had the whole afternoon ahead of me, I decided to visit Kelleher and ask her point blank if she knew Byron. Suddenly, my interview with Kingston, which I had considered a dead loss in spite of his self-congratulatory offer of a reward, seemed another step along the path to enlightenment. Or so I told myself while checking the brochure for the address of Patchwork Creations.

Back in my truck, I headed south on I-75/I-85. I swung left at Exit 100, then drove down Ponce de Leon to Moreland Avenue, hung a right, and ran straight to Little Five Points, an erstwhile hippie district now mostly given over to black-clad androgynes with dyed hair, body piercings, and such an aloof ethereal air that you almost expected them to sublime away, like spilled ouzo.

I parked on Euclid, near the Variety Playhouse, and walked back up to Moreland. Aging punks and credit-card-toting trustafarians strolled through the odors of baking pizza, evaporating wine, and fresh dog crap. This unholy mix of smells made it easier to ignore my mounting midday hunger.

Soon, I stood in front of Patchwork Creations. Kelleher's boutique occupied the ground floor. Its display window hosted one mannequin: a figure with a clock head, a drum torso, a baseball bat and a floppy dryer-duct for arms, and a welded chain and a wicker column for legs. In the second-floor window stood a conventional tailor's dummy, naked, hinting at the atelier or design studio that sprawled above the trendy shop.

Unlike Kingston Ventures, Patchwork Creations had virtually no security. Opening the broad glass door, I heard a jingle akin to that of temple bells. I ambled past displays of handbags, women's shoes, and belts; past racks of feathery dresses, leather skirts, geometrically patterned carcoats, and plush fur stoles and capes: a fashion menagerie.

A young woman dressed like a zebra intercepted me at a junction of striped scarves and immense hats with parrot plumes or snakeskin bands. "Ah, your first visit to our shop, I see."

"How can you tell? Don't I look savage enough?"

The clerk—an alert, white-tressed anorexic—stood back to appraise me. "You definitely haven't gotten in touch with your inner animal self yet. Maybe we can help you."

"No offense, but I may need some heavy-duty consultation to accomplish that. Any chance of my seeing Alberta Kelleher?"

The clerk turned to shout up a set of plank stairs at the rear of the store. *"Alberta! Guy down here wants to talk to you!"*

Twenty seconds passed. "Maybe she's busy."

"Well, of course. She's always busy. She's Alberta Kelleher."

Someone in an acetate swirl of scarlet, emerald, and peacock skirts began to descend the steps. Four steps down, she bent at her ample waist to disclose the face of a jowly henna-haired woman in her late fifties or early sixties. Her eyes glittered like bits of blue broken glass.

"Don't make me come all the way," she said. "Three up-and-down trips a day is my limit, and I've already made two."

I said, "No, ma'am, I won't."

When she clomped back up in heavy shoes that her long skirts had concealed, I followed.

Her studio-cum-workshop spread out across a wide column-studded bay, the whole enterprise humming like a dynamo to which Kelleher, as chief engineer, made continual minor adjustments, scurrying from one employee to another. Seamstresses labored at sewing machines, assistant designers pored over photographs and patterns. Sloping shelves organized hundreds of bolts of fabric; garment racks on wheels held finished creations; several flat bundles of hides and a couple of plastic trashbags spilling feathers composted beside the windows. Finally, Kelleher broke away from a fretful employee and led me to her desk in a rack-bordered niche, where she waved me to a stubby wooden stool.

Once we'd both sat down, she said, "You don't appear to be in the rag trade. What do you want?"

Her bluntness amused rather than irked me. "What if I *were* in the rag trade, a competitor on a spying mission?"

Kelleher reached over to touch my cheek, not flirtatiously, but to remove a gold sequin that clung, now, to her fingertip. Laughing, she said, "Dear, I doubt you know a seam from a gusset. What could you possibly report back to anyone?"

"Maybe the source of your exotic materials."

"I see." Kelleher pulled back from me. "You're a muckraker from the *Journal-Constitution* or a TV station. You imagine we're hiding some scandalous story involving the poaching of lizardskin, leather, and feathers, right?"

"No, ma'am, I—"

"What happened during sweeps week? Did your segment on hookers with high IQs bomb? You damned *germalists* make me sick. I should tell Ian to kick your ass down the stairs." She shoved a garment rack aside, revealing a black man in a plum-colored turtleneck at work pasting up a catalogue. *"Ian!"* Despite his prissy shirt, Ian looked like a sparring partner for Evander Holyfield.

"Ma'am, I'm not a 'germalist' of any kind. My name is Will Keats. My interest in your business touches only on its connection to Erroll Kingston."

Kelleher waved Ian off. "Okay. Tell me more."

"Does Kingston ever help you secure your exotic materials?"

Annoyed, she said, "Why do you want to know, Mr. Keats?"

"Odd as this may sound, the information could have some bearing on the recovery of a missing child."

Kelleher literally harumphed, then looked away from me, mulling this disclosure. "Can you really imagine Erroll Kingston hauling a bag of egret feathers up those steps and into this place?" she said finally.

"Not Kingston himself. But a henchman or two, yes."

" 'Henchman'? My, you have a melodramatic turn of mind."

"You haven't actually told me no, Ms. Kelleher."

She peered at me sourly. "You're reaching, Mr. Keats. All that Patchwork Creations acquires in the way of fabric, skins, or accessories, we obtain from legitimate licensed suppliers."

"Do any of your raw materials come from South Georgia?"

"As in the Okefenokee? A few maybe, but none from the portion set aside as a refuge. Did you know that American alligators don't rate full protection anymore? They're flourishing. And we never make use of caiman skins. Poachers have completely extirpated the creatures in some areas of the Amazon and Orinoco River basins. I insist on environmental responsibility in the design and fashioning of all our garments."

"Forgive me, ma'am, but how do you enforce that?"

Kelleher lifted a pile of paperwork from her desk and dropped it with a rude *thuuunk*. "The documentation on these shipments is exhaustive. We deal only with countries and organizations that have subscribed to CITES, the Convention on International Trade on Endangered Species. We would never patronize anyone harvesting in a wildlife refuge like the Okefenokee. In fact, most of our gator skins come from farms in Florida."

"And the feathers?"

Kelleher laughed. "The majority are from poultry. More exotic sorts come from unprotected cattle egrets or waterfowl. I've never handled feathers from endangered swamp species. No kingfishers, or herons, or, God forbid, ivory bills."

"God forbid." Her defense stymied me.

"Tell me, Mr. Keats: How does any of this information bear on the recovery of a missing child?"

"It's simply a hunch. Maybe her abductor's carried her to a forbidding place like the Okefenokee, and maybe the culprit works for Kingston."

"He'd have to *know* the place to take the child there. Do you have a suspect in mind?"

"Actually, I do."

"Not Kingston himself, I hope. Most Atlantans, including me, regard him as a community asset; a benefactor."

"That opinion doesn't translate to real innocence."

Kelleher's bottle-blue eyes flashed at me. "Don't you know, Mr. Keats, that the strong appearance of innocence often serves a business person better than innocence itself?" Before I could answer or even parse this remark, she shook the garment rack again and shouted across the studio, "Dear God, Brittany, that'll never do! Recut! Recut!"

As at Kingston's tower, I let myself out.

My hunger overcame my reluctance to eat in Little Five Points, and I bought two slices of pizza and choked them down sitting in a narrow booth. All about me scruffy student types lifted beers and laughed at jokes beyond my comprehension.

Returning to Tocqueville, I decided that no matter what Alberta Kelleher had told me, Patchwork Creations almost certainly made use of contraband materials—with or without her knowledge. Some of them undoubtedly came from Waycross, Folkston, Fosterville, and other small towns in the vicinity of the Land of the Trembling Earth. Whether this inference placed me any closer to recovering Olivia, however, I had no clue.

Somehow I had managed to accomplish both my interviews and my jaunt back home before the end of the school day. I drove straight to Nicholas Cooper's office and found him at his desk poring over a series of reports. A picture of painful concentration, he looked frozen in his chair, one elbow glued to his desktop. He leapt when I cleared my throat.

"Lord! I'm going to strangle Bonnie for not buzzing me when visitors arrive. You nearly gave me a heart attack. What's up, Will?"

I told him of my visits to Kingston and Kelleher. As I spoke, his mouth tightened.

"You have the sense of a drainpipe spider," he finally said. "Less, maybe. Stay away from Erroll Kingston. He's a sorry piece of work, even if his neighbors in the Big Peach love him. If he ever takes it into his head to mess with you, Will, you'll regret it forever."

"What about his posting a reward?"

"Just more headaches. Every kook in the country will barrage us now." Cooper's lower jaw slid back and forth on the oil of his repressed fury. "You might as well make a pallet on your porch for Oscar Greenaway."

"Have you heard anything from Fearing?"

"Not much. He stays in the field. The FBI forensics people have a deformed bullet, but no casing, that matches a bullet from an unsolved murder in Birmingham. No gun yet, though."

"What does that mean, Nick? It hardly sounds like progress."

"Maybe it isn't. But we'll make even less if you continue your manic amateur detecting. Go home, Will."

I drove home. Adrienne arrived just as I pulled in. We walked arm in arm to the house.

While we made dinner, I recited my glib jury-rigged fictions about the financial business I had transacted for LaRue. I also mentioned dropping in on Cooper, and how he still frowned on our efforts to assist the investigation. I let Adrienne believe that Cooper's current irritation stemmed from my telling him of our Saturday visit to Fosterville.

"In other words," Adrienne said, "Cooper now considers you and me part of the problem, not part of the solution."

"Exactly." A witty epigram from a wise fellow Georgian, a bipedal possum named Pogo, sprang to mind, and I said it aloud: " 'We have met the enemy, and he is us.' "

Thirty

On Wednesday evening, as I had asked her to do, Mrs. Lapierre phoned to remind me that I had an interview next morning with the director of the Community in Schools program, Ocie Lee Degginger. I thanked her and went upstairs to look for a presentable suit of clothes. Laundry and dry-cleaning had not topped very many of our recent to-do lists. Adrienne followed me.

"Don't let the pay cut dampen your enthusiasm," she said.

"Listen, I just want to work. This job could eventually feed me back into the Speece County school system with restored benefits and pay. I have to do well tomorrow."

"You'll ace the interview. Stop worrying."

"Mrs. Degginger has other candidates, and whatever pressure she feels from Mrs. Lapierre on my behalf could boomerang. She may resent me so much that she selects someone less qualified, just to signal her independence."

"Is your description white-counselor code for 'another black'?"

"God forgive me, maybe it is. No one wants to talk about what all of us already know in our guts, that race factors in to folks' decisions. I'll say this, though: In Mrs. Degginger's position, I'd probably want to slap me down too."

"I know Ocie Lee. She's a good woman. She'll pick you because you deserve it." Adrienne draped her arms over my collarbones as I rummaged through my side of the chifforobe.

Moving the first padded hanger, I suddenly recalled the back of the wardrobe's opening out onto a vast stormy plain, a dream memory that flashed like lightning but that did not strike again.

Oblivious, Adrienne said, "Would you like me to rehearse the interview with you?"

I found a pair of pleated navy trousers. "Right now, I think I just need these ironed."

Adrienne kissed my neck and slowly withdrew her embrace. "All right. I do that too."

I reached Ocie Lee Degginger's office on Old Cofield Road a full thirty minutes early. The secretary, a pretty young woman sporting elegant cornrows, looked at me every now and again as I shifted in my chair. Her expression conveyed mild surprise at the presence of a white male in an office where African-Americans made up three-quarters of the staff and clients. Every time she looked at me, I smiled self-effacingly. I needed all the allies I could recruit.

I felt more anxiety than I had expected, my feet as cold as iced flounders, my intestines coiled like serpents around a staff. Reassurance lay in the facts that my interview represented a mere formality and that it would deposit me in a job that I had already performed well. But whether my raw disquiet stemmed from my sense of myself as a brusque intruder, or from the oddity of sitting in a bona fide work environment again, or from my oppressive unrelenting awareness of Olivia's seven-week absence, I could not definitively say. Probably the last.

Because I missed Olivia. I missed her with a terrible somatic ache, dreading that no matter how long or hard we searched for her, we would never hold or even see her again. To escape this dread, I would have gratefully left my body, removing to a plane of spirits or shadows. An observer peering into that waiting room, a person ignorant of my angst's origins, would have seen only a man in the throes of pre-interview jitters. But a saint, a man as perceptive, say, as Roshi Rakestraw, would have penetrated to the true source of my disquiet: the fear that all I most cherished on this material plane—Adrienne, Olivia, my work—would leap irreclaimably out of my grasp into a limitless void.

"Show some muskrat courage, Will." I murmured this with just enough volume to provoke a strange look from the secretary. "Song lyric," I told her, improvising. " 'Muskrat Courage, Won't You Take Me Home?' Ever heard it?"

"No sir. Don't think I ever have."

A short while later, she led me into Mrs. Degginger's office and shut us up in it together for my interview.

An elongated wooden pyramid with a brass nameplate on the side facing me stretched across the front of Mrs. Degginger's desk. The woman behind the desk did not immediately look up, but motioned me into a chair and slammed a staple into a sheaf of papers with what struck me as sublimated anger. The stapler jumped under her palm like a mechanical toad.

In her lavender suit, with a blouse of intermixed ivory and violet, Mrs. Degginger seemed actively seeking to smuggle spring into early winter. She had at least ten years and fifteen pounds on me, but maneuvered behind her desk with an athelete's agility. For almost three minutes she shuffled papers, fussed with manila folders, opened and closed drawers. I felt like an empty computer carton awaiting disposal.

Finally, I said, "You don't really want me for this position, do you?"

Ocie Lee Degginger looked at me. "Did somebody speak?"

I raised my hand to chest height. "Will Keats."

"Ah, Will Keats." She laced her fingers and set her hands on her desk like a rock. "The man who pulls strings."

"Sometimes I use puppets in my work, but never the kind with strings."

"Please don't joke, Mr. Keats. You may or may not do fine in this position. You've got a nice record and strong references, but I don't like anyone telling me beforehand I *have* to take somebody. It sort of nullifies an interview's purpose, don't you think? It turns me into a rubber stamp."

"Interview me. If I don't pass muster, hire someone else."

"I may just do that. Never mind that the superintendent of schools, the director of counselors, and some other bigheads would fall on me like a mortarless chimney." She set her hands before her, showing me ten hard scarlet nails. "Okay, Mr. Keats, sit up straight and we'll get started."

I was sitting as straight as I knew how. "Go."

She went. She asked me to evaluate my own strengths and weaknesses, to list for her what I knew about available community resources, to blue-sky a special counseling program that I would implement if I had the requisite time and money, and to tell her forthrightly how well or ill I ordinarily worked as a team member. I said that I scored high in the empathy and advocacy departments, low in the areas of patience and candlestick-polishing. I cited personal contacts in DFACS, the Speece County Lions Club, various Parent-Teacher Organizations, and the business community. I blue-skyed for her about a summer grief camp, where I would work with Tocqueville Hospice and local pastors to counsel kids who had lost people important to them within the past year.

"Can you take coaching?" Mrs. Degginger said when I ran down. "Can you hand the ball off as well as run with it?"

I thought of my many solo flights as a children's advocate at Oakwood Elementary and of my independent sorties as an unlicensed investigator.

"Well, Mr. Keats?"

"Yes, ma'am, I can." Then I qualified that truth: "If I have a good coach."

Mrs. Degginger stared back with the poker face of a Memphis gambler. Then she said, "Thank you for your interest, Mr. Keats. I have three other applicants to see. I'll probably make up my mind over the weekend, but don't expect to hear anything until next Wednesday."

"Should I telephone?"

"If you don't mind, yes." She turned back to her paperwork. "But not before next Wednesday."

Leaving, I realized that my departures from several recent meetings all had a sad common denominator: I had shown myself out each time. Maybe I needed to enlist Adrienne to help me work on my interpersonal skills.

After a dinner of French bread and minestrone soup, Adrienne and I lay on our four-poster talking.

"It looks more and more like a longshot," I said.

"You might feel worse if you get the job. The backbiting and politicking at my school have escalated like mad. You could face the same thing, or worse, with CIS. Some of Ocie Lee's colleagues and staff might actively resent you."

"Well, I'd like a chance to win them over."

We spent twenty minutes elaborating utopian schemes for school reform and interracial harmony, then lay quiet as wind buffeted the trees around Roogy's paddock.

Then Adrienne said, "We've heard nothing from Agent Fearing since Thanksgiving."

"I know."

"What about Cooper and Stratford and their crew?"

"I imagine they're hard at work, but every time I visit their headquarters Buddy Ebsen's favorite detective has his skinny butt planted in front of his Toshiba."

"Maybe we should hire a private investigator."

"Like who?"

"How about that fellow who started the National Alliance for Lost and Stolen Children? He's brought kids home from as far away as Lebanon."

I sat up and studied Adrienne's bright abstracted face. "He specializes in custody cases. He doesn't handle snatches stemming from sheer malignant perversity."

"Maybe Olivia's kidnapping qualifies, Will. Byron's been gone too long now. His disappearance has to bear on what's happened to Olivia. If the police could just find him—"

I cut her off: "I know someone who knows his whereabouts right now."

"Who?"

"DeLynda Gaye."

Adrienne pouted self-mockingly, as if considering this idea. Then she placed a fist on either side of her chin. "So what do you think we should do, Sherlock? Beat it out of her?"

"Visit her. Talk to her. Convince her to tell us more."

"And you want me to go along?"

"Of course, Watson. Don't you have your Sidekicks' Union card handy?"

"I never leave home without it."

· · ·

The following day I telephoned the number for the loft above Owsley's Anvil & Bellows, only to hear a digital voice tell me that BellSouth service no longer extended to that address. Why? I wondered. Had the converted carriage house burned down?

Next, I telephoned Nick Cooper.

"We know exactly what's happened, Will. DeLynda got tired of waiting for Byron to come home. She thinks he's reneged on his promise to support her. She has no income. So she locked up the building, canceled the utilities, and moved away."

"Do you know where?"

"Of course. Back to Columbus, Will. Do you need a road map to her place of employment?"

"Victory Drive," I said without hesitation. "The Glass Cat."

"Good. You'll earn that detective badge yet."

"I—Adrienne and I intend to go see her."

"Of course you do," Cooper said. "Well, have fun. I hear that Friday at the Glass Cat is Ladies' Night."

Thirty-One

As soon as Adrienne got home from work, I told her where we needed to go to question DeLynda Gaye. An undoubtedly sleazy strip club on a two-mile stretch of borderline-legal establishments: massage parlors, sex shops, private photography dens—even illicit cockfighting pits, for all I knew. A demimonde catering to GIs in training, frat boys, and a wide assortment of local men, married or single, with hyperactive libidos.

"If Byron lured DeLynda away from that world," Adrienne said, "he deserves a medal."

"Don't start handing out medals yet. Before he took up with DeLynda, Byron liked to visits those kinds of places himself. He met her in one. I just want you to know what you have in store if you come along."

"Wonderful," Adrienne murmured.

"You don't have to, you know."

She laughed. "You expect to wander unaccompanied through acres of exposed female flesh? Think again, boyfriend."

We ate a light dinner, walked Roogy Batoon around the paddock, took or tried to take naps, then drove the Camry down I-185 into Columbus to the Victory Drive Exit north of Fort Benning. Friday night traffic slithered and swooped around us, headlights muted to pale disks in the glare of the boulevard's signage.

From almost three blocks away, I could see the Glass Cat, a stucco-faced building with a calico paint job, a turret on each corner, and a neon sign incorporating a sinuous prancing cat whose super-long tail scripted the club's name. Dozens upon dozens of automobiles occupied the parking lot, their metal bodies reflecting the kaleidoscopic lightshow around them.

"Do I belong here?" Adrienne suddenly said.

"A woman?"

"A surgically unaltered woman in cotton clothes and flats."

"Well, you do violate several local zoning standards. But I've got to dance with what brung me."

"Thanks for the vote of confidence. Will, you've got to help me out. I feel like I'm crashing a humongous Neanderthal bachelor party."

I pulled into the parking lot. "Would you feel safer staying in the locked car? I'll leave you the keys, and you can even keep the motor running."

"So that I can take off and strand you in some terrible mess when the shit hits the fan? Think again."

"Will do," I said.

I drove past the valet, a skinny kid in jeans and a riverboat gambler's vest, and parked behind the club. I kissed Adrienne on the forehead. Then we climbed out and walked arm in arm to the front. The valet and a stocky Latino bouncer bowed deferentially to Adrienne as we approached the entrance, a door padded in purple vinyl. We paused to study a row of boxed posters on the outside wall, each one depicting exotic dancers in revealing feline getups, as if from an R-rated production of *Cats*. One showbill proclaimed "The Return of Ruby Slippers!" and featured a photo of DeLynda Gaye dressed as a twelve-year-old farm girl in pigtails.

Inside, the posters—more explicit now—marched along a corridor leading to a smiling red-haired hostess clad in a tuxedo jacket, blue fishnet stockings, and sequined high heels. She gave us a lovely but plastic smile.

"We have a ten-dollar cover charge per person, please."

"Isn't a cover charge something of an oxymoron here?" Adrienne said.

"Ma'am?" said the clueless young woman.

I gave her a twenty—obviously, Nick Cooper had been joking about Ladies' Night—and pushed Adrienne into the pulsating club proper. Or improper.

We stood on a gallery with steps leading down at intervals into a table-filled pit, along three of whose walls ranged booths of fake black leather. The stage occupied the remaining wall, a pair of runways projecting from it at sharp angles, two or three brass poles arising from each catwalk. Most of the tables already hosted patrons, who stared glassily from their places or hooted loudly enough to be heard over the migraine-inducing techno music. The noise level reminded me of that of an underground station when two trains arrive at once.

Six young women performed, their movements as machinelike as that of industrial robots. They showed a variety of costumes and flesh. Three still wore the club's trademark feline tailoring, while three had worked down to shiny G-strings. None appeared to be DeLynda Gaye, but the smoke convoluting in the colored lights, as well as the distance between us and the stage, left real margin for doubt.

At my elbow, Adrienne cried, "Those gals had better all have handicapped parents at home, or I'm going to start ranting!"

"Maybe they all have kids whose daddies don't send support payments!" I shouted back.

"Right! Men with snake kidneys for brains!"

For the first time since leaving our farm, I took a close look at Adrienne's outfit: tan loafers, a blue denim halter dress over a white jersey, and a white cardigan decorated with yellow school-bus and red schoolhouse appliqués. She stuck out like Janet Reno at a mob picnic. I took her hand and led her along the gallery.

Moving along it, we encountered several tall wanly lit display cases. Glass figurines of nude women, supernatural-looking cats, or anthropomorphic hybrids of the two filled their shelves. Some of these pieces, including an antique bottle shaped like a sphinx, struck me as aesthetically fine. One good brawl, however, would have reduced the entire expensive menagerie to a few cents' worth of recyclables. That the management had mounted such an exhibit attested to its confidence in its customers or its iron hand with troublemakers.

"Never expected to see an art show here!" Adrienne said.

"You don't think the dancing counts?"

She gave me an exasperated look, and I guided her down the nearest steps. A party of buzzcut GIs barely old enough to drink, and three flushed older men in suits, gave us curious looks as we passed. I saw a table littered with empty glasses, unrecovered tip money, and the hulls of peanuts. I led Adrienne to it and pulled out a chair for her.

She never spoke, but I could read her thoughts: *This place reeks— spiritually, morally, literally.* I could not disagree. The Gag Reflex, which my father had owned with Satish Gupta, had generated similar levels of noise, smoke, and drunkenness, but the Glass Cat's writhing nude dancers imparted to this club a surreal Boschian atmosphere. You half expected beaked devils with tridents to jump out and chivvy everybody on the premises down a lightning-disclosed stairway to Hell.

"Are you sure DeLynda even performs tonight?" Adrienne said, leaning near.

"I telephoned. Mr. Saudek, the manager, told me she has her own spotlight segment"—I checked my watch—"in twenty minutes. He said we could go backstage afterwards to see her."

"By then, we may need eardrum transplants."

A brunette woman in gray tails, a thong, and sorrel stockings came to take our drink orders. I asked for two Rolling Rocks and a basket of party mix. When she returned with these items, she also left a tab for nearly fifteen dollars.

"I hope you have a gullible client footing your expenses," Adrienne said.

"Check your driver's license for her address."

The current set finally ended, with the dancers either slinking offstage like panthers or, in one case, riding a lift to a hidden exit. The piledriving techno music yielded to ballads by Sinatra, Mathis, and Connick at a volume level almost tolerable. But before I could speak to Adrienne again, a fresh-faced blond soldier in his weekend greens approached. His nametag said "Motes." He nodded at me but addressed Adrienne.

"Ma'am, I wanted to tell you how much the guys and I're looking forward to seeing you step out of that schoolmarm getup. I've had a thing for teachers ever since preschool, and that outfit's hotter than a Waxahatchie sidewalk in July."

"Stop," Adrienne said.

"It's okay, ma'am. You deserve the ego boost. All of us think so.

So when you climb up and start unwrapping, you can count on me and the fellas to whoop you right out of your garter belts."

"You really don't want to tell me this."

"Ma'am, we do. It's no trouble to offer a little encouragement to a lady as original—as classy—as you."

"Private Motes, I *am* a teacher."

Motes openly admired her. "Boy, you really know how to stay in character. We can hardly wait." He ambled away, as if he had just kissed his prom date good-night.

Adrienne turned to me. "He thinks I strip here!"

"An honest mistake."

"Listen, that smirk doesn't become you."

"Face it, kid. Teachers just naturally exude sensuality."

"I ought to geld the whole simpering lot of them."

"Do it, tiger." But I pushed the basket of party mix over to distract her, and the tactic worked. She nibbled obsessively, eyeing me as if I were a pod-person who might split open, disclosing another randy army recruit who'd proposition her.

Then the P.A. system cranked up a staticky recording of Judy Garland singing "Somewhere Over the Rainbow," and DeLynda Gaye, as Ruby Slippers, stepped from a gap in the curtains into a traveling spotlight. Along with nearly everyone else in the club, we watched her performance from beginning to end, a series of deft movements resulting in the graceful divestment of article after article of clothing—until she posed at center stage, one leg discreetly in front of the other and one arm thrown back in triumph, naked save for her garters and trademark slippers. Immediately, cheering men crowded forward to stuff the garters with folding money.

"We're doomed," Adrienne said.

I glanced back at her. "What do you mean?"

"That woman spent weekends teaching Olivia to bump and grind. One day we'll wind up in some other sin den watching our daughter take off her clothes for money."

If we're lucky, I thought. Aloud I said, "I seriously doubt that." As DeLynda made her final circular strut before leaving the stage, I got to my feet. "Come on."

Adrienne followed me, and we made straight for the door to the dressing rooms. The Latino bouncer we had seen outside halted us, took our names, and consulted a list on a clipboard.

"Okay," he said. "It's got your names, but one at a time, *por favor.* Glass Cat policy."

Adrienne said, "Surely that applies only to men. You can see we're a couple."

"Don't matter," the bouncer said. "Rules say one customer at a time back there with any girl." He showed us the tiny boilerplate regulations at the top of his list.

Adrienne shook her head in disgust. I asked her if she wanted to go first.

"I only want to go home. You go. I'll wait here."

"Would you keep on eye on her?" I asked the bouncer. "A couple of those GIs thinks she's a performer."

"Sure. But rules also say you can't touch waitresses, dancers, or lady customers."

"What a bill of rights," Adrienne said. "Go on."

Beyond the door, I found myself in a warren of concrete boxes. Several of the open dressing-room doors had removable placards in their slots: "Tupelo Honey," "Rhonda Wonder," "Tara Blue Belle," "Divinity," "Julep." The smells of sweat, powder, hairspray, lipstick, and the acrid hot plastic of curling irons mingled into one sweet fetor. The dancers—costumed, half-dressed, or robed—mostly ignored me as I moved along the central defile. Out of the spotlights and the hungry gazes of men, their makeup peeled away and their cheeks shockingly gaunt, several of the women exuded weariness and defeat rather than glamour.

Finally, a Peter-Pan-sized gamine in a tangerine chemise asked me who I wanted. When I told her, she said, "Keep going. Last girl hired always gets the farthest pen, even if she's worked here before."

The door with "Ruby Slippers" on it hung ajar. The strains of classical music, probably Bach, issued from the cubicle. I knocked and looked in.

"You again," said the erstwhile Ruby, dressed in a short kimono of profound shimmering black. She slumped in the room's lone chair before a pegboard wall to which wigs and costumes clung. A boombox sat on a shelf beneath a mirror. "Where's Byron's ex?"

"Out front. Would you rather talk to her?"

"I'd rather take a trip to Paris. But I can't. How'd you all like the act? Think your girlfriend picked up any moves?"

"We liked it fine."

DeLynda snorted. "Try harder to pretend I didn't turn you on."

I crossed my arms and leaned against the door because I didn't want to squat like a coolie. "Cut the crap, okay? We had a reason beyond my depravity or Adrienne's long-standing interest in modern dance in coming down here tonight. Maybe you'd like to hear it."

"And maybe I wouldn't."

"Earlier this week, I saw Erroll Kingston in his headquarters tower in Marietta."

DeLynda straightened in her chair. "You visited the ogre in his castle? And escaped to watch me dance? What did the bastard have to say?"

"That he doesn't know Byron. That he's never *met* Byron."

"What absolute bullshit!" She slumped again. "But why do I get worked up over either of those scumbags? On the other hand, Byron may've run out and dumped me back into Mr. Saudek's lap, but Kingston is Satan himself."

"What makes you say that, DeLynda?"

"The fact that the son of a bitch could easily go straight, but won't. He runs dozens of profitable legit businesses, but he can't stop mucking around in all sorts of nasty shit."

"Like what? Poaching?"

"Oh, yeah. He's got a maniac's Ph.D. in poaching."

"What else? Pot growing?"

"Not for years. Pot doesn't have the sting or stamina for him. Doesn't hook its users deeply enough."

"What does?"

"Try crank. Crystal meth. Half the girls here have a habit, Mr. Keats. Keeps the flab off, puts a sparkle in the eyes, gives the old strut a pretty bodacious bounce."

"Do you use crank, DeLynda?"

"How stupid do I look?" She snorted. "Don't answer that. Anyway, even crank wears off, and when users like my girlfriends here need another dose, who do you think they turn to?"

"Erroll Kingston."

"Bingo! I wouldn't give the toad the satisfaction of owning me that way. I only strip between six and two. Kingston owns my body then, but every other hour's mine. I do my thing without a fat KV branded on my soul."

"Kingston doesn't deliver drugs here himself."

"Use your head! A fellow named Armando packs the stuff in. But Armando draws his paycheck from one of Kingston's aboveboard enterprises."

"Maybe your Armando is a lone wolf, a freelancer. How can you know Kingston enters the crank picture at all?"

"He wanted to make Byron his top lieutenant in its manufacture and distribution, William."

"Byron told you this?"

"Right before he left."

"But Byron refused the offer."

"Yeah. I think it flattered the shithead, but he didn't want to risk that big of a bust. He wanted to stick with poaching. You know, fines instead of jail time."

"And Kingston agreed to let him?"

DeLynda frowned. "Kind of hard to picture Kingston taking a kiss-off with a smile and a handshake."

"You think he had Byron killed for refusing?"

"Hit? Yeah, I think so." DeLynda glanced at herself in the mirror, then closed her eyes. "Best way in the world to keep a body quiet. Forever."

"But you've come back to work in a place owned by the man who may've had your lover killed?"

"You see me sitting here."

"Why would you do that, DeLynda?"

She studied me appraisingly. "The Glass Cat pays the highest wages in town, Mr. Keats." She let the wings of her kimono fall open. "And I'm worth every scarlet cent this dump wrings from you lecherous bastards."

Thirty-Two

I found Adrienne seated at our table with two men, the Hispanic bouncer and Private Motes, who had admired her "costume." Motes and the bouncer were talking animatedly about the president's sex life, while Adrienne sipped the dregs of her beer and tapped her index finger on the tabletop like a telegraph key. Her message dit-dit-dotted frustration, impatience, and distaste, but, seeing me, she grinned in spite of herself.

"Finally!"

"Gentlemen," I said to her chaperones, "forgive us, but we've got to go. Thanks for keeping Adrienne company."

"Our pleasure," said Motes, standing up.

"Yeah," said the bouncer, who remained in his chair. *"De nada, hombre."*

I grabbed Adrienne's hand, hoisted her up, and pulled her on a jog-march from the club, around back to the Camry. Within seconds I had my key in the door lock.

Adrienne gripped my arm. "Did you learn anything backstage, or were you too busy ogling the merchandise?"

" 'Breasts to the left of me, breasts to the right of me, into the valley of cleavage strode the bold gumshoe. Mine not to reason why, mine but to spy and sigh, into the—' "

"Knock it off, Alfred Lord Peepingtom."

"Sorry." I let Adrienne in, then went around and climbed in my door. "Listen, whenever possible, I kept my eyes averted but sometimes my options narrowed to a straightforward look. Do you want to hear what DeLynda told me?"

"Of course."

I started the car, backed out of our spot, and regained Victory Drive. As we rode, I told Adrienne about Byron's work for Kingston as a poacher and Kingston's efforts to recruit Byron as overseer of his methamphetamine operations. We ran north on the Lindsey Creek Bypass, then west on the Airport Expressway—a conspicuous detour from the most direct route home, but a detour that Adrienne failed to notice as she questioned me about crank abuse among the women at the club and about DeLynda's suspicions that Kingston had had Byron murdered.

"We have to tell Cooper and Fearing," she said.

"Sure. As soon as we get home, okay?"

For the first time, Adrienne realized that I had driven us into Green Island Hills. "What are we doing here out here? Isn't this where Gupta lives?"

Instead of answering, I made a final turn onto a tree-lined access road, where Golconda, the mansion belonging to Satish Gupta, my father's former business partner, burst into view. As always during the holiday season, the entire estate—castlelike house, topiary shrubbery, and immense lawn—blazed with thousands of strings of fairy lights, Gupta's egotistical but earnest tribute to the Christ child's birth. We parked on the hidden road, tuned the radio to a seasonal NPR broadcast, and for ten or fifteen minutes sat before the staggered white torches of the trees and Golconda's shimmering reflection in Lake Oliver.

At length, Adrienne said, "Thanks, Will."

"Sure."

"A nice antidote to the strip club. Even if we both know that Gupta is a mercenary, murderous bastard."

I started the car. "I just figured that next to Kingston, old Satish would look like a saint."

Within five minutes of our arrival home, I called both the Speece County Sheriff's Department and the special number that Asa D. Fearing had given us. Unfortunately, I reached a desk jockey at the first number and a machine at the second. Cooper's subordinate advised me to talk to Cooper in the morning. On Fearing's machine, I briefly outlined the new information we had learned from De-

Lynda Gaye about Byron's connection to Kingston. Then, Adrienne having already preceded me, I went to bed.

At five o'clock Sunday morning, after a night dozing in uneasy squalls, I lay staring at the ceiling. The telephone rang once. I snatched receiver from cradle, expecting to hear either Cooper or Fearing's voice, and said, "Keats here."

"Can you talk?" said a male voice initially unfamiliar to me.

Adrienne, facing the other wall, did not stir. Good. I wanted her to sleep.

"Give me a minute," I whispered. "Let me switch rooms." I carried the portable handset down the hall to the *zendo,* where, shaking with cold in only my skivvies, I watched starlight twinkle on the soapstone lineaments of the Buddha before I spoke into the handset again: "Okay, who is this?"

"Can't you guess, chickenshit?"

"Byron! Listen, Byron, you—"

"No, *you* listen, jerk. Don't wear out my name, it's all I've got left."

"By your own choice."

"And if you keep using it over the fucking phone," Byron said, "the cops'll haul me in just to polish their badges. Pay attention: I need to talk to you. Face to face."

"Where?"

"You remember where Olivia learned to swim?"

The question threw me. Then I understood that Byron did not wish to tip any hypothetical listener to our meeting place. Olivia had taken her first successful independent strokes at a small beach on West Point Lake, about ten miles from our house.

"Okay, I know the spot. When?"

"Right away. Don't tell Ade. Don't call the cops. Don't drag in any of your meddling buddies, either."

"Okay, okay."

"Swear to it, Keats, or I'll vanish for good."

"You'd take my word?"

"You're such a fucking Boy Scout, you wouldn't sell out even a son of a bitch like Kingston if you gave him your word. So, yeah, I'd take it. Swear, Keats. Swear now."

"All right. I give you my word."

Byron chortled. "Amazing, Mr. Counselor. See you in twenty, eh?" My compliance had simply added fuel to his disdain.

After I found some warm clothes in the dryer downstairs and an old pair of tennis shoes in the mudroom, I dressed in the kitchen. If I could keep our meeting short, I could almost certainly return to the farm before Adrienne awoke. Given our recent activities, I imagined her sleeping until eight, at least.

The Tacoma fishtailed out of the yard without backfiring, and I rumbled westward into a fog that gave the darkness a motile woven dimension, like spiderwebs blowing in a storm. My mind raced, but in muddy troughs allowing no real progress. Only one point seemed clear: Byron, having probably called from a hideout in his native Alabama, would approach West Point Lake from that direction. About twelve minutes into my trip, I saw an armadillo waddling away from the mangled corpse of a dog, looking in my high beams exactly like a peripatetic toaster-oven.

At the lake, I parked next to a boat-loading ramp near the small beach where Olivia had conquered her fear of the water—something I had not yet done myself. Out of my truck, I walked down the ramp to the lake. With the eastern sky lightening, I heard the ghostly voices of two fishermen in a skiff debating the merits of a high-school scatback. I pulled my windbreaker tight and peered about like a lost hiker.

A hissing sounded behind me. A sotto voce command followed this hiss. "Keats! Get your ass over here!"

Silhouetted at the top of the ramp, Byron Owsley beckoned me, then withdrew. I followed his retreating shadow into a row of pines, and caught up with him in a small damp glade. Traces of reflected sunlight from the lifting fog lent Byron's forehead and cheeks a spectral sheen. Before I could say anything, he patted me down.

"You didn't bring a gun, did you?"

"I usually don't do guns, Byron. How about you?"

"Only in deer season. But I'd damn sure rather hold one than face one."

The fishermen in their skiff drifted into view. To Byron's surprise, I grabbed his elbow and steered him deeper into the pine thicket.

"Voices carry over water," I said. "We don't need to broadcast our talk to those guys."

Byron shrugged off my grip and trudged away, rattling foliage and breaking twigs. We halted in another chilly copse, pine-needle fans overhead and subsiding mulch underfoot. I could hardly make out Byron's features, but his cheeks had a haggard angularity and his eyes a struggle-haunted radiance. When he spoke, he honored my caution about the fishermen by whispering.

"For the moment, Keats, Olivia is still alive. Rest easy on that score."

"How do you know?"

"A little hooded warbler told me. He also told me who offed Polk James."

I expected Byron to tell me more, but he merely hunched his shoulders and blew plumes of breath from his nostrils like Roogy Batoon.

I said, "What's up, Byron. I'm glad Olivia's okay, but you didn't call me out here just to tell me that."

Byron pulled his hands from his pockets. "I brought you out here to—well, to confess."

My heart felt like the lightbulb inside a closed refrigerator. "To confess what, Byron?"

He refused to meet my eyes. "I had Polk grab Olivia for me. I told him when to do it, how to time it. I gave him your schedule, more or less, and a plan of the house and barn. I even told him where to find the pruning hook for cutting the wires. He carried Olivia to that hunter's cabin over by Gadsden because I told him no one would ever find them there."

A frosty rage infiltrated my lungs and iced my spine. "You stupid miserable bastard!" I said. "What in Christ's name did you *think* would come of that shitty scheme?"

Byron came back defiantly. "Polk would hold her—take good care of her—for three or four months. Then I'd show up to fetch her to me again, and we'd've started ourselves a new life free of all you stuck-up goody-goodies. A daddy and his sweet little girl, somewhere in Mexico, like maybe Baja California, where a guy with my skills can still make a decent living, and you can kick back on the beach and watch the whales run." The defiance ebbed from his eyes, and something like wretchedness flowed in. "But a lot of crap went wrong, Keats. A lot of crap went wrong."

"I'd say. Someone shoots your buddy, then the shooter kidnaps Olivia again. A brilliant plan, Byron, the tiptop genius summit of your asshole life. Where does that leave us?"

"Not at a dead end. I told you, I know who killed Polk."

"Okay. Tell me."

"A guy named Monk Lewis, one of Kingston's suckass goons."

I pictured the tonsured man who had shown me his collection of porcelain and Erroll Kingston's penthouse natural-history museum. I imagined him cradling a Ch'ing dynasty vase, then envisioned him squeezing the trigger of a well-oiled pistol. "I've met Lewis," I told Byron.

"Good. Then you can believe what I'm about to tell you. For years now, I've poached for Kingston. Skins from protected gators, feathers from rare birds. Cranes, herons, kingfishers, egrets—some really beautiful plumes. I've even taken down bear for the Asian love-potion markets."

"Byron, make your point."

"A buddy worked with me, Farrel Quadrozzi, a Creole-Italian guy. He comes from Rainbow City, up near Gadsden. He put me on to the cabin where I told Polk to lay up till I could meet him there and take Olivia off to Mexico."

"And Quadrozzi spotted them there?"

"Yeah. A fluke, a total fucking fluke. I thought Farrel was still in Alaska! Anyway, Farrel had a hunch that what he'd learned might matter to Kingston so he ratted Polk and Olivia out. This earned him big points with Kingston, who wanted leverage over me." Byron fell silent.

Sparrows, wrens, and hideous speckled starlings began racketing around us. Constellations faded and vanished one by one behind the sky's evolving blue. "How did you learn all this?"

"Farrel had a change of heart after the killing. I mean, we're buddies. He spilled everything to me."

"Maybe he's setting you up for something else."

"I don't think so. Farrel liked Polk. It really browned him off that Monk shot him. Besides, Farrel couldn't help me put my hands on the most important part of the puzzle."

"Olivia's whereabouts?"

"Right. I figured that out myself."

"So tell me, Byron. It's almost the only part of your story I care about right now."

"Lewis took Olivia to the Okefenokee. Kingston has a compound in the swamp on a peninsula he calls Kingston's Island. It's really several acres of marshy ground poking from the mainland into Mynant Prairie, with cypress, gum, and even magnolia on it, but Kingston fancies he's got a sort of hidden fort with a moat around it. He dredged just enough of the spit's landward end to make it all look unreachable. But if you know how, you can drive straight in across the dry edge of Chesser County. I've spent time there myself, back when Kingston still thought me his golden boy." First Huberdeau as disappointed mentor; then Kingston, whom Byron had also rejected—either wisely or foolishly, depending on the outcome of their next real run-in.

"How do you know Olivia's on Kingston's Island?"

"Monk hit Fosterville last night. Kingston was probably with him, out of sight. Anyway, a friend of mine down there sold Monk the supplies they usually pack in when they visit the peninsula for a little R and R."

"And that means Olivia's there too?"

"They wouldn't give her to anybody else. Whoever has Olivia stands neck-deep in the sinkhole of a murder, and Kingston wouldn't admit his own involvement to just anybody. She's there on Kingston Island, I'd bet my soul—if the devil still wants it."

"What exactly do you want me to do?"

"First of all, don't tell the cops."

"Jesus, Byron. To me, keeping the cops out feels like signing Olivia's death warrant."

"You'll set her up if you *do* call them. The police can't storm the place without tipping Kingston off hours in advance. So either he cuts and runs, or he makes a stand. If he makes a stand, Monk will probably just put a bullet in Olivia's head. He's blown away plenty of others just for the thrill for it."

"But you have a plan to keep that from happening?"

"I offer myself as bait. Kingston doesn't want to kill me. He still wants me for a partner—hell, for his son and heir. He'll hand Olivia over if I agree to his conditions. That's why he took her, to get to me. Once I have her, I'll somehow pass her along to you, Keats."

"So you can stay there and let Kingston's evil empire put you under wraps again?" Only then did I realize that Byron wanted me to accompany him on a crazy reverse-kidnap mission to Kingston's Island.

"No way! Once I know you've gotten Olivia safely out of there, I make my own escape."

"That sounds like suicide for you and a dangerous voyage home for Olivia and me."

"No—no, it isn't. Kingston wants me back with him. You and Olivia will make it because I won't sign on again—not totally— until I know you all've cleared the island."

"No offense, Byron, but your track record stinks. What makes you think this plan holds out any more chance of success than some of your past me-first fiascos."

Byron turned to one side and stripped bark from a pine with his fingernails. "This thing isn't a me-firster, Keats—I'm doing it for other people too."

"If not for your own selfish stupidity, you wouldn't have to do anything now. Olivia would've never wound up in the straits you've put her in."

"Okay, Keats, I admit it. I fucked up. I've fucked up before, and I fucked up big-time when I asked Polk to grab Olivia. But now maybe I can make amends."

I gave a low incredulous whistle. Byron merely looked at me from his raw haunted eyes. That look decided me. "When do we make this insane excursion?"

At first, Byron did not react. Then he allowed himself a hedgy smile. "Hang loose, Keats. Hang loose."

Thirty-Three

As I'd predicted, Adrienne awoke at eight. She came downstairs to find me in the kitchen with a pot of decaf on the hotplate. She drank a single cup heavy with cream and sugar.

"Didn't I hear you go out? What time was that?"

"Maybe forty minutes ago. I fed Roogy."

"Oh. Good for you." She leaned over and kissed me.

By nine, we had eaten. Then Adrienne aggressively vacuumed the upstairs corridor while I stayed at the table inattentively reading the *Constitution*'s editorial pages.

Nicholas Cooper telephoned. "You had a message for me, Will?"

I tried directness. "Adrienne and I went to the Glass Cat last night. DeLynda Gaye says Erroll Kingston controls methamphetamine production and distribution in Georgia."

"You angling for a special commission in the GBI? Pass that info to Trent Badcock and friends, with *proof*, and they'll make you an honorary agent."

"Give me their number."

"Okay. Here's Badcock's direct line." He gave me the number. "Now, what's the crank trade have to do with finding Olivia?"

"DeLynda claims that Kingston tried to recruit Byron as his top lieutenant. Byron declined."

"Keep talking."

"Now Byron's gone missing, just like his biological daughter. Wake up and smell the pepper-gas, Nick." Part of me wanted to confide in Cooper what Byron had told me that morning. A bigger part wanted to resist that impulse. What if my telling resulted in a gun battle in the swamp between Kingston's party and the police? What would happen to Olivia then?

"You really think an investigation of Kingston would turn up links to both Owsley and Olivia?"

"I do. I certainly do."

"Respectfully noted. Anything else?"

"Could you guys get your asses in gear and end this nightmare?"

After a long pause, Cooper said, "We're shifting into overdrive this morning, Will. Hang in there." He rang off.

At noon, as Adrienne slid a grilled cheese sandwich out of the skillet and I ladled tomato soup into bowls, we heard a vehicle rumble up to the house. Its engine cut off, and a well-made door slammed.

Adrienne and I hurried to the front door and opened it to find Asa D. Fearing standing there with an upraised fist. Seeing us, he lowered it and smiled enigmatically. "Good to see you all. You left a message, Mr. Keats? Something about Byron Owsley's past dealings with Erroll Kingston?"

We had not seen Fearing since Thanksgiving Day and our panicky retreat from New Hampshire. He reminded me simultaneously of that unexpected visit and the weird confidence that his stolid presence could evoke in us. We led him to the kitchen.

"Would you like some soup?" Adrienne asked him.

"Tomato? Yes'm please." When she also offered to grill him a sandwich, he said, "Yes indeed. Reminds me of winter lunches my sweet departed mama used to fix."

With Fearing looming over his bamboo placemat, the kitchen felt little roomier than Olivia's treehouse. Steam fogged the paddock-facing windows, and Fearing's lime-scented cologne overpowered the food smells already present. Fearing took three quick spoonfuls of soup, then stopped and looked at us.

"I've spent most of my time lately fact-gathering, consulting, and chasing down leads. I've learned almost too much to lay out. So tell me what your phone call meant."

As Fearing virtually inhaled his soup and sandwich, I filled him in our trip to the Glass Cat. My longing to tell him about my meeting with Byron battled with my promise to remain silent until Byron and I could rescue her—just as they had in my talk with Cooper. So my brief recitation left me drained.

Sensing my exhaustion, Adrienne said, "Now tell us what *you've* learned, Agent Fearing."

He chewed a last chunk of sandwich, swallowed, and said, "Never play cards with anybody named Doc. 'Course I learned that a coupla years before I joined the Bureau."

This glib attempt at levity infuriated me. I imagined that Fearing's shuck-and-jive was meant to conceal his and the Bureau's egregious lack of accomplishment.

"Look," I said, "we don't need a joke to cheer us up. We need you to tell us one indisputable lead you've uncovered."

Fearing instantly sobered. "I wish you folks'd learn to trust us a little." He held his thumb and forefinger a fly's leg apart. "We're *this* close to breaking Olivia's case wide open and bringing you all's little sweetheart home. As we speak, major players're laying down some next-to-foolproof snares. Why, I'd—"

Out in the yard, a horn like a Klaxon blew five or six times. I left the table and headed straight for the porch. Fearing and Adrienne followed.

Next to Fearing's sleek '98 sedan trembled a headache-green Nissan of indeterminate age. A green raccoon tail drooped from its antenna, a yellow plastic budgie served as hood ornament, and some sort of painted Tibetan mandala decorated the roof. The doors bore a more familiar insignia: a white G inside a white O. Inside the car, Oscar Greenaway waved like a clown arriving at center ring in an absurd bozomobile, then opened his door and tumbled out, dressed in a quiet gray suit.

"Greetings, Mr. Keats, Miz Owsley, and imposing Nubian guest." Greenaway bowed like a courtier.

I went down the steps to prevent him from climbing them. His characteristic stoop and his baggy clothes gave him the look of a wizened 1930s university prof, but I doubted that inside our house he would prove quite that deferential or self-effacing.

"No one telephoned you, Mr. Greenaway. No one invited you here to trade on our heartbreak again."

Greenaway appealed past me to Adrienne. "Must he stand in the teeth of the storm and plead for a hearing?"

"Who's this 'he' he's speaking for?" Fearing asked me.

"Himself," I said, exasperated. "He refers to himself in the third person."

"It mocks our God-given powers of speech to talk in such a damned confusing way," Fearing told Greenaway. "Don't you have the sense God gave a child?"

Her arms crossed, Adrienne stared at her feet. "Incredible," she murmured.

Greenaway raised a hand to the cloud-addled firmament. "Oscar comes in answer to a heavenly summons. He did not send himself, ye faithless vipers."

I said, "He insults people he claims he wants to help."

As if screwing the sun more tightly into its socket, Greenaway twisted his upraised wrist. "Do you think Oscar willingly forsook his comfortable castle and his delightful budgies to travel on mere whim to Tocqueville? Never! Dream lore and karmic necessity, the twin flails of fate, compelled him!"

I said, "You've interrupted our lunch with bombast and drivel."

Adrienne came down the steps, gently lowered Greenaway's arm, and said, "Come inside, Mr. Greenaway. We can offer you some soup and a sandwich."

Like a kid thwarted in some trivial desire, I kicked a small dirt clod off the Nissan's bumper.

"Does Oscar not hunger like others of his species? Do not his intestines rumble with that immemorial longing to make the empty full? Oscar accepts your kind invitation, ma'am."

Fearing shook his head. "Man keeps talking like that, I expect I'll have to leave."

Inside, Adrienne opened another can of soup and built a fourth grilled cheese. Greenaway, diffusing a stale tweedy odor, sat with us like a gnome among giants. When Adrienne set his bowl before him, he tapped its rim with his spoon three times, as if signaling the start of some fairy parliament.

"Oscar expects only such payment as those he assists see fit to bestow. He neither wishes nor expects charity."

"Agent Fearing kicked in three bucks toward *his* lunch," I told Greenaway maliciously.

"Will!" Adrienne gave me a scowl and Greenaway a sandwich cut diagonally.

I finished my cold food, then leaned back to watch Fearing and Greenaway compete, first one spooning up soup and then the other in a slurpy "Anvil Chorus." Both Fearing and Adrienne finished ahead of Greenaway, who downed his last bite of sandwich two hours before I became eligible for Social Security.

Adrienne leaned toward him across the table. "What do you know about Olivia, Mr. Greenaway?"

He waved off the question and patted his lips with a napkin. "A small talking dog visited Oscar last night. It leapt out of a bureau drawer and right into his lap."

I scraped my chair around to face Greenaway. "What did this talking dog say?"

"The dog called itself Olivia. It related to Oscar many details of its current ordeal. It spoke of swimming, and of storms that churn the waters, and of the ugly studded saurians that lurk in them. It insisted that some of these cold-blooded creatures have mutant human faces."

"What hogwash," said Fearing. "You're trying to defraud these folks with your crazy hoodoo."

"Oscar knows how much you'd like to believe him a humbug, sir, for you rebuke him to disguise your own empty-kettle status." To taunt Fearing, Greenaway made a cork-popping noise.

Fearing rose to his feet. "Goodbye. Thank you, Miz Owsley, for a most delicious and nostalgic lunch."

"The charlatan departs, the seer remains," said Greenaway.

Adrienne walked Fearing out of the kitchen. I leaned across the table and laid a hand on Greenaway's wrist. "Describe the dog that came to you in your dream."

"A wiry animal, with upjutting ears. Its breath smelled of bologna and peppermints."

When Adrienne returned, I told her that Greenaway's vision of Olivia as a tiny dog duplicated one of my own. The synchronicity of these visions erected the hairs on my arms.

Adrienne said, "Did the dog in your dream wander into swamp waters?"

"Oscar has spoken all that he may disclose without two small inducements."

"Money and what else?" I said.

"First, the metrical symmetry of a C-note appeals to Oscar."

Between us, Adrienne and I rounded up five twenties. Greenaway tucked the bills into a vest pocket.

"And the second inducement?" Adrienne said impatiently.

"If only Oscar could visit the girl child's room . . . ?"

We led Greenaway up the stairs like landlords showing a Keebler elf his new flat. In Olivia's room, he gawked at the artificial armada of clouds and balloons on the walls. He picked up the bow to her violin and placed it gently across the out-of-tune strings. Reverentially, he fingered the pleats of her dresses, mouthed the titles of her books, and, without touching any of them, studied the toys in her cedar chest.

"Ah," said Greenaway, chancing upon Davy Quackett. "Oscar sees an old acquaintance. May he not hold him?"

Adrienne handed the loose-limbed duck to Greenaway, who jounced it as a mother might her baby. This grotesque sight annoyed and spooked me, but after thirty seconds or so, Greenaway returned the figure to Adrienne.

"Alas, I can learn no more. I must go."

" 'I'? Don't you mean 'Oscar'?"

"No, no," Greenaway said. "If I stay longer, I'll surely suffer the very breakdown that you two have so far superhumanly resisted."

All at once, Adrienne sat down on Olivia's bed, Davy Quackett collapsing in her lap. When I could not get her to move again, I took it upon myself to lead Greenaway outside to his car.

When Greenaway opened the driver's door, I got my first close look at the Nissan's interior. He had removed the rear seat and placed a mesh partition between the front and the back seats. Five or six budgerigars perched on swinging dowels in this portable aviary, while another two or three birds clung to the otherwise useless door handles. Guano streaked the side panels and spotted the metal floorboards.

"Trust yourself," Greenaway advised me, gripping his steering wheel. "You know ever so much more than you think you do."

Then he drove away, fat-faced little birds flashing in his rear window like pastel traffic lights.

Thirty-Four

B yron did not try to contact me again that Saturday. Nor did I hear from him on Sunday morning. Too anxious to go out, I did not attend church in Mountboro, and even convinced Adrienne to feed and exercise Roogy Batoon—on the pretext that she could use the work and fresh air. In the afternoon, she went upstairs for a round of sitting more disciplined, and more helpful, than yesterday's fugue with Davy Quackett.

During her meditation, the phone rang. I picked it up in the living room and said, "Talk to me."

Byron said, "What time does Adrienne leave for work tomorrow?"

"Seven."

"She doesn't come home for lunch, does she?"

"No, it's too far. She'd only come home if she fell ill."

"Then eat an early lunch. I'll pick you up a little after noon."

"You've talked to Erroll the King?"

"Christ, man, don't joke around on the line that way." Before I could apologize or ask another question, Byron hung up.

Tomorrow afternoon, we would drive to Fosterville and then as far as we could onto the cypress- and conifer-cloaked peninsula known as Kingston's Island, a finger poking into the eye of Mynant Prairie, a tea-colored, plant-clogged marsh surrounded by mostly solid steppes of palmettos, galberry bushes, and blackthorn vines.

My gut shifted.

Allegedly, Monk Lewis had murdered Polk James and others; and Erroll Kingston, his city work ethic and designer clothes aside, cultivated a matching ruthlessness as primeval as the Okefenokee. If these two pitiless men—and their anonymous flunkies—held Olivia captive in the swamp, how could I justify going in after her without the support of the law?

First, Byron had made a strong case that only he could stand surety for Olivia and free her from Kingston. Second, none of the authorities had made—or anyway reported—the kind of progress inspiring confidence. I had interviewed almost as many people as Cooper, the GBI, and Fearing, with results as good as or better than theirs, or so I believed in these late demoralizing stages of the investigation. Byron had shown himself to me, rather than to the police, because he needed a confederate and because he understood that Olivia meant as much to me as to him. Third, Oscar Greenaway had confirmed our suspicions about Olivia's whereabouts while casting doubt on Asa D. Fearing's claims of a breakthrough. He had also counseled me to trust myself. Fourth, I remembered that with the help of my friend J. W. Young, I had found my father's missing dummy, Dapper O'Dell, without involving the police. I set aside the crucial difference that our current search focused not on an inanimate ventriloquist figure, but on a vulnerable flesh-and-blood child.

"Will, what are you doing?"

An early December darkness shrouded the living room as I sat on the sofa jiggling my leg and mulling the wisdom of what Byron and I planned to do. "Nothing, I guess."

Adrienne dropped down beside me. "If you like doing nothing, why not do it beside me in the *zendo*?"

"Never," I said.

She gouged me with an elbow. "Yeah? Why not?"

"Remember my motto? Death before ego-dissolution." I leaned to kiss her and slipped a hand under her sweater to find her naked beneath it and her breast consolingly warm.

"What a charmer," Adrienne said. "He philosophizes even as he cops a feel." But she kissed me back and ran her own hands under my shirt. Kissing, we stroked each other—less as foreplay than as mutual solace. This lasted a long time. Then we rolled onto the floor and tenderly made love.

. . .

After Adrienne left for work on Monday morning, I had second, third, and seventy-sixth thoughts about my impending jaunt to the Okefenokee with Byron Owsley. I kept seeing Monk Lewis forcing us to our knees and shooting us dead. Not only did we fail to bring Olivia home in this scenario, but we squandered our own lives in a misguided attempt to upstage the cops. Immediately, I pushed this vision from my mind and reviewed again my reasons for joining Byron in such folly.

In Olivia's room, I found her favorite hardcover copy of *The Wonderful Wizard of Oz* and sat down on her bed with it. On its front flyleaf, I carefully wrote out the essential details of what we intended to do today. I wrote for ten minutes, then signed the explanation *"Love, Will."* I had almost set the volume aside when I decided to add a P.S.: *"Remember muskrat courage."* Then, instead of returning it to Olivia's bookcase, I leaned it against a bolster on her bed.

Byron drove up at noon in a vintage brown junkyard Mercury with a customized grille and dual exhausts. From the porch I watched it slue to a stop. A teenage sodbuster from Alabama would have seen this Mercury as the acme of cool—thirty years ago. (Of course, that description fit Byron's roots almost exactly.) Byron kicked the balky door open and climbed out, his jeans and burgundy leather jacket grease-stained, his boots extravagantly scuffed.

"Ready to go, Keats?"

"As I'll ever be. Where'd you get that tenth-rate Batmobile?"

"On the lam, smart-ass, a fella borrows whatever comes along."

"Maybe we should take my truck."

Byron snorted. "So Ade can call in an APB when she realizes you're late coming back from the beauty parlor. Smart."

"We'll make Fosterville about when she gets home. Once there, I can call her and win us some extra time."

"Okay, do that. But no truck that cops can easily spot. Remember, if you offer somebody a chance to fuck up your plans, even if they mean to do you good, you can damned sure bet they'll take it. Now, get behind the wheel."

"Me? Why me?"

"I don't plan on speeding, but if a cop stops us, I want him to look at *your* license, not mine. Something about my face makes cops think I'm running coke or AK-47s."

I came down from the porch and circled the Mercury. It had an up-to-date Alabama tag and a bumper sticker reading MORE FOB. Its tattered but roomy cockpit held a small Igloo cooler, a blanket, empty fast-food cartons, and a stack of *Juggs* magazines, which, if I viewed their presence charitably, *might* have belonged to the Merc's previous owner.

I took the wheel, Byron slid in beside me, and we circumvented the sheriff's department and jail facility by following backroads to I-185 well south of Tocqueville. Now what? I found it hard to imagine passing five hours of close confinement in this growling rustbucket with the semifelonious Byron Owsley. The wreck's shock absorbers had failed during Watergate, and the dash had more wires hanging from it than a shrapnel-struck piano.

I clicked the radio on anyway. Miraculously, it played. I tuned through Christian and country-western stations until I hit a Garth Brooks ditty that I thought Byron would approve, "Friends in Low Places."

"You like that shit?"

"I can stand about ten minutes of it at a stretch."

"But you figured *I* liked it?"

I shot him a glance. "Given the stations in South Georgia, it was either that or Steven Curtis Chapman."

"Or NPR, the egghead channel, right? I bet you get off on— what's it called—'Adventures in Good Music.' " He said this with a convincingly haughty patrician accent.

"Not really," I said.

Byron banged the dashboard. "But you just go ahead and assume *I* like this honky-tonk shit, damn it! Fact is, I hate these whining line-dancing wusses! They give me a fucking migraine! Now do me a favor and cut that garbage off."

"Yes sir." I clicked the radio off.

"And pass that stinking chicken truck before the stench from it makes me puke!"

I pinned the accelerator to the deck. The Merc shuddered, drew alongside the big truck and slowly beyond it, my knuckles on the wheel as white as the flyleaf in Olivia's book. For the next five miles, until it turned, that truck seemed magnetized to our bumper, a demonic juggernaut in our rearview.

Byron tapped his fingers on his knees. His boots ticktocked back and forth on the worn floormat. His worry filled the Merc's cockpit as palpably as raucous line-dancing music.

I said, "We don't have to do this, Byron. We can still call in the police."

"Those blame-shifting bastards! Those do-nothing pissants!"

I stifled a laugh. "We pay their salaries, Byron. They train for situations like this."

"Christ, you've got K-Y Jelly where your spine should be. Do you really want the feds laying seige to Kingston's Island—after Philadelphia and MOVE, or Ruby Ridge, or Waco? Do those names mean ratshit to you, Keats?"

"But *your* plan will work?"

"Damned straight! We float around the peninsula to keep some antsy perimeter guard on land from blowing us away. Then we sneak into the compound, where I show myself and deal. When Kingston lets Olivia go, you take her and skedaddle. If they kill me before things get that far along, you scoot on back to Fosterville and tell Sheriff Donovan. But only as a last resort."

"Can I get all this in writing?"

Byron stared at me incredulously for a few seconds, then burst into guffaws. "Keats, maybe you've got some promise after all." He opened the small cooler and pulled out an amber bottle. "Have a beer? I bought these to repay you for that six-pack I toted into my apartment. I've got some ice cream here too."

"No thanks. I'm your designated driver, remember?"

Byron uncapped his longneck and noisily gulped from it. Then he wiped his mouth. "Right. Another stroke of genius on my part, Keats." And he laughed again.

For maybe ten miles, we had nothing more to talk about. Byron quit after one beer, traffic thinned out, and the countryside—still green from our hurricane-watered autumn—revolved about us like a patchwork quilt on a turntable, bringing vast arabesques of kudzu and weed-spangled meadows into view. Occasionally, Byron's stomach rumbled. We both ignored it.

"Two years ago," Byron said without preamble, "I got word that my mama in Rainbow City had died. I didn't live with anybody then—no arrangements to make—so I put on a shirt and tie and drove over there to pay my respects, which I never did in my daddy's case at all. When I got out of the navy, Mama'd wanted me to come back to help her take care of Goodloe, 'cause other folks' illnesses ate at her like lye soap, but I didn't heed her and figured my face at his funeral would've struck her as an insult."

I said nothing, already aware that Byron intended to see this confession through to the end. In fact, he took a chest-expanding breath and continued:

"Folks I hadn't seen in thirteen years—friends of my mama's, old girlfriends, second cousins—greeted me pretty kindly, taking everything into account. I was like the prodigal son getting hugs, food, flowers; boy, you name it. Made me feel like shit *I* hadn't brought anything. I started to think that under this big welcome lurked some heavy resentment. At the cemetery I really felt their bad vibe. I started to beat myself up for the sorry-ass way I'd treated my mama. She'd really cared. Even shooting at a fucking Co'-Cola truck hadn't turned her against me. So when they lowered her into that hole, Keats, I *cried*. Tears flowed down my face like somebody'd twisted a couple of spigots." Byron's feet ticktocked on the floorboard, even when he pressed his palms to his knees in an attempt to stop them.

I said, "That must've been tough, Byron."

"Yeah, well, crying *helped*. Probably three quarters of the folks there thought my tears were phony, but some kind of lever tripped inside me, went from off to on. Sure, I may've cried some of those tears for myself, but most of them I cried for that woman going into the ground, for how I'd dishonored her and Goodloe." For the first time since telling this story, Byron looked directly at me. "You understand any of that, Keats?"

"Sure. At my daddy's tomb in Mountboro, I felt some of what you felt at your mama's funeral in Rainbow City."

Byron thought on my comparison, then said, "I know I haven't acted like a damned disciple since then. I've screwed up—bad. But what happened to me over there's finally starting to sink in."

"A heart transplant?"

"Yeah." Byron liked the image. "A heart transplant."

In spite of some guarded sympathy for him, I said, "You haven't given DeLynda Gaye any evidence of it. You left her."

"Look, I skipped to keep her safe. So Kingston'd have no call to go anywhere near her."

"Too bad. Because DeLynda went straight back to the Glass Cat, where Kingston can drink her in whenever he wants."

Byron slumped as if I'd struck him. "I didn't know she'd gone back. I swear, I had no idea."

"She had no income. What did you think she'd do?"

"I never meant to—" Byron struck the dashboard and leaned away to mull the natural results of his own actions. In how many different roles could he mull them? As faithless son, deceitful apprentice, unreliable husband? As poacher, kidnapper, deserter? Driving, I thanked God that my own worries were sufficient to keep me wired. How would I have coped with Byron's?

Thirty-Five

Teenagers passing us in gleaming Audis or SUVs or late-model Mustangs eyed our Merc as if it had just returned to Georgia from Havana or Cairo, a third-world expatriate miraculously back in the U.S.A. Between Tifton and Enigma, a state trooper pulled onto the highway and followed us at a distance of a hundred yards all the way to Alpaha. I watched him in the rearview, my palms clammy, waiting for him to decide if we fit his profile for heroin mules and to set his eerie blue spinner flashing. He stopped following us, I think, only because we looked too much like criminals to have foolishly committed a crime.

"You sweating like I am?" I said.

Byron checked over his shoulder to make sure the cruiser had veered off. "No. I'm starved. That ice cream didn't do it for me, Keats." He had put away the whole pint of my alleged payback Cherry Garcia from the Igloo cooler.

"Where do you want to stop—if a fast-food franchise doesn't suit you?" He had vehemently nixed every such place we'd passed.

"Look, if you put a dipstick down my throat, it'd come back up registering four or five quarts of grease. I need something decent for a change."

I recalled the food on the table in Byron's Dogtown loft: cold cereal and a dried-out ingot of cheese. He could have fared little better these past couple of weeks on the run. Of course he longed for a respectable meal.

"Let's not stop at the Tupelo Gum in Fosterville," I said. "If

Sheriff Donovan or any of Kingston's thugs spies us, your plan goes down in flames."

"Relax. I like a place where Monk Lewis always used to stop— the Appalachee Indian Village south of Pearson on 441."

"Is that a tourist trap or a restaurant?"

"A little of both. They've got roasting ears, shaved pork, Brunswick stew, and gator wrestling in season. Monk had me stop with him there three or four times. Quadrozzi too. Quadrozzi liked the alligator steaks."

I thought a moment. "Did you and Quadrozzi supply the meat after poaching the gator skins?"

Byron grinned. "Shame to let the carcasses rot. And it meant extra cash straight into our pockets. I doubt Ol' Erroll would've minded even if he'd known."

Byron Ramses Owsley, the King of Denial. He began to hum, peppering his kneecaps with rhythmic finger tattoos. Several miles passed before I recognized the tune, Bobby McFerrin's "Don't Worry, Be Happy." I resisted an impulse to lean over, jack open his door, and shove him out.

At Pearson, we turned right on U.S. 441 and in less than five minutes hove up before the Appalachee Indian Village, a combination restaurant, trading post, petting zoo, truck stop, and animal show that sprawled over the landscape like a tawdry oasis. A fence of round-topped red planks—giant Popsicle sticks dipped in blood or Mercurochrome—encircled the buildings. Huge Masonite cutouts of aboriginal warriors, deer, birds, bears, and alligators decorated the fence, advertising in painted word-balloons milkshakes, peanut brittle, pralines, leather goods, and trinkets. A stand-alone sign with removable wooden placards gave the show times, in-season, for guided tours, gator-wrestling exhibitions, and lectures on snakes. I pulled into the ragged asphalt lot and parked between a GM truck and two Harleys.

"No gator-wrestling between November and March," Byron said wistfully.

"We'll have to come back on April first," I said. What more appropriate day?

Byron shot me a look, said, "Maybe you will," then led me into a restaurant the size of an aircraft hangar.

Light the color of white latex paint poured down from lofty fluorescents, washing out the faces of patrons occupying many of the
fifty or more tables scattered across the dull cement floor. Up front,
near the entrance, display cases stocked with gimcrack souvenirs
alternated with flimsy racks of T-shirts ("3 for $10!"), most with
obvious manufacturing flaws. A bank of pay telephones against the
entrance-side wall caught my eye.

"I need to call Adrienne. If she's not home yet, she will be pretty
soon."

"You can't talk to her, Romeo."

"Just let me leave a message. It'll buy us time. If I don't, she'll
imagine the worst."

"She always had a talent for that."

I turned back to Byron. "I can't deliberately cause her any more
pain. Can you?"

The dig hurt him. "Go on, then. Don't tell her where you're
calling from, though. Don't tell her jackshit."

I used a long-distance card to get through. The voice that greeted
me belonged to Olivia: *No one can talk to you right now, but
Adrienne Owsley, Will Keats, Olivia Owsley, and Roogy Batoon still
want to hear from you. After the beep, start to cheep!*

Intellectually, I knew that we had never erased her recording in
favor of a message of our own, but actually hearing her voice sand-
bagged me. I stepped back, pulling the metal-cased cord to its full
length. The rapid *beep-beep-beep* of the prompt caught me with no
coherent thought in my head.

Finally, I spoke, "God, Adrienne, to hear her voice again—it
reminds me of how much I love you both. That's why you won't
find me there when you get home. Try not to worry, though, and
keep up your muskrat courage."

I hung up and leaned my forehead against the coinbox. Anyone
looking on would have probably thought I had just learned of the
deaths of my entire family in a plane crash.

A jukebox somewhere in the hall began playing "Will the Circle
Be Unbroken" by the Staple Singers. I pushed away from the pay
phone and turned around. A hostess had already escorted Byron
across the immense floor to a vacant table. I hurried to join him,
but Byron shook his head and steered the hostess past the table to

a booth abutting a glass counter full of cakes, pies, danishes, and cobbler dishes.

"I think I could eat half that lemon meringue for dessert," he told her. "Welcome back, Keats."

The hostess smiled and left.

We slid into the booth opposite each other, and Byron said, "Monk always sits here. Gives him a good view of all the entrances and a handy exit out the kitchen if he needs it. He orders a big plate of barbecue, a side of fried green tomatoes or popcorn okra, and a basket of steak fries. His eyes never stop roving even while he feeds his face."

"And you aspire to the same swinish paranoia?"

"Fuck you, Keats. His attitude's what I want to escape."

Eventually, the jukebox began pouring out Linda Ronstadt's take on Roy Orbison's "Blue Bayou," her homesick voice filling the room but sounding as close as that of an embracing lover. Byron tilted his head to listen.

A heavyset but nimble waitress brought us water and a pair of vinyl-jacketed menus.

"This man's got an angry hunger," I said. "If you don't feed him pretty quick, he may bite my head off."

The waitress looked Byron over and smiled at me. "Will do, honey. We can't have a fine-looking specimen like this un wasting away. You all tell me what you want."

Byron's scowl stayed put, but steam stopped billowing from his ears. "A full rack of ribs, extra-hot sauce, some cornbread, the okra, and the collards." He thought again. "Plus a side of beans and a Molson Ice."

"Yes sir. I'll get the buckboard ready." She looked at me. "And you, mister?"

"A pork sandwich, chipped. And a ginger ale."

"Thanks, fellas. Be right back with your drinks." She waddled off—gracefully, speedily.

"A ginger ale? Jesus, Keats, why don't you just order a Shirley Temple?"

"My stomach's kicking up. You'd better thank Vulcan yours is made of iron."

"You know," said Byron, gazing past me, "*I* should be nervous, but I'm just not. The nearer we get to Kingston and the swamp the easier it goes for me. First time I put a foot in the Okefenokee I felt like I'd come home. The place filled me up through my pores. Prairies, islands, gator holes, hive trees—hell, I learned them faster than I ever did algebra or Spanish. Animals just don't give you the same kind of shit people do. Cypress trees and blackthorn vines don't knot your gut like truck payments or broken appliances manage to do. So I've got a sense—like something left over from my turnabout at Mama's funeral—that we'll slip Olivia out okay and spit in Kingston's eye when we do."

"Loan me a little of your confidence, Byron."

He looked at me again. "Take some. I got plenty."

"Yeah, well, excuse me while I make a trip to the head before our meals arrive."

I made my way between tables to the elaborate doors fronting the restrooms. Roseanne Cash's "The Summer I Read Colette" began to reverberate through the hall, a jukebox selection that surprised me. Predictably, most of the diners paid more heed to their meals or their table conversations. ("As they should," Adrienne would have said.) Above the restroom doors hung the mounted heads of a black bear, a twelve-point buck, and a Florida panther, almost as if—depressing thought—Erroll Kingston had chosen the restaurant's decor.

Inside the big restroom, I relieved myself, splashed cold water on my face, and tried to straighten the mussed part in my hair with a pocket comb. Idly, I read the notices that the owner had posted on the burgundy and navy tiles: "EMPLOYEES MUST WASH HANDS BEFORE RETURNING TO WORK/PLEASE LEAVE THIS FACILITY CLEAN FOR THE NEXT PERSON/BY ORDER OF THE MGT.—NO SWEARING, LOITERING, OR SPITTING.

One posting among the bills, especially given these upper-case imperatives, leapt out as incongruous. Somebody had apparently ripped a page from a printed book, folded it in two, and affixed it to the tiles with two gold stars of the kind that teachers use to reward good work. I peeled off the stars, took the page down, and opened it out.

And recognized it instantly. A drawing of two flying monkeys carrying a small girl between them on their locked hands identified the text from which it had come: I was holding page 147 from a mass-market paperback edition of *The Wonderful Wizard of Oz.* Across the top of the page in pencil, as neatly as if she had written the message in school, Olivia had printed: *"Help me. Call the police. Olivia Mildred Owsley."* A bolt of cold lightning flashed down my spine.

I left the restroom and returned to our booth. George Jones's "He Stopped Loving Her Today" had long since replaced the Roseanne Cash song, while Byron had just begun to bite into the sugary black crust of an enormous pork rib.

"If I'd known you needed help shaking it, Keats, I'd've sent some desperate queer along with you."

"Take a look at this." I set the page from the first *Oz* book in front of Byron. He squinted at it, focused, read the penciled message, and reread it as if he had stumbled upon a paragraph as abstruse as anything in a chaos-theory text. Still bewildered, he took a bite of the rib and read it yet again.

"Olivia wrote this."

"Apparently."

"No. I mean, she *really* wrote it. She hates her middle name, but she uses it here."

"To prove to whoever finds her note that it's legit, Byron. Bless her heart, the kid's always thinking."

"Her mama coming out," Byron said, his sauce-smeared mouth looking like a swamp cat's after a good kill. "That's definitely her mama coming out."

Thirty-Six

Back in the Mercury, Byron asked me where Olivia had gotten the book. ("She probably begged Lewis for it," I told him. "You know how Olivia can make you do stuff you don't want to.") He asked why she had entered the restaurant's men's room. ("Monk needed to take a leak but didn't want Olivia roaming free as he did.") He asked if we had a legal obligation to hand over the evidence I'd found to the police. ("Probably.")

We cruised into Fosterville in the thickening dusk of a day one week shy of the year's shortest, sliding past lighted storefronts and through pools of dim radiance cast by streetlamps. Near the busy Tupelo Gum Café, I wondered if Jimmy Wayne held down a counter stool or if the skinny dishwasher still had his arms up to the elbows in soapy water. Not until we had reached the town's eastern outskirts, beyond the last muddle of crackerbox houses and the last ramshackle filling station, did Byron speak again.

"Stop. I'll drive. I know where we're going, and no cop's likely to pull us over now."

Byron went around the Merc while I slid over into the shotgun seat. Despite our stop at the Appalachee Indian Village, my muscles ached from so many hours behind the wheel, and I welcomed the respite. Once underway again, though, I felt powerless, prey to the same nervous excitement that had caused Byron to fidget and hum. I resolved not to indulge in this behavior: Whereas I had resisted my impulse to shove Byron out the door, Byron might well choose to act on his.

We bumped past a lost church of some aggressively primitive

denomination, a clapboard garage with a crude homemade steeple. An illuminated signboard on wheels carried the message "The Beast Draws Nigh/Gird Up Your Loins." Then we whirred northeast on droning treads along State Highway 177, an asphalt hogback with palmetto fields to our left and palmettos or the interlocking fingers of the sluggish swamp to our right. A dirty sliver of waning moon hugged the horizon, and two or three vehicles returning from Stephen C. Foster State Park whooshed past us.

About six miles along this ridge, Byron slowed the Merc to a crawl, and our lights picked out a double-rutted road that I would never have seen. We turned and edged along it at a cautious ten miles per hour. Our passage through this hinterland of marshes and slow-sprawling streams stirred wildlife into flight. A barn owl—locals called them monkey-faced owls—dropped from the sky toward our windshield, but providentially veered off and vanished into a copse of sweetbays. Turkey oaks and ragged conifers began pressing in as the nearby waters stewed provocatively.

Byron halted at a point that I regarded as indistinguishable from any other. "Okay, from here we go on foot." Suddenly, the reality of what we had planned hit home, and I balked at climbing out. Byron, already moving, said, "Hurry up, chickenshit," and I joined him at the Merc's trunk, from which he rummaged a big black Z-Lite lamp with a rubberized grip. He thrust this lamp at me and then fished out a holstered pistol.

"Combat Commander forty-five. Think you can shoot it?"

The heft of the gun satisified some ache inside me. "No sweat. I did a little target-shooting in college."

Byron chuckled darkly. "Shooting people feels a lot different from shooting targets, Keats. We don't need any casualties from friendly fire. Now, strap it on."

I set the Z-Lite down and struggled to buckle the Sam Browne belt. The snap-down military holster rode on my hip like a boil, alien and painful. Byron straightened the belt and passed me a spare seven-round magazine, which I pocketed.

"Where'd you get the gun, Byron?"

"I cannot tell a lie: I stole it."

"So I drove all the way down here with a stolen firearm in the trunk?"

"Hey, I liberated the Merc too. You're now a bona fide felon, Keats. What do you say to that?"

"I owe it all to expert mentoring."

Byron snorted, then set out toward the swamp. I clicked on the Z-Lite, aimed the beam at his heels, and followed. After only a few steps, he stopped, turned, and handed me the Merc's keys. "If something happens to me, you'll have to get back here with Olivia. So pay damn close attention to the trail."

We hiked farther in. Stars sparkled like dagger points amid the leaves of magnolias, cypresses, and oaks. Katydids chorused. Night birds quarreled. The temperature had stalled in the high fifties, and far fewer insects than I had expected flitted about. The humidity lodged in my lungs, though, while the straps of my various belts slid over my sweat. A series of alarming crashing noises prompted Byron to halt me and whisper, "Deer," even though they sounded to me like ludicrously klutzy representatives of their kind. I never saw even one of them.

At the sudden end of our overgrown road, we struck a borderless ditch, a moat of cold coffee. Cypresses reared, wetly black at the base, spiderweb-silver higher up. Flecks of starshine on the water suggested eyes, and I wondered if alligators hunted at night. In spite of myself, an enmired log near the shore looked disturbingly like a scaly reptilian torso. To my surprise, Byron shuffled sidelong to the log, knelt, and laid a hand on it. "Give me some light here, Keats."

I painted the log with the Z-Lite. Some local boatwright had felled an immense cypress bole, then cunningly hatcheted, burned, chiseled, and dressed it out as an aboriginal dugout. It had no seats, but held two long paddles with blades like waxed shark fins, and a bamboo stob pole.

"We'll go the rest of the way in this," Byron said.

I eyed it dubiously. "What makes you think it'll float, much less travel any distance?"

"Here in the Oke, you'd rather have this sweet baby than some stupid beer can of a canoe. Get friendly with it, Keats. Who knows when you'll have to pilot it?"

I knelt beside Byron, and together we freed the dugout from its mucky trench. Once it had begun to drift, we clambered in. I took the front and, as we paddled quietly along the shoreline, tried to repress my fear of the water—a lifelong phobia, stemming from my inability to swim—by concentrating on my paddle strokes. I must have disappointed Byron in this work, though, because he eventually shipped his paddle and used the stob pole to propel us forward. I had only to push us away from stumps or entangling foliage. Owls called to one another from flannel-lined throats, and a freshening breeze off Mynant Prairie caressed my hot skin.

"All right," Byron said. "The trail's gone to water, but it's still a trail. Memorize the landmarks."

Landmarks? The swamp looked everywhere the same, a many-armed maze with lily pads or shiny never-wets floating in its corridors and cul-de-sacs. "Byron, If I have to find my way out without you, I may as well confess my unfitness now."

"Spoken like a complete citified wuss. See, there's Kingston's Island." A line of anchored vegetation created a dense shadowy wall to our right. "Keep that shadow to your left coming out and you'll do just fine."

"I'll do even better with you in the stern."

"Can't count on that, so get ready to count on yourself."

We kept poling, gliding along, until our steady motion and the starshine on the water had induced in me a waking trance. A mild disinterested curiosity had displaced my fear. Even an alligator bumping our dugout or a cottonmouth falling into it from a bay limb would have had no power to panic me. The stink of decaying peat, marinating wood, rotting fish, and nameless vegetation added to my preternatural calm, like incense in a *zendo*.

Abruptly Byron said, "Ship your oar. Stay low in the boat."

I obeyed him without question. A new smell turned in the air, a contrast to the other blended stinks: the aroma of fresh-brewed coffee. Byron braced himself on the gunwales and lifted an owlish three-note call—*hoo-hoo, hoooooo!*—that echoed over the water. Instantly, a high-sustained whistle that might have issued from a bird, a human being, or a teakettle sounded in response, prompting Byron to grunt and pole us forward again.

Between pickets of cypress knees and hurrah bushes, the landing on Kingston's Island showed as a thin belt of white sand. Stoles of moss fringed the opening, into which our dugout glided and crunched to a rocky standstill. Well inland, up the beach, a light flashed three times. We both stepped clear of our boat and squatted at its bow in almost accidental parley.

"Wait here five minutes after I leave," Byron whispered. "Then follow me to Ol' Erroll's hideaway. Hunker down where you can see his front door."

"How do I get Olivia away from him?"

"Leave that to me. When it seems we've reached an agreement, I'll signal, and you can bring Olivia here to the dugout and pole her back to safety."

"Simple," I said dubiously.

"Yeah. If I do my part, and you don't fuck up." He started to leave, but I grabbed his wrist.

"What about this gun? Who do you want me to shoot?"

"Not me, for Christ's sake. Beyond that, use your judgment. I can't draw you a fucking blueprint." He shucked me off and started to duck-walk forward.

"Byron!" I stage-whispered.

He looked back. "*Shhhhh!* Yeah, what?"

"Do this right, okay? For all our sakes."

"That's the plan, chickenshit." He rose to his full height and trudged up a bleak defile between shadowy trees.

As he had ordered, I hung back, periodically pressing a button on my watch to summon the eerie blue light allowing me to read its face. When five minutes had passed, I advanced upslope in a D-Day invader's crouch toward Kingston's hidden compound. After fifty yards, a minefield of snapping twigs and treacherous burrow holes, I stumbled into a half-acre clearing.

A rickety palmetto-thatched cabin with screen windows dominated the clearing. A Coleman lantern hanging from a hook on a porch strut provided the only feeble light, but, crouching amid foliage at the clearing's edge, I heard Kingston himself distinctly voice a question: "Did you pat him down?" "

"Oh, yeah. He's as clean as Nevada hooker." Monk Lewis in his self-defining arrogant-moron mode.

About forty feet beyond the far corner of the cabin's elevated verandah hulked the formidable trailer of an eighteen-wheeler. Who could say why? The trailer sat at right angles to the cabin, its pale-yellow flank visible in the lantern light. The company name flourished there in modified Old English script:

ROYAL TANGERINE PORCELAIN
FINE CHINAS FOR THE DISCRIMINATING

More than likely, Kingston and Company had hauled this monstrous cargo hold on wheels into his well-camouflaged retreat from the mainland. That task had required considerable effort. Even more than likely, then, the trailer contained stolen goods or concealed illicit activity. Butchering gators? Plucking egrets? Nothing outward betrayed its interior use.

Squatting on the clearing's edge, I waited. I could no longer hear the voices of the cabin's occupants well, but I saw no faces at its windows, no guards patrolling the clearing's edges. The smells of swamp gas and Deet bug spray irritated my nostrils, increasing my impatience to move. If I could make the transition, the trailer's huge wheels would provide a shelter from behind which I could more safely watch the cabin. Duck-walking, I edged along the clearing's outer circle of light until the trailer rested between me and the cabin. Then I dashed from the woods to the concealing balloons of the trailer's gigantic tires.

From my new vantage, I could see that about twenty feet behind the cabin stood a separate shanty, which a crude portico of poles and thatch connected to the larger building. Light poured from the shanty's only window, silvering the battered padlock on its door. I instantly assumed that Kingston and Lewis had locked Olivia in this outbuilding. I forsook the trailer to creep toward it and traversed one whole wall of the cabin without alerting anyone to my presence. For several minutes, then, I lurked outside the shanty breathing in the peculiar stench emanating from it, an odor that from the beginning had constituted a subtle component of the baleful perfume arising from Kingston's Island.

Chancing capture, I stood and glanced into the shanty's lone window. Shelves held rows and rows of boxes and bottles. On two propane stoves, industrial-scale cookers bubbled like Shakespearean cauldrons, but nothing in this makeshift laboratory suggested that

Olivia had ever huddled here. Clearly, this was Kingston's crank factory—his *personal* crank factory—which he had built apart from the main cabin for safety reasons. The Okefenokee had aided in its establishment by providing cover and by masking its telltale stench with smells exclusive to the swamp.

Hurriedly, I retreated from the crank lab to the trailer and squatted behind its tires. I regretted that I had not told Cooper and Fearing of our plan. Kingston would never let anyone who had spied his lab, and whom he did not trust, depart Kingston's Island alive. The full weight of my folly bent me beneath it, and I felt adrift on perilous waters.

Unintelligible murmurs reached me from the cabin. Suddenly, I feared that Byron had decided to sell me and Olivia out, to enlist again in Kingston's private SS, and to cooperate with Kingston and Lewis in our murders. I took off my shoes, unholstered the Combat Commander, and crossed to the cabin's verandah with the unhurried stride of a KV confederate. This tactic obviously demonstrated my irrationality—my insanity, even—but I had to learn what Byron had done, in what vile way he had delivered me up for sacrifice and himself for unending servitude.

More important, I had to learn if Olivia still lived.

Thirty-Seven

I climbed onto the solidly built verandah and crept soundlessly under one window until I could stand between it and the only other window on that wall. With my back to the cabin, the .45 in hand, and my heart galloping like a mis-shoed horse, I hazarded a glimpse through the window to my right.

Erroll Kingston sat in the sparsely furnished room in a kitchen chair, his pale thighs protruding obscenely from his khaki shorts, his trail-booted feet hooked around the ladderback's forelegs, his hairy arms gripping each other across a white dress shirt that he wore open to the breastbone. He faced inward on a revealing angle, his crossed arms a rebuke to all supplicants, including the man now before him.

Byron stood as poker-straight as possible with his wire-wrapped wrists thrust out before him, like those of a POW. A headband of sweat shone on his brow, and his eyes flashed like dirty pennies. Behind him jutted the end of an iron bedstead, and a man eclipsed by Byron's intervening bulk stood by the bed. To calm my heart, I concentrated on the urgency with which Byron bargained for Olivia's release.

"—do anything you want me to, Erroll. Camp out here for a year. Oversee the cooking, package up the goods, any damned thing you want, from shitwork to heavy-duty supervision. Just let Olivia go home to her mama."

"Where she'd be now, Byron, if you hadn't hired a small-town retard to bag her and cut for the woods. What the hell were you thinking? That you'd abandon Kingston Ventures and become a wealthy cactus farmer in Baja California? What does all that say about your sworn fealty to Erroll the King?" Kingston slapped his thigh. A pearl of spittle shone at his lip corner as if a jeweler had pierced a hole for it there.

Byron hesitated before saying, "Come on, Erroll. I confessed, right? I came back, right?"

"You think I couldn't have figured out your selfish scheme by myself?"

"Snatching Olivia had nothing to do with you and me, Erroll, one way or the other. Put yourself in a daddy's place for a minute or two. Then you'll see why I did it."

Kingston leaned forward, his fists between his thighs, as if considering Byron's defense. " 'Put myself in a daddy's place'? Is that what you just said?"

"Yes sir."

"But you know I can't father a kid, Byron. I've seen my seed under a microscope. The little bastards don't move—they can't. They lack motility."

"Erroll—"

"Motility, Byron. They lack it. I've told you this story before, haven't I?"

"Yes sir, you have."

"But you've just asked me to 'put myself in a daddy's place'—so that I can imagine how *you* feel?"

Byron had no reply.

"Well, hold on to your cojones, Byron, but I know *exactly* how you feel, how any goddamned father feels when a valued child goes missing. Can you believe that?"

Byron still had no reply, but he turned his head a few inches toward the window. Could he see me? Would he take comfort from my presence if he could?

"It feels like having a fucking condor tread your heart. Like a flock of vultures eating your guts out, coil by coil. Does that sound right to you, Byron?"

"I guess so," he said.

I guessed it did too. Kingston's on-target summary here—his sensitivity—startled me, and the raised .45 in my hand began to rack my forearm.

"How do you think a childless chump like me, a guy with blanks in his clip, can come so close to describing how it feels to lose a precious child?" Kingston said.

Helplessly, Byron hunched his shoulders.

"You know, don't you?" Kingston shouted at him. "You *know*! Because I had a foster son in you, an heir to part of my empire, and you turned your self-righteous back on it!"

"Erroll, I just couldn't go the crank angle."

"Oh, really? Why not, do you suppose? Too idealistic? Too principled?"

"Crank takes people down," Byron said. "It eats out their noses and veins. Scabs them up with sores. Some end up looking like they've lived years in a concentration camp, Erroll." His earnestness had a desperate edge.

Kingston barked a laugh. "And you feel *pity* for them? Don't insult us with pseudo-moralistic drivel, Byron. Monk and I know what you've done out here."

"Poached animals!" Byron said hotly. "It's not the same! I couldn't sleep if somebody like DeLynda got a habit because of me, and I don't want it ever happening to Olivia."

"But good fathering would save Olivia, Byron. Good fathering or good sense. Neither Monk nor I ever succumb to the temptation of crank, for example. Do we, Monk?"

"No way," said Lewis's unmistakable voice. "Leastwise, not by that name."

Byron took a short step toward Kingston. "But I'm *not* a good daddy," he said. "And who can do a decent job when dope and such garbage exist to trip folks up? How can *anybody* resist the pretty poisons you all set out?"

"Free will," Kingston said. "Free will in a free country."

"Please let Olivia go," Byron said, chin on chest. "She can't do a damned thing for you all, but I can. And I will too, anything you all want me to."

" 'Let her go'? Shall I turn the tyke loose in the swamp and let her stumble home? Or do you expect me, personally, to conduct her to her doorstep?"

"Erroll—"

"Don't ever suppose I'll let *you* out of my sight to escort her back to Mama."

"Just send her down to the landing, Erroll. I left Will Keats by our dugout. He'll take her home, and you'll never hear word one about this whole screwed-up business again."

Monk Lewis's voice said, "Right."

I had winced at Byron's mention of my name, and now my gun hand threatened to rattle against the cabin wall, revealing my location exactly.

Kingston clapped his hands and leaned back in his chair. "All right, Byron, you've got a deal. To seal it, though, I want you to swear your renewed allegiance by kneeling."

"Kneeling?"

"Sure. Like all those who stick by me through thick and thin, you deserve a Kingston Ventures knighthood. But how can I knight you, Byron, if you refuse to kneel?"

"Kneel, peckerhead!" said Lewis from behind Byron.

Byron said nothing, but permitted his knees to bend a little. Then they locked, and rather than kneeling, he swayed upright like a soldier at attention.

"I thought not," Kingston said. "Such a waste. Monk."

Wearing a blue mechanic's coverall, Lewis stepped into view at Byron's left side and, with a scythelike kick, swept his feet out from under him. Byron crashed to the floorboards. As he struggled to rise, Lewis straddled him and shot him calculatingly in the back of the skull. Once.

The sound of the gunshot expanded to fill the entire swamp. Its reverberations pinned me against the cabin's wall, freezing me, trapping me in a bubble of indecision and shock. Kingston and Lewis, on the other hand, would move quickly. Because they knew I had accompanied Byron onto the island, unless I acted now, one or the other would shoot me dead within the next few minutes. Nor would they have any difficulty disposing of our corpses out here, where they could lose us forever by filling our pockets with rocks and sinking us in some remote gator hole.

I released the .45's safety, prayed silently to Jesus, Buddha, and any anomalously bloodthirsty saint or bodhisattva listening in, and stepped to the window screen in a two-handed shooter's stance. Lewis had bent over Byron's body to check the results of his single shot. In fact, he had just nudged a lock of hair off Byron's brow with his gun barrel when I pumped out three bullets, catching him in the face and upper chest, driving him back so that he struck the iron bedframe and toppled. *"Jesus!"* Kingston shouted. Before I could shoot him too, he scrambled from his chair and bolted through a doorway into another room.

I considered kicking in the screen and giving chase, but knew without thinking that he'd retreated for a weapon and that other bodyguards lurked either here in the compound or on the island's landward border. I hesitated, staring down through gaps in the verandah's planking at used aerosol cans, pharmaceutical bottles, and ventilator tubes, trash from the crystal-meth factory in the shanty out back. Move, I told myself, and leapt to the patch of well-lit sand below the porch. Jackknifed low, I zigzagged toward the path leading to the water.

Nearly there, I risked a look back. Kingston emerged from the cabin carrying a submachine gun with a suppressor on its barrel. He saw me and squeezed off a fusillade, rattling the foliage and kicking up stinging sand pellets. I hurled myself deeper into the trees, thinking that I had four bullets in the socketed clip, and seven in the clip in my pocket.

"Farrel! Reggie!" Kingston called. "Get your sorry asses down here!"

Where could I go? The dugout would draw Kingston's thugs as surely as carrion summons crows. I began to wonder if I had shot Monk Lewis more out of fear and outrage than necessity. Killing him had briefly seemed wise as well as expedient, but now I feared that I had put myself and Olivia at inordinate risk. If I failed to escape Kingston's Island alive, she would also die, and Adrienne would have the rest of her own life to wonder at and curse my foolishness, not only in permitting Polk James to abduct Olivia but also in suppressing my better judgment in favor of the asinine heroics of Byron Owsley, who had plotted his own daughter's kidnapping in the first place.

I angled away from the path to the dugout, moving on a slant in my stocking feet toward the western side of the compound. At one point, I looked through gnarled cypress trees and vines at a grotto of water in which a corrugated shield rose to the surface and shone in the star glitter like a mocking emblem of the sham knighthood that Kingston had wanted to bestow on Byron. A stubby phallic head emerged from one edge of the shield, peered about, and vanished as the shield sank again, dropping through its own incandescent boil. A soft-shelled turtle, and a good omen if I had seen it active so late in the year. Whether I really had or not, I stalked upslope with boosted resolve.

A bitter smell drifted toward me. It originated in the crank shanty. I defined a careful loop through the woods toward the back of Kingston's cabin. Kingston, Reggie, and Farrel—the Farrel Quadrozzi who had betrayed Byron—fired no more bullets into the undergrowth. Nor did any of them shout again, choosing not to give away their positions.

Briefly, I thought about using the two-edged skill that Skipper had drilled into me. Maybe throwing my voice would distract my pursuers. But ventriloquism depends in part on visual misdirection, and the intervening baffle of the trees would thwart its effectiveness here. Besides, I could not see Kingston's crew any better than they could me, and making *any* sound might disclose my own location.

At last I squeezed between two slash pines and gained a view of the crank kitchen. No one occupied any part of the intervening compound. I held my breath and ran past a natural muscadine arbor to the shanty, where I pressed myself against the back door in the shelter of its thatched overhang. Here I took in a lungful of air and almost gagged on its mephitic taste. The stench of sulfuric acid, pseudoephedrine, sodium metal, and other witch's ingredients, all cooking together, scalded my throat.

Listening hard, I heard movement in the undergrowth near the beached dugout and surmised that Kingston had sent his grunts down there to find me. My hypothesis nerved me to chance a look around the corner of the lab.

Erroll Kingston stood at the foot of a metal ramp extending about twelve feet from the rear of the cargo trailer to the oily white sand surrounding it. He had just pivoted back toward the cabin, Ingram M11 in hand, as if he had intuited my presence. In that instant I realized that he had locked Olivia inside the Royal Tangerine Porcelain trailer.

I stepped into the open, lifted the .45, and shot Kingston in the gut. He staggered backward a step before sitting down with a hollow bang on the ramp.

Thirty-Eight

F or the second time in less than fifteen minutes, I had shot a living human being. I, a counselor trained to ease suffering, had acted in a way that many religions, Adrienne's among them, declared a doorway to untold eons of pain. The exigencies of the moment did not allow me to consider this idea now, but, if I survived, at some point I would have to exhume it and stare hard into its pitiless face.

Erroll Kingston's submachine gun had fallen from his hand when he collapsed to the ramp on his butt. The midsection of his white shirt darkened with blood.

"Oh God, Oh God, Oh God," he moaned.

I holstered the Combat Commander, ran the entire length of the shanty and cabin, and knelt beside Kingston. He had once vowed not to forget me, but despite Byron's telling him of my presence here and his own attempt to gun me down from the verandah, he seemed not to know me. He stared at me out of empty reptilian eyes, as if I had dropped from the moon.

From the woods, one of his goons cried, "Mr. Kingston! Are you all right? What the hell's happening?"

Kingston started to speak, but I put my palm over his mouth. Mimicking his supercilious voice, I shouted, "Fine! Everything's fine! Keep looking for the bastard!"

Reggie—or Farrel?—did not call out again, giving me to think that my imitation had deceived him, but Kingston put an end to this self-congratulatory fantasy by biting me between my thumb and forefinger. I pulled my bleeding hand away and reflexively bounced his head off the ramp. I snatched a handkerchief from my rear pocket, twirled it around itself, and gagged Kingston with it. I could have saved time and trouble by shooting him, but even given the emptiness of his eyes, proximity kept me from pulling the trigger, as Lewis had pulled it on Polk James and Byron. Maybe my civility—or my squeamishness?—would spare me an eon or two of karmic torment.

Or maybe not. I grabbed Kingston by his shirt and, leaning into his face, said, "Surrender Olivia, lizard-man. Give her up, you hear?"

His eyes looked shielded, as if with a membrane, while his head lolled like a ragdoll's. I dropped him, slung his submachine gun over my shoulder, clambered up the ramp, and rotated the big handle to unpin the trailer's doors. The right-hand door swung open. Wan light, as if from a failing battery-powered lamp, spilled out. To conceal from Kingston's hirelings the fact that I had shot him, I returned to Kingston, dragged him up the ramp into the trailer, and shut the door from the inside.

The Royal Tangerine Porcelain trailer featured a bed, a desk, a lantern on a crate, and shelf after shelf of raw planking on which Monk Lewis had set out his treasures: bisque figurines, jars with dragon-and-cloud motifs, place settings of antique and contemporary china, vases, sauceboats—so much frangible stuff that, yanking Kingston to a sitting position under one of the shelves, I could not take it all in. What sickening pretense! I wanted to inter Kingston and Lewis with all Lewis's useless pottery, just as that ancient Chinese emperor had buried himself with thousands of terra cotta soldiers.

Across the cabside end of the trailer stretched a gypsumboard wall that hid this improvised jail's chemical toilet, evident by smell alone. At one end of the wall, a hollow-core door stood open a fraction of an inch. As Kingston alternately moaned and gibbered, the door began to move outward so slowly that I knew someone was cautiously pushing it open.

A frightened someone: Olivia.

I turned toward the door. "Olivia, it's Will. Come on out." Realizing that a gunman could just as easily appear, I pointed the submachine gun at the door.

A nearly bald child stepped out. The child stared at me from sunken eyes with a terrifying absence of expression, as if I were an upright snake. I stared at the child as if I had never seen one before. Then recognition dawned for both of us. Wearing a flannel shirt, loose-fit dungarees, and thick-soled sneakers, the child, Olivia herself, self-consciously massaged her knobby skull with one gaunt hand.

"My God, you look like a boy," I said.

She hurled herself at me, wrapped her arms around my waist, and pressed her shaven head into my stomach. "I know," she said. "But I'm still me."

I returned Olivia's caress and put my lips to the strange furze mantling her skull.

"Mr. Kingston!"

The shout came not from the woods, but from the compound—in fact, from very nearby. Olivia's eyes widened, her body trembled. She looked so much like Byron's son, or as Byron must have looked at her age, that I imagined the young Byron quailing before his enraged father after some petty domestic infraction like spilling his juice—as if the child-ghost of the man lying milky-eyed in Kingston's cabin had come now to possess his daughter.

I shook off this hallucination and knelt before Olivia. "Go back to your hiding place." I gestured at the partitioned end of the trailer. "Lie flat on the floor."

"For how long, Will?"

"Don't worry—I'll come for you."

Olivia took my face in her hands and studied me as if trying to confirm my reality. "When?"

"Soon," I told her. "As soon as I can."

Her hands dropped back to her sides. "Don't you forget me."

"Never." I kissed her temple, and, without a backward glance, she trotted to obey me.

"Mr. Kingston, are you in there?"

Kingston looked at me from his spot below one of Monk Lewis's ridiculous china-displaying shelves. The outrage in his eyes was the first quasi-human emotion I had seen in them since shooting him. Footfalls sounded on the metal ramp. I put a finger to my lips and hefted his weapon as a warning, but he merely clutched his wound and moaned around his gag.

As the man on the other side of the door began to open it, I knelt behind the trailer's child-sized bed and propped the threaded barrel of the Ingram on a pillow.

Reggie—or Farrel—stepped into my sights. Kingston chose that moment to kick out and topple the crate on which the battery-powered lamp had sat. I fired a burst from the submachine gun, but Kingston's foot soldier, seeing his boss, had automatically yanked open the trailer's right-hand door and leapt clear of the ramp. He returned fire from outside, but from an angle allowing him to rake only the shelves of china to my left. These shattered, leapt into the air, and further fragmented, hurtling all about in a chaos of noise and powdery shards. In fact, one shelf unbracketed, striking the one below and producing a deafening chain reaction of dropping shelves and splintering porcelain. I fired again, to keep the shooter from trying to reenter, then jumped over the bed and took shelter behind the unopen door half.

Kingston rolled his eyeballs high, smiling malevolently at my frustration. Squatting beside him, I had no idea what to do next. Then I heard more gunfire—from dozens of yards away, not from the base of the ramp. What did it mean? Had Reggie and Farrel inexplicably turned their weapons on each other? Or had some new combatant arrived either to challenge them both or to take sides with one against the other?

You'll never find out cowering here, I told myself. I leapt to the open half of the door, bent at the waist, and swiveled to scan the compound. No one. I trotted down the ramp and started for the cabin, but another rattle of submachine-gun fire made both my heart and my scrotum clench. I halted, fully expecting the next burst to perforate me from forehead to groin.

Instead, there followed the loudest explosion I'd ever heard—a rolling cascade of explosions. Their concussive waves bowled me over and buffeted the trailer on its struts. Dropping back, the trailer lost a sand shoe and tilted drunkenly. Porcelain crashed again, clattering from the last fixed shelves.

I regained my feet and backed toward the trailer. What had happened to Olivia? And Kingston? I had no time to answer these questions because, all about the meth lab, unholy chaos had arrived.

Uprushing, oxygen-drinking, orange-and-crimson flames crackled in self-devouring splendor. Soon the cabin would catch, and the muscadine arbor, and the encroaching trees.

From out of this inferno, however, staggered a burning man, a submachine gun fused to his fingers, a burnt steak for a face. He took several impossible steps and pitched forward to the glittering white sand.

Either Reggie or Farrel had decided to cut and run. But first he had deemed it prudent to destroy the evidence of an illegal drug operation. His death would have come more easily if he had simply shot himself. With help like this, who could wonder that Kingston had fixed so ruthlessly on bringing Byron back?

Flaming debris rained down on the main cabin, igniting the palmetto thatch. Soon, the entire compound would stand blazing, bellowing, roasting the very air. I hurried to the trailer and walked carefully up its tilted ramp. The conflagration from the meth lab lit the interior luridly, as if a lighting technician at the Glass Cat had tried to simulate hell on one of the club's runways. Broken china carpeted the floor, and Kingston, bleeding from his belly and hands, even from around his gag, had fetched up against the head of Olivia's bed.

"Olivia!" I called.

She opened the door to the toilet, then picked her way across the smashed porcelain, and around Kingston, to join me. I clutched her to me, smoothing nonexistent hair away from her brow and trying to process the fact that a second killer still lurked somewhere in the compound. Either Reggie or Farrel had died setting the crank lab on fire. The other, if he hadn't already hightailed out of the swamp, remained as a threat.

Solemnly, Olivia said, "That was really loud." She had a red mark on her jaw, apparently from the trailer's partial collapse.

"Yeah," I said, touching it. "Can you run?"

She nodded, once, and her stare—this time—held a glimmer of the old Olivia Owsley feistiness.

Good. She would need it. *I* would need it. Fire continued to roar in the compound, lapping at the woods around us, threatening our escape from the island. Should we go back to the dugout? Or strike

out through the woods along the camouflaged road by which Kingston's men had brought in their absurd trailer? I had no clear idea.
Olivia, meanwhile, gazed up at me as if I had planned every move
in this catch-as-catch-can operation weeks ago.

"Come on, kiddo." I took her hand.

Thirty-Nine

I led Olivia through the porcelain debris to the gaping trailer doors, which framed a Dantean scene so radiantly surreal that I did not want to enter it.

As we hesitated on its brink, Kingston croaked some word. Both Olivia and I looked back at him crumpled by the bedstead, his body black with blood from neck to waist, his eyes supernaturally alive because firelight glittered in them. To my astonishment, I felt a burst of empathy for him.

Olivia squeezed my hand. "Take that out of his mouth? So he can breathe?"

Watching our exchange, Kingston tried to speak again, and the word he managed around his gag sounded like my name, *"Keats!"*— an accusation and a plea.

I returned to him, knelt, and fidgeted with the handkerchief knot that I had tied behind his neck. His eyes peered beyond me, as if I had no more substance than a ghost, until I drew the gag from his mouth. Then he spat a gob of blood and saliva, which hit me in the throat.

Olivia—not by the doors, but at my side—screamed like a broken-backed rabbit, for she had followed me in and Kingston had clamped a greedy hand around her ankle. Before I could strike him, Olivia's hand inscribed a swift descending arc toward Kingston's face. He clutched his eyes with both hands and screamed as Olivia had screamed, but even more loudly and with a sonorous fury almost prehistoric. Still roaring, he pulled a spikelike object from his eye and flung it haphazardly across the trailer. Amazed, I registered the spike in mid-arc as a bloody pencil.

I caught Olivia under the arm, picked her up, and hustled her down the ramp to the sandy floor of the compound. Then I set her on her own feet, and we scrambled across the clearing and down the mulch-carpeted path to the beach where Byron and I had landed the dugout. The dugout was gone. Apparently, Kingston's one surviving bodyguard had used it himself. I peered out over the water, seeing nothing but half-imagining that I did.

Then I looked at Olivia, marveling at how much she resembled an escapee from a boy's bootcamp.

"How did Monk Lewis bring you to this place, kiddo?"

"In some sort of Jeep. I know where he parked it."

"Can you show me?"

"Sure." She took my hand and led me back up the slope toward the fire-bright compound. Going back unsettled her; as we moved, she clung to me like a smaller Siamese twin.

Halfway there, I halted and knelt before her. "Olivia, you did okay in the trailer. You did fine."

"I hurt him."

"He wanted to hurt us. He *did* hurt us. He had Monk Lewis kill your daddy." Maybe I should have saved this revelation for a less stressful time—if one ever arrived—but acknowledging one more nightmare in the midst of the great nightmare engulfing us seemed a lesser evil than failing to undercut Olivia's guilt. I don't think she fully registered the news.

"Monk Lewis gave me that pencil," she said.

"That surprises me, kiddo."

"I told him I wanted to write stuff, like I did when Polk had me with him."

"And he brought you the pencil?"

"After a while. I kept it sharp rubbing it on stone."

"You did fine, Olivia. You did exactly right."

"Come on." She seized my hand again and dragged me into the clearing. The cabin had begun to blaze from the roof downward. Olivia led me past both it and the porcelain trailer to a chapel of turkey oaks and bayberry trees east of the main compound. Here sat a mud-encrusted copper-colored Chevy Tahoe with Autotrac four-wheel drive. No one had locked its doors, but the ignition held no keys.

"Who had the keys, Olivia?"

"Monk, I guess."

We jogged back to the cabin. Flames carpeted the roof. I told Olivia to stay put and darted inside.

Smoke hazed the room holding Byron's and Monk's bodies, making breathing and searching difficult. I grabbed Monk's ankles and dragged him outside, looking away when his head triple-bumped the verandah steps. Olivia watched gravely as I stretched Monk out and returned to the cabin. Byron I gripped by the wrists and, owing to his bulk and my own fatigue, wrestled outside with an even greater struggle. I panted like a spent greyhound as I ranked him alongside Lewis in the yard.

"Is that my daddy?" Olivia said, pointing at Byron.

"I'm afraid so. He sacrificed himself to rescue you. Do you understand?"

Olivia said nothing, then nodded yes, then said, "No," backed up a few feet, and squatted. Firelight fingerpainted her features as she pondered Byron's stillness.

While I searched the pockets of Lewis's coveralls, the rear half of the cabin's roof caved in with a sound like a papier-mâché 747 crashing. I found no keys, but did not reenter the funeral pyre of the cabin to see if they'd fallen from Lewis's pockets as I dragged him out.

I went to Olivia, took her by the hand, and led her to the base of the trailer ramp. "Wait here." I walked the warped ramp and bent over Kingston's slumped body. If his heart still beat, it did so like a metronome winding down. His bloody left eyesocket had a real hole in it this time, but looked scarcely any emptier than the right one. I reached into the lumpy front pocket of his shorts and extracted a keyring.

The key to the Tahoe hung between a miniature knife and a photo cameo of Byron. I clambered back down the ramp to Olivia, wholly indifferent to what might befall Kingston now, and together we ran into the copse concealing the SUV.

I hoisted Olivia into its passenger seat and buckled her in. Then, behind the wheel, I turned the key and listened to the motor snarl gratifyingly to life.

"Which way out, kiddo?"

Olivia pointed at a shadowy gap in the thicket, one that might denote the opening of a twin-rutted trail. I shifted into drive, and Olivia touched my arm.

"Please don't leave my daddy here."

I backed into the clearing, far enough to feel some of the furnace-like heat radiating from the fire, put the Tahoe in park, and jumped clear.

"Lock your door and stay put."

Dragging Byron over to the vehicle proved the easy part. But I could boost him inside only by gripping the lapels of his jacket, flopping his torso over the rear seat, and then, with my elbows behind his knees, levering him up and back. I left him scrunched into place with his knees awkwardly bent.

Again in the driver's seat, I said, "Don't look at him," but Olivia had no need of my warning. She stared straight ahead with zombielike fixity. I accelerated, and we shot out of the burning camp down uneven trial ruts through whipping foliage. The Tahoe's leaps made me feel that we had broken a crucial physical barrier, of sound or of light, but the speedometer never registered higher than thirty-five.

My hands shook, but not solely because of our jouncing progress through the swamp: I had just spent an hour in hell.

A helicopter Osterizing the air above the Okefenokee's jungle threw its searchlight on us—then passed over on a headlong tilt, its eerie clatter also vanishing.

"Were those friends?" Olivia asked.

"Of course." Surely, only the law would mount a 'copter mission out here, and not Kingston Ventures.

We lurched onward, slued, righted, clawed ahead again—until I had to slow to cross the trench of water and quicksand linking Kingston's Island to the mainland.

Then, on the move again, we saw two sets of lights approaching us blindingly at ground level. Had Kingston's second bodyguard—

Farrel Quadrozzi?—escaped to summon reinforcements? Should I floor the accelerator or stomp the brake? My heart swelling to the size of a whale's, I stomped the brake and bit my tongue as we slid to a galumphing halt.

An unmarked Oldsmobile sailed over a bushy hummock and slammed down in front of us like a tank jettisoned from a C-147. A black sedan followed, swinging to a stop behind the Olds as a trailing parade of cars closed in more cautiously.

Asa D. Fearing barged from the Olds with pistol drawn and badge held high. "FBI!" he shouted, pointing his gun at the Tahoe. "Out of the vehicle with hands behind your head! *Now!*"

I got out with my hands behind my head, but Olivia sat frozen. "Will Keats!" I shouted. "Will Keats and Olivia Owsley! For God's sake, don't shoot us now!"

Fearing bounded directly to me, holstering his .38 Special under his windbreaker. He jerked my arms down with sinew-popping force, then thrust his face into mine to confirm my identity. Sheriff Donovan of Chesser County, looking incongruously natty in his black-and-tan uniform, halted five or six feet away, covering us with his own firearm.

Now certain that he knew me, Fearing wrapped me in his arms and squeezed me like a python. "A note!" he shouted. "A Jesus-loving note in a Jesus-loving kiddies' book!"

Evidently, Adrienne had found my message in Olivia's copy of *Oz*. I worked myself free of Fearing as Sheriff Donovan ambled over holstering his own pistol.

"Mind telling us how you set the swamp on fire, Mr. Keats?"

I stepped past him to the SUV's passenger door and opened it. "Come on out, Olivia." She climbed down, and I picked her up and perched her on my hip like a toddler. Overhead, the police 'copter had returned, clattering obnoxiously as it banked back toward the conflagration.

"That's your *daughter?*" Donovan asked.

Fearing said, "Good Lord, those devils scalped her."

Squinting into the battery of headlights, Olivia lifted a hand to her gold-glinting fuzz.

"It'll grow back," I told her. "It'll grow back in no time at all." Then I turned to Fearing and said, "One of Kingston's men caused the fire. Another escaped. Monk Lewis and another gunman lie dead in the compound, Kingston's dead or dying in a porcelain company's cargo trailer, and I put Olivia's daddy"—I nodded at the Tahoe—"in that thing's backseat. Lewis shot him dead at point-blank range."

Fearing whistled. "Busy night, Mr. Keats. Is the child okay? Does she need medical attention?"

"Not for any bodily injury," I said.

With neither fear nor amazement in her voice, Olivia said, "I stuck a man in the eye with my pencil."

"If it was Erroll Kingston," Donovan said, "he deserved it."

"I'd do it again too. Only harder."

"Shhh," I said. "Think of something more pleasant, kiddo—like seeing your mama again."

Fearing pulled a candy bar from his windbreaker pocket. "You hungry?" Olivia stared at the candy with no visible interest or objection. Fearing peeled the wrapper back and placed the bar in her hand, closing her fingers around it. She took a big predatory bite, and then another. "Maybe you all'd like to accompany me to a Dairy Queen in Fosterville. Appears Little Miss Droopy Dungarees here has got herself an appetite."

Donovan, a Chesser County deputy, and two men in windbreakers with "FBI" stenciled on the back moved in on the Tahoe. They would survey every item of evidence connected to the vehicle, including Byron's corpse, and sort and file them as incidentals in the story of Olivia's kidnapping.

Olivia and I transferred to the backseat of the Olds, while Fearing and a blond agent with faint sideburns and a boil on his neck sat in front. Fearing radioed a "Mr. Grey," whom he told to meet us at the Dairy Queen, then pulled a three-point turn that almost enmired the Olds before a hard jab at the gas pedal sent it careening toward Fosterville.

For the next several miles, Kingston regaled us with anecdotes about the best barbecue joints in Atlanta—"black-style barbecue, I mean"—while I pictured neither spare ribs nor chipped pork but a gunman staggering from a burning meth lab.

Forty

"M r. Grey" wore a familiar face. At high speeds and against department protocols, Captain Nicholas Cooper had driven Adrienne from our farm on Antioch Church Road to Fosterville to await the outcome of a joint operation between the FBI and the Chesser County Sheriff's Department. Without our knowledge, the authorities had planned to launch their raid of Kingston's Island—on local maps, Boatwright Island—the following morning. But entering the swamp on our own initiative, Byron and I had triggered the assault twelve hours early.

Nick Cooper and Adrienne sat across from each other in a booth in the Dairy Queen, which the franchise's owner had decorated like an immaculate cowbarn, with yokes and harnesses on the walls. I felt a surge of gratitude: it reminded me of Roogy's stall and the welcome imminence of our trip home.

Adrienne sat facing away from the door and did not see us come in, but Cooper tapped her on the wrist, and she quickly swung her head around. Her stare combined relief, exhilaration, and offended perplexity. Whose bald boy-child had I brought out of the swamp, anyway?

Then recognition developed—with the gradual suddenness of a photo emerging from a tray of chemicals—and Adrienne had no eyes for me. She swept from the booth and toward us, Olivia moving to meet her with a peculiar stiff-legged trot so that only feet from the door Adrienne scooped her up and started helplessly rubbing her scalp. Olivia knotted her ankles in the small of Adrienne's back, and the two twirled in slow motion, like porcelain figures atop a music box. The other patrons—only a few at this hour—looked on bemusedly.

Without warning, Adrienne shouted, *"Yeeooooow!"* like a cowgirl or a sports champion, and the customers tumbled to the fact that a momentous reunion had just occurred. Tears washed down Adrienne's face, brightening it, and she held her mouth open in both amazement and an attempt to breathe more easily. Olivia lay her head against her mother's chest and smiled with the gentle suspicion of a foundling adopted by a billionaire.

Fearing stood beside me—his partner still in the Olds, to monitor its radio—and smiled more broadly. "Would you lookit that. Makes a man forget how hungry he is."

Eventually, Adrienne calmed enough to peck me on the lips and ask if I were okay. I wasn't. I kept seeing Monk Lewis, self-made connoisseur, shooting Byron dead, and Olivia's arm descending to stick a pencil in Kingston's eye. Not images I wanted to divulge just now. Not images to boost the revelry level of a long-deferred party.

"I'm fine," I said.

Fearing and Cooper conferred apart from us. Discussion quickly finished, Cooper turned away from his compatriot and said, "After Olivia eats, we need to get her to the Chesser County Medical Center for an exam. You too, Will, if you think you could use one."

"All I need is a couple of months of uninterrupted sleep. Let Adrienne go with her."

And so, after deliberately putting away two cheeseburgers, an order of fries, and a butterscotch sundae, Olivia proceeded to the hospital with Adrienne and Fearing, the latter carrying an Oreo Blizzard and another cheeseburger.

Cooper and I remained alone in our booth, Cooper regarding me with a scowl similar to the one Kingston adopted when he no longer chose to suffer fools. "Congratulations, Keats."

I stared out the window at the neon bathing beauty on the sign in front of Vulliamy's Body Shop next door. I trembled all over—not from any current fear, but from the thousands I had suppressed on the island.

"What?" I said.

"Your derring-do warrants congratulations. You bulled in where civilians don't belong and somehow managed not to get that innocent girl killed." He nodded toward the door. "But you left a trail of dead bodies a mile long and you brought out a child a fucking sight less innocent than she went in."

I put my hands palm down on the Formica to stop their shaking. "I did what I thought I had to."

Cooper opened and closed his fingers, fisting and unfisting them as if he wanted to use his arthritic knuckles on me. Then he smiled lopsidedly. "Plenty of heart and balls, Will, but next time put your brains into play too."

I relaxed, slumping back against the padded booth. Apropos of nothing but the rubble in my head, I said, "I never saw so much broken china in my life." I related some of what had happened in the trailer where Kingston had confined Olivia.

"A year and a half ago," Cooper said, "that truck and trailer disappeared from the face of the earth. Monk Lewis pretty clearly hijacked the whole rig and shot the teamster. If we searched all the gator holes around Kingston's Island, we'd probably find the entire cab with the driver's body still in it."

"I don't get it—Lewis's porcelain hangup."

"Beautiful things break, Will. Monk couldn't reverse that law, but he figured he could maybe live with it if he had some say over when and to what degree the breakage occurred. He didn't have any *real* say of course, but he liked the illusion that he did. Who among us is so terribly different?"

I shook my head, then looked out the window at the winking blue and green bathing beauty.

On Wednesday morning, after a full day's rest following a midnight ride home from Fosterville in Nick Cooper's patrol car, Adrienne and I balanced on a fence rail watching Olivia trot Roogy Batoon around our paddock. Olivia perched bareback, using only a simple rope hackamore and periodically leaning forward to whisper nonsense in Roogy's ear. Roogy responded with either a curious attentiveness or a vigorous toss of her head. Olivia invariably tossed her own head, and laughed, and glanced toward Adrienne and me with mischief and radical glee in her eyes.

A piquant glory suffused the windy gray sky. Christmas loomed, only eight days away, but we already had our heart's desire.

Adrienne slipped her arm around my waist. "You doing okay, tough guy?"

"Getting there, I guess. You?"

"The same. More or less. Everything that happened before we brought Olivia home has grown more and more dreamlike." She pushed a canary's wing of hair from her eyes. "Maybe I'll do better once we've had Byron's memorial service."

In the absence of any near surviving kin, we had taken these arrangements upon ourselves. After Byron's cremation, we would commemorate his life at a simple ceremony in Owsley's Anvil & Bellows on Friday afternoon. To date, only Nick Cooper and DeLynda Gaye had promised to come.

I said, "You still think Olivia should go?"

"She can't *not* bid her father farewell, Will."

"I just don't want to dredge all yesterday's pain up again for her. How can we tell just how much this whole freaking nightmare has traumatized her?"

"We'll find out in due course." Adrienne put her chin on my shoulder. "Remember when you wanted to celebrate Halloween? You said we couldn't just avoid observing certain events."

"Yeah, I remember."

"Well, the same rule applies now that we have Olivia back."

Olivia wore a red stocking cap with a white snowflake design to cover her buzzcut and keep her warm. I half expected her to snatch it off and wave it about like a rodeo rider.

I said, "I guess she'll learn that her father loved her enough to steal her. Enough even to overcome his dislike of me to enlist my help getting her back."

"Enough to die for her. That wrong-headed, arrogant, selfish, insufferable bastard loved her that much."

Olivia made Roogy Batoon gallop toward us at a brisk clip and veer off at the last moment so that tail hairs actually snapped against our knees. Olivia's laughter drifted back to us even over the thudding of Roogy's hooves.

A car horn beeped, and I looked over my shoulder to watch a Mercury Tracer the shade of purple lip-gloss turn into our driveway and creep toward the house.

"Who'd have the gall to bother us this morning?" I said.

"J. W. Young. Or a reporter. Or Hutchinson Payne. Or Oscar Greenaway. Or—"

"Okay, okay. But I have the right to sledgehammer whoever climbs out of that motorized eggplant."

"Tough guy," Adrienne said; a josh and a reproach.

I calmed myself enough to watch the driver emerge: she wore a tailored lavender jacket and skirt, and walked on grape-colored high heels that sank into the turf, hobbling her approach.

"Isn't that your prospective new boss?" Adrienne whispered. "Go help her, you idiot."

I hopped down and strode across the yard to take Ocie Lee Degginger's elbow, assistance that she neither shrugged off nor explicitly acknowledged. Together we wobbled to the fence, where Adrienne now stood smiling earnestly. Extending her hand, Adrienne said, "Adrienne Owsley, Ms. Degginger. We met once at a seminar in Columbus."

Ms. Degginger shook her hand briskly. "Glad to see you got your little girl back okay." She watched Olivia ride. "She seems to've come home with her spirit unbroken, praise the Lord."

"We hope so," Adrienne said. "Welcome."

Ocie Lee Degginger turned to me with a softer look than I had managed to generate from her to date. "The rumors flying around Tocqueville say you really put your butt on the line to get little Olivia home."

"I'd've never figured you to put much stock in rumors, ma'am."

Out of Ms. Degginger's view, Adrienne drew two fingers across her throat: *Cut the smart stuff, Will!*

"I do if my sources check out, Mr. Keats. And these do. They say you walked that extra mile. A thousand, maybe. And that sort of commitment impresses me."

"Thank you," I said. Adrienne smiled.

"So I'm here to say if you want that Community in Schools job you interviewed for, you've got it."

"Yes'm I want it."

"Just one condition."

"Name it."

Ocie Lee Degginger smiled, a first in my experience. "Don't carry a gun into Mrs. Lapierre's quiet school. Nobody over there needs that kind of persuasion."

Two days later we received a telegram. My mother, LaRue Keats, had terminated her South American cruise early. She, Kelli, and Burling Whickerbill would arrive from Miami at Atlanta Hartsfield International Airport on Saturday afternoon. Could we pick them up and deliver them safely home to Columbus?

"Good thing we hadn't made other plans," Adrienne said. "LaRue wouldn't appreciate sitting curbside on her luggage until it became clear we weren't going to show."

"In that case, Burling would've hired a limo so they could zip home swilling gin and tonics from the backseat wet bar. Their asking us to pick them up—in your Camry?—actually shows LaRue practicing a kind of family-values *noblesse oblige.*"

Adrienne, snickering, clamped a hand over her mouth.

Neither my truck nor the Camry could seat six people, but the Camry could comfortably hold four. This meant that I would have to drive to the airport alone. I did not want to go without Adrienne and Olivia—we had not allowed one real separation among us since Olivia's return—but as I drove north, my irritation gave way to warmer feelings. LaRue had her dotty, exasperating side, but she had always loved and supported me, and she had survived Skipper's career-dictated neglect and multiple adulteries with bizarre good humor, even dignity. Also, I wanted to see how my sister, Kelli, had fared on this extravagant autumn cruise.

Ordinarily, the people one waited for at an airport concourse gate always hobbled into sight dead last, whey-faced and exhausted. Not this time. The Keats women, and Burling Whickerbill, had flown first-class, with champagne, filet mignon, and extra pillows. They strolled into the incandescent sprawl of B Concourse bright-eyed, giddy, and gregarious. In fact, they fell upon me almost before I realized that passengers had begun to disembark. Burling looked astonishingly tan and fit, Kelli had blossomed into a self-assured young woman, and LaRue exuded a manic cheerfulness—as if some debonair deckchair Romeo had paid her harmless court every evening of the entire cruise.

"William!" she cried. "Our dutiful boy! Our stay-at-home savior!" I kissed her on her lightly rouged cheek. "Welcome home. It looks as if the sunny Latin climes agreed with you all."

"Oh, they did, they did! Let's claim our luggage, William, and I'll spill every juicy detail."

We rode a subway car to baggage pick-up, found the appropriate carousel, and began our wait. LaRue seized me by the shoulders in the midst of the other milling claimants and pushed me out to arm's length. Kelli gave me a sympathetic wink. Burling slouched at the end of the carousel, people-watching.

"How do you feel?" LaRue asked me. "Has the pressure of your joblessness begun to get to you?"

"I have a job now."

"Wonderful! Such a load off my mind!" Typically, she did not bother to ask me about the job, but abruptly changed tacks: "Now, you can't *imagine* the time we had—the festivities, the food, the charming native peoples, the portside adventures! Nor can you know the great pity I feel for those who never experience what *we* were privileged to experience."

"LaRue Keats," Kelli said, digging me in the ribs, "the Mother Teresa of those without valid passports."

"Already I can feel the threat of boredom setting in," LaRue went on. "I love Georgia, but sometimes it's so mundane. How can you stand it, William? How can you exist here—without a job, I mean—in anything other than terminal boredom?"

"I don't know. Courage, I guess. Muskrat courage."

LaRue, glancing sidelong at the carousel, ignored my odd turn of phrase. "Our bags! William, please grab them."

I plucked the bags off the conveyor. They were heavy, but nothing I couldn't handle.

About the Author

Novelist Clyde Edgerton called Philip Lawson's previous novel, *Would It Kill You to Smile?*, "a page-turning suspense-filled search for truth and trouble." *Muskrat Courage* exhibits those same virtues while exponentially raising the stakes. As for Lawson himself, he has lived enough for two people. He occupies homes in Pine Mountain, Georgia, and Providence, Rhode Island, using a different alias in each place—to keep the locals ignorant of his nefarious past.